Hannah's List

**Center Point
Large Print**

Also by Debbie Macomber
and available from Center Point Large Print:

Cindy and the Prince
Bride on the Loose
Same Time, Next Year
Mail-Order Bride
Return to Promise

and

The complete *Blossom Street* series

Hannah's List

DEBBIE MACOMBER

CENTER POINT PUBLISHING
THORNDIKE, MAINE

LP
Mac

This Center Point Large Print edition is published in the year 2010 by arrangement with Harlequin Books S.A.

The text of this Large Print edition is unabridged. In other aspects, this book may vary from the original edition. Printed in the United States of America on permanent paper. Set in 16-point Times New Roman type.

ISBN: 978-1-60285-769-8

Library of Congress Cataloging-in-Publication Data

Macomber, Debbie.
  Hannah's list / Debbie Macomber. -- Center point large print ed.
    p. cm.
  Originally published: New York : Harlequin, 2010.
  ISBN 978-1-60285-769-8 (library binding : alk. paper)
  1. Large type books. I. Title.
  PS3563.A2364H36 2010
  813'.54--dc22
2010003387

To
Maggie Peale Everett
in appreciation
of a
wonderful idea

May 2010

Dearest friends,

My readers tell me they enjoy learning the genesis of a story. The idea for *Hannah's List* came into being in September 2008, when I had the honor of dining with Paul and Maggie (Peale) Everett. Maggie told me about a friend of hers who knew she was dying. Like my character Hannah, she gave her husband a list of women she felt would make him a good second wife. I was deeply touched by what I'd heard and recognized immediately what an act of love such a letter would be. It wasn't long before the premise took shape in my imagination. Soon after that, the central character of Michael, the young pediatrician, appeared. And the rest is . . . this story.

While this is peripherally a Blossom Street book, it's more along the lines of *Twenty Wishes* in that it takes place away from A Good Yarn, Lydia Goetz's store. If you've read the Blossom Street stories, you'll remember Winter Adams, the owner of the French Café. And, naturally, you'll be getting updates on some of your favorite characters. Still, this book belongs to Michael and in many ways to Hannah, whom I grew to love and admire in the process of writing the story.

When *Hannah's List* begins, she's been gone a year. She died of ovarian cancer, which is often called a silent killer. Ovarian cancer claimed my own friend, Stephanie Cordall, who was one of the original members of my Thursday morning breakfast group. I encourage you to check out the following Web site, which explains how to identify the symptoms: http://www.mayoclinic.com.

As always I'm eager to hear from my readers. Your feedback has guided my career all these years. You can reach me either through my Web site at www.DebbieMacomber.com or at P.O. Box 1458, Port Orchard, WA 98366.

Debbie Macomber

Chapter One

I am not a sentimental guy. I've been known to forget Mother's Day and, once, when Hannah and I were dating, I even let Valentine's go unnoticed. Fortunately she didn't take my lapse too seriously or see it as any reflection of my feelings. As for anniversaries and birthdays, I'm a lost cause. In fact, I'd probably overlook Christmas if it wasn't for all the hoopla. It's not that I'm self-absorbed . . . Well, maybe I am, but aren't we all to a certain extent?

To me, paying a lot of attention to people because it's their birthday or some made-up holiday is ridiculous. When you love someone, you need to show that love each and every day. Why wait for a certain time of year to bring your wife flowers? Action really does speak louder than words, especially if it's a loving deed, something you do for no particular reason. Except that you want to. Because you care.

Hannah taught me that. Hannah. A year ago today, May eighth, I lost her, my beautiful thirty-six-year-old wife. Even now, a whole year after her death, I can't think of her without my gut twisting into knots.

A year. Three hundred and sixty-five lonely days and empty nights.

A few days after her death, I stood over Hannah's

casket and watched as it was lowered into the ground. I threw the first shovelful of dirt into her grave. I'll never forget that sound. The hollow sound of earth hitting the coffin's gleaming surface.

Not an hour passes that I don't remember Hannah. Actually, that's an improvement. In those first few months, I couldn't keep her out of my head for more than a minute. Everything I saw or heard reminded me of Hannah.

To simply say I loved her would diminish the depth of my feelings. In every way she completed me. Without her, my world is bleak and colorless and a thousand other adjectives that don't begin to describe the emptiness I've felt since she's been gone.

I talk to her constantly. I suppose I shouldn't tell people that. We've had this ongoing one-sided conversation from the moment she smiled up at me one last time and surrendered her spirit to God.

So, here I am a year later, pretending to enjoy the Seattle Mariners' baseball game when all I can think about is my wife. My one-year-dead wife.

Ritchie, Hannah's brother and my best friend, invited me to share box seats for this game. I'm not fooled. I'm well aware that my brother-in-law didn't include me out of some mistaken belief that I'm an inveterate baseball fan. He knows exactly what anniversary this is.

I might not be sentimental, but this is one day I *can't* forget.

As a physician, a pediatrician, I'm familiar with death. I've witnessed it far too often and it's never easy, especially with children. Even when the end is peaceful and serene as it was with Hannah, I feel I've been cheated, that I've lost.

As a teenager I was involved in sports. I played football in the fall, basketball in winter and baseball in the spring, and worked as a lifeguard during the summers. The competitive spirit is a natural part of who I am. I don't like to lose, and death, my adversary, doesn't play fair. Death took Hannah from me, from all of us, too early. She was the most vibrant, joyful, loving woman I have ever known. I've been floundering ever since.

Although I've fought death, my enemy, from the day I became a doctor—it's *why* I became a doctor—I learned to understand it in a different, more complex way. I learned death can be a friend even while it's the enemy. As she lay dying, Hannah, who loved me so completely and knew me so well, showed me that ultimate truth.

A year's time has given me the perspective to realize I did my wife a disservice. My biggest regret is that I refused to accept the fact that she was dying. As a result I held on to her far longer than I should have. I refused to relinquish her when she was ready to leave me. Selfishly, I couldn't bear to let her go.

Even when she'd drifted into unconsciousness I sat by her bedside night and day, unable to believe that there wouldn't be a miracle. It's stupid; as a medical professional I certainly know better. Yet I clung to her. Now I realize that my stubbornness, my unwillingness to release her to God, held back her spirit. Tied her to earth. To me.

When I recognized the futility of it all, when I saw what I was doing to Hannah's parents and to Ritchie, I knew I had to let her go. I left Hannah's room and got hold of myself. I hadn't slept in days, hadn't eaten. Nor had I shaved, which means I probably looked even more pathetic than I felt. I went back to our home, showered, forced down a bowl of soup and slept for three uninterrupted hours. When I returned, the immediate family had gathered around her bedside. Hannah's heart rate had slowed and it was only a matter of minutes. Then, just before she died, she opened her eyes, looked directly at me and smiled. I held her hand and raised it to my lips as she closed her eyes and was . . . gone.

That last smile will stay with me forever. Every night as I press my head against the pillow, the final image in my mind is Hannah's farewell smile.

"Hey, Michael. A beer?" Ritchie asked. He doesn't call me Mike; no one does. Even as a kid, I was never a Mike.

"Sure." My concentration wasn't on the game or on much of anything, really. Without glancing at the scoreboard I couldn't have told you who was ahead. I went through the motions, jumped to my feet whenever Ritchie did. I shouted and made noise along with the rest of the crowd, but I didn't care about the game. I hadn't cared about anything for a long time—except my work. That had become my salvation.

"How about dinner after the game?" Ritchie asked as he handed me a cold beer a few minutes later.

I hesitated. All that awaited me was an empty house and my memories of Hannah.

"Sure." I didn't have much of an appetite, though. I rarely did these days.

"Great." He took a long swig of beer and turned back to the field.

I hadn't done my brother-in-law any favors by agreeing to attend this game. These weren't cheap seats, either. Ritchie had paid big bucks for box seats behind home plate, and I'd basically ignored the entire game. I should've made an excuse and let him take someone else. But I didn't want to be alone. Not today. Every other day of the year I was perfectly content with my own company. But not today.

The game must have been over because, almost before I was aware of it, people were leaving.

"Great game," I said, making the effort.

"We lost," Ritchie muttered.

I hadn't been paying enough attention to notice. Ritchie slapped me on the back and headed out of the stadium. That was his way of telling me he understood.

Half an hour later we sat in a friendly sports bar not far from Safeco Field. I stared at the menu, wishing I could conjure up an appetite. Over the past year I'd lost nearly twenty pounds. Food was a necessity, and that was the only reason I bothered. I usually ate on the run, without interest or forethought. I needed something in my belly so I grabbed a protein bar or a vegetable drink. It served the purpose, although I derived no pleasure from it.

Hannah had been exceptionally talented in the kitchen, just like her cousin Winter Adams, who owned the French Café on Blossom Street. She loved experimenting with recipes and took pride in preparing meals. Hannah's dinner parties were legendary among our friends. As a hostess, she was a natural—charming and gracious.

"What are you thinking about?" Ritchie asked.

His question startled me until I saw that he was gazing at the menu. "Grilled salmon," I replied.

"I'm leaning toward the T-bone," he said.

I've always associated steaks with celebration, and this wasn't a day I'd consider celebrating. Long before I was willing to accept that Hannah had lost her battle with cancer, she'd told me that when she was gone, she didn't want me to grieve. She said her wake should be as much fun as her parties. At the time I didn't want to hear her talk about death. By then she'd resigned herself to the outcome; I hadn't found the courage to do so.

The waitress took our order, brought us each a beer and left. I held the amber bottle between my fingers and frowned at the table. I wished I was better company for Ritchie.

"It's been a year," my brother-in-law murmured.

I nodded, acknowledging the comment, but not elaborating on it.

"I miss her."

Again I nodded. As painful as it was to talk about Hannah, I had the burning desire to do exactly that. I wanted—no, needed—to hold on to her, if not physically, then emotionally.

"Hard to believe it's been twelve months." I heard the pain in my own voice but didn't try to hide it.

"You doing okay?" Ritchie asked.

I shrugged rather than tell the truth—I wasn't okay. I was damn mad. Still. How *dared* this happen to a woman as wonderful as Hannah. How dared it happen to me!

Hannah and I were married as soon as I graduated from medical school. We decided that my internship and residency would be too demanding to allow us to start a family right away. Hannah worked for a regional department-store chain as a buyer and loved her job. When I'd get home too exhausted to think, she'd entertain me with stories of the people she'd met. People whose names I soon forgot but whose foibles lived on. The smallest incident became a full-fledged anecdote, complete with wickedly funny observations. She had a way of making the most mundane details fascinating. If I close my eyes I can still hear her laugh. I can smile just recalling the early years of our marriage and the struggles we endured, the things we enjoyed. Memories sustained me that first year without Hannah.

The day I finished my residency and specialized training and was able to join a Seattle practice was the day Hannah threw away her birth control pills. We talked endlessly about our family. I love children and so did Hannah. She wanted three kids; I would've been satisfied with two. Hannah felt an odd number would be best, so I said yes to three.

But Hannah didn't get pregnant. We'd assumed it would be so easy. She worried constantly, and I was convinced the stress she felt was the real problem. After eighteen months she wanted to see a fertility specialist and I agreed. That was when we learned that getting Hannah pregnant was the very least of our concerns. Within a week of our first visit to the specialist, Hannah was diagnosed with stage-four ovarian cancer. By the time the discovery was made, it was too late to save her.

I couldn't help feeling I should have known, should have suspected that something wasn't right. As a medical professional, I blamed myself for the fact that Hannah went undiagnosed as long as she did. If I'd paid closer attention, I told myself, I might have picked up on the clues. I'd been busy, preoccupied with work. I had other things on my mind.

Friends have argued with me, friends like Patrick O'Malley, who's another pediatrician and one of my partners. They frequently reminded me—as did Hannah herself—that ovarian cancer is notoriously lacking in symptoms until it's too late. I knew all that. What I realized was that I *needed* to feel guilty, to punish myself; I think I felt better if I could blame myself for not noticing.

"Remember the night Steph and I had you and Hannah over for dinner?" Ritchie asked, breaking into my thoughts. "The last night?"

I nodded. It'd been a Friday evening, the final time we'd gone out as a couple. We'd received news that afternoon that had rocked our world. The latest test results had come in—and they showed that the chemo had done little to slow the progression of the disease.

Devastated, I'd wanted to cancel dinner, but Hannah insisted we go. She'd put on a bright smile and walked into her brother and sister-in-law's home as though nothing was wrong. I was an emotional mess and barely made it through the evening. Not Hannah. If I hadn't known, I would never have guessed.

"Yeah, I remember."

"She asked me to do something for her that night," Ritchie went on to say.

"Hannah did?" Unable to hide my surprise, I looked up from my beer.

Now Ritchie glanced away. "While you were playing a video game with Max, Hannah spoke with me privately."

I moved to the edge of my seat. The noise from the television blaring above the bar seemed to fade into the background. Every muscle in my body tensed, almost as if I knew what Ritchie was about to tell me.

"She said the doctors had delivered bad news."

I focused on an empty bar stool on the other side of the room. "I wanted to cancel dinner. Hannah wouldn't let me."

"She had a good reason for wanting to come that night," Ritchie explained. "She told me there wasn't any hope left and she'd accepted that she was going to die."

I wasn't in the mood to hear this.

Ritchie exhaled loudly. "She wasn't afraid of dying, you know."

"Why should she be? Heaven was made for people like Hannah."

Ritchie nodded, agreeing with me. "She'd made her peace with God long before that night. She never had a fatalistic attitude. She wanted to live. More than anything, she wanted to live."

At one time I'd doubted that. "I begged her to let

me take her to Europe because I'd read about an experimental treatment there. She wouldn't go."

"It was too late," Ritchie said simply. His hand tightened around the beer bottle. "She knew it even if we didn't."

That was Hannah—not only was she wise, but forever practical. While she was willing to accept the inevitable, I clung to every shred of hope. I spent hours studying medical journals, calling specialists, doing online research. But my crazed efforts to cure her didn't make any difference. In the end Hannah had been right; she'd reached the point of no return. She died less than two months later.

Even now I was shocked by how quickly she slipped away. It was the only time in our marriage that I became truly angry with her. I wanted Hannah to fight the cancer. I shouted and paced and slammed my fist against the wall. Gently she took my bleeding knuckles between her own hands and kissed away the pain. What she didn't seem to understand was that no amount of tenderness would ease the ache of her leaving me.

The waitress brought our meals, but I couldn't have swallowed a single bite had my life depended on it. Ritchie apparently felt the same because his steak remained untouched for several minutes.

"Hannah asked me to give you this," my brother-in-law finally said. He pulled an envelope from his jacket.

"A letter?"

"She asked me to wait until she'd been gone a year. Then and only then was I to hand this over to you. It was the last thing my sister asked of me."

I stared up at Ritchie, hardly able to believe he'd kept this from me. We worked out at the gym three mornings a week and had for years. In all these months he'd never let on that he had this letter in his possession.

"The night of the dinner party I promised Hannah I'd give you this," Ritchie said. "I put the letter in our safety-deposit box and waited, just like she wanted me to."

Not knowing what to say or how to react, I took the letter.

We left the sports bar soon after. I don't remember driving home. One minute I was in the parking garage in downtown Seattle and the next time I was aware of anything I'd reached the house and was sitting in my driveway.

Once I'd gone inside, I dropped my keys on the kitchen counter and walked into the living room. I sat on the edge of the sofa and stared at the envelope. Hannah had written one word on the front of it.

Michael.

I looked at my name, mesmerized as grief rippled through me. Unbelievable though it seemed, it felt as if her love for me vibrated off the paper.

My hand shook as I turned over the envelope and carefully opened it.

Chapter Two

I don't know how long I stared at the letter before I found the courage to unfold it. It consisted of four sheets.

The first thing I noticed was the date. March 13. This was another date that had been burned in my memory—the Friday of our appointment with the medical team, when we'd received the devastating news.

Hannah had written the letter that day? That was impossible. I'd been with her every minute from the appointment until dinner with Ritchie and Steph. That meant . . .

I fell back against the sofa cushion and closed my eyes. Hannah must have written the letter *before* the appointment. She knew even before we got the final word. She'd always known. In some way I think I did, too, only I couldn't face it. I'd refused to accept what should have been evident.

I returned my attention to the letter. She'd written it by hand, her cursive elegant and flowing. I felt a visceral reaction to seeing her handwriting, which had once been so familiar. I tensed as if I'd just taken a punch to the gut.

My darling Michael,
   I know this letter will come as a shock to you and I apologize for that. It's been a year

now and I imagine it's been a difficult one for you, as well as our parents and Ritchie. I would've given anything to have spared you this grief.

Even on the verge of death, Hannah didn't think of herself. Instead, she was thinking of me, our parents and her brother and how terribly we missed her and how deeply we'd loved her.

For the past few weeks I've been giving serious thought to what I wanted to say and what my last words to you would be. Please bear with me as I have quite a lot on my mind.

I know people laugh when they hear about love at first sight. I was only eighteen when we met, and young as I was, I knew instantly that you were the man I was going to love . . . and I have, from that moment forward. I will love you until the day I die and beyond. And in my heart I know you'll love me, too. I want to thank you for loving me. Your devotion to me through everything I've undergone since the cancer was diagnosed has been the greatest gift of my life. You have made me so happy, Michael.

I closed my eyes again, fearing I didn't have the emotional strength to continue. I knew when Ritchie handed me this letter that reading it would be hard, but I didn't know *how* hard it was going to be. I dragged in a deep breath and went on.

The early years of our marriage were some of the most wonderful days of my life. We had so little, and yet all we needed was each other. I loved you so much and was . . . am so proud of you, of the caring pediatrician you've become. You were born to be a physician, Michael. And I was born to love you. Thank you for loving me back, for giving so much of yourself to me, especially during these past few months. You made them the very best months of my life.

I don't want to die, Michael. I fought this, I honestly did. I gave it everything in me. Nothing would have made me happier than to grow old with you. I'm so sorry that, for me, the end has to come so soon.

Please don't ever believe I had a defeatist attitude. When we first got the diagnosis, I was determined to fight this and win. It's just in the past week that I've come to realize that this cancer is bigger than I am. There's no use pretending otherwise.

I had to stop reading a second time, regretting once more my insistence that Hannah travel to Europe for the experimental treatment I'd wanted her to receive. It'd been far too late by then. I took a moment to compose myself, then went back to her letter.

I've asked Ritchie to give you this a year after my death. Knowing you as well as I do, I suspect you've buried yourself in work. My guess is that you spend twelve hours a day at the office, eating on the run. That isn't a healthy lifestyle, my darling. I do hope you're still meeting Ritchie at the gym three times a week.

I smiled. Yes, Hannah knew everything about me. Right down to the long hours and skipped meals. I'd tried to quit my exercise regime, too, just like I'd dropped Thursday-night poker with the guys. But Ritchie wouldn't let me. It became easier to show up than to find an excuse.

Two weeks after Hannah's funeral he arrived on my doorstep in his workout clothes and dragged me back to the gym. A couple of early-morning calls from my brother-in-law, and I decided I couldn't fend him off anymore, so our workout became part of my routine once again.

This next section of my letter is the most painful for me to write. Although it hurts, I have to accept that there's no hope now. I suppose it's only natural when facing one's mortality that regrets surface, along with the knowledge that the end is close. The greatest of those regrets is my inability to have children. This is harder for me than even the discovery that my cancer is terminal. I so badly wanted your baby, Michael. A child for my sake, yes, but yours, too. You should be a father. You will be a wonderful father. Oh, Michael, I so wanted a child.

Once more I was forced to stop reading as a lump formed in my throat. "I wanted a child, too," I whispered. I rested the letter on my knee and wondered if I could finish without giving in to the weakness of tears. And yet I had to read on. I had to know Hannah's last words to me.

I have one final request of you, my darling, and I hope you will honor it.

"Anything." I would do anything for Hannah.

What I want, what I need from you, is this, my dearest love. I want you to marry again.

I gasped. No way! I'd already thought about this, and I couldn't do it. I'd had the love of my life and I'd be foolish to believe it could happen twice. If I did remarry, I'd be cheating the new woman I pledged to love. I'd be cheating us both because my heart would always belong to Hannah and only to Hannah.

I can see you shaking your head, insisting it isn't possible. Michael, I know you. I can almost hear your protests. But this is important, so please, please listen. Loving another woman won't diminish the love we had. Nor does it mean you'll love me any less. I will always be a part of you and you will remain a part of me.

The thing you must remember is that my life's journey is over.

Yours isn't.

You have a lot of living left to do and I don't want you to waste another moment grieving for me. You made me completely happy, and you'll make another woman equally so.

I wasn't sure I agreed with Hannah, wasn't sure I was capable of loving another woman, not with the same intensity, the same depth. She didn't understand what she was asking of me. I had no desire for another woman, no desire to share my life with anyone else ever again.

Knowing how stubborn you are, I realize you're going to require a bit of help, so I've compiled a short list of candidates for you to consider.

What? A list? Hannah had supplied me with a list of possible replacements? If it wasn't so shocking I would've laughed. Still, curiosity got the better of me.

Remember Winter Adams, my cousin? She was a bridesmaid in our wedding. Winter has a big heart and she loves children. She'd make you an excellent wife. She's also a chef and will cook you incredible meals. In addition to being my cousin, she's been a good friend. I want you to seriously consider her.

Of course I remembered Winter. She and Hannah had been close. We hadn't seen as much of Winter after she opened her restaurant, the French Café on Blossom Street, not far from my office. Hannah and I had visited the café a few times and enjoyed coffee and croissants. I recalled her keeping in touch with Hannah, mostly by phone. If I remembered correctly, Winter had been going through some relationship crisis shortly before Hannah was diagnosed, and, Hannah, being Hannah, had offered her comfort and encouragement.

Winter had been at the funeral and had doubled over in tears at the cemetery. I hadn't heard from her since, although I vaguely recalled a sympathy card she'd sent me after we buried Hannah.

I liked Winter, but I wasn't interested. Despite Hannah's confidence in her cousin as a potential wife, I had no intention of remarrying. Besides, all Winter and I had in common was our memories of Hannah.

The second woman I want you to consider is Leanne Lancaster.

The name was somewhat familiar, but I couldn't immediately figure out why. She wasn't a friend of Hannah's that I could remember.

Leanne was my oncology nurse. She was always kind to me and so caring. As a nurse she'd have a special understanding of the stresses you face as a physician. Leanne and I talked quite a bit and if I'd . . . if I'd had the chance, I feel Leanne and I would've become good friends. I admire her emotional strength. She's divorced and had a rough time of it. I don't know her as well as I do Winter, but my heart tells me she'd suit you. Meet with her, Michael, get to know her. That's all I ask.

Meet with Leanne . . . get to know her. I doubt Hannah had an inkling of what she was really asking. I had no interest whatsoever in seeking out this woman. As I thought about it, I realized I did remember the oncology nurse. And Hannah was right. Leanne was a kind and caring person—but that didn't mean I had any desire to know her better!

The third person on my list is Macy Roth. I don't think you've met her. She's a part-time model I became friends with while I was still able to work. We met because of some fashion shows I was involved in and some catalog work she did for the store. When Macy learned I was in the hospital she sent me notes of encouragement—cards she made herself with adorable sketches of her cats. Remember? And she knit me socks and a shawl I wore during my chemo. She's funny and clever and multitalented; she models and paints murals and has two or three other jobs. As I was thinking over this list, her name came to me because I know she'll make you smile. She'll bring balance to your life, Michael. I'm afraid that when I'm gone, you'll become far too serious. I want you to laugh and enjoy life. The same unrestrained way Macy does.

Once again, Hannah was right; I hadn't laughed much in the past two years. The fact is, I couldn't remember the last good belly laugh I'd had. Life *was* serious. I'd lost my wife and, frankly, I didn't have much reason to smile, let alone laugh.

I didn't remember this Macy, although no doubt she'd featured in some of Hannah's stories. As for those gifts—the sketches and socks—they'd be among Hannah's things, the stuff I'd brought home from the hospital. I'd thrown everything into a box and shoved it in the back of a closet. And I'd never looked at it again.

I've given you three names, Michael. Each is someone I know and trust. Any of them would make you a good wife and companion; with any one you could have the children you were meant to father.

I'll be watching and waiting from heaven's gate, looking down at you. Choose well.
Your loving wife,
Hannah

I folded the sheets and set them on the coffee table while I tried to absorb what I'd read. That Hannah had written this letter when she did was shocking enough. Then for her to suggest I remarry—and go so far as to name three women—was almost more than I could take in.

If she was watching over me, then she had to know what hell this first year without her had been.

I'm not much of a drinking man. A few beers with the guys at a sporting event is generally my limit. All at once I felt a need for something stronger.

I remembered a bottle of Scotch stashed in a cupboard somewhere in the kitchen. My father gave it to me when I graduated, claiming it was for "medicinal" purposes. If ever there was an occasion for a medicinal drink, it was now.

I spent nearly fifteen minutes searching for it. Hannah had stored it in the pantry, the last place I thought to look. Not surprisingly, it turned out to be single malt, since that was what my father drank. His favorite brand, too—The Glenlivet.

Reading the label, I saw that it had been aged eighteen years and I'd had it for at least a decade. None of that ten-year stuff for dear ol' Dad.

I got a clean glass out of the dishwasher, added ice cubes and poured two fingers of my twenty-eight-year-old Scotch before I settled back down on the sofa. Kicking off my shoes, I rested my feet on the coffee table and reached for Hannah's letter. I would read it again with an open mind and see if I could possibly respond to her last request. I didn't think so. Hannah was all the woman I'd ever need. The only woman I'd ever love. I already knew I'd find anyone else sadly lacking—even the three women my wife had so carefully selected for me.

Chapter Three

Wednesday morning I was at the gym by six. Ritchie was on the treadmill, his iPod plugged into his ears, when I stepped onto the machine beside his.

He looked over, saw it was me and stared expectantly. I knew I was in for an inquisition as soon as we entered the locker room. I hadn't shown up on Monday morning and ignored his phone calls for the past two days. I wasn't ready to talk about Hannah's letter, not even to my best friend.

Ritchie finished his routine first. Just as I'd suspected, he was waiting for me in the locker room, sitting on the bench with a towel draped around his neck. He leaned forward, elbows braced on his knees. When I appeared, he glanced up.

"You didn't return my phone calls," he said, as if I needed to be reminded.

"I was busy."

"Doing what?"

I was reluctant to tell him, although I knew that he of all people would understand. "I got drunk on Sunday after I got home," I admitted. The hangover on Monday had been a killer. From this point forward I was sticking to beer. Maybe my father could handle the strong stuff, but not me.

"Because of Hannah's letter?"

I nodded and lowered myself onto the bench. I leaned forward, sitting in the same position as my brother-in-law. "Hannah wants me to remarry."

Ritchie's eyes widened. "Get outta here."

My sentiments exactly. "She went so far as to give me a list."

Ritchie's mouth sagged open. "A list? You mean of *women?*"

I nodded again.

"Why would she do that?"

Explaining Hannah's reason was beyond me. I didn't understand it, although I'd read the letter a dozen times.

"Hannah seems to think I won't do well on my

own and that I need a wife." I avoided mentioning that she wanted me to be a father, too.

"She actually gave you a list?" He seemed as shocked as I'd been when I first read the letter.

I didn't respond.

"Who's on it? Anyone I know?"

I looked away. "Your cousin, Winter."

"My cousin?" he repeated.

"Do you know someone else named Winter?" I snapped, sorry now that I'd said anything.

"No," he said sheepishly. "Who else?"

"Leanne Lancaster. She was Hannah's oncology nurse."

"Don't remember her. What's she like?"

I wasn't sure what to tell him. "Quiet. Gentle. A good nurse. Hannah really liked her."

"No kidding."

I ignored that.

"Anyone else?"

"Someone I've never met. A model she worked with by the name of Macy Roth."

Ritchie released a low whistle. "A model, you say?"

"Hannah says Macy will give me a reason to laugh again," I told him, unable to disguise my sarcasm. "And that's practically a quote."

My brother-in-law chuckled. "I bet Steph wouldn't tell me to marry a model if anything happened to her."

I knew Ritchie was joking; still, I couldn't let the

33

comment pass. "Just pray to God nothing does."

My brother-in-law frowned. "It was a joke, Michael. Lighten up, would you?"

He was right; I didn't need to take every little comment so seriously. "Sorry," I muttered.

Ritchie nudged me. "You going to do it?"

I shook my head. "I doubt it."

"Why not?"

The answer should've been obvious. "I'm not ready."

"Will you ever be?"

Good question. "Probably not," I said honestly. I'd lost my wife, my soul mate. I couldn't ever forget that or blithely "move on" with my life, as various friends and acquaintances were so fond of telling me I should.

"I thought you'd say that," Ritchie said. "Hannah knew you'd hibernate for the rest of your life, which is why she forced the issue. My sister loved you and—"

"Listen, Ritchie, I don't need a lecture."

"I don't intend to give you one. Answer one simple question and then I'll shut up."

"Okay, fine. Ask away," I said, resigned to the fact that he wouldn't leave me alone until he'd said what he wanted to say.

He stared at me for a long intense moment. "Do you suppose it was easy for her to write that letter?"

I sat up straighter.

"What woman wants to think of her husband with someone else?"

"That's two questions," I said.

"They're one and the same," he argued.

I closed my eyes. Insensitive jerk that I was, I hadn't given a single thought to what Hannah must've been feeling when she wrote the letter.

"If the situation had been reversed, could you have offered up the names of men you'd trust to be her husband?"

I didn't need any time to think about *that* one. "No."

"Me, neither," Ritchie confessed. "That said, the least you can do is take her letter to heart and get in touch with these women." He chuckled. "If it was me, I'd start with the model."

Very funny. It'd been years since I'd asked a woman out. I wouldn't even know how to go about it. "Dating . . . me?"

"Dating—you. Sure, why not? You're young and you've got a lot of years left."

Hannah had said almost the same thing.

"You already know Winter. If you're more comfortable with her, then give her a call."

"And say what?" I asked. My fear was that the only subject we had in common was Hannah. If we went to dinner, Hannah was all we'd have to discuss, and we'd both be crying in our soup before the main course was served.

"Hell, I don't know."

"I'd want to talk about Hannah."

Ritchie didn't seem to think that was so terrible. "So would Winter. They were good friends, even as kids, trading clothes, spending the night at each other's houses." He smiled. "Once when we were all in our early teens, our two families went camping. The restroom was clear on the other side of the campground.

"In the middle of the night, I could hear Hannah and Winter whispering that they had to go to the bathroom really bad." Ritchie's eyes gleamed with a look of remembered mischief. "Neither of them wanted to make the long trek across the campground so they decided to walk into the woods close to our campsite."

I knew what was coming.

"I waited until they had their drawers down, then turned my flashlight on them."

I grinned. Ritchie had always been a practical joker.

"You wouldn't believe how loud they screamed," he said, laughing. "I swear they woke up half the campground. People thought there was a black bear on the loose. Those two girls single-handedly caused a panic."

Years earlier, when we were first dating, Hannah had told me the story. I had to admit it was funny. But the most I could manage now was a weak smile. Maybe she had a point; maybe it *was* time I found a reason to laugh again.

"Call Winter," Ritchie urged.

He made it sound easy, but it wouldn't be. I had no idea what to say, how to approach her. "Do you see her often?"

"Hardly ever," Ritchie said. "Life's strange, you know?"

"Tell me about it," I groaned.

"Our families were close when we were kids and we both live and work in Seattle, but the only time we see each other is at weddings and funerals."

He winced and I could see he instantly regretted the reminder.

"It's the same with my cousins," I said. We'd drifted apart through the years without any intention of doing so. Life got busy and people scattered, and those connections were hard to maintain.

"Give her a call," Ritchie urged a second time.

If we could talk about Hannah, it might not be so bad.

"Better yet . . ." Ritchie looked pointedly in my direction.

"What?"

"Stop by her place."

"Her house?" That seemed rather presumptuous.

"No . . . that restaurant she has. I can't think of the name."

"The French Café," I told him.

"Right. I remember now. I don't know why she

called it that. Our background's English, not French."

My guess was that her reason had to do with the menu. "They serve great croissants."

That got Ritchie's notice. "You mean to say you've been there?"

"With Hannah. We checked it out a few times. It's on Blossom Street."

"Hey, man, that's not far from here. You could stop by casually on your way to work. If you call her it becomes sort of a big deal. Going to the restaurant would be more natural."

"You're right," I said, my decision made.

"Want me to walk over there with you?"

"No." I didn't need my brother-in-law holding my hand. If this worked out, fine—and if not, that was fine, too.

We showered and dressed for the office and headed out. Ritchie's a chiropractor. His office is north of the downtown area, whereas mine's just off Fifth. Blossom Street's a few blocks from there, not that far from Pill Hill where Virginia Mason, Swedish Hospital and several other medical facilities were located.

I took off at a clipped pace. My office opens at eight, so I didn't have a lot of time—and I wanted to get this over with. I saw the French Café as soon as I rounded the corner of Blossom Street. Two people entered the restaurant as three others came out. The place was doing a brisk morning business. I was happy to see that it was such a success; Hannah would be pleased for her cousin.

I liked the atmosphere with the striped awning and the tables set up outside. I was sure they hadn't been there on my earlier visits with Hannah. The line was about ten people long when I joined it; I saw that we were being served by one clerk and one cashier. Impatiently, I glanced at my watch. I really didn't have time and yet I couldn't make myself walk away. My attention went to the glass case, which displayed a number of baked goods from croissants to doughnuts and sweet rolls. I decided on a latte, along with a croissant.

My mind, however, wasn't on my order. When I finally reached the counter I felt light-headed and nauseous. "Can I help you?" the clerk asked.

"Coffee and a croissant," I said quickly. A latte would take too long.

"What size coffee?"

"Uh, medium."

"Do you want me to leave room for cream?"

"I drink it black," I said and retrieved my wallet. With my pulse pounding, I asked, "I don't suppose Winter's here?" My throat was so dry I could barely speak.

The clerk looked up. "Just a minute and I'll check for you."

I could see that the other customers didn't appreciate me holding everything up, so I stepped aside while the clerk went into the kitchen, taking the opportunity to pay. She returned half a minute later and shook her head. "She isn't in yet."

"Oh." That response sounded incredibly stupid, even to me.

"Would you like to leave her a note?"

"Ah . . . sure."

She grabbed a pen and pad and handed them to me. I took them, together with my coffee, and found an empty seat. My coffee was lukewarm before I gave up trying to write anything; I was already late for the office and a cold sweat dampened my brow. This was senseless. I had nothing to say to this woman. Wadded-up sheets of paper littered the tabletop, and I felt pathetic and angry with myself for listening to Ritchie. I should've known better.

Eventually I walked back to the counter and returned the empty pad. "Just tell Winter that Dr. Michael Everett stopped by this morning."

"Will do," the friendly clerk said.

"Thanks," I mumbled as I shoved the crumpled sheets in a trash can, then made my way to the door, hoping I wouldn't run into Winter on Blossom Street.

Feeling I'd wasted my time, I hurried to the office. In our partnership of three—Patrick O'Malley and Yvette Schauer are the other doctors—each of us has our own office and head nurse. Linda Barclay, my nurse, has been with me from the beginning. The rest of the staff is shared—a receptionist, one person who does transcriptions and two all-purpose clerks who also work on forms for insurance companies and government agencies.

Linda looked concerned when I dashed into the office several minutes later than usual. She didn't ask where I'd been, for which I was grateful. I hadn't arrived late in so long she must've known that whatever delayed me was important. I reached for my white jacket, jerking my arms into the sleeves, and wordlessly headed down the hallway to the exam room, where my first patient waited. I made an effort to push all thoughts of Hannah's cousin out of my mind and concentrate on my appointments. Nothing out of the ordinary—some vaccinations, checkups, a case of strep throat.

At the end of the day, I stepped into my office to make the phone calls that tend to dominate the late afternoons. That's when I generally review prescriptions that need to be refilled, read over lab reports and deal with any other messages that require my attention. I often spent two or three hours at my desk after the rest of the staff had left. Since I didn't have a reason to rush home, it didn't bother me. The quiet following the hectic pace of the day was a welcome respite.

Several pink message slips were neatly laid out on my desk. I set them aside to look at when everything else was done.

It was after six before I got to the last message. In Linda's distinctive handwriting it read: *Winter Adams phoned. She said it was a private matter.* She'd written the phone number below.

Chapter Four

Macy Roth tore through the disorganized mess that was her bedroom. Her Mexican ruffle skirt had to be in here *somewhere*. She really had to get everything sorted out and she would, she promised herself—one of these days. She tossed discarded clothes aside in a frantic search for the white skirt, moving quickly around the room. Clean sheets, fresh from the dryer, resting on top of her bare mattress meant she'd have to make the bed later, only she wasn't sure what time she'd be home. The chore she disliked more than any other was making the bed; it always seemed so pointless, since she'd be sleeping in it that night and messing it up all over again. Same went for dishes. Well, it couldn't be helped. That was just the nature of housework.

"Snowball!" she yelled as her long-haired white cat bounced onto the mattress and snuggled into the mound of clean sheets, luxuriating in their warmth. Waving her arms, Macy cried, "Scat! Get out of here."

The cat paid no attention, which was fairly typical. The only time Snowball recognized her voice was when Macy called him into the kitchen to eat. "Fine, I'll change your name." She'd acquired Snowball as a fluffy white kitten, but he'd turned out to be a male and seemed to object to his name. "I'll think on it, buddy, okay? Now get out of those sheets."

Peace, hearing the commotion, raced into the bedroom and leaped onto the bed in a single bound. Lovie followed. Now all three of her cats romped in the dryer-warm sheets, rolling around in the tangled pillowcases. They appeared to be having great fun. If she hadn't been in such a hurry, Macy would've taken time to play with them.

"Do any of you know where I put my skirt?" she asked.

The cats ignored her.

"Did one of you drag it off?" she demanded.

Again she was ignored. "Ungrateful beasts," she muttered as the oven timer dinged. "The casserole." Oh, my goodness, she'd forgotten all about it. Hurrying into the kitchen, Macy grabbed the oven mitts and took the dish from the oven. The recipe was a new one and the casserole smelled divine.

She switched off the oven and started toward the back porch, where several piles of laundry awaited her. She really did need to get a handle on her chores and she would—one day. But right now she had to find her white skirt, take the casserole dish over to Harvey and drive to the recording studio. Most important of all, she had to arrive on time. Her job depended on it.

Digging through a pile of dirty clothes, she sighed with relief when she located the skirt. Looking it over, she decided it could stand one more wearing and stepped into it, adjusted the waistband and tucked in her multicolored blouse. All she needed now was her sandals.

On her way to the bedroom, she checked her reflection in the bathroom mirror. Frowning, she ran a brush through her curly red hair and used a clip to sweep one side above her left ear and secure it. She needed a haircut, too, but she couldn't afford that until she was paid for recording the radio ad. She really, really couldn't be late again.

The producer had warned her last week, when she was a few minutes late for another radio spot. She'd had a good excuse, but Don Sharman wasn't interested. He kept saying that if she couldn't show up when she was scheduled, they'd find someone who could. He was unwilling to listen to her explanation—that she'd been at the vet's with Snowball, who'd had a bladder infection.

No, Macy absolutely could not lose this gig. It was perfect for her. She'd been told her voice had a melodious quality, and it must be true because she'd read several commercials for this agency.

The money wasn't bad, either. She always got a kick out of hearing her own voice on the radio touting the benefits of Preparation H, a hemorrhoid medication currently marked down by Elburn's, a locally owned pharmacy.

Her grandmother had drilled into Macy the importance of never leaving the house without lipstick, so she added a bit of color to her lips. And while she was at the mirror she applied some coppery eye shadow that highlighted her green eyes. Satisfied that her grandmother would be pleased, she slipped her feet into her sandals.

"I've got to get this casserole to Harvey," she told the cats, who'd deserted the bed and gathered around her. "Watch the house for me."

Lifting the glass dish with her tiger-striped oven mitts, Macy opened the screen door with her hip and started down the front steps, avoiding her bicycle at the bottom. She took a shortcut across the lawn and ran up the steps to Harvey's place.

The World War II veteran had been her grandmother's next-door neighbor for more than forty years. They'd been good friends and neighbors all that time, and although neither would've admitted it, Macy was convinced they were—as her grandmother might have said—"sweet" on each other.

The front door was open, so Macy called out. Normally she wouldn't have bothered with formalities like announcing herself or ringing the doorbell, but it was difficult to open the screen while she was loaded down with a hot casserole dish.

"Go away." Harvey's voice came from inside the kitchen.

"I can't."

"Why not?" he barked.

Macy had learned long ago that his gruff exterior disguised a generous, loving heart. Apparently, his mission in life was to hide it.

"I brought you dinner."

"It's not even noon," he shouted.

"I know, but I won't be home by dinnertime," Macy shouted back. She made an effort to open the screen only to discover it was locked.

"Come on, Harvey, open the door."

"I locked it for a reason." Taking his time, he ambled into the living room and reluctantly unfastened the screen. He looked none too happy to see her. "I've got more important things to do than answer the door, you know."

"Of course you do." She glided past him and into the kitchen. The newspaper lay on the table, the crossword puzzle half-completed. Harvey read the paper from front to back every day.

Macy set the casserole on the stove, then pulled off her oven mitts and set them aside.

"What's that?" he asked, nodding at the casserole and grimacing with exaggerated disgust.

"Food."

"Don't get smart with me, little girl."

Macy grinned. "It's a new recipe."

"So I'm your guinea pig."

"In a manner of speaking." Harvey had lost weight in the past year. His clothes hung on him and she couldn't help worrying. At eighty-six, his age had finally begun to show. He used to work in his yard year-round and had always taken great pride in his garden and flower beds. Twice now, Macy had mowed his yard for him. If he noticed he didn't say. She had an old push mower that had been her grandmother's, and it was better exercise than working out at the gym. Less costly, too.

Macy avoided anything that required monthly payments, other than those that were unavoidable, like water and electricity. Since she didn't have a steady job, she couldn't count on a regular income. There were a lot of months when she had to resort to digging in the bottom of her purse for lost coins.

"It smells good," Macy said, leaning over the casserole dish and giving an appreciative whiff.

"What's in it?" he asked suspiciously.

"Meat and rice."

"What kind of meat?"

"Chicken," she said. "But when did you get so choosy?"

"I've got my standards," he insisted.

She smiled; it was true—but those standards were starting to slip. She saw dirty dishes stacked in the kitchen sink. That wasn't so unusual at her house, but it was for Harvey. He liked organization, thrived on it, while she was most comfortable in chaos. Perhaps *comfortable* was putting it too strongly. Saying she was accustomed to chaos would be more accurate. One day she really did intend to put everything in order; she'd have Harvey teach her.

"I don't need you looking after me," he said. "Haven't you got better things to do than feed an old man?"

"Not really," she told him. Granted, she had to get to the studio, but Harvey was a priority. Even if her grandmother hadn't asked Macy to keep an eye on him, she would've done it anyway. "Besides, *I'm* the one who needs *you*."

He snorted and sat back down at the table, picking up his pen. "I don't intend to argue with you all afternoon."

"Fine." She tucked the oven mitts under her arm. "Now promise me you'll eat dinner."

He glared at her and shook his head.

Macy sank into the chair across from him with a deep sigh.

"By the way, what's the name of that singer your grandmother liked? It's seven letters."

"Barry Manilow?"

"Yeah, that's the one." He filled in the squares, then immediately started working on the area around that answer.

Macy exhaled again, just to remind him she was still there.

"What are you doing *now?*" he grumbled, briefly glancing in her direction.

"I'm staying here until you promise me you're going to test my new recipe."

"Well, you'll have a long wait. I haven't been hungry in five years."

"I've got time," she lied.

"Thought you had a job today."

"I do."

"You're going to be late."

"In that case, they might not ask me to work for them again." Actually, that was more of a guarantee. In Sharman's world, as he'd repeatedly pointed out, time was money.

Harvey snorted once more. "I suppose you're going to blame me if you lose this job."

"I'll probably lose everything," she said dramatically.

"You could always sell your art. That is, if you ever finished a project."

Macy shrugged. "Not much of a market for it in this economy."

He muttered something under his breath. "If I agreed—and I do mean *if*—would I have to eat the whole thing in one sitting?"

"Don't be silly."

"You're the silly one," he said. "Don't know why you can't leave an old man alone."

"But, Harvey, you're my best friend."

"Me and all those cats you're constantly feeding. What you need is a dog."

"I prefer cats." It was really the other way around; the cats seemed to prefer her. She had Snowball, Peace and Lovie, who were her inside friends, and there were an additional four or five who showed up at irregular intervals, expecting a handout. They'd sort of adopted her. She'd never gone looking for pets; they just seemed to find her.

"Get," Harvey said, waving both hands at her. "Go on. Get out of here."

"Sorry, can't do it until you give me your word."

"You're as bad as your grandmother."

"Worse," she returned. "Or so you've told me dozens of times."

"Okay, worse. No need to quibble about it. I'll have you know this was a nice, peaceful neighborhood until your grandmother moved in. Just my luck that she willed *you* the place. Between the two of you, I haven't had a moment's rest in over forty years."

"You love me." He'd deny it to his dying day, but Macy knew otherwise. He'd loved her grandmother, too—more than he'd ever admit.

"No, I don't," he stated emphatically. "I tolerate you. Your grandmother turned out to be a good friend, but you need someone to keep an eye on you and it's not going to be me."

"We need each other," she said and meant it.

Harvey was her last link to her beloved grandmother. Lotty Roth had adored Macy and her curly red hair and her quirky personality. Macy had always been . . . different. While other children got involved in sports and music and dance, Macy had been what her grandmother referred to as a free spirit. She'd never had any interest in organized activities, and her artistic abilities were developed on her own. She'd rather stand in front of a painting at a museum or a gallery, absorbing its beauty and skill, than analyze the artist's techniques in a classroom.

She could remember once, in sixth grade, being called upon to answer a history question about the Civil War. She'd stood quietly next to her desk, and the teacher had repeated the question. Macy knew the answer, but she'd been thinking about something else that seemed far more important at the time—her plans to draw one of her cats and how much fun it would be once she got out of class to sit down with Princess and a pencil and pad. When her teacher demanded an answer, Macy started talking about Princess and her antics, and soon everyone was laughing—except Mrs. Moser, who'd sent her to the principal's office for disrupting the class. As her father used to ruefully say, Macy was a few French fries short of a Happy Meal.

Her grandmother had been her one ally when it seemed Macy didn't have a friend in the world.

Grandma Lotty's home was her refuge. Like Macy, Lotty Roth had possessed an artist's soul, and that was something they'd had in common. They'd seen the world in a similar way, from their passionate love of animals to their delight in unconventional people and places. When her grandmother died two years earlier, to everyone's surprise she'd left Macy her house.

Macy had loved this old home with its gingerbread trim and immediately painted it yellow with bright red shutters. The white picket fence was still white but only because she'd run out of paint. Harvey frequently complained that the house looked as if someone from Candy Land had moved in next door.

"You're gonna be late," Harvey said now.

"Guess so," she said with an exaggerated yawn.

"Didn't you just tell me that if you showed up late one more time they wouldn't use you again?"

"Yup. That's what Mr. Sharman said."

Harvey closed his eyes and threw back his head. "So when you lose the house, you'll tell me I should let you live in one of my spare bedrooms."

"Could I?" she asked cheerfully.

"No," he snapped.

"All it'll take to avoid a complete upheaval of your life is a simple promise."

"That's blackmail."

"But it's for your own good." She glanced pointedly at her watch. "It'd be a real shame to lose this job, not to mention a potential career in radio commercials."

"For crying out loud," Harvey said and slammed down his pen. "All right, I'll eat some of the casserole."

Relieved, Macy grinned, leaped up from the chair and kissed his leathery cheek. "Thank you, Harvey."

The old man rubbed the side of his face, as if to wipe away her kiss. He frowned in her direction.

Macy, on the other hand, couldn't have been more delighted.

"Gotta scoot," she said as she bounded out the door. "See you later."

"Don't hurry back," he shouted after her.

Macy grinned. Harvey loved her the same as he had her grandmother. She'd figured out years ago that the louder he fussed, the deeper his affection.

Home again, Macy grabbed her purse and car keys and hurried outside. If she made every green light, she wouldn't be more than five minutes late.

Mr. Sharman might not even notice.

Chapter Five

I didn't call Winter and she didn't try to reach me again, either. The truth is, I've never been much good at this dating thing. When I first met Hannah, she made everything so easy. I was attracted to her; she was attracted to me. I like that kind of honesty and straightforwardness. You so often find it in children, less often in adults, which is one reason I chose pediatrics. I'd make more money in another specialty, but I've only ever wanted to work with kids.

Frankly, I regretted going to the French Café. I wasn't ready to go out into the world; life was complicated enough. Still, Winter's phone number sat on the corner of my office desk and seemed to taunt me. I lost track of time while I looked at it. Then indecision would overcome me once again and I'd glance away.

Friday nights were always the worst for me. Hannah and I had made a practice of doing something special on Fridays. She called it our date night. That didn't mean we went out for fancy dinners and dancing or stuff like that. We couldn't have afforded it in the early years. But on Friday nights we spent time together, no matter what. Our "date" could be cuddling on the sofa, watching a rented movie and ordering pizza, or—especially later on—it might be a full-blown dinner party with three or four other couples.

Hannah loved to host parties. She enjoyed cooking and having friends over. She made everything look effortless and possessed a gift for making others feel comfortable. I'd come to enjoy these occasions far more than I'd ever expected.

Now, without Hannah, Friday nights seemed especially bleak and lonely. That was the reason

I'd started volunteering Friday evenings at a health clinic in Seattle's Central District. I usually arrived around six and stayed until eight or nine and went home exhausted. Not only did working those long hours help me get through what had once been a special night for my wife and me, but afterward I could almost guarantee that I'd be able to sleep.

Aside from the benefits I received, deep down I knew Hannah would approve of my volunteering.

I sat at my desk and it seemed that pink message slip with Winter's phone number wouldn't let me be. It might as well have been a flashing neon light the way my gaze kept returning to it. I felt as though Hannah herself was reminding me that calling these three women was the last thing she'd ever ask me to do.

"Oh, all right," I muttered. I grabbed the slip and glanced at the ceiling. "I hope you're happy."

As I may have mentioned, I often spoke to Hannah. That was our secret, mine and hers. I didn't admit this to other people, even Ritchie, because I was afraid they'd suggest I stop conversing with my dead wife. They'd say it was time I got on with my life and accepted the fact that Hannah was dead. Well, I *did* accept it, but I wasn't about to give up talking to her when I found such comfort in it. In more ways than I could count, I felt she was still with me.

Sighing, I picked up the phone. I didn't know

what I'd say when Winter answered. Apparently, she had the same problem because she hadn't contacted me again, either. I wondered if she felt as ill at ease as I did and assumed that was probably the case.

I exhaled when the call connected, and closed my eyes, praying for inspiration.

"The French Café," a pleasant-sounding woman announced.

"Oh, hi," I managed to say. "This is Dr. Michael Everett. May I speak to Winter Adams?"

"Hi, I'm Alix. Winter said you'd be phoning."

That was encouraging.

"Unfortunately she isn't here at the moment."

"Oh." So I was to receive a second reprieve. I smiled. I'd done my duty; Hannah couldn't fault me for not making the effort.

"Winter left instructions that if you called I was to give you her cell number."

I clenched my teeth. No reprieve, after all. It'd taken me three days to respond to her message and now the situation was going to drag on even longer. "Okay," I said. "Give me the number."

Alix recited it, I wrote it down and then repeated it. "Correct?" I asked.

"Yes," Alix confirmed. "I know Winter's anxious to speak to you."

Oh, good, now pressure had been added to the mix. Winter expected to hear from me. "I'll call her right away," I said and disconnected.

I knew I should follow through immediately, or else I'd leave the number sitting on my desk over the weekend. Another three or four days would pass, making it harder than ever. I hung up the phone and leaned back in my chair.

Folding my hands behind my head I analyzed my options. I could call Winter now, as I'd said I would, but I'd have to be quick, since I needed to leave for the clinic in ten minutes. Still, a lot could be said in that length of time.

The exchange of chitchat wouldn't take more than a minute, two at the most. I'd ask how she was and she'd say fine, and then she'd ask how I was getting along and I'd lie and tell her every-thing was going well. She'd express her condo-lences and then—what? Silence?

I wasn't going to mention Hannah's letter. I sup-posed I could ask about the café. That might take another minute or so. Eventually I'd need to get around to the reason I'd phoned her. It'd been almost a week since Ritchie had given me the letter and I felt as much at a loss now as when I'd first read it. The down-and-dirty truth was that I had no desire to remarry and resented being forced into confronting something I didn't even want to consider. Hannah was the only woman on earth for whom I'd do anything as crazy as this.

I stared at Winter's cell number so long that when I happened to look at my watch I realized I'd wasted my remaining ten minutes debating what I'd say. It was too late to call now. A sense of relief settled over me as I headed out of the office to the clinic.

The clinic provided free parking behind the five-story brick structure. A couple of the doctors' vehicles had been broken into so I preferred to take my chances on the street. Low income and high crime seemed to go hand in hand. Never mind that I was volunteering my time; I was putting my safety and my vehicle at risk.

The Central District Health Clinic waiting area was filled to capacity when I stepped inside. The volunteer staff sorted the order in which cases were to be seen based on the severity of need. As much as possible, they steered the children to me, although I saw my fair share of adults.

My first patient was a young woman named Shamika Wilson, who had a badly swollen right eye. She'd come to the clinic because she thought her arm was broken. I read over the chart and saw that she claimed her injuries had occurred as a result of falling down the stairs. An instant red flag went up. Apparently, Shamika Wilson made a habit of "falling down the stairs" because this was her third visit to the clinic with possible fractures in as many months.

The young woman refused to look my way as I started asking her questions.

"You fell down the stairs?" I pressed.

She nodded.

I refrained from mentioning the number of times this had happened. "When was the . . . accident?"

"Wednesday night."

Two days earlier. "Why did you wait so long to come to the clinic?" I asked, noting the pain she was in.

Shamika stared at the floor. "I thought it would get better on its own . . . but the pain just seemed to get worse."

Seeing that her arm was badly swollen and how she screamed at the mere touch of my fingers, I could only imagine the agony she'd endured for the past two days. "I'm ordering an X-ray," I said.

She bit her lip and nodded. Shamika knew as well as I did that the technician would need to move her arm to do the X-ray. It would cause her excruciating pain, but I had to know what I was dealing with before we could progress any further.

"Did someone bring you to the clinic?" I asked.

"My . . . husband."

"Is he in the waiting room now?" I asked. My anger was close to the surface and I struggled to hold it back. I wasn't entirely sure who was the object of this fury. The young woman must've seen that she wasn't fooling me with this tale of tripping on the stairs. She'd avoided eye contact when she referred to her husband, another telltale sign. The husband was some loser who used his wife as a punching bag to take out his own frustrations.

"Yeah, Kenny's waiting for me," Shamika said, again without meeting my gaze.

"I'll see you in a few minutes," I told her and left the room. I asked for a volunteer to escort Shamika to X-ray. Once she was out of earshot, I went to the waiting area. I asked to speak to Kenny.

A skinny, wiry man stepped forward. "How's Shamika?" he asked.

I stood in the doorway and looked him in the eye. "I've ordered an X-ray, but I'm fairly sure the arm's broken. It'll need to be set."

He sighed. "How long is that going to take?"

"I won't know until I see the X-rays." I glanced out at the crowded waiting room. "Shamika insists she fell down the stairs. I find that interesting because she's fallen down the stairs three times in the past few months."

Her husband shrugged. "What can I tell you? The bitch is clumsy."

I might've let the matter go if he'd referred to Shamika as anything but a bitch. "*Clumsy?* Now listen up, Kenny. You and I both know this accident on the stairs is pretty much a lie. Don't you realize how lucky you are to have a wife?" Whether they were legally husband and wife—I suspected they weren't—was irrelevant.

He looked up, and his eyes narrowed with challenge. He almost dared me to continue, and I was happy to defy his warning.

"You have a good woman, and you treat her like this?" I said from between gritted teeth. "Do you enjoy hitting a woman?"

He didn't answer.

I had the attention of everyone in the waiting area, which was what I wanted.

"She deserved it. The bitch's got a mouth on her."

"And I've got a temper," I said and shocked myself by grabbing his collar and lifting him off the ground so that he stood on the tips of his toes. I knew I might be asked to leave the clinic for pulling this stunt, but at the moment I didn't care. He had a wife and chose to mistreat her, while I would've given anything to have Hannah back.

"You're a little man," I spat out. "You hit your wife again and I will personally see to it that you're sorry. Do I make myself clear?" I carefully enunciated each word so there'd be no doubt in his mind that I was serious.

He fought to break my hold, but I had a firm grasp on his collar.

"Do we understand each other?" I asked, shoving him against the wall.

He managed to nod, which wasn't easy, seeing that I had his shirt wadded up to the point that he could hardly breathe.

"Good." I glared at him, our faces so close our noses practically touched.

"Dr. Everett." Mimi Johnson, who ran the clinic,

had her hand on my arm. She repeated my name again and then a third time.

I didn't know how long she'd been standing there or what else she'd said.

Reluctantly, I released Kenny, but maintained my stance, glaring at the other man, letting him know I wasn't backing down. He, on the other hand, couldn't get away from me fast enough.

The piece of scum brought his hand to his throat as if he'd been in mortal danger of being choked to death. If he hurt Shamika again, I'd have no qualms about making sure he suffered. I doubted Shamika would press charges against him. I'd seen this type of situation far too often; bullies and abusers rarely got the punishment they deserved.

Under normal circumstances, I'm not a violent man, but my limit had been reached. I wanted Kenny to feel embarrassed and humiliated and at the same time I was fairly confident that he understood there'd be consequences if I ever heard of him hitting this woman again. I'd make sure a police report was filed, but it wouldn't do much good unless Shamika pressed charges.

We scowled at each other and then he turned and fled the room, slamming the door behind him.

Mimi asked me to come into her office, which I did. Needless to say, the lecture that followed was completely justified. I listened and nodded at the appropriate times. My job wasn't to judge, but to treat the sick and injured to the best of my ability.

It was up to the authorities to handle cases of domestic violence. And it definitely wasn't my place to take matters into my own hands.

"Do you understand?" Mimi asked.

"Yes." Although I couldn't guarantee it wouldn't happen again.

"If this aggressive behavior is repeated," Mimi warned, "I'm going to have to suggest that you might not be an appropriate fit for our clinic."

I said nothing.

"Do you need to leave? Shall I call for a replacement?"

"I'll behave," I assured her like a repentant youngster.

"Good." She sighed with relief.

We both knew it would be difficult to find a replacement, especially at the last minute like this.

I finished the shift without incident and left with barely a word to Mimi and the others. As I pulled into the driveway, I was shocked anew by my own behavior. In all my years in the medical field, I'd never once stepped over the line the way I had that evening. It was time to bow out. Mimi realized it and I did, too. I'd send a letter of resignation on Monday.

Inside the house, I tossed my car keys on the counter and then sat on the edge of the sofa. "I lost it," I told Hannah. "I just lost it." Kenny deserved everything I'd said and done, and in that sense I didn't regret it. However, I'd been called upon to treat the sick and injured—nothing less and certainly nothing more.

Generally, I picked up something to eat on my way home from the clinic. But I hadn't thought of food all evening, although I hadn't eaten since noon. My stomach growled.

I located a can of soup, heated that and ate it over the kitchen sink. When I finished I set down the bowl and just stood there. I was still angry. My hands became clenched fists.

"I can't do it anymore," I told Hannah.

How I missed her. How I needed her. She would've been horrified by the regular attacks on Shamika and concerned about my uncharacteristic loss of control. Undoubtedly she would've found the perfect words to comfort me and ease my mind.

But Hannah wasn't here. She never would be again and I'd need to deal with instances like this on my own. I'd acted foolishly. But while I regretted cracking, I didn't regret threatening that wife-beater.

It was midnight before I'd calmed down enough to go to bed, but sleep didn't come. After tangling the sheets, rolling one way and then the other, I decided to sit up and read. That didn't help, and in an act of pure desperation, I reached for the photo of Hannah. It was one of my favorites—she was walking in an open field, carpeted with blooming wildflowers. I'd taken it on a day trip to Hurricane

Ridge several years before. I kept the framed photograph by my bedside and now I set it on the pillow next to mine.

As I suspected it would, having Hannah's picture close soothed me and I finally fell asleep.

I woke to the bright light of morning and lay on my back, gazing up at the ceiling as I replayed the events of the previous night. I turned my head to one side to look for Hannah's photograph, planning to replace it on my nightstand. I was surprised to find it missing.

I sat up and looked around. It took me a few minutes to discover that at some point I must have thrashed around and caused the photograph to fall to the floor.

I leaned over to retrieve it and found the glass shattered and the frame broken.

Chapter Six

I work out at the gym three days a week, but on Saturday mornings, I usually run. After my five-mile jog, I stepped into the shower and let the spray beat down on my back while my thoughts churned. I couldn't get the vision of Hannah's broken photograph out of my mind. It felt almost as if she was telling me how upset she was that I hadn't done what she'd asked, which I realized was ridiculous. And yet . . . the glass had shattered. Why *now*, I wanted to know, after the countless times I'd placed it on the empty pillow next to mine?

I'm not a superstitious man; I believe in science and rational behavior. But I couldn't help wondering if Hannah was the reason I instantly recalled Winter's phone number. Of course, the fact that I'd stared at it for ten minutes yesterday evening might have something to do with it.

I waited until nine-thirty, then called. Winter answered on the second ring.

"Hello."

"Hi, Winter. It's Michael," I said. Actually, I'd been hoping the call would go to voice mail and I could escape talking to her. No such luck.

"Michael! It's so good to hear your voice. How are you? No, don't answer that, I know how you are."

"You do?"

"You miss Hannah. Oh, Michael, I do, too."

So I'd been right. Hannah would be the primary focus of our conversation.

"I can't believe it's been a year."

"Me, neither," I muttered. In some ways, though, it felt much longer.

"I heard you stopped by the café," Winter continued. "I'm sorry I wasn't there. I hope you'll come again."

"Sure."

"How about now?"

"Now?" I repeated.

"Unless you've got other plans. We can have coffee, spend a few minutes catching up."

Perhaps it would be best to get this over with quickly. I'd fulfill my duty and then go back to missing Hannah. She wouldn't be able to fault me once I'd made the effort. "It'll take me fifteen minutes to get there."

"That's perfect. How do you like your coffee?"

"Black," I told her.

"I'll start a fresh pot. It'll be ready by the time you arrive. Would you like a croissant?"

I wasn't turning one down. "That would be wonderful."

"Great. I'll see you soon."

"Bye." I hung up and paused while I considered what had just taken place. All week I'd worried about what I'd say, but so far, dialogue on my part had hardly been necessary. Winter seemed pleased, even excited, to hear from me, although I hadn't seen her in more than a year.

All at once an idea struck me. Was it possible that Hannah had written letters to the three women on the list, as well? This hadn't occurred to me before, and it paralyzed me.

After a few minutes, the pounding of my heart subsided as I decided on a plan of action. I'd sound Winter out. Naturally I'd broach the question carefully. If the letter to me was the only one Hannah had written, then I didn't want Winter— or anyone else—to know about it. Ritchie knew, of course, but I could trust him to keep his mouth shut.

I left the house and made the short drive to Blossom Street in less than ten minutes. The downtown area was starting to show signs of life as business owners opened for the day. I noticed the yarn store across from the French Café and pulled into an empty slot in front of it. Cody Goetz was a patient of mine and I'd met Lydia, his mother and the shop's owner, on a number of occasions. The family had recently adopted a twelve- or thirteen-year-old girl. Hannah had always wanted to learn how to knit. She'd intended to knit our baby a blanket and had signed up for classes at A Good Yarn just before we learned she had cancer. The classes were forgotten, although Hannah had been so eager to knit that baby blanket. . . .

A baby blanket!

I turned my thoughts away. No need to depress myself more than I already was.

I jaywalked across the street and entered the restaurant. I saw Winter right away.

"Michael!" She stepped out from behind the counter, extending her arms toward me, hugging me as I drew close.

"Hello, Winter."

She held me as I stood there limply, my arms dangling awkwardly by my sides. After a moment I hugged her back.

She smiled up at me. "It's wonderful to see you."

"You, too." I forced a bit of enthusiasm into my voice.

She was lovely, and although I looked hard for a resemblance to Hannah, I didn't see any. Winter was blonde with blue eyes. Hannah had dark hair and dark brown eyes. They were about the same height, but the similarity ended there. As I studied her, I recognized the expressive, mobile face Hannah had liked so much. A face that was very different from her own.

"Come sit over here." Winter led me to a table by the window. The day was overcast; otherwise, I would've preferred to sit outside. The entire café had an inviting ambience, however, with flowered tablecloths, comfortable chairs and warm lighting.

While I pulled out a chair and sat down, Winter motioned to a young pregnant woman at the counter who efficiently delivered two mugs of steaming coffee and a plate of croissants.

"You have a nice place," I commented as I reached for the coffee. "I was here the other day and it was busy."

"We do a good business," she said. "I didn't know what to expect with the downturn in the economy, but I've been pleasantly surprised."

I noticed that her prices were reasonable. For those fortunate enough to have a job nearby, it would be convenient to stop in for coffee on the way to the office.

"What are your hours?" I asked.

"We open early," she replied. "Alix, our baker—" she gestured at the woman who'd served us "—comes in around five and does the baking, including the croissants. Then Mary arrives at six and takes care of the morning crowd. We have a steady flow of regulars."

I nodded.

"Business quiets down around midmorning and then picks up again with the lunch crowd. We serve soup, salads and sandwiches."

The specials for the day were listed on the blackboard out front. The soup was beet with ginger and the salad was spinach with blue cheese and dried cranberries. Colorful and creative, I thought.

"We stay open until nine-thirty."

"So you serve dinner, too."

"The menu's the same for lunch and dinner," she explained. "I wasn't sure evenings would work, but I was wrong. There are enough people living in the neighborhood to make the longer hours worth my while."

"That's great." I glanced around appreciatively. Pictures of the Eiffel Tower, the Seine and other distinctive French scenes decorated the walls.

"I've worked hard to make this café a success," Winter told me, her voice ringing with pride. "Hannah used to encourage me . . ." Her voice trailed off.

I stared down into my coffee. "Like you said, it's hard to believe Hannah's been gone a year."

"It is," Winter agreed quietly.

I held my breath. "I'm starting to clear out her things." A bold-faced lie if there ever was one. "I wondered if there was anything of hers you'd like to have."

Winter's eyes misted and she brought her hand to her heart. "Oh, Michael, that's so thoughtful of you."

"Hannah loved you. You were her favorite cousin."

Winter looked as if she might cry. Other than Hannah's, I never could deal with other people's emotions. Since her death, I often find myself in the role of comforter. It's difficult to ease someone else's pain, especially when my own is so debilitating.

"Is there anything of special significance? Anything you'd treasure?" I asked.

Winter shook her head. "I treasured my cousin. I didn't realize how much until she was gone."

I understood the feeling. I took a croissant, ripped off a piece, but didn't eat it. I was afraid if we headed down this path of memories it would depress us both.

"I can't think of anything I'd want. Whatever you'd like to give me is fine."

"What's the connection with France?" I asked, changing the subject.

Winter regarded me for a long moment. "I went there with Pierre."

"Pierre?"

"Pierre Dubois. We . . . we used to be involved."

"You met in France?" I was trying to remember if Hannah had mentioned any of this. The name sounded familiar.

"No, we met here in the States. At one time we worked together, but that was ages ago now," she said, lowering her voice slightly. "I flew over to meet Pierre's family and loved every minute—the food, the culture, the people. Being there inspired me. When I decided to open my own café I wanted to duplicate those memories."

I smiled, caught up in her words. Then I remembered Hannah telling me about Winter and some Frenchman she'd been dating. A guy she'd worked with at a classy restaurant. The same guy who'd caused her grief.

"I suppose you're wondering about me and Pierre?" Winter asked. "I'm sorry we were never able to attend the dinner parties you and Hannah had. With our work schedules, it was impossible. But maybe that was just as well."

"Ah . . ." I wasn't sure how to respond.

"He and I are taking a break from each other," Winter said.

I didn't know exactly what that meant. "A break?"

"A few months," she elaborated. "We split up once before and then got back together, but the same old problems cropped up again. All we seemed to do was argue." A look of sadness came over her. "Some people are meant to be together, I guess, and others aren't, no matter how strong the attraction is." She shook her head as if she wasn't sure how any of this had happened.

If I understood her correctly, Winter had reunited with Pierre after a long break and recently split up again. Hannah had obviously written her letter after the first separation. "What about dating others during this . . . break?" I asked without any subtlety or finesse.

"Well, that hasn't really come up, but I don't think it would be a problem."

"I see. If someone encouraged you to date . . . say, someone like me, would you be inclined to do so?" I asked. What I really wanted to find out was whether Hannah had written her a letter condoning—or even suggesting—a relationship between the two of us.

"If someone encouraged me?" She watched me curiously. "Like who?"

"You know. Someone like a friend or—" I hesitated "—or perhaps a relative."

"You mean Ritchie?"

"Not specifically." Obtaining the information was harder than I'd expected.

"I wouldn't need anyone to encourage me, Michael," she said, smiling across the table at me. "I've always thought the world of you."

I smiled back, thanking her, but I had no idea what else to say. I hadn't actually asked her out—not intentionally, anyway—but she'd assumed I was trying to initiate a relationship. This was embarrassing. I wasn't sure how to extricate myself now that I'd brought it up.

We left it open-ended, so that she'd get in touch with me. A short time later I walked away, confused and bewildered.

With no better alternative, I drove to Ritchie's house. My brother-in-law was in his garage; the door was open and I could see him puttering around inside.

He went out to the driveway to greet me. "Hey, this is a surprise. What's up?"

"I just had coffee with Winter."

"So you two finally connected." I followed him back to the garage and leaned against his workbench.

"Where are Steph and Max?" I asked.

"Shopping. Max has a baseball game later this afternoon. I'm taking him to that. Wanna tag along?"

I didn't need an excuse to see Max. I was fond of my nephew. He loved his Xbox and, because of that, I'd cultivated the skill; we spent hours battling each other. He had top score and it wasn't because I wasn't trying. The kid was a natural. "Glad to," I told Ritchie.

We were silent for a moment. "Well, don't keep

me in suspense," Ritchie said, crossing his arms. "How did the meeting with my cousin go?"

I shrugged. "All right, I guess." Before I could say anything more, Ritchie started talking.

"I've been thinking over what you told me about Hannah's letter."

"What about it?"

"My sister put Winter's name first for a reason."

"Which is?" I was only coming to terms with this whole letter thing now, but I wasn't convinced that I could do what Hannah had asked.

"Hannah knew Winter the best and—"

"Winter's involved with some Frenchman," I said, cutting him off. "They've been seeing each other for quite a while. It makes me wonder why Hannah would even include her. Pierre and Winter must've been on their first, uh, hiatus, but still . . ." In any event, I wasn't up to hearing what a perfect match the other woman was for me. Not from Ritchie and not from Hannah, either.

"She's involved with someone else?" This quickly flattened Ritchie's enthusiasm. "You ever heard of this guy?"

"Maybe. I'm pretty sure Hannah told me about him. Also that he and Winter split up—but then they got back together. After Hannah died, I guess."

He stared at me blankly and I felt compelled to continue. "Now they're taking a break from each other. They haven't broken up, they're taking a break," I repeated, trying to emphasize the difference.

"What's that mean?" he asked.

"Hell if I know. Sounds like something a woman would think up."

"How long is this break?"

"A few months, she said."

"Did she mention how far they were into this . . . temporary break-up?" he asked.

I hadn't thought to ask. "No. But," I added, "she's going to call me."

Ritchie nodded. "What she's telling you is that there are problems in that relationship," Ritchie explained knowledgeably, as if he had a post-graduate degree in Understanding Women.

"That would be my guess," I agreed amiably enough.

"So you're free to step in."

"No," I said automatically. "I don't think so."

"How come?"

"Problems or not, she's in love with Pierre." At least the two of us could talk about the people we loved. And it wouldn't be each other.

"Don't be so willing to give up. Ask her out."

I chortled, reluctant to admit what a mess I'd made of our meeting. "Winter more or less assumed I'd contacted her for exactly that reason. But I didn't ask her out."

Ritchie cocked his head to one side. "She's

interested, though, if she said she'll get back to you. Isn't that obvious?"

Nothing was obvious to me at the moment. "Do you think Hannah might have written more than one letter?" I needed Ritchie's opinion on this. I suspected she hadn't, but her brother knew her well, almost as well as I did . . . had.

My question apparently gave him pause. Then he shook his head. "Who would've delivered them?"

"Good point." That settled it in my mind. There was only the one letter.

"Hannah might suggest dating these other women to *you*, but I doubt she'd discuss it with them." Ritchie rubbed the side of his jaw. "No," he added. "I'm fairly confident Hannah just wrote one letter. Yours."

I nodded slowly, reassured on that count. My encounters with Winter and the other two women—if I called them—would be awkward enough without more letters from Hannah.

"If Winter's interested, then I say go out with her," Ritchie urged.

"No," I said adamantly. "It'd be a waste of time for both of us."

"Don't be so sure. Remember, Hannah put her name first on the list, and there was a reason for that."

I sighed. "Yeah, I know."

"It's what she wanted, Michael. You aren't going to ignore my sister's last wish, are you?"

Leave it to Ritchie to hit below the belt. "I'll think about it," I muttered. But I already had a feeling that Winter and I would never find happiness together.

Chapter Seven

Maybe she shouldn't have been surprised, but it'd been good to see Michael again.

Winter Adams wasn't sure how to react when she got the message that her cousin's husband had stopped by. She hadn't called him right away; she'd had no idea what to say once she did. She'd always liked Michael and missed Hannah terribly. Her relationship had been with Hannah, though, and because she was usually working the dinner shift, she hadn't socialized with them as a couple all that much. Which made the whole situation a bit uncomfortable. Nevertheless, she felt she had to return his call.

"Did he ask you out?" Alix asked when Winter carried the plate and two empty coffee mugs to the dishwasher.

She nodded.

"Are you going?"

"I don't know," she answered honestly. Still mulling over the conversation, she went into her office and closed the door.

Michael might be interested, but Winter belonged with the man she loved. Pierre Dubois.

The past three weeks without him had been painful. Bleak. Her life was complicated and she'd probably done Michael a disservice by not explaining the situation better. She *was* involved with Pierre and had been for a long while, although they'd decided to take a three-month break from each other.

As she'd told Michael, this wasn't the first time they'd split up. Technically, this wasn't a split; it was more of a breather while they analyzed what was wrong with their relationship. Two years earlier Pierre and Winter had broken it off for good. At the time it had seemed for the best, since they were constantly arguing, constantly at odds. They spent fifteen months apart. Winter had been miserable without him.

During those months, she'd visited Hannah often, both at the hospital and at home. When Michael was busy, Winter sat with her cousin and poured out her heart. Hannah had been such a sympathetic listener. She'd assured Winter over and over that one day she'd meet a man who would make her happy.

Then, shortly after Hannah's death, she'd run into Pierre in downtown Seattle. Winter's heart had started beating furiously at the sight of him. She'd missed Pierre each and every day, but had worked hard to convince herself that she'd gotten along fine without him. At first their meeting had been awkward. They'd exchanged the briefest of pleasantries and gone their separate ways.

Then they'd met again, a few minutes later in a department store. They'd laughed, a bit nervously, Pierre had made a joke about it and they'd headed in opposite directions—only to meet a third time outside the store. Pierre had laughed and suggested they have coffee at a nearby Starbucks. They'd talked for three hours. He said he'd never stopped thinking about her. Winter admitted how much she'd missed their quiet, intimate evenings together. The nights they cuddled in front of the television and discussed menus and cooking techniques while the program aired with barely a notice. They were two of a kind in their perfectionism and their passion for food and cooking; that shared interest had drawn them together in the first place. Unfortunately, they were both stubborn and so sure of their own visions—about food, life and everything else— that they tended to clash. Winter had come to recognize that she could be uncompromising. But no more than Pierre!

At the end of that day, they'd decided to give it one more try, determined to make their relationship work. They felt that if they made a sincere effort, and it succeeded, they should consider marriage. They left the coffee shop with their arms tightly around each other.

Nine months later they were at odds again. Winter didn't know how it'd happened. All she knew was that they were miserable—miserable together and miserable apart.

In view of their history, they'd agreed to take a three-month "sabbatical" from each other. Pierre had gone so far as to set the date they'd meet to make a final decision. Winter had marked it on her calendar and circled the day. Until then, they were to have no contact at all. July 1, they would either go forward or end the relationship once and for all. This time there'd be no going back. They were in love, but what they needed now was a way to make their love work—a way that brought them happiness and fulfillment.

When they'd first met, Winter had recently graduated from cooking school and Pierre had been her boss at a seafood restaurant—part of an upscale chain—that catered primarily to tourists. He'd been recruited by the chain after receiving his training in France. His parents were chefs, too, and the family had moved to the States for a few years when he was in his teens. They'd eventually gone back to France. Pierre, however, considered Seattle home.

One night at the waterfront restaurant, he and Winter had sat and talked for hours after closing. Talked and kissed . . . Winter had shared her dream of starting her own restaurant.

Pierre had encouraged her. He'd helped her with the business plan and filling out the loan documents. After weeks of working on the project, they'd been practically inseparable. While they were waiting to hear from the bank, Pierre had taken her to France for what he called a "culinary vacation," which included meeting his family, who'd charmed her completely. Although her French was terrible, she felt welcomed and loved. Thankfully they all spoke excellent English. She'd had one spectacular meal after another, some in bistros and restaurants, others prepared by his parents.

When Winter announced that she was naming her new venture the French Café in honor of Pierre and his family, he'd let her know how pleased he was.

Then for reasons she never quite understood and couldn't seem to change, their relationship had gone steadily downhill. They lived together briefly, but it just didn't work. Her schedule often conflicted with his. Some days she'd go home after a long shift at the café and make his dinner. But Pierre showed little or no appreciation for her efforts, which annoyed her. She'd sulk or make some derogatory comment, and he'd react swiftly with one of his own.

Other times she'd talk about her day and Pierre would be so fixated on some incident or other in his own kitchen that he couldn't or wouldn't listen. Soon they'd be bickering, furious with each other, finding fault.

Then it'd all blown up and they'd separated. A

year and three months had passed before they met again and admitted they'd both been wrong. They'd each had an opportunity to examine their roles in the breakup. Yet here it was, happening all over again.

The problem was that they were too much alike—both perfectionists, both volatile. Sooner or later, usually sooner, a clash was inevitable.

A few months after they reunited they'd slipped back into the old patterns. Nothing had changed, despite their determination to make the relationship work.

This time Winter had been the one to suggest they separate and Pierre had been all too eager to comply. Watching him walk away had nearly broken her heart. She couldn't believe that two people who'd been so enraptured with each other could let it all fall apart.

They both hoped that during this separation they'd be able to figure out a way to fix what was wrong.

At the beginning of this second breakup, not having Pierre in her life had been a relief. The sudden lack of tension had lifted a gigantic weight from her shoulders. It felt good to get home at the end of the day and not worry about doing or saying something that would set him off. She could relax, listen to the music she enjoyed, watch her favorite TV programs without having to defend her choices. She cooked what she wanted to eat without being subjected to his complaints.

The honeymoon period without Pierre had carried her for nearly two weeks. Only in the past few days had Winter realized how empty her life was without him.

She'd heard that he'd changed jobs and wondered if some of their problems might have been related to the stress he was under as head chef at the seafood restaurant. She'd learned from a mutual acquaintance that Pierre had taken over as executive chef for the Hilton Hotel. The position entailed far greater responsibility, with a large staff, huge banquet facilities and less creative freedom. The trade-off must've been worth it if Pierre was willing to make such a drastic move. It hurt that he hadn't talked to her about his decision. Still, she reminded herself, that was their agreement. No contact.

When Winter had suggested the terms of their pact, she'd fully expected Pierre to break it. He broke every other one they'd made. Oh, that wasn't totally fair. When they'd shared a place, he did occasionally prepare dinner, but not on a reliable basis. Often he'd be too tired or he'd simply forget, so she did most of the cooking. Even when she left a notation on the calendar it hadn't helped. And he hadn't exactly done his allotment of household tasks, either. If Pierre couldn't manage to pick up his dirty socks, she wondered how he'd ever deal with being a husband and eventually a father.

Despite their agreement, it bothered her that he hadn't made a single effort to contact her. She hadn't tried to reach him, either, but that was because he'd always been the one to make the first move, the one who sought peace after their quarrels. So, admit it or not, she'd *expected* to hear from him.

Pierre's temper flared hot and erupted like a volcano, and when he was finished it was over. He was ready to kiss and make up. Not so with Winter. She blew like a factory whistle, and when she finished, it *wasn't* over. She wanted Pierre to react, to change, to learn and grow. Instead, he just walked away until she became what he called "reasonable" again. He'd make overtures to see if that "reasonable" state had been achieved and when he decided it was safe, he'd act as if nothing had happened. Until the next time . . .

Now something unforeseen had turned up and she wasn't sure how to handle it. Michael had come to visit and he'd made it plain that he was interested in her. At least that was what she'd assumed. While setting their rules, neither Pierre nor Winter had provided for such a contingency. The question remained. Did she want to go out with her cousin's husband? Winter still didn't know.

By midafternoon, she'd talked herself into breaking the agreement with Pierre and seeking him out. She had a valid excuse. While she wasn't eager to acknowledge it, her real reason was that she was starved for the sight of him. These past few weeks had been a revelation.

She missed Pierre. She loved him and, in the weeks apart, that hadn't changed. Closing her eyes, she heard the lilt of his accent and her heartbeat accelerated at the memory. She missed his touch, his whisper when he woke early in the morning and kissed her. In a crazy kind of way, she even missed the excitement, if that was the appropriate word, of their quarrels. What it came down to was that nothing seemed right without him.

Now Michael had offered her the perfect excuse to see Pierre. Her pride would stay intact and she could present Pierre with this new situation and gauge his feelings. If he truly loved her, he'd move heaven and earth to join her in solving their problems. The possibility of another man's interest should galvanize him into declaring his own. Her goal wasn't to make him jealous, but to get him to recognize his feelings. The more she thought about it, the more hopeful Winter became.

Sitting at her desk, she called his cell phone, let it ring once, then abruptly disconnected. She wanted to do more than speak to Pierre. She wanted—*needed*—to see him. One look would tell her if he missed her half as much as she missed him.

Decision made, Winter waited until later that

afternoon, in the lull between lunch and dinner. She contacted the Hilton and confirmed that Pierre was indeed working that day. She pictured walking into the kitchen, pictured Pierre raising his head, meeting her eyes. He'd stop whatever he was doing and come toward her as though drawn by an invisible rope. Then she'd rush into his arms and he'd tell her how unhappy he'd been without her.

Figuring she had time, Winter went shopping at a fancy little boutique off Blossom Street owned by Barbie Foster, whom she'd met through Anne Marie Roche. Anne Marie had the bookstore diagonally across from the café and was also a friend of Alix's. On a whim she purchased a new outfit. The classic "little black dress." Elegant yet sexy, it was ultraexpensive and worth every penny because of the way it made her feel. She was going to give Pierre an eyeful of what he was missing, just in case he'd forgotten.

When she'd changed clothes, she took a cab to the Hilton. She announced herself to one of the dining-room staff.

"I'm Winter Adams, a friend of Pierre Dubois," she explained. "If you tell him I'm here, I'm sure he'll see me."

She wasn't left to wait more than a few minutes. In that time she reviewed what she wanted to say. The staff member returned, smiling, and said, "Chef Dubois will see you in his office."

"Thank you." Winter followed the other woman into the kitchen.

Its size made her own small café look insignificant by comparison. Winter lost count of how many people she saw working at various stations. Everyone was busy with meal preparation. One thing was obvious; Pierre had his hands full. If nothing else, this experience would teach him some organizational skills, which in her opinion were sadly lacking.

It took about two seconds to realize that her assumptions about her reception—and his improved organization—were off base. His desk was in a state of chaos.

He stood when she entered the room, but he didn't advance toward her. Worse, he showed no signs of being happy to see her. He wore his chef's toque and white uniform and appeared all business. Nothing in his expression revealed any curiosity about her visit after all these weeks.

Winter blinked. "Hello, Pierre," she said softly, letting her voice betray her feelings.

He ignored her greeting and gestured for her to sit down, then seemed to notice that the chair was stacked with papers, catalogs and menus. He scooped up the whole pile and set it on the corner of his desk, where it promptly slid off and tumbled to the floor.

Winter bent down to help him retrieve the assorted pieces of paper.

"Leave it," he snapped. He hated it when she felt the need to tidy up a room.

Swallowing, she straightened, then sat in the chair while Pierre dealt with the fallen papers.

He didn't say anything the entire time he was reassembling the stack. Neither did she.

When he'd finished, Pierre threw himself into his own chair. The room wasn't big, but it was much more spacious than her tiny office at the café.

"How are you?" she asked with a small, tentative smile.

"Busy."

In other words, he was telling her to get to the point and be on her way.

"I hadn't heard from you," she said, hoping the comment sounded casual and carefree.

"We agreed there'd be no contact. It was your suggestion, as I recall."

"We did say that," she said, nodding. If he wanted this to be strictly business, fine. "So you understand I wouldn't be here now if it wasn't important."

His gaze narrowed. "Are you pregnant?"

She stared, hardly able to believe what he'd said. "You know better than to ask such a thing."

"Do I?"

"Yes," she flared. *She* was the responsible one. After the first week, it became abundantly clear that she'd have to be in charge of birth control. As a matter of fact, she'd continued with the pill, which was ridiculous since they hadn't even touched in weeks.

"If you aren't pregnant, what's so important that you have to interrupt me in the middle of the day—on a Saturday, no less?"

Winter hadn't stopped to consider that he might have two or three different banquets scheduled during a weekend.

Nonetheless, she forged ahead. "An interesting situation has come up that I felt I should discuss with you."

"By all means," he murmured with more than a hint of sarcasm.

"My cousin Hannah's husband—"

"Your cousin who died?"

"Yes. Hannah's husband's name is Michael. He came to see me."

"And?" Pierre prompted, obviously in a hurry to be rid of her.

"He wants to go out with me." There, she'd said it. If she was looking for a reaction from Pierre, she didn't get one; his expression didn't so much as flicker. It was as if she'd pointed out that this spring was cooler than normal for the Pacific Northwest.

Pierre held her gaze. "We never discussed anything like this," she felt obliged to remind him.

"How foolish of us," he returned, his words heavy with scorn.

She didn't respond to his unpleasant tone. "Well?" she pressed.

He shrugged. "I don't see the problem."

"You don't mind?" she blurted out, unable to hide the hurt she felt.

"Why should I?"

"But . . ." Pain and disillusionment gathered in her chest. Rather than explain, rather than reveal how deeply his total disregard and lack of concern had cut her, Winter bounded to her feet and headed out the door.

"Winter . . ."

"I thought we could have a decent conversation for once," she said, struggling to hold back her own anger.

"You come to me after weeks of silence because you want my permission to date another man?"

"I didn't say that!"

"As a matter of fact, you did."

"Are we going to argue about semantics?" she asked. How quickly they'd fallen back into the same old patterns. A few minutes earlier, Winter had been nearly breathless with anticipation. Now she was close to tears.

"If you want to date this other man, don't let me stand in your way."

"I won't," she said and smiled sweetly. "He's a doctor, you know."

"Who cares?"

"Oh, that was mature."

"About as mature as telling me you're dating a doctor. Just leave, Winter, before I say something I regret."

"*I'm* the one with regrets, Pierre. I never should've come here, never should've assumed that being apart would make any difference. I can see nothing's changed. I thought I loved you . . . I thought you loved me, too, but I can see how wrong I was." She rushed through the kitchen, blinded by anger and sorrow, and almost ran to the exit.

Pierre didn't follow, and that was just as well. She'd learned the answer to her unspoken question. Pierre was completely and utterly indifferent to her. His one concern was whether she might be pregnant. He was no more ready to be a husband and father than . . . than the man in the moon.

Hurrying into the street, Winter paused, her pulse beating in her ear like a sledgehammer. Breathless, she leaned against the building and placed both hands over her heart.

The meeting had gone so much worse than she'd expected. Pierre didn't need three months to decide about their relationship. Apparently, he didn't even need three weeks. His decision had been made. Which meant hers was, too.

It was over.

Her life with Pierre had come to an end.

If Dr. Michael Everett was interested in pursuing a relationship, then Winter needed to open her heart to the possibility.

Chapter Eight

Monday morning I met Ritchie at the gym. The Saturday afternoon we'd spent together had lifted my spirits. Max's softball game had gone well—his team had won—and it felt good to sit in the bleachers with the other parents and cheer on my nephew. Max, at almost nine, was a terrific kid. Afterward, the two of us played Xbox until Steph called us down for dinner. As soon as we'd finished, we both went upstairs again, eager to get back to our game. Ritchie eventually joined us, but his expertise was on a level with mine. Max beat us both.

The boy had been a great favorite of Hannah's. She'd loved spending time with him; she used to buy him books, take him to movies and attend his Little League games whenever she could. Losing his adored aunt was hard for Max, and he hardly ever mentioned Hannah anymore. That didn't bother me. I knew Max treasured his memories of Hannah the same as I did. I saw her picture in his bedroom when he showed me the latest addition to his baseball card collection. My gaze fell on the photograph, and Max, ever sensitive and kind, had simply walked over and hugged me. I hugged him back. We didn't need to talk; his gentle embrace said far more than words.

"Did you hear from Winter?" Ritchie asked as we walked out of the gym.

I'd wondered when he'd get around to asking me that. I'd just about made a clean escape, but I should've known my brother-in-law wouldn't let it pass.

"She left a message on Sunday afternoon."

"You weren't going to tell me, were you?" Ritchie chastised.

"Nope." No point in lying.

"That's what I thought." We walked toward the parking garage, and I hoped that would be the end of the subject. Wishful thinking on my part.

"You didn't pick up, did you?" Ritchie said when I didn't elaborate.

I was continually surprised by how well Ritchie could predict my behavior. It was almost as if he'd been sitting in the same room with me. "No," I admitted reluctantly.

"What did she say?"

I shrugged. "Nothing much. She asked me to return the call when it was convenient."

"How long do you suppose it'll be before you find it convenient?"

My delaying tactic wasn't working as success-fully as I'd hoped. "I thought I'd give her a call later this afternoon." Maybe. I wasn't convinced Winter and I were a good match, despite what Hannah seemed to believe.

"Don't disappoint me," Ritchie warned.

I was grateful when I reached my car, eager to bring this awkward conversation to a close.

"How about poker on Thursday night?" Ritchie asked.

Sometimes I swore he had radar and knew exactly how hard to push before backing off.

"Steve's got a meeting," he went on, "and can't make it."

I shook my head. I used to play with Ritchie and the other guys every Thursday. In fact, I'd been the one to instigate the poker game. Patrick O'Malley, one of my partners, Steve Ciletti, an internal-medicine specialist, Ritchie and I used to get together for poker every week. At first we took turns hosting and then we settled on Ritchie and Steph's place because it's centrally located and easily accessible to all of us. We never played past midnight and the wagers were friendly. I'd given up poker and all other unnecessary distractions after Hannah was diagnosed with cancer.

"I don't think so," I said automatically.

"Bill's been substituting for you for two years now. Isn't it time you rejoined the group?"

"Maybe I will," I said. I wasn't sure why I hesitated. I used to enjoy our poker nights, and I didn't understand my own reluctance.

I had hospital rounds that morning. We did it on a rotation basis and this was my week. Because Hannah had spent so much time in this hospital, I'd had the opportunity to see the situation from two different perspectives—first, as a physician, and secondly, as the spouse of a patient. I could write a book on what I'd learned.

When I arrived at the hospital, I noticed signs everywhere for the annual picnic. The children's ward put on a huge charity function each year, one specially designed for children with cancer. This wasn't a fund-raising event. The sole purpose was to let them be kids and forget about chemo and surgery for an afternoon. Hannah and I had volunteered at the picnic for several years and since I often had a patient or two in the pediatric oncology ward, it was very personal for us.

"Michael." Patrick O'Malley called my name as he walked down the wide corridor to meet me. I hadn't expected to see him; he must've been there for one of his patients. "What's this I hear about you?" he asked.

"What?" I didn't know anyone had much of anything to discuss about me. I'd pretty much stayed under the radar, especially when it came to social activities.

"Friday night at the clinic."

"Oh, that." Actually, I was embarrassed by the altercation and wished I'd kept my cool. I'd just . . . snapped. I didn't know what had brought it on and had regretted it ever since.

"I hear you threatened some guy within an inch of his life."

I didn't want to talk about it. "His wife *fell down*

96

the stairs—" I made quotation marks with my fingers "—three times in three months. I figured someone should do something."

"She wouldn't press charges?"

"Apparently not. She wouldn't admit the guy even touched her." I might have maintained my professional attitude, but her chart confirmed that her injuries had become more extensive with each assault. Shamika didn't seem to realize she was risking her life if she stayed with the creep. Still, I was appalled by my own behavior; the audacity of it was completely unlike anything I'd ever done.

"You only did what all of us have felt like doing a dozen times."

No matter, I'd been out of line. "I don't think the clinic wants me back."

"Are you kidding?" Patrick said. "It's hard enough for them to get volunteers. They'll look the other way, at least this once."

I thought so, too, but my decision was made. I'd resigned. My uncharacteristic act of violence simply disturbed me too much. A replacement doctor had already been found, according to Mimi, but I didn't tell Patrick any of this. He'd find out soon enough.

"Speaking of volunteers," Patrick said, glancing pointedly at the posters decorating the hallway. "The picnic's on Saturday."

"It's a little early this year, isn't it?" I asked, stalling for time.

"Not really. It's always in May."

I hadn't attended last year's. Hannah's funeral had been only a couple of weeks before that and I was barely coping.

"We could use a few more volunteers."

"I've got plans," I said, although it wasn't true. Again, my own reluctance baffled me. Until Hannah's illness and death, I'd enjoyed being part of the event.

"Can you change your plans?" Patrick asked. "We're really shorthanded. We need someone to help with the games."

I sighed.

"We need a volunteer to flip burgers, too, if that's more to your liking."

I could see Patrick wasn't going to make this easy. "I might be able to come."

"We need every worker we can get."

"How long would I need to be there?" I asked, hedging. If I could find a way out of this I'd gladly take it.

Patrick shrugged. "A couple of hours should do it."

"Okay, I'll rearrange my plans," I said, continuing the farce. The only thing I had scheduled for Saturday was my routine five-mile run.

"Thanks, buddy." He slapped me on the back and hurried off.

The word that I'd signed up as a volunteer at the Kids with Cancer event spread faster than a

California brushfire. Clearly Patrick hadn't wasted any time.

A couple of other physicians stopped me during my rounds to say how pleased they were that I was socializing again. In my opinion, the news that I was volunteering at a charity function shouldn't be treated like a public announcement.

Besides, I wasn't socializing. I'd been pressured into helping what I considered a good cause. I wouldn't be doing this at all if Patrick hadn't cornered me and practically blackmailed me into it. Naturally, I couldn't say that. I smiled at the two physicians and quickly extricated myself from the conversation so I could go about my business.

I hadn't taken more than a few steps when I noticed a couple of the nurses with their heads together, whispering. They looked up a bit guiltily as I approached them, and I realized they were probably talking about me.

"Morning, Dr. Everett," the first one said. She seemed impossibly young and energetic.

"Morning," I responded and picked up my pace. Over the course of the past year I'd received quite a bit of attention from certain women in the medical field. I was fairly young and presentable . . . and I was available, at least in theory.

Emotionally, I was worlds away from being ready for another relationship. The fact that I'd even talked to Winter on the subject of dating confused me.

I resented the way some people thought that because a year had passed, my time to grieve was over. They seemed to think I should've awakened a year after Hannah's death, prepared to "move on" with my life—an expression I'd come to hate. I also hated people's assumption that all I'd need to get over her loss was three hundred and sixty-five days. On day three hundred and sixty-six, I should be running around acting all bright and cheery as if—sigh of relief—I'd completely recovered from my wife's death.

"I hear you're going to be at the picnic," the same young nurse said. She nearly had to trot to keep up with me.

I nodded, not wanting to encourage conversation.

"Our whole shift has volunteered. It's such a wonderful idea, isn't it?"

Again I nodded.

"I'll see you there," she said, sounding breathless. Before I could speak, she veered off, making a sharp turn into a patient's room.

I made the rounds, filled out the paperwork and left the hospital with my head spinning. First Hannah, then Ritchie and now Patrick. It seemed everyone wanted to help me, and while I appreciated their efforts, I wasn't prepared for any of this. From the hospital I drove to the office. Linda

Barclay looked up from her desk when I entered through the private door reserved for staff.

"Good morning, Michael."

Linda's the only person at work who uses my first name. She's nurse, surrogate mother and friend all rolled into one middle-aged woman.

"Good morning, Linda." I walked past her, then turned back. "Why is it," I asked, still perplexed over what had taken place at the hospital, "that everyone seems to have this opinion that I've grieved long enough? What unwritten decree is there that I only have one year?"

"Ah . . ." Her eyes widened, and I could see that my question had startled her.

"Apparently, I'm volunteering at the children's picnic on Saturday," I explained, inhaling a calming breath.

"Good for you. It's about time."

"Et tu, Brute?" I muttered, and Linda laughed.

"My family's after me to date again," I said, growing serious. Linda would understand. "I'm not ready."

"Of course you aren't."

Her soothing voice took the edge off my irritation.

"I've basically been manipulated into going out with Hannah's cousin."

"The one who owns that restaurant?"

I nodded, surprised Linda would remember.

"Are you going to do it?"

"No." There, I'd said it. My mind was made up. I refused to be controlled by another person's wishes, even if that person happened to be my dead wife.

I loved Hannah—I would always love her—but that didn't mean I was willing to get involved with Winter or anyone else just because Hannah felt I should. Like I'd told Linda, I wasn't ready and I didn't know when I would be.

Perhaps because the morning had started off wrong with Ritchie interrogating me about Winter's message, I felt out of sorts all day. I didn't intend to call her back. She was obviously in love with her Frenchman, and I clung to my memories of Hannah.

By the time I got home, I was cranky and tired and hungry. The fridge and cupboards revealed a depressing lack of anything quick or easy. I knew I should avoid processed foods whenever possible, but there were many times, such as tonight, when I would gladly have pulled a frozen pizza from the freezer and popped it in the oven.

A trip to the grocery store was definitely in order. I ended up eating a cheese sandwich and a bowl of cold cereal without milk. It wasn't the most appetizing dinner of my life, but it filled my stomach. When I'd finished, I sat down in front of the computer, logged on and answered e-mail.

I was just beginning to feel human again when the phone rang. The sound jarred me. It seemed to have an urgent tone as if something bad had happened, or was about to.

Caller ID informed me it was Winter Adams. I stared at the readout but couldn't make myself pick up.

Winter didn't leave a message, which was actually a relief. I didn't want to be rude; all I wanted was peace and quiet. Okay, so maybe I *was* being a jerk, but this was a matter of self-preservation. The refrain *I'm not ready* clamored in my head and I couldn't ignore it.

Chapter Nine

"What is that noise?" Macy Roth asked Snowball, who'd planted himself on the closed toilet seat and studied her as she brushed her teeth. It was late and Macy was tired. She had a photo shoot in the morning; she planned to work on her knitting for half an hour or so and then go to sleep.

A car horn blared not far away, followed by the sound of screeching tires.

Macy turned off the water and then it happened again—a driver repeatedly hitting the horn.

Walking barefoot through her living room, the toothbrush clenched between her teeth, Macy decided to investigate. Peeking through the front window, she saw the lights of an oncoming car illuminate a large dog who stood, paralyzed by fear, in the middle of the street. Although Jackson Avenue was in a residential neighborhood, there was quite a lot of traffic, even at night. If the animal remained where it was, sooner or later it would be hit. Someone had to do something and, despite the noise, she didn't think anyone else had noticed.

Opening her door, Macy hurried outside, disregarding the fact that all she had on were her cotton pajamas. Her toothbrush was still in her mouth. She grabbed the trembling dog by the scruff of his neck and urged him onto the sidewalk.

Her heart pounded furiously as she led him toward her front steps. He was terrified enough to allow himself to be dragged, offering no resistance at all. Macy drew him into the house and closed the door. He was a large, long-haired brown dog of indeterminate breed—or breeds. Once inside, he stared up at her with a forlorn expression that would've softened the hardest of hearts. His pitiful brown eyes seemed to thank her for coming to his rescue. He continued to tremble as she bent to stroke his head.

She removed the toothbrush from her mouth and saw him gaze at it longingly. "Nope, this isn't very tasty," she said, tucking it behind her ear. The dog thumped his tail.

"Who are you, fellow?" she asked. Not surprisingly he had no collar and she doubted he'd have a microchip or a tattoo.

The poor dog looked as if he'd been lost for quite a while. He was emaciated, his thick hair matted with mud and grime.

"You're hungry, aren't you?"

He sat down on his haunches and stared at her with trusting eyes.

"You might as well come into the kitchen and I'll see what I can find, but be warned—I only have cat food." As if he understood every word, he got up and trotted behind her.

Snowball stood guard over his dish; he took one look at the dog, arched his back and hissed.

"Hush," Macy said. She placed her hand on the dog's head. "You'll have to pardon the lack of welcome from Snowball. Don't take it personally."

She removed a can of cat food from the small stack on her shelf. "Sorry, this is all I have. I hope you like salmon." From the looks of this mutt, he'd eat practically anything.

She was right.

He gobbled down the cat food almost as fast as she could spoon it onto the paper plate. The dry food disappeared just as quickly and when he was finished he gazed up at her as if to plead for more.

"Poor boy," Macy whispered. Lovie and Peace strolled casually into the kitchen to inspect the newcomer. Snowball, on the other hand, viewed him as an interloper and was having nothing to do with him.

Lovie edged close to the dog and began to purr. He's kind of cute, she seemed to be saying. Can we keep him?

"No, he can't stay," Macy informed her. "He's lost and we need to find his owner, or, failing that, a decent home."

Peace joined her friend, apparently taking up the dog's cause.

"Not you, too!" Macy groaned. "Okay, just for tonight, but that's it." She regarded the dog a second time. He was filthy. "However," she added, "if I let you stay the night, you're going to have a bath."

As she took the pet shampoo out from under the sink and opened it, all three cats scattered in different directions. "I wasn't talking about the three of *you,*" she said with a laugh. Lovie and Peace hated water, although Snowball rather enjoyed playing with it. He frequently stuck his paws or his tongue under the faucet. It was a brave front, Macy suspected, aimed at showing up the two females. But he wasn't any fonder of baths than they were, no doubt recalling the time he'd escaped into a muddy, rainy night and come home to face the consequences—being doused with this same antiseptic-smelling shampoo.

The dog cocked his head to one side.

"You need a name," Macy said. She wasn't sure why animals found their way to her door. It'd started when she was a child. They seemed to sense her love, her appreciation and her joy in their presence. While mice and spiders terrified her family and friends, Macy saw them as utterly fascinating. She couldn't imagine a home without pets, or herself without a host of animals.

"How about Sammy?" she suggested.

The dog lay down on the cold kitchen floor and rested his chin on his paws.

She patted his head. "Okay, Sammy it is. Now, don't you worry, we'll find you a wonderful home." Seeing that he was such a well-behaved dog, she couldn't help speculating on what might have happened. Had he wandered off when someone opened the door? Or perhaps he'd escaped from a farm miles away. Worst of all, he could've been abandoned, maybe because his people had moved to some apartment building with a no-animals clause. She'd make an effort to return him if he had an owner—and if that owner was looking—but she suspected the task of relocating him would be up to her.

"We're going to clean you up and make you good as new," she murmured. He didn't seem to mind the cats' food and she figured he'd have no problem with their shampoo.

She led him down the hallway to the bathroom. Snowball hissed from Macy's bed as if to declare that this was *his* territory and Sammy had better not trespass.

"Oh, honestly, Snowball, your hiss is worse than

your bite. Now, be nice. Sammy's our guest." She went into the bathroom, the dog at her heels, and filled the tub with warm water. She read the label on the shampoo bottle. Thankfully it would eliminate any fleas.

It took some doing to convince Sammy that he needed a bath. By the time she'd finished, she was soaked from head to foot and the bathroom looked as though a tornado had struck. Towels lined the floor and mud spatters reached all the way to the ceiling. Brushing Sammy's hair proved to be an impossible task, so Macy sat on the floor with a pair of scissors and did what she could.

When he was relatively clean and kempt, it was nearly one o'clock. All three cats had gone to sleep and Sammy was obviously worn out. Still, she knew he was appreciative because he turned his head just once and licked her face.

"I'd let you sleep on the bed, but I don't think that's a good idea," she said as she gathered up all the wet towels. "Snowball tends to be the jealous sort. Sorry about that." Back in the kitchen, she made a comfortable bed out of an old blanket. The dog immediately curled up on it, sighed and closed his eyes.

"Night, Sammy," she said with a yawn and turned off the light.

Exhausted, Macy fell asleep right away and woke with the alarm. The sun was shining through the bedroom window and onto her face. Her cats had settled, the three of them, on her pillows, sur-rounding her head.

Snowball jumped down and left the room. Macy assumed he'd gone to investigate whether Sammy was still in the house. A couple of minutes later she heard him voice his opinion of their house-guest and then race back, yowling a long list of complaints.

"He isn't staying," she promised. "He's lost. How would *you* feel if you were lost?"

In response, Snowball turned his back and ignored her completely.

"Fine, if that's how you're going to be."

Macy dressed in white jeans and an olive-green sweater, then ran a brush—not the one she'd used on Sammy—through her tangle of red curls. The makeup people would see to her hair and face later. This assignment, a photo shoot for a yarn company catalog, was scheduled for eleven. Radio was more fun, but the money she made from modeling put food in the cats' dishes.

She let Sammy into the yard, where he relieved himself against the fence—good thing Harvey wasn't out yet. A moment later he came back in and she refilled bowls and made a pot of coffee. Taking her cup, she wandered outside, which was part of her morning ritual. Sammy was busy wolfing down his breakfast.

Harvey had come into the backyard by now, a hoe in his hands, weeding his garden. She sat down on the step, savoring the cool spring air.

"Good morning, Harvey," she greeted him cheerfully.

He ignored her and continued hoeing. After a minute or two he muttered, "Don't see anything good about it. Seems like every other morning to me."

"I had company last night," she told him.

"Anybody I know?"

"Don't think so. He's a real sweetheart, though."

Harvey straightened and leaned against the hoe. He frowned. "You hiding a man inside your little house?"

"Definitely a male."

"I suppose you took in another stray. How many cats are you feeding, anyway? Your grandmother would be shocked if she knew you've turned her home into a cat house." He grumbled some other remark that she couldn't quite hear.

"I need a favor."

"Can't do it," he said and returned to weeding his garden. He lowered his hat over his eyes as if to shut her out completely.

"It's not a cat," she said as she walked to the fence and sipped her coffee. Sammy needed a place to stay until she could locate his owner or find a new one, and Harvey needed a friend. As far as she was concerned, it was meant to be. A perfect match.

"I'll bet it isn't a man, either," Harvey said.

"Now *that's* something you could use. I don't understand what's wrong with you."

Admittedly, she had problems with relationships. She'd dated lots of men and even fallen in love a time or two. But eventually the men in her life seemed to grow disenchanted with her. They found her too disorganized, too eccentric, too impulsive. Initially her unconventional nature appealed to them, but then they decided they wanted a more "nine-to-five kind of woman," as one of them had put it.

"There's nothing wrong with me."

He snorted.

"Are you going to help me or not?"

"Not."

"I'm counting on you, Harvey."

"Don't care, I'm not doing it. You aren't getting me involved in one of your schemes, so don't even ask."

Sammy poked his head out the back door and padded carefully down the four back steps.

"Harvey, meet Sammy," she said, gesturing toward the dog.

Harvey glanced in her direction, then rolled his eyes. "It isn't bad enough that you're feeding cats. Now you've added a dog to your menagerie."

"He's a stray. Look at him. Doesn't he just melt your heart?"

"Are you the one who gave him that ridiculous haircut?"

111

"I didn't have a choice, his hair was so matted."

"You bathed him, too?"

"I had to. He was filthy."

"Probably infested with fleas."

"Probably, but I got rid of them last night."

"So you say."

"Listen, I have to leave in a few minutes. I'm doing a photo shoot for that yarn company I was telling you about. They need me for hair and makeup at ten."

"Don't let me hold you up. Go." He waved her away.

"I can't leave Sammy here alone."

"Why not?"

Macy edged her way along the fence line, following him as he hoed. "Snowball's taken a dislike to him."

"At least one of your cats shows some intelligence."

"Harvey, will you watch him while I'm gone? Please?"

He shook his head emphatically. "Not me."

"It'll only be for a couple of hours."

"Tie him up in your backyard."

Macy had already considered that option. "How would you like a rope around your neck?" Unfortunately the yard wasn't fully enclosed.

Harvey didn't respond.

"Sammy's lost and frightened."

"I'd be frightened, too, if I had Snowball giving me the evil eye."

"Two hours," she murmured pleadingly. "Three at the most."

"Ten."

"Ten what?"

"Hours. I know how you operate, Macy Roth. You have no concept of time. One hour or six— it's all the same to you. I am not looking after that dog, so you might as well accept it right now."

Sammy ambled over to the fence and stared up at Harvey.

"Don't *you* start." He pointed an accusing finger at the dog, then turned to Macy. "Did you teach him to look at me like I'm his last friend in the world?"

"When would I have had time for that?"

"Go back inside because you're wasting your breath. I'm no babysitter to a flea-infested mutt."

She bent down and whispered to Sammy.

"What did you just tell that mangy dog?"

"Nothing."

"Yes, you did," he insisted. "I saw your lips move."

"If you must know, I told him not to pay any attention and to just go on over and visit."

Harvey buried the hoe in the freshly turned dirt. "Why is it you ignore everything I say? I don't know why I even bother to talk to you."

"Because you love me."

"No, I don't. Now kindly leave an old man alone."

"Can't do that. Sorry. I guess I'll call and cancel my part in the photo shoot."

Harvey removed his hat and wiped his brow. "That trick isn't going to work this time, so you can forget it. I don't care if you lose your job." He wagged his index finger at her. "And you aren't moving in with me if you lose your grandmother's house, either. I refuse to let you blackmail me."

"Not to worry, I told Sammy to stay here and keep an eye on you."

Harvey scowled. "If he's on your side of the fence, it's fine. But I don't want him digging in my garden."

"I'll make sure he knows to wait right here and I'll tell him to look after you, too."

"You do that, because if he sets one paw on my land, I'm calling the dogcatcher."

"Harvey, you wouldn't."

"Don't tempt me."

Macy rolled her eyes. "I'll be back in a few hours."

"Whatever."

"Look after him for me, Harvey."

"I said I wouldn't, and I won't."

Nevertheless, Macy figured it wouldn't be long before Sammy won over her neighbor. She'd let the two of them sort it out.

She put out fresh water for her animals and threw the dirty towels in the washer before grabbing her backpack and heading out the door. She left Sammy in the backyard, confident in Harvey's kindness despite all disclaimers to the contrary. Her cats were inside the house.

When she went to start the car, she saw that she was desperately low on gas. Considering what a nice day it was, she decided to ride her bicycle.

She got it out of the garage and pedaled down the street. It really was a lovely morning.

Chapter Ten

I've always been fascinated by how wise children often are, especially those with cancer. Despite the fact that they've been dealt a crummy hand in life, these kids are impressive. In my observation, children, by their very nature, are optimistic and in most cases far more realistic than their parents. I hadn't been looking forward to this picnic, but my reasons had nothing to do with the kids.

My fear had to do with my colleagues. I was afraid some of them—like Patrick—would use the opportunity to set me up with one of their friends. My concerns were well-founded, judging by the way they'd reacted to the news that I planned to attend.

Saturday morning I arrived at the park around ten-thirty. The weather had cooperated, although there was a huge gazebo for shelter in case of rain.

The rhododendrons and azaleas were in full bloom, just as they were in Hannah's garden at home. Splashes of soft color all around reminded me of a Monet painting. Children raced around, some with hair and others without. Today was a day for fun and laughter, games and prizes, food and friends. For this short period they could forget about everything associated with cancer. Their parents, too, could put aside their worries and fears and simply enjoy the day.

As I walked to the picnic area I saw Patrick O'Malley strolling toward me. He grinned and held up his hand in greeting. Although we worked in the same practice, we didn't often get a chance to talk. I owed Patrick. He'd covered for me so I could be with Hannah, especially toward the end. That had made turning down his request nearly impossible. Patrick had asked me to help and I could do nothing less.

"Glad to see you made it," Patrick said when we met. "And congratulations. I heard you've been nominated for Fischer-Newhart's Pediatrician of the Year. That's huge!"

I shrugged off his praise. The pharmaceutical company, which specialized in medication for children, gave a major award once a year in four regions of the country. This was my first nomination and it *was* a big deal. Of course, Linda knew and my parents, too, but I hadn't mentioned it to anyone else. Being singled out sort of embarrasses me. Always has. My goal is to be a good doctor and to make children well. That's it. I don't need any public acknowledgment.

The award was to be presented at a large banquet, the type of event everyone hates but feels obligated to attend. The thought of sitting through the evening alone held no appeal. I could invite someone; I just didn't know who.

I rubbed my hands together, eager to mingle with the kids. "Where do you need me most?"

"We could use some help with the games," Patrick said, reminding me of his original request.

"Perfect."

"Then *later* you can flip burgers." He slapped me affectionately on the back.

Within minutes I was laughing and horsing around with the kids. I regretted my bad mood earlier in the week. I blamed Hannah's letter for that. I wanted to argue with her, tell her I'd rather forget the outside world as much as possible, and she seemed to know that. I resented, at least a little, that a woman who'd been gone a year still had the power to manipulate me into something I had no interest in doing. Yet how could I refuse her?

A couple of hours later I was exhausted. I'd participated in the three-legged race, teaming up with James, a ten-year-old boy who probably wouldn't see his eleventh birthday. We crossed the finish line first and James wore his blue ribbon proudly.

Somehow or other, I got conned into being a partner with Kellie, a six-year-old with leukemia, for the egg toss. We lost—the egg broke in my hands, much to Kellie's delight. I wasn't any luckier with the water-balloon toss, but managed to jump far enough back to avoid getting soaked. After that, I put on an apron that read The Cook Is King and stood in front of the barbecue, grilling hamburgers. I noticed James wolfing his down and saw tears in his mother's eyes as she watched her son eat. I suspected it'd been a long time since he'd had this much of an appetite.

It was the oddest thing. I could feel a weight lift from my shoulders. I'd woken that morning just like I did every day, instantly aware that Hannah was gone. She was the first person I thought of every morning and the last person every night. The pain had settled in my chest the way it always did. Yet here I was, only a few hours later, and it almost felt as if she was there with me, laughing, teasing, encouraging me to enjoy the event.

Despite the satisfactions of being with children, today reminded me that I'd most likely never have any of my own. Hannah had written in her letter that her greatest regret was not being able to have our child. I regretted it, too, and knew I'd miss out on that aspect of life. Hannah would've been a wonderful mother. I didn't intend to remarry, regardless of her letter and her list, so I wouldn't have the opportunity to be a father. That saddened me and yet, as I watched the children racing about the park, laughing and teasing one another, I couldn't help wondering if maybe Hannah was right—at least in her insistence that I stop focusing on the past and look to the future.

By this point I'd read her letter so often I'd practically memorized it. Maybe I *should* look ahead instead of keeping myself locked in old memories. Still, I wasn't sure that could ever include remarriage. My fear, I suppose, was that I'd never be able to recapture the special bond I'd shared with my wife. I was afraid I'd measure every woman I met against Hannah. That would be unfair to Hannah and to the other woman.

When I finished my cooking shift, I grabbed a paper plate and helped myself to a cheeseburger. Potato salad's a favorite of mine and I piled on a big scoop of that, as well as a giant pickle and a small bag of corn chips.

I found a spot and sat down on the lawn, legs stretched out, and balanced the paper plate on my thighs. I picked up my burger and took my first bite. As I glanced about the park I saw several other volunteers and friends. Each was paired up with someone else. For the first time since I arrived, it struck me how truly alone I was.

Patrick sat on the lawn with his wife, Melanie, and when he saw me he gestured that I should join them. I hated to barge in, but I didn't want to eat by myself, either, so I stood and walked toward them.

"It's so good to see you," Melanie said as I lowered myself onto the lawn. Patrick's wife is a nurse at the hospital and one of the kindest people I know.

I took another bite of my hamburger, surprised by how delicious it was. I realized I was hungry; no wonder, since the kids had kept me physically active for a couple of hours. I was actually *enjoying* the taste, a sensation I hadn't experienced since Hannah's illness.

"Who's that?" Melanie asked, pointing out someone else who was sitting alone some distance away.

Patrick looked in the direction his wife had indicated, and I did, too. The woman seemed familiar. I'd seen her earlier while I was involved with the children. I thought at the time that I knew her, but I didn't remember from where.

"Isn't that Leanne Lancaster?" Melanie asked her husband.

I nearly dropped my cheeseburger. "Leanne Lancaster?" I repeated.

"Do you know her?" Melanie asked.

I slowly nodded and a numbness spread down my arms. "She was one of Hannah's oncology nurses." More than that, Leanne Lancaster was the second name on the list Hannah had given me. Trying not to be obvious, I squinted at her. Leanne looked different—thinner, gaunt, pale. That must've been why I hadn't immediately recognized her.

"I hate to see her eating alone," Melanie said. She turned to me, then started to get up. "I'll go over and sit with her."

"Why don't you invite her to join us?" Patrick suggested. "Do you mind, Michael?"

"Patrick," Melanie warned in a low voice.

"What?"

"I don't want Michael to think we're matching him up."

"It's fine," I said, interrupting. Little did they know Hannah had already done that. "Invite her if you'd like." I hadn't seen Leanne in a year. That we should come across each other now felt like more than coincidence. I couldn't shrug off the feeling that Hannah had somehow arranged this.

As Melanie walked over to chat with Leanne, Patrick said, "So, how well do you know Leanne?"

"Just professionally." I was cutting off any matchmaking effort before it could get started.

"She's had a hard time."

"Oh?" I wasn't sure what he meant. "How so?"

"Her divorce." As he said that, I recalled the comment in Hannah's letter.

"Her husband was Mark Lancaster," Patrick went on to explain.

The name caught my attention. "What about

him?" I asked. "Who is he?" Hannah hadn't given me any details about the divorce.

"He's the guy who embezzled money from that charity benefit the hospital had a couple of years back. He's an accountant and volunteered to collect the funds. An audit a month later showed a discrepancy of twenty-five thousand dollars. As it turned out, Mark supposedly 'borrowed' the money."

I nodded. The scandal had shocked the hospital community, but for me, of course, it had been eclipsed by our personal tragedy.

"I don't remember the outcome," Patrick was saying, "other than the embarrassment Leanne went through and the divorce."

My guess was that Hannah knew all about Leanne's troubles; she was the kind of person others confided in.

My thoughts were interrupted when Melanie returned with Leanne. I stood as the two women approached.

"You remember Michael Everett, don't you?" Melanie asked Leanne.

"Oh, yes. Hello again."

She had a nice smile, I noticed. I also realized how much she'd changed. Leanne wore her dark brown hair shorter than she had a couple of years ago and she seemed . . . deflated somehow. Her style was very different from Hannah's—"careless casual," I'd call it—and she was taller by several inches.

My perusal came to an abrupt halt. I was doing the very thing I'd sworn not to, and that was comparing her to Hannah, at least in appearance.

"Do you still work at the oncology center?" I asked, making conversation while I considered the last time I'd seen her. It would've been two weeks before Hannah's death. Since almost everyone, Hannah included, knew there was no hope, other medical professionals had started to withdraw. This emotional detachment is a protective device common in my field. Leanne had been the exception. She had remained Hannah's friend to the very end, chatting with her, bringing her small gifts. Flowers, a magazine, some chocolate now and then. I'd been so consumed by my own efforts to deal with the fact that I was losing her, I hadn't paid much attention at the time. I remembered it now and was grateful.

"I'm still at the hospital," she confirmed.

"Leanne organized the volunteers this year," Patrick said. "You and I both know what a big job that is."

Patrick and I had done it several years ago, and it'd been a huge task. Thankfully, Hannah and Melanie had willingly lent a hand and made dozens of phone calls on our behalf.

"I had a lot of help," she said, dismissing his praise.

"Patrick's the one who coerced *me* into volunteering," I told her.

"Me, too." Leanne grinned and I had to admit she was lovely. She smiled less often than she should, I felt. I sensed a sadness about her and wondered if it had to do with her divorce. After close to two years, shouldn't she be over that by now? It occurred to me with a sudden shock that I was thinking about her the same way others had about me. That my allotment of grief had come to its end.

The four of us sat and talked for a while. Not once did Leanne bring up Hannah's name, which I appreciated. It wasn't that I didn't want to talk about her; Hannah was always on my mind and in my heart. But I preferred to reminisce about her life rather than her death. In not bringing up the subject, Leanne revealed a sensitivity I found rare among my friends. Most people seemed to feel obliged to tell me how sorry they were, especially if I hadn't seen them since the funeral. I particularly hated being told that they understood how I felt. They didn't; they *couldn't*. I was thankful we didn't need to travel down that troubled path. Perhaps Leanne avoided mentioning Hannah's death because she didn't want to discuss her own divorce. Either way, I was content to chat about the picnic, the children or just about anything else.

When we'd finished our meals, Patrick and Melanie drifted away and I was sitting alone with Leanne. I felt a moment of panic, not knowing what we had to say to each other without the buffer of my friends.

"This turned out to be a beautiful day," I said and wanted to jerk back the inane words as soon as they were out of my mouth. Apparently, the weather was the most stimulating topic I could come up with.

"I'm glad. It's always a risk when you plan a picnic in May."

"Then why hold the picnic this month?" I asked. "We could count on sunshine in late August or early September."

"I looked into that. When the picnic first began, the only time we could book the park was in May."

I nodded; other organizations would have made reservations long before, seeing how popular this park was.

"Then later, when the committee tried to book another month, they ran into all kinds of roadblocks," Leanne explained. "So it was decided to keep the May date and to count our blessings."

That made sense.

An uncomfortable silence followed. I started to speak at the same time as Leanne.

"I—"

"Would you—"

We both stopped and looked at each other. I motioned for her to speak first. She was a bit flushed, as though she found this situation as awkward as I did.

"I was about to say I'm grateful Patrick and Melanie invited me to join them."

"I am, too," I echoed, then realized she might misunderstand my meaning. "I was sitting alone, too."

She glanced down at my wedding band. I'd never removed it. I considered myself married. That was when I noticed the slight indentation on the ring finger of her left hand.

"I still feel . . . naked without my wedding ring," she whispered as though reading my mind.

"I would, too," I said, as if that was explanation enough. I continued to wear mine because I wouldn't feel like myself without it.

"Sometimes it isn't easy to let go of the past." She didn't meet my eyes.

"It isn't," I agreed.

"I loved my husband. I trusted him," she said, gazing down at the lawn. "I never thought he was capable of doing something so wrong."

"You weren't to blame."

"I know, but I felt responsible."

I didn't remember any of the details, nothing beyond what Patrick had mentioned. The scandal took place soon after Hannah was diagnosed and I had other things on my mind. I did hear about it, but honestly I hadn't made the connection when I heard Leanne's name. She was Hannah's nurse and that was it. Hannah hadn't said anything, either, and surely she knew. It simply wasn't important to her or, for that matter, to me.

"Do you get tired of people telling you to get over it and move on?" Leanne asked.

I snickered because she mirrored my own feelings so precisely. "Do I ever," I mumbled. "I'm sick of hearing it, sick of people telling me I only have a certain number of months and then I'm supposed to be done with grieving."

Her eyes met mine, and understanding blossomed between us. "Yeah. And I'm sick of people trying to set me up on dates with their cousin or brother-in-law!"

"It's been so long since I've been on a date that I'd feel like a fish out of water." That wasn't the most original analogy, but it got my point across.

"I know what you mean."

I plunged in, recognizing the irony of what I was about to do. "Do you think it'd be okay if I called you sometime?" I could hardly believe I was asking. And yet it felt . . . good. I wasn't ready to date and she didn't appear to be, either. Maybe if we met casually a few times it would help both of us ease back into the world of the living.

She looked up at me and grinned. "I think that would be a nice idea."

"I do, too."

Midafternoon I headed home in a better mood than I'd been in a long while. I climbed into my car and rested my hands on the steering wheel.

"I hope you're happy," I said to Hannah. "Next time you want to arrange a meeting with a woman on your list you might be a bit more subtle."

I started the car and I could swear I heard Hannah's laughter over the sound of the engine.

Chapter Eleven

Her brief talk with Michael Everett at the picnic had been a turning point for Leanne. She'd hardly been able to sleep that night as snippets of their conversation played back in her mind. Michael was the first man who seemed to understand, and that was because he, too, was intimately aware of loss.

Oh, the circumstances were drastically different. Mark was very much alive, whereas cancer had taken Hannah's life. But Mark had made it abundantly clear that as far as he was concerned she might as well consider him dead. Only he was alive and Leanne couldn't make herself pretend otherwise.

Her ex-husband had embezzled twenty-five thousand dollars. As a result, Mark had spent a year in prison. Leanne still felt shocked and mortified by what he'd done. When she'd first learned of the discrepancy, the missing funds, she'd refused to believe Mark could be responsible. It made no sense that he, a respected accountant for a long-established Seattle firm, would resort to something like this. Something so underhanded. So wrong.

In the beginning she'd defended him, put her own reputation on the line. Later she'd been humiliated when, without a single word to her,

Mark had stepped forward, his attorney by his side, and admitted guilt. Two years later, she still found it difficult to comprehend. Not once had he discussed the situation with her. She hadn't even realized he'd hired an attorney. He wouldn't answer when she'd demanded to know why he'd taken the money. As his wife, his staunchest supporter, she felt she was entitled to more than his tight-lipped refusal to give even the most rudimentary explanation.

If he was going to "borrow" funds, then why, oh, why did he have to take money from a charity event for the hospital where she worked? Where she was left to face everyone once the truth came out? Surely he understood how embarrassing this was for her. All Mark would say, all he'd confess to, was that he'd needed the money and planned to return it. He didn't tell her, his parents or anyone she knew—not even his attorney—why he'd so desperately needed that amount.

Shamed in front of her peers and shaken to her very core, Leanne felt she had no option but to file for divorce. Apparently, Mark wasn't the honorable man she'd assumed. When he was presented with the divorce papers, he hadn't offered the slightest resistance. If she wanted out of the marriage, he was willing to let her go.

When the decree arrived, he signed it, worked out a plea bargain with the prosecution and served his time, which ended up being a year.

Her marriage in ruins, her life in shreds, Leanne had floundered. She dragged her pain and disillusionment with her from one day to the next. Thankfully, in the two years following Mark's arrest, the talk, the rumors, the unpleasantness, had mostly died down.

She hadn't spoken to him since the divorce was final, although she'd made a couple of pointless efforts to write him while he was in prison. Mark had never acknowledged her attempts to communicate or responded to her letters. All she'd wanted to know was why he'd taken the money.

A short while after she'd mailed the second letter, Muriel Lancaster, Mark's mother, had phoned at his request. It seemed he'd asked that Leanne not write to him again. They were divorced and he suggested she move on with her life, the same as he intended to do.

Now, however, Leanne regretted the divorce. She'd filed in anger, believing it was the best thing to do under the circumstances. No matter how many times she'd pleaded with him to explain, he'd remained silent. Hindsight being what it was, she wished she hadn't reacted as quickly as she had. Especially in light of what she'd learned since.

Mark was close to his younger sister. Denise was in a bad marriage with an abusive husband. She'd been living in California, and no one in the family was aware of how dangerous the situation was until she'd tried to leave Darrin. Her husband had immediately filed for custody of the two children and Denise was forced to fight him in court. Attorneys' fees added up and the couple had to put their house on the market.

Thankfully, Denise won full custody of the children, but she knew she'd never be safe living in California where Darrin had access to her and the two little girls. With her half of the proceeds from the house, Denise would be able to pay off the attorney and start over in another state. She could make her escape, buy airline tickets and leave for a new life.

Desperate, she'd called Mark at the last moment. All she needed was twenty-five thousand dollars for less than ten hours. She'd FedEx Mark a cashier's check from the sale of the house the very next day. She couldn't involve her parents, since her father had recently retired and their income had already been reduced. Denise was in a state of panic. Leanne and Mark had taken out a home-equity loan to remodel their kitchen and with the work in progress they were at their credit limit. Knowing how frantic Denise was to pay her bills and get out of California, Mark had sent her the funds from the charity drive at the hospital.

Then the deal on Denise and Darrin's house had unexpectedly fallen through. Caught up in her own drama, Denise took the money and ran, fleeing with her children and going into hiding.

With the help of a women's organization, she went underground for six months. It was only when she resurfaced that she learned what had happened to Mark. Denise had no idea Mark had "borrowed" the funds, no idea of the consequences he'd suffered as a result. She'd pleaded his case before the court and Mark's sentence had been reduced from the original five years to one.

By the time Denise contacted Leanne and explained, it was too late. The divorce was final. The house never did sell and eventually went into foreclosure. She ended up with nothing—except guilt over what she'd caused her brother.

The only contact Leanne had with Mark's family now was through his mother, Muriel. Brian and Muriel lived in Spokane, and her former mother-in-law called Leanne periodically. The entire situation had been devastating to all of them. Brian had been an anchor, supporting both of his children, but he seemed to have a hard time forgiving Leanne for walking out on his son when Mark needed her most.

Leanne regretted her lack of faith in her husband—and his lack of faith in her. Mark wasn't faultless in this. He should've explained, should've trusted her. She felt that if they'd worked together, faced this as a couple, everything might have turned out differently.

Now here she was, two years later, divorced and

miserable. The house was long gone, and she was renting a high-rise apartment. Denise, on the other hand, lived in Nebraska with her kids and was working toward repaying the money, although it was nearly impossible on what she made as a waitress.

Leanne didn't keep in touch with Denise. She couldn't help blaming her, at least a little, for the disaster that had befallen Mark, although none of it was intentional. And she suspected Denise blamed *her* for not staying with him.

The conversation with Michael the day before had brought Leanne a new resolve. She woke Sunday morning knowing she had to make one last effort to sort things out with her ex-husband. The divorce had happened so fast. She wanted—no, she *needed*—to see him. Perhaps they could assess the situation and find out if their love, along with their marriage, was completely dead. If so, she'd wish him well and move on. And "moving on" could include seeing Michael Everett. . . .

Leanne had found out from Mark's mother that after his release from prison, he'd gone to Yakima, assisting migrant workers there, helping them with government forms and immigration papers. Apparently, this was part of the community-service hours he'd been ordered to serve. Muriel had reluctantly supplied his address. All she'd asked was that Leanne not tell Mark how she'd learned it.

So Leanne was going to Yakima. She dressed carefully, choosing tailored pants and a silk blouse Mark had purchased for her the last Christmas they were together. She hoped it would be a reminder of happier times. He wouldn't want to see her; returning her letters and not calling or visiting since his release made it more than clear. Still, that didn't deter her.

Despite everything, she wanted him to ask her to reconsider, to give their relationship another shot. Almost two years had passed and maybe, just maybe, they could start again. But the request had to come from him, and Leanne knew there wasn't much likelihood of that.

He'd done nothing but shove her away from the moment he'd surrendered to the authorities. He'd let her know, through his attorney, that he didn't want to see her at the jail or in court. Leanne had complied, out of anger and hurt feelings. Later, she decided that he'd wanted to separate her from this scandal as much as he could. It was the only explanation that made sense.

Today she was about to confront Mark for the first time since his sentencing.

She set off, considering the sequence of events that had brought her to this point. It seemed only minutes later that she was over Snoqualmie Pass on I-90. The next two hours passed quickly as she took the exit in Ellensburg and headed toward Yakima. Before long, thirty minutes or so from where she'd left I-90, she arrived at the freeway exit. The address she'd put into her GPS led her to a small apartment complex in a neglected part of the city. The two-story structure was badly in need of renovation. The outside railing had once been brown, but was now rusted where the paint had peeled off. Mark's apartment was on the upper level.

Leanne parked the car and sat inside it for several minutes, gathering her courage. Her stomach was queasy. She had to do this, she told herself. Had to know. Had to make one last effort.

Before she lost her nerve, she slid out of the car, squared her shoulders and drew in a deep breath. As she climbed the rickety steps to the upper level, she held on to the handrail, although it was too shaky to provide much support.

Standing outside his apartment door, she rang the bell.

No response.

Foolish though it seemed, she'd never considered that Mark might not be home. Then it occurred to her that the doorbell might be defective, as everything else at this complex seemed to be. She knocked hard. If Mark was inside, he had to know there was someone at his door.

"Hold on."

Hearing his voice after all this time startled her. He sounded angry, gruff, unlike the man she'd known and loved. But after a year in prison she had to assume he was no longer the man she remembered. Tightening her jaw, she stepped back and waited. She had only a few seconds to compose herself before the door was flung open.

Mark stood on the other side and it would've been difficult to say who was more surprised. Her assumption was correct, at least with regard to his appearance, which was completely altered. The neat, clean-cut accountant she'd married bore little resemblance to the man who faced her now.

His hair grew over his ears and it didn't look as if he'd shaved in two or three days. He wore a faded T-shirt and jeans. His eyes were sunken and his expression was that of a man without hope.

For an instant, the tiniest moment, she was sure his gaze softened as he recognized her.

"Leanne." Her name was more breath than sound. He recovered from his shock, and his eyes hardened. "What are you doing here?"

She disregarded the lack of welcome. "I'd like to talk, if that would be possible?" Right away she realized she shouldn't have added the last part.

"Everything that needed to be said was said a long time ago."

Leanne refused to be so easily dissuaded. "Could I come inside?"

"No. I'm not receiving company." His voice was brusque. Sarcastic.

"Oh."

Mark stared at her. "Why are you here?"

At one time he'd been gentle, but it seemed that every bit of tenderness he possessed had been ground out of him. He held himself stiffly on the other side of the threshold.

"We never talked about . . . any of this."

"No need. It's too late now. We're divorced. Our marriage is over and the sooner you realize that, the better."

"You should've told me." This was an old argument and one he obviously didn't want to hear. She'd begged him incessantly to explain, back when he was out on bail awaiting his hearing.

"I don't want you here," he said. He looked around, then briefly closed his eyes. "You don't belong in this place. Just leave—and don't come back."

Her throat had closed up so tightly it was impossible to speak. Although he was outwardly angry, Leanne had to believe their love wasn't entirely dead. At the very least, she had to give it every chance to resuscitate itself, even if their relationship changed in the process, as it inevitably would.

"I don't think it's too late. We can talk, work this out, the way we should have in the beginning," she said urgently. Perhaps if she was willing to share her own regrets, Mark would acknowledge the role he'd played in all this.

"You did us both a favor," he said, backing away from her. "You weren't the only one who wanted out of the marriage."

"I don't believe that." It was a lie, and she refused to accept it.

"Believe whatever you like," he said coldly. He betrayed himself, however, when his eyes couldn't seem to meet hers.

For a few seconds, she thought she sensed a yielding in him. But if that *was* the case, it had been all too fleeting.

"Don't you get it?" he said, his voice low. "Do you honestly think it was just the money?"

She blinked in confusion.

He took a step backward. She advanced, unwilling to let him escape. If he had something else to tell her, something that had never come up before, she was going to insist on hearing it.

"What are you saying?" She hated the way her voice quavered.

"You don't want to know."

"You're wrong."

"Fine." He paused. "Frankly, I'd hoped to spare you this."

She reached out and grabbed the doorknob, instinctively knowing she'd need its support.

"Did you ever wonder why I didn't fight the divorce? I figured it was for the best for more reasons than you realize. There were other women, Leanne."

She felt the color drain from her face. It would've hurt less had he thrust a knife in her abdomen. Then she frowned, suddenly sure of one thing. His words were nothing but a ploy, a trick to convince her to forget him. "That's a lie." *Another* lie.

He hung his head. "I wish it was. Now you know. You saw me as this decent, honorable man and the truth is, it was all an act. You're better off without me." He looked at her. "We aren't good for each other, Leanne."

She found it difficult to breathe. "I still don't believe you." He was sacrificing himself and she wouldn't allow him to do it.

"Like I said, believe what you want, but know this." He spoke slowly and distinctly. "I don't want to see you. I don't want you here." He glanced over his shoulder, the gesture deliberate.

Leanne blanched. He was signaling that there was someone inside the apartment, waiting for him. A woman. She couldn't hear anyone, but that didn't prove a thing.

What if this *wasn't* a lie?

Leanne clasped her hands, because she desperately needed to hold on to something and that something had to be herself. No one else was going to shore her up. She was on her own and had been from the moment Mark was arrested.

"Get on with your life," he added. "I have."

Leanne stiffened her spine. "Funny you should say that."

He locked eyes with her, which he'd avoided doing since he'd opened the door.

"I met someone," she told him.

"Good."

"He's the husband of one of my former patients. She died . . . I was her nurse."

He said nothing.

"I ran into Michael at a picnic. I've been doing a lot of volunteer work. It keeps me occupied."

He looked down at his scuffed running shoes as though bored.

She ignored his rudeness. "Michael was one of the other volunteers at the event."

"And this interests me why?"

"We talked."

"I hope he asked you out." Again he gave the impression of boredom.

"Is that what you want, Mark?"

He raised his shoulder. "Go out with the man, okay?"

She stared at him. He didn't mean what he'd said. He *couldn't.* "You've changed," she whispered, trying to gauge the truth about his feelings. This was what she'd feared—the man she'd fallen in love with ten years earlier no longer existed. The one who stood in front of her was a stranger.

"Trust me, a year in prison will change any man."

She swallowed hard.

"I don't want to be cruel," he went on. "I appreciate that it took a lot of courage for you to come here today, but it's too late. What we had is over. Just accept that."

Clenching her fingers so tightly they hurt, she struggled to find the right words, but he spoke first.

"Don't let yourself get bogged down in useless sentimentality. We aren't the same people we once were."

Leanne felt more confused than ever. "What you said earlier isn't true, is it? You were always faithful." She *had* to believe that, because the alternative was too devastating to consider.

He didn't answer.

As she blinked back tears, he stepped inside and quietly closed the door.

Stunned, Leanne stood there, rooted to the spot, while she took in what had just happened. She closed her eyes and felt in the strongest possible way that Mark was on the other side of the door, his heart beating in unison with hers, crying out in pain, the same as hers.

After several minutes, she turned away. She climbed carefully down the stairs and got into her car. She had to make several attempts before her hands stopped trembling enough to insert the key.

She had her answer. The time had come to reconcile herself to the fact that she was divorced.

If and when Michael Everett phoned to ask her out, she'd respond with an unequivocal *yes*.

Chapter Twelve

"D o anything special this weekend?" Ritchie asked as we left the gym Monday morning.

Once again my brother-in-law seemed to have some kind of intuition about what was happening in my life, almost as if Hannah was whispering in his ear.

"Why do you ask?" I probably sounded more defensive than I meant to because Ritchie turned to look at me, arching his eyebrows as though surprised by my reaction—or overreaction.

"I guess that touched a nerve," he said with a grin. "So tell me what's up."

"I volunteered at the hospital picnic for children with cancer on Saturday."

"You said you were going to."

I inhaled and held my breath, then slowly released it. "While I was there, I ran into Leanne Lancaster."

Ritchie stared blankly at me.

"Leanne is one of the women on Hannah's list."

In typical fashion, Ritchie started to laugh. "I can see my sister's fingerprints all over this."

The problem was, I could, too. I was convinced that Hannah had been directing my life, as well as Leanne's. Not that I approved or was even interested in her plan. Or so I immediately told myself.

"Did the two of you talk?" Ritchie asked.

It took me a moment to realize he was referring to Leanne. "For a few minutes. She's divorced."

Ritchie looked thoughtful. "Hannah must've known that if she put her on the list."

The timing was right. Leanne had said her divorce was final nearly two years ago. That meant Leanne had been dealing with it when Hannah was undergoing chemotherapy.

"What's she like?" Ritchie asked.

"How do you mean?"

"Physically. Is she blonde, brunette? Tall or medium height?"

"Something like that," I said, as I reviewed our time together. Brunette, but I saw no reason to tell Ritchie that. Besides, physical appearance wasn't significant; what was far more important was the emotional connection I felt with her.

Ritchie shook his head, his expression amused. "Are you going to call her?"

Actually, I hadn't decided. "We talked about it, Leanne and I. She isn't over the divorce yet and you, better than anyone, know how raw I still feel."

"Ask her out," Ritchie urged. "What can it hurt?"

"We're two wounded people."

"See?" he joked. "You already have something in common."

I had to admit Ritchie had a point. I grinned. "Maybe I will." We reached the street, ready to part company.

"You have plans for next weekend?" my brother-in-law asked.

I mentally scanned my social calendar, which took all of two seconds. "Not that I can remember. Why?"

"It's Max's birthday. Steph's throwing him a party. I thought you could keep me company."

"Count me in." I appreciated the way Ritchie and Steph included me as both family and friend.

"Great. I'll give you the details about Saturday when I have them. See you Wednesday morning."

"Wednesday," I repeated and headed for the office.

The morning was fairly typical of any Monday in a pediatrician's clinic. The phone rang constantly and I had appointments scheduled practically on top of one another. A new influenza was going around; I saw three cases first thing. The big danger when children have the flu is dehydration, and I sent one four-year-old to the hospital.

I stepped into my office at lunchtime and shut the door. I'd ordered a Greek salad from the deli across the street and it sat on my desk. I pried open the lid and pierced some lettuce with my plastic fork. As I took my first bite, Leanne came to mind. I couldn't help wondering if she'd thought about me on Sunday. She'd occupied *my* thoughts, and I wasn't happy about it, either.

I leaned back in my chair as I contemplated my course of action. Although I'd mentioned getting in touch, I hadn't jotted down her phone number. As I'd pointed out to Leanne, I was rusty when it came to this dating business, but I didn't realize how much until that moment.

I checked the online telephone directory and found nothing listed for Leanne Lancaster or L. Lancaster. I doubted she'd still have a phone listing under her husband, but it wouldn't hurt to look. Only I couldn't think of his name. Mack? Matt? It definitely began with an *M*—didn't it?

I tilted back my head and closed my eyes in an effort to remember. Then it came to me. Mark. His name was Mark Lancaster.

I set my salad aside, scooping up a kalamata olive and popping it in my mouth. The online telephone listing held dozens of Lancasters, but not a single one with the first name Mark.

I had no way of getting in touch with Leanne, unless I contacted the oncology center at the hospital. That, however, I was reluctant to do, perhaps because of all the memories associated with calling that number. Then again, I didn't have any other option.

I decided to make the call before I lost my nerve.

The receptionist answered in a cool professional-sounding voice that I didn't recognize. I asked to speak to Leanne, giving my name only as Michael, hoping that would alert Leanne to the fact that I'd followed through on our discussion.

I didn't have to wait long. "This is Leanne," she said after picking up.

While I'd made a point of placing the call quickly, I'd neglected to consider what I wanted to say.

"I . . . didn't get your phone number," I blurted out. "Your home number," I added.

"Is this Michael Everett?"

"Yes. If there's a restriction on personal calls, I apologize."

"No . . . no, it's fine. I'm taking a late lunch."

I glanced at the clock and saw that it was past one. I had patients waiting. Any moment now, Linda would be knocking on the door to remind me.

"I thought Saturday went well," I said.

"Thanks, but I had lots of help."

Leanne assumed I was referring to the picnic when I was actually talking about our conversation. I can be oblivious, as Hannah frequently—and often laughingly—used to point out. Leanne had done an impressive job of organizing the volunteers and deserved the credit. I'd completely forgotten.

"We discussed getting together," I said.

"Yes . . ." She sounded almost as hesitant as I did.

"Do you have any particular time in mind?" I realized as soon as I'd asked what a ridiculous question that was. "I mean, is one day better than another for you?"

"Not really. What about you?"

"Ah . . . anytime, really. Well, other than work hours, of course."

"Me, too."

Linda knocked at the closed office door. "I need to go." I got to my feet.

"I should, too."

"Tonight?" I said. "I could do dinner tonight."

"Dinner?"

"So we can talk?" Feeling like a bumbling fool, I pressed my hand to the top of my head. I wasn't sure why, other than to keep my head from exploding before I embarrassed myself further.

"I could meet you after work," she said.

"Sure. Thanks, Leanne." I was about to hang up when she stopped me.

"What time?"

"Oh, yes. Is seven too late for you?"

"No, seven's good. I suppose we should choose a restaurant while we're at it."

"Do you have a preference?"

"No, do you?"

"Not really." My mind whirled with possible suggestions.

"We could always meet at Ivar's on the waterfront."

"Fine. See you there." My office and the hospital were both in downtown Seattle, so we could walk to the waterfront without the bother of moving our cars. The fish-and-chip place was a well-known northwest institution and served great food. Dining was casual. We could order at the counter and then sit at one of the picnic-style tables that lined the pier. We wouldn't have a waiter fussing over us and could come and go as we pleased.

Linda knocked a second time, reminding me once again that I had patients waiting. "I'll see you at seven," I said. I started to hang up when I heard Leanne call my name.

"Yes?" I said, eager now to get off the line.

"I just wanted to thank you for taking the initiative and contacting me. I wasn't sure I'd hear from you and . . . I guess I wanted you to know I'm happy you called."

"Oh . . . Me, too," I mumbled.

The rest of the afternoon passed in a flash. I refused to let myself dwell on the awkward conversation with Leanne. We'd make quite the couple, both of us out of practice when it came to establishing a relationship. But friendship would be enough, I told myself. Friendship was all I really wanted for now.

My staff had left the office by five-thirty. Since I generally stayed later to finish up paperwork and read over lab results, I sat in my office and made a genuine attempt to concentrate. Yet all I could think about was my dinner date with Leanne.

I'd made a mistake earlier when I'd called and

hadn't figured out what to say. This time I was determined that wouldn't happen. Retrieving a pad from my desk drawer, I planned to write out a list of topics we might discuss. I thought of this as a cheat sheet—and frankly I needed one.

Naturally, we'd talk about Hannah. Well, I'd want to talk about her at any rate and I'd be a willing listener if Leanne chose to enlighten me about her divorce. There'd be any number of medical professionals we both knew, including Patrick, and I wrote down several colleagues' names.

So far, my list contained three items. It was a start; I hoped Leanne wouldn't rely on me to carry the conversation. I wasn't good at that. Winter, Hannah's cousin, had made our brief meeting relatively painless. I hoped that would be the case with this evening, too.

I gave myself fifteen minutes to make the short trek down the hill from Fifth to the waterfront. Summer was fast approaching, and in a few weeks the Seattle waterfront would be crowded with tourists, many of whom come here a day or two in advance of boarding cruise ships that would sail up the Inside Passage to Alaska.

Hannah and I had always dreamed of taking that cruise. Medical-school bills and the cost of joining an established practice had prohibited such luxuries. After that, our schedules interfered and then Hannah's illness. . . .

I approached the ferry terminal and had to wait while a line of cars disembarked. Ivar's was just down the street and I saw that Leanne had arrived before me. She noticed me at the same time and waved.

I waved back and my stomach tightened. A surge of panic went through me until I felt the wadded-up list in my pocket.

Once the sidewalk was clear, I walked over. "Thanks for agreeing to meet me," I said. Smiling at her, I suddenly realized what an attractive woman she was.

"Thank you for asking me," she said.

I'd already lost my train of thought. We stood, uncomfortably silent, until Leanne said, "Should we order?"

I wished now that I'd suggested a restaurant with a bar. A glass of wine would've helped us both relax.

"Okay." This wasn't a hopeful beginning. We lined up and I studied the menu, listed on a board above the counter. "What would you like?" Thankfully I had the presence of mind to ask.

"I love Ivar's clam chowder," she said.

"That's all you want?"

"I'll have it in a bread bowl."

That sounded good to me, too. The thick chowder was ladled into large sourdough buns, which then served as part of the meal. I doubted I'd eat much, considering how unsettled I was. I felt the same way I had the first time I'd asked a girl out on a date. I'd been fifteen.

I paid for our order, then carried the tray to the adjacent area where picnic tables were set up. We sat for a moment and neither of us seemed inclined to eat or speak. We did a fairly good job of not looking at each other.

Leanne reached for her spoon and I reached for mine. She took her first bite and I did, too. Then she set the plastic spoon down on her paper napkin.

She finally looked at me. "I suppose you want to know about Mark."

I met her gaze head-on, unsure why she'd introduced the subject of her husband so soon. At some point in the evening I'd expected her to mention him, but leading off with Mark as the main topic was disconcerting.

"Everyone wants to know," she elaborated. "It's probably best to get it out of the way."

"Okay," I said and gestured toward her. "If that's what you want."

"It isn't, but it's only fair to tell you that he's done his time in prison and . . . and moved on with his life."

I nodded, encouraging her to continue.

Leanne lowered her eyes. "As I said, he's gotten on with his life. I . . . I guess I should, too."

Chapter Thirteen

"Mark's stealing from the hospital was the worst shock of my life," Leanne said. She'd stopped eating. "I knew something wasn't right just from the way he behaved after the charity event, but he wouldn't talk about it. I assumed it had to do with his job, but I wish I'd . . . asked more questions."

I understood that better than she realized. "I'm a physician. Although I couldn't have *known* Hannah had cancer, I feel I should've at least suspected she wasn't well."

I saw the sympathy in Leanne's eyes. "You can't blame yourself any more than I can take responsibility for what Mark did."

I knew that; nevertheless I did blame myself. I'd been so wrapped up in my own career, in my own needs and wants, in our shared comforts and routines, it never occurred to me that anything might be wrong with my wife. As a husband and a doctor, I couldn't help feeling that I'd failed Hannah.

Consequently I'd failed myself, too. I wasn't sure I could ever get over the guilt of that, irrational though it undoubtedly was. Hannah would be the first to reassure me. Again and again she'd reminded me that ovarian cancer is difficult to detect and there are few, if any, symptoms. There was no reason—no unusual fatigue, no pain or nausea, no family history, nothing—to suggest she might have this disease.

"You must've been surprised when Mark was arrested," I said, preferring not to discuss Hannah, even though I'd assumed we would.

"I was speechless." Leanne shook her head. "His parents, too. I think what confused me the most was the fact that Mark's one of the most honorable people I know. He has . . . had more integrity than any other man I'd met."

"You're still in love with him?" I asked, although the answer was obvious.

Reluctantly, Leanne nodded. "Although I don't really want to be . . . As you can imagine, I was outraged and embarrassed. Mark refused to explain himself, so I felt I had no option other than to file for divorce. I . . . I wish I'd waited—knowing what I do now." She paused, closing her eyes. "Still, after recent . . . revelations, perhaps I made the right decision, after all."

"Was Mark involved with someone else?" It was a painful question and I could see from the way she flinched that I'd touched the emotional equivalent of a bruise.

"I'm positive he wasn't. Mark might've been able to deceive me when it came to embezzlement, but not . . . our marriage." She sent me an agonized look.

I leaned over to lightly clasp her hand, releasing it after a few seconds.

"In my heart of hearts I have to believe he was faithful during our marriage . . . but I don't know about now. He might be seeing someone else, although I don't really think so. If he was dating again, I'm sure his mother would've told me. We're still in touch."

"Did Mark want the divorce?" To me, it didn't make sense that he'd throw away his marriage, along with his freedom and his career.

"Apparently. He certainly didn't resist when I told him that was what I wanted. He signed the final papers without a second's hesitation."

That must've been devastating to Leanne. "He probably didn't want you involved in his legal troubles," I offered as a possible explanation.

"Maybe, but how could I not be?" she asked. "He was my husband, so I was already up to my neck in it, and then to have him walk away from our marriage without a backward glance . . ."

I remembered reading about the case and of course Patrick had mentioned it, but my recollection of the facts was vague. "Was there a trial?"

"No. He accepted a plea bargain."

She took a deep breath. "Mark served a year in prison and has to make restitution. He also received a substantial fine. His mother told me he owes forty thousand dollars."

While I didn't want to dwell on Mark's legal problems or his financial mess, I had to ask one last question. "How did this ever happen?" From what

Leanne had said, Mark Lancaster was—or had been—a good, honorable man. Why had he become an embezzler? Surely there was some underlying problem—drugs, gambling, who knows what.

"I didn't find out until much later that he took the money to help his sister. I won't go into the whole story, but Denise was desperate. She thought she had the money, but it fell through at the last minute."

"He went through all this for his *sister?*" I asked, a bit incredulous. I could only hope Denise appreciated what he'd done, no matter how wrong and misguided it was.

"They're close."

"Even now?"

Leanne nodded. "To be fair, Denise—well, she had no idea Mark had, um, borrowed the money. She thought he'd gotten a loan and would simply be covering the interest until she could repay it. She didn't know what this so-called loan had cost him until it was too late. She did plead for leniency before the judge and is doing what she can to pay back the money."

I noticed she hadn't touched her chowder since the first spoonful. I continued eating, but at a slow pace.

"Have you had any contact with him since he got out of prison?" I asked.

I could see her struggle to hide her feelings. "Not really," she said in a low voice.

I wasn't sure what that meant, but had the distinct impression she didn't want to talk about it. That was fine. I wouldn't press her to tell me anything she found distressing.

"He says he wants nothing more to do with me. According to him, I should get on with my life." She bit her lip. "I saw a counselor for a while. She said essentially the same thing."

"Have you?" I asked. I remembered how Leanne and I had talked about this—the way we disliked that kind of advice; I figured I was the only one who could decide when and how to "move on." And yet . . . Hannah herself was, in effect, saying it, too.

"I made one other attempt to date. Besides tonight," she clarified.

"How did that go?"

She grinned. "Awful."

"Is tonight starting off any better?"

Again she smiled, and the worry lines between her eyebrows relaxed. "Much better."

That was comforting. I smiled back.

"What about you?"

"Me?"

"Have you tried to socialize again since you lost Hannah?"

Rather than explain that this was my first date with another woman since my early twenties, I shrugged. "Some." I was counting the coffee with Hannah's cousin as a sort-of date.

"How'd it go for you?"

I thought about my time with Winter. "All right, I guess."

"Hannah was an extraordinary woman."

Extraordinary didn't begin to describe my beautiful wife.

"At work I care for people undergoing cancer treatment and they all have different attitudes," Leanne said. "Some are angry, some are defeated or resigned. Hannah was always cheerful and optimistic. She helped others see the positives instead of the negatives." She was silent and thoughtful for a moment. "Even at the end, she found things to be grateful for. When she died, I can't tell you the number of people who told me what an inspiration Hannah was to them."

"She inspired me, too." I was a better man for having spent twelve years as her husband.

"I want you to know how sorry I am that I couldn't attend her funeral."

I shook my head, dismissing Leanne's apology. I hardly remembered who was there and who wasn't. My own grief had been so overwhelming that such details were of little concern. The church was packed and the service was moving—that's about all I took in.

I saw that Leanne was now eating her chowder and I was the one who'd stopped.

"It's been a difficult year for you, hasn't it?" Leanne murmured.

"It's been a year," I said in a weak attempt at a joke.

"Mark and I were divorced two years ago. I assumed everything would get easier."

"It hasn't?" This wasn't a good sign.

"In some ways it has. When I say my name now, people don't automatically ask if I'm any relation to the accountant who stole the hospital's money."

"How do you cope?" I asked, hoping for ideas to lessen the emptiness in my own life. Or if not ideas, at least some reassurance. "Do you miss him any less?"

"No," she said starkly. "I miss him every single day."

Although I would've liked a more encouraging answer, I didn't really expect one. "I miss Hannah the same way."

"A divorce is a loss of another kind," Leanne said, "but it's still a loss."

No argument there.

We finished our meals and I dumped our leftovers in a nearby receptacle. I wanted to suggest we walk for a while, but wasn't sure how Leanne felt about extending our time together.

"It's a lovely evening," she said, gazing out over Puget Sound. The lights on the boats, reflected in the green-blue water, seemed festive to me, even though this was an ordinary weekday evening. Or maybe not so ordinary . . .

"Would you care to walk along the waterfront?"

I asked, thinking she might not object, after all.

"I'd love to."

We strolled down the sidewalk, but neither of us seemed talkative. I pointed out a Starbucks and proposed a cup of coffee to conclude our evening. I hesitated to use the word *date*. This didn't feel like one.

"I'm comfortable with you," I said after I'd paid for our coffee and we continued down the walkway past the Seattle Aquarium.

"Thank you. I'm comfortable with you, too." She looked over at me and smiled. It was a pleasant smile and I caught myself staring at her and wondering what it would be like to kiss her. I wasn't going to do it; neither of us was ready for anything physical. Still, the thought had entered my mind and I didn't feel instantly guilty. That was progress.

When we'd drunk our coffee, I escorted Leanne to the parking garage where she'd left her car, despite her protests. I couldn't in all conscience let her walk into a practically deserted garage alone.

"Can I drive you to your car?" she asked when we got there.

"No, thanks. The exercise will do me good."

I took the stairs out of the garage and emerged onto the sidewalk. Since my car was ten blocks away, I started the strenuous climb up the Seattle hills.

"Well, what did you think?" I asked Hannah,

burying my hands in my pockets. Glancing toward the sky, I resumed my ongoing conversation with her. "I think it went well, don't you?"

There were certain times I felt her presence and this was one of them.

"I hope you're pleased," I said. "I've gotten together with two of the three women on your list."

I couldn't immediately remember the name of the third woman, whom I'd never met. Her cousin I knew fairly well, although we hadn't been in contact since Hannah's death. Until last week. Leanne Lancaster I'd known on a casual basis, and Macy . . . yes, Macy Roth, that was her name. I knew absolutely nothing about her.

"Why Macy?" I asked.

Silence greeted my question.

"Okay, you're right, I haven't met her yet. I will." Although I hadn't come up with a way to do it . . .

"You have any bright ideas?" I asked Hannah. "You want me to meet Ms. Roth, so it would help if you had a suggestion or two on how to go about it."

Still no answer. "I am not making a cold call, so you can forget that," I told Hannah. I definitely wasn't phoning this woman out of the blue!

"If you want me to meet Macy, you'll need to show me how." I nodded my head decisively so Hannah would know I was serious.

I reached the parking garage. The night-shift attendant knew me. Paul had been at the garage from the day I joined the practice. It'd been a while since I'd chatted with the older black man.

"Evening, Dr. Everett."

"Hello, Paul."

"Staying extra late tonight?"

"A bit," I agreed. "Good night now." I started to walk away.

"Dr. Everett," Paul said as I turned.

"Yes?"

He smiled and there was a note of approval in his voice. "I hope you don't mind me saying this, but you seem better."

"What do you mean?"

"You're healing," Paul said. "When you first lost the missus, I was real worried about you. But I can see that you're looking more alive. Your step's a bit lighter."

I thanked him with a smile.

"It really does get easier with time."

"Does it?" I asked, not really believing that was possible.

"It did with me. I lost my Lucille three years ago."

"I'm sorry, Paul, I didn't know."

"No reason you should. I didn't let on, figured professional men and women like yourself don't want to hear about my troubles."

I felt bad that he'd borne this alone.

161

"Have you . . . remarried?" I asked.

"No, but I got myself a girlfriend. We play bingo at the VFW on Saturday nights and she talked me into taking dance lessons." He chuckled and shook his head with its patch of unruly white hair. "If only Lucille could see me now. She'd get such a kick out of me on that dance floor."

"You ready for *Dancing with the Stars*?" I joked.

He laughed outright. "I don't think any TV producer's going to be interested in me."

I raised my hand in farewell.

"Nice talking to you, Dr. Everett."

"You, too, Paul," I said and headed in the direction of my car. I noticed I was smiling when I happened to catch my reflection in the car window.

I glanced upward, imagining Hannah with a satisfied little smirk on her face. "I suppose you're responsible for that conversation, too."

Chapter Fourteen

Ever since my dinner date with Leanne Lancaster, I hadn't been able to get Hannah's list out of my mind. I'd entered into this scheme of hers kicking and screaming and now . . . Well, now I was still fighting it, but my objections weren't as loud.

I'd connected with Leanne. I wasn't romantically interested in her, but I felt that at some point

162

I could be. I believed the same was true of her. We'd put no pressure on each other. We'd both suffered great loss and while that might be a fragile bond, it gave us each a reprieve from loneliness. Simply put, I enjoyed the evening with her. The hardest part about being alone is . . . being alone.

Tuesday morning when I got to the office I still felt good, which I attributed to my dinner with Leanne. What had helped, too, was my chat with Paul, the parking garage attendant. That brief conversation had filled me with hope. Like me, he'd lost his wife, but had been able to move forward in life. Granted, with him it'd taken three years but at least he'd shown me that this grief, this all-consuming pain, would abate. Leanne had reminded me that others suffered, too, that I was not unique in my pain, regardless of how it felt. Paul had assured me that, with enough time, suffering became bearable.

At noon I found a message from my brother-in-law and returned Ritchie's call while I ate lunch.

"It's me," I said when he answered the phone. "You called?"

"Yeah, I wanted to give you the details for Max's party."

"Go ahead." I reached for a pen and a pad.

"Saturday at eleven. Steph's taking Max and five of his friends to the arcade and out for pizza afterward."

"Are we expected to tag along?" I asked, grinning, knowing Ritchie was a kid at heart.

"You mean you don't want to accompany me and six highly active screaming boys to the arcade, where they'll go through quarters faster than a slot machine?"

"I wouldn't miss it."

"I didn't think so."

"I'll make a point of arriving early this Saturday," I told him.

Then that radar of Ritchie's seemed to kick in. "Anything new with you?"

"How do you mean *new?*" I asked, stalling for time.

"With you and that oncology nurse."

I hesitated, then decided I'd tell him about meeting Leanne. "I went to dinner with her last night."

"Dinner? You actually asked her out?"

"Yeah."

"How'd that go?"

"Good." I didn't elaborate.

I felt more than heard Ritchie's uncertainty. "Define *good.*"

I should've realized he wouldn't be satisfied with a one-word response. "Okay, if you must know, we spent three hours together."

Ritchie released a sharp whistle. "Sounds like the two of you hit it off."

I wasn't convinced I should be discussing this with my brother-in-law. Sure as anything, on

Wednesday when we met at the gym he'd besiege me with questions. Questions I had no intention of answering.

"Leanne and I have a lot in common," was all I was willing to tell him.

"That's a great start," he said enthusiastically. "You've met with Winter and now with Leanne."

Apparently, he was keeping tabs.

"Of the two of them, who has the strongest appeal?" he asked.

"Leanne," I said. "Not that I don't like Winter," I added quickly, remembering they were cousins.

"What's the name of the third woman again?"

"Macy Roth." I had no connection with her at all, no way of casually running into her as I had with Leanne. And it wasn't as if I could stop by her restaurant for coffee and a croissant.

"What do you know about her?"

"Practically nothing."

"No, wait. She's the model." Ritchie wasn't giving up. "What else did Hannah say about her?"

"I don't remember." A lie. In her letter Hannah had mentioned the fact that Macy held several jobs. She'd also written that she thought Macy would make me smile.

"Are you going to call her?" Ritchie asked.

"Macy? I wouldn't even know how to get in touch with her."

"Come on, buddy, you're smarter than that."

I wasn't interested in meeting the third woman

165

on Hannah's list. I liked Winter, but I had more of a connection with Leanne. Adding a third woman to the mix would confuse me, especially if I felt any kind of affinity with her, the way I did with Leanne.

"Hannah wanted you to meet her," Ritchie pointed out—as if I'd forgotten.

"Then I'll let Hannah arrange it."

"You know what? She just might."

"I can handle that," I said, not altogether sure I could. I looked down at my lunch of broccoli soup and a hard roll. I realized I'd spent most of my break talking to Ritchie. "I've got to run."

"See you in the morning."

"See you." With that I disconnected.

I wondered why Hannah had chosen *three* candidates. Why not two? Or four? Maybe because three's a magic number, the number that always appears in fairy tales. If I was going to complete all my tasks like a fairy-tale hero, I had to meet this third woman.

"Okay," I muttered, sensing her dissatisfaction with me. If not hers, then Ritchie's. "I'll meet Macy. Somehow." I wasn't happy about it. I was astonished by how susceptible I was to guilt. And both Hannah and Ritchie were piling it on.

When I'd finished my lunch, Linda came by, all smiles. She tended to be a sober woman and her amusement caught my attention.

I asked her about it.

"Have you seen Dr. O'Malley's office?" Linda asked me.

"Not recently." I saw Patrick two or three times a week but rarely visited his office at the opposite end of the floor.

"He had a mural painted for the children. It covers the entire hallway, both sides. It's the cutest scene with fire trucks and bulldozers on one side for the boys, and on the other is a castle with a coach and horse-drawn carriage for the girls."

"A mural," I repeated slowly.

"I was thinking this is something we might want to consider, too."

Hannah had done it again. She'd given me the perfect excuse to contact Macy Roth. In her letter she'd mentioned that one of Macy's many professions was that of artist. She painted murals. Therefore I'd hire her to paint the office wall; that would allow me to meet her without any expectations. Well, other than for the job I was hiring her to do.

"A mural's an excellent idea," I said.

"Would you like me to ask Susan in Dr. O'Malley's office for the artist's name?"

"No . . . ah, sure. But I already know the name of a woman who could do this."

"I'll get the phone number of the one who painted Dr. O'Malley's mural, as well," Linda told me. "Then if the artist you know doesn't work out, we'll have another option."

"Great." This was what I appreciated most about Linda. She thought of everything.

I waited until the end of the day to call Macy. I found her phone listing in the online directory and punched out the number.

The phone rang four times and I was preparing to leave a message when a breathless voice greeted me. "Hello?"

"Macy Roth?"

"That's me." She sounded as if she'd run a long distance.

"This is Dr. Michael Everett."

"Is it about Harvey?" she demanded, panic in her voice. "I asked him to give my name as an emergency contact. He's terribly ill, isn't he? I've been so worried! He didn't tell me he made a doctor's appointment, but there's a lot Harvey doesn't tell me."

I had to wait for her to take a breath. As soon as she did, I jumped in and assured her this had nothing to do with Harvey, whoever that might be. "Actually, I'm phoning on an entirely different matter."

The line went quiet. "This *isn't* about Harvey?"

"No," I told her again. "This is about a job. I understand you paint murals."

"I do," she said brightly. "I'm good at it, too."

And modest about her talent, I noted.

"Would you like me to paint a wall for you? I charge reasonable rates and I'm creative and dependable."

I chose to ignore the finer qualities she felt obliged to enumerate. "I'm thinking of having a mural painted in my office." I wasn't willing to commit myself until I'd had an opportunity to meet Macy.

"I'd be happy to paint a mural for you."

"Do you have pictures of what you've done?" I asked.

"I do . . . somewhere. I'm not sure exactly where they are, but I do have photographs of my work."

"Can I see them?" It seemed a logical request.

"I'll have to hunt them up. I'm afraid that might take a while."

The woman clearly didn't possess much of a business mind, let alone any organizational skills. "Would you like to know what I want painted?" I asked, half amused and half irritated.

"It's a wall, right? That's where most people want their murals."

"A hallway."

"Okay. Have you chosen a subject? Like . . . like goldfish in a pond. Or a farm scene. Or—"

"I'd like to hear your ideas. When would it be convenient for you to stop by?"

"I'm not doing anything right now," she volunteered. "If you want, I could drop in tonight."

It would be nice to deal with this matter after hours, rather than between patients. "How soon can you be here?" I asked after giving her the office address.

"Oh, you're close. I could make it in twenty minutes."

"I'll alert the security guard to let you into the building."

"Thanks." She hesitated, then asked, "If I'm a few minutes late, it's not a problem, right?"

"Well . . ."

"I'll do my best," she promised and the line went dead.

"A few minutes late," as Macy called it, turned out to be thirty-five minutes *past* the time she'd mentioned. I paced the office, disgruntled and annoyed. I insist on promptness, especially in business situations; when I tell someone I'll arrive in twenty minutes, I keep my word. If I'm held up for some unforeseen reason, I contact the person in question and explain.

Almost an hour after our phone call, I heard the office door open and came out to meet Macy Roth. To my surprise, I did know her. When Leanne had apologized for not attending the funeral, I'd said I hadn't been aware of who was there and who wasn't.

With one exception.

The woman in red. The woman who'd worn a bright red outfit and a wide-brimmed hat with curls of carroty hair poking out beneath. She'd stood out like a lone apple tree in the middle of a meadow. Everyone else had worn black or dark clothes for mourning. Not Macy. Just seeing her there as though dressed for a party had set my teeth on edge. Obviously the woman had no discretion. No common sense, either, since she'd chosen to wear such cheerful clothes to a funeral. Today she had on a pair of yellow leggings, a leopard-print tunic and ballet-style shoes. Her long, red hair was pulled into a ponytail high on her head. Macy Roth must have been thirty, but in that get-up she looked about eighteen. She certainly didn't exhibit the professional appearance I would've expected at an interview.

She stopped abruptly when she saw me and her eyes met mine in sudden recognition. "You're Hannah's husband," she whispered.

I nodded.

Macy's eyes went soft with pain. "I loved Hannah."

"Thank you," I said curtly. I wasn't going to discuss my wife with this woman I'd disliked on sight.

"I remember the time she—"

"You're late." I knew I was being rude, but I couldn't help it. I was astonished that Hannah had seen this woman as a suitable wife for me.

She snapped to attention like a raw recruit. "Oh, yes. Sorry about that."

"You said twenty minutes."

"I had to get the shoe box down from the closet and then Lovie got trapped inside when I closed the door, except I didn't know that. All I could hear were these frantic cries. It took me five minutes to discover that she was still in the closet."

I had no idea who Lovie was and could only assume she was either an animal or, God forbid, a toddler.

"I found the photos you wanted to see. They were in the shoe box, the one in the closet. I have them in my purse." She fumbled with the zipper and chattered away nonstop. "You see, Sammy wanted to be friends with Lovie, and Lovie wasn't interested. Normally Sammy's over at Harvey's place." She paused. "I really am worried about Harvey. He just isn't himself lately."

"The mural?" I said. "For the hallway?"

"I'd like to see it."

"I'd like to show it to you." I directed her to the area behind the receptionist's desk. A series of five doors off the long hallway. One opened into my office and the other four led to exam rooms for patients. There was an alcove on the opposite side for Linda.

"Did you have anything in mind?" she asked.

"Not really. What I'd like is a scene that would create a sense of comfort. The children I see are sick, and some of them are afraid they'll need a shot or that someone's going to poke a needle in them and draw blood. I want to convey that the doctor's office isn't a scary place."

Macy frowned. "It was for me."

I frowned in return. "Then make sure this one isn't."

She hesitated, and I could see she disliked me as much as I did her.

Then she smiled. "I'll sketch a concept and bring it in for your approval," she said pleasantly.

"When can I expect that?"

She shrugged. "It shouldn't take more than a couple of days."

I questioned that, considering her attitude toward punctuality. "And your fee is?" I asked.

She glanced down the hallway and I could almost see the wheels turning in her brain. When people know I'm a physician, they usually jack up the price. If she attempted to gouge me, I wouldn't tolerate it. Linda had given me the amount charged by the artist Patrick had employed, so I had a rate to compare Macy's to.

"I can see this running about seven hundred dollars." She looked at me assessingly. "That's half of what I normally charge—but I need a favor."

"What kind of favor?" I immediately asked.

"A small one. I'll tell you once we've agreed on a scene. Okay?"

I nodded, just so we could move this process along. I could always decline and find another artist.

"Go ahead and sketch out your idea and bring it over when it's convenient," I said.

"Okay."

I started out of the office, grateful this meeting was over.

"I'm sorry I was late," she said as she began to leave.

"Apology accepted. Oh, can I see the photos you brought?" I remembered that was why she'd kept me waiting an additional thirty-five minutes.

"Yes, I almost forgot. I think Lovie might've chewed on the corners of a couple of them, but you'll get a good idea of the work I do."

I still didn't know who Lovie was, nor did I want to ask.

She brought the photos out of her purse and handed them to me. The edges had been chewed on—and recently, I noticed, since they were moist. I shuffled through the first few and thought she did an adequate job. Her work was at least as good as that of the artist Patrick had used.

"Well?" she said expectantly.

"You'll do. Based on the acceptability of the sketches, of course—and the terms of this so-called favor."

Anger flashed in her eyes. "I'll get back to you next week."

"Fine."

She yanked the photos out of my hand, turned and walked out the door.

For the life of me I couldn't imagine why Hannah would ever think I'd be interested in someone like Macy Roth.

Chapter Fifteen

D r. Michael Everett was a jerk.

Macy couldn't understand why a woman as kind and compassionate as Hannah would marry such a . . . a stuffed shirt.

She left the office building and drove home, muttering under her breath. She couldn't get away from that unpleasant man fast enough. He'd gotten all bent out of shape because she was a few minutes late. It wasn't like the entire world revolved around *him!*

Back in her own neighborhood, Macy released a deep sigh and felt the tension ease from her neck and shoulders. Men like Dr. Everett were one reason she couldn't hold down a regular nine-to-five job. She'd never survive in an office, because she couldn't bite her tongue; it just wasn't in her.

Ten minutes with him had been a severe challenge.

When she reached her front porch, Macy found Sammy curled up on the welcome mat, his chin resting on his paws.

"Did Harvey lock you out again?" she asked. Poor Sammy didn't know where else to go. Macy had dutifully taken him to the vet for a checkup, hoping he'd have a microchip; of course he didn't. The good news was that he'd been neutered—one less expense for her. It also proved that once upon a time he'd had a loving, or at least decent, home. She'd posted Sammy's picture on every telephone pole in a mile's radius, along with her cell phone number. So far she hadn't received a single response. He was such a gentle dog and he'd done wonders for Harvey, although her neighbor would never admit it.

Despite his protests to the contrary, Harvey liked Sammy. He grumbled about how much the dog ate and that he brought fleas into the house, which wasn't true. Still, she saw Harvey place his hand on the dog's head and pat it. Sammy provided companionship when she wasn't around and he was a good watchdog, too. No squirrel had gotten into Harvey's backyard bird feeder since Sammy's arrival.

"Where's Harvey?" Macy asked, bending down to stroke his fur.

Sammy looked up at her with his doleful dark eyes.

"I'll bet he just forgot and locked the door," she reassured him. This had happened a couple of times already. When it did, Sammy wandered over to Macy's and set up residence on her porch. Unfortunately Snowball objected vigorously whenever Macy let him in the house. The cat apparently considered it his duty to maintain a dog-free zone.

Sammy rose and started down the steps. He

paused halfway to look over his shoulder, as though urging her to follow.

"Okay, I'll come," she said.

Instead of heading for Harvey's front door as he usually did, Sammy led her to the backyard.

Macy saw Harvey's hat first. Harvey was never outside without his hat. Immediately, she felt a jolt of alarm. Increasing her pace, she trotted anxiously into his yard, clambering none too gracefully over the low picket fence.

"I should charge you with trespassing," Harvey mumbled.

Macy whirled around to find him sitting on a lawn chair. From his position she was sure he'd collapsed into it. The fact that he was in the chair without his hat told her he'd been too weak to retrieve it.

"Harvey," she cried, kneeling down in front of him, giving him his hat. "What *happened?*"

"Nothing."

He was deathly pale and seemed to have trouble breathing. Macy didn't know what to do. "I'm calling 9-1-1." She heard the panic in her voice despite her efforts to remain calm.

"Don't," he said, his breathing labored. He pressed one hand over his heart and held her forearm with the other.

"Harvey! Something's wrong with you."

"Is not," he argued. "Now leave me alone."

"I am not leaving you."

"Scat, girl. Get off my property."

"If I do that, then I'm calling emergency services."

Harvey managed a grin. "You're an evil woman."

"Uh-huh." Macy sat cross-legged on the lawn. She pulled up a blade of grass as if she felt carefree and relaxed when her heart was actually beating at an alarming rate. "I'm staying here until I'm convinced you're all right."

Harvey muttered under his breath.

Sammy lay down next to Macy and focused his gaze on the old man. She could tell he was worried, too.

"I just met the most unpleasant person," Macy said, figuring that if she could distract Harvey he might agree to let her call for help.

"Anyone I know?"

"I doubt it." She made a face. "He got all nasty because I was a few minutes late."

Harvey grinned. "You're always late."

That was a gross overstatement. "Not true! I *try* to be on time." And she did. But the world seemed to conspire against her. Invariably something would delay her. Like today—She couldn't leave the house while Lovie was crying. Besides, that man had asked to see pictures of her work. Then he had the audacity to complain because she'd taken the time to comply.

Despite her efforts, she'd been cursed with this

proclivity for being late. If it wasn't one reason, it was another: a missing cat, an unexpected delivery, a desperate phone call from a friend. The timing was uncanny.

"He's such a pompous jerk."

"Who?"

"This doctor I met," she said, wondering why he still lingered in her mind.

"What kind of doctor is he?"

"A pediatrician who believes he's the center of the universe. He had a really wonderful wife, too."

"Had?"

"She died." Macy grew quiet. "I liked her so much. She had the most gentle, loving spirit."

Harvey snickered.

"Oh, come on, Harvey, haven't you ever met someone who's truly good? Someone you feel an instant camaraderie with?"

"No."

"Not even me?" she teased.

Harvey snickered again. "Hardly. You're lucky I put up with you."

"Am I really that difficult?" Okay, so she wasn't everyone's idea of the perfect neighbor—or girl-friend or employee. Macy tried to conform when-ever possible, but she wasn't too successful at taking directions from others. She needed her freedom, always had. Her Grandma Lotty had called her a free spirit, but unfortunately, even free spirits needed money, which meant Macy had to work. Her problem, aside from a resistance to following orders, was the fact that she got bored if she had to do one thing for any length of time.

Painting murals, for instance. She'd tackle a project and would work on it intensively for a week. Once she was finished, she was *finished;* she never wanted to see that painting again. She'd be physically exhausted and mentally depleted. Two or three days would pass before she found the energy to accept another assignment. It was the same with knitting. She probably had a dozen half-completed projects lying around. The vest for Harvey was the current one, and she was determined to get it done by the fall.

She needed variety.

"This doctor upset you, didn't he?"

Macy nodded. "He was a major disappointment." She'd expected more of the man Hannah had married. He must have *some* redeeming quality, although it hadn't been apparent in their initial meeting.

"Don't do it," Harvey advised.

That had been her first inclination, too. "You mean you think I shouldn't paint the mural?"

"You don't like him?"

"Well . . . I suspect it was more of a case of him not liking me."

Harvey shook his head. "That I can understand."

"Harvey!" She slapped his arm. He was feeling better, she could tell; still, she wasn't prepared to leave until she was sure he'd completely recovered. They'd happened before, these spells of his. She thought it might be his heart, but there was no real way of knowing unless Harvey underwent a physical exam. And Harvey, being Harvey, was dead set against stepping foot inside a medical office. No amount of wheedling would convince him to make an appointment.

"Tell the doctor you're not interested in the job," Harvey said again.

"I need the money."

"What for?"

"Oh, I don't know," she said playfully, raising her arms in a shrug. "It's just that I've grown accustomed to certain luxuries—like *eating regular meals.*" She'd like to see Harvey placate three hungry cats without any cat food on hand. That was one lesson she'd learned the hard way. Her cats had not been fooled nor were they amused when she'd served them Cheerios for breakfast. Okay, fine, that had only happened once, but they'd made their disgust quite plain. At least they'd lapped up the milk.

"Speaking of meals," she began.

"Were we?"

"Yes, I was talking about how fond I am of little things like breakfast, lunch and dinner."

"Right," he muttered.

His agreeing with her was unusual enough to get her attention. "When's the last time you ate?"

He frowned as though deep in thought. "A while ago."

"Can you be more specific?"

"This morning."

That might explain why Harvey appeared to be light-headed.

"I think," he added.

Well, no wonder, then. "Stay put," she ordered as she rose to her feet.

"You talking to me or that mangy mutt?"

Macy smiled. "Both of you. I'll be right back."

"Don't hurry on my account and don't be bringing me anything from your fridge. I remember the last time you decided I needed to eat." He cringed at the memory, and Macy rolled her eyes.

"You liked it," she told him.

"Until I learned I was eating *health* food." He nearly spat out the word.

"Tofu is excellent for you. And you didn't mind it when you thought it was chicken." She'd told that little white lie for his own good.

"I had indigestion for a week."

"I'll bring you canned soup," she promised. Her cupboards were looking like Mother Hubbard's, except for a case of tomato soup she'd picked up a month or so earlier. A bowl of that would be easy on Harvey's empty stomach. She'd heat some up and bring it to him.

"What's it got in it?"

"Tomatoes."

"How can I believe you?" He snorted. "You already tried to fool me once."

"You don't have to eat it if you don't like it," she told him.

"I don't like it."

"You haven't tasted it yet."

"I won't like it," he insisted.

"You sound like a two-year-old."

Macy refused to argue with him any further. "I'll be back in a jiffy."

"Take your time," Harvey said. "In fact, take all the time you want—like a year or two."

"A bad mood is merely a symptom of being hungry or tired."

"Maybe that was your doctor's problem. Maybe he was hungry or tired."

Macy pretended not to hear as she climbed over the fence and walked in her back door. She really should remember to lock it. Someone might actually break in one day. Not that a thief would ever find anything.

Heating up the soup took only a few minutes. She carried out a bowl using both hands, with a sleeve of soda crackers tucked under her arm. Harvey's eyes were closed and his hand rested on Sammy's head. He removed it when he heard her coming.

"I was napping," he complained. "You woke me up."

"Here."

"I said I don't want that."

"Harvey, don't make me spoon-feed you."

He seemed to weigh his options, then sat up straighter and reached for the bowl.

Macy waited until he'd taken his first spoonful. His eyed widened and he looked genuinely surprised. "This isn't bad."

"Told you so."

Macy returned to the kitchen and prepared a second bowl for herself. Her cats weren't pleased to see her go, especially so soon after she'd come home. They wove between her feet, purring loudly in protest.

"I'll be back in a little while," she said, bringing her own soup outside.

She stepped over the fence again and reclaimed her place on the lawn next to Harvey. Sammy gazed at her bowl of soup and seemed to decide she could have it all to herself. Macy ruffled his ears.

"Find the owner of that dog yet?" Harvey asked.

"Nope."

"He can't stay here."

"Okay, Harvey."

"I mean it this time."

"Of course, Harvey."

"Why do you agree with everything I say, especially when we both know you don't mean a word of it?"

She grinned and helped herself to a couple of crackers. "It's just my nature, I guess."

He ignored that and looked at her thoughtfully. His soup was only half-eaten when he set it aside. "You figure out what you're going to do?" he asked.

"About what?"

"That doctor."

"Oh, him." Macy had almost managed to forget that unpleasant man and wasn't happy about the reminder.

"You didn't like him."

"No."

"Then don't work for him."

"You're right, I shouldn't." Michael Everett would probably criticize every detail of the mural. Working for him was guaranteed to be completely and totally frustrating.

Macy glanced at the house and saw all three of her cats sitting on the windowsill, watching her. It was their dinnertime. She'd need to buy cat food soon, since she didn't want a repeat of the Cheerios incident. Harvey had a point; she could turn down the job. But that would be foolish, especially when the first of the month was fast approaching.

"You thinking about what I said?" Harvey asked.

"I am."

"What did you decide?"

She settled back on the grass, supporting her weight on the palms of her hands. "I'm thinking I'll paint that mural."

The old man grinned as if he'd known all along that was what she'd do.

"But I won't like it," she added emphatically.

Chapter Sixteen

I'd had an enjoyable weekend with Ritchie and Stephanie. Max had turned nine and we'd celebrated his birthday long after his rambunctious friends had departed. Max requested the leftover cake and ice cream for dinner, so that was what we ate.

Perhaps because the weekend had been such a highlight, my week started off well. Wednesday morning I arrived at my office after meeting my brother-in-law at the gym and was greeted with a surprise.

Winter Adams was there waiting for me.

Linda told me she'd brought Winter to my office. "Did I do the right thing?" she asked uncertainly.

"It's fine," I assured her.

Winter stood when I entered the room. She gave me a warm smile and I saw a large plate of fresh croissants on the corner of my desk.

"I know it's rude to stop by unannounced," Winter said, "but I hope you don't mind."

"On the contrary, I'm delighted." And I was—but I hadn't expected anything like this.

Winter moved toward me and I met her halfway. I didn't plan what happened next. As she drew near I leaned forward and kissed her on the cheek. To anyone else it might seem a little thing, but to me, at this stage of grieving, it was major. I was actually comfortable kissing, albeit rather formally, another woman. I wasn't sure how to explain it, other than that it seemed appropriate.

"I hadn't heard from you," Winter said, "and thought I'd drop by. I hope you and your staff enjoy the croissants."

I heard the hesitancy in her voice and realized she was uneasy about appearing forward. "I appreciate it," I said. "So will everyone else."

"My pleasure, really." She walked over to my desk and I saw she'd also brought a paper bag. She took out a stack of paper plates, napkins and several small jars of jelly and foil-wrapped pats of butter.

"Thank you. This is very generous, Winter."

She bobbed her head. "You're welcome. I know you're busy, and I should be getting back to the café. My baker, Alix, is pregnant. I mentioned that before, didn't I? The entire staff watches over her. So I've been coming in extra early and . . . Well, anyway, I wanted you to know I've been thinking about you." She didn't look up as she spoke and I noticed that her hands trembled slightly. They made small jerky movements as she arranged everything on the desk; then she didn't seem to know what to do with them anymore and dropped them by her sides.

"Thanks again," I said awkwardly.

"Your nurse said you have a busy schedule this morning so I won't keep you." She picked up her purse, yanking the strap over her shoulder as she edged her way to the door. "Enjoy."

I walked with her. "Can I call you later?" I asked.

She looked up at me as a slow smile slid into place. "I'd like that." She moved past me and gave my elbow a gentle squeeze as she left.

For a minute, maybe longer, I stood rooted to the spot, analyzing what had just happened. I hadn't talked to Winter in more than two weeks. I was doubtful there was any chance of a romantic relationship between us.

Winter and Hannah had been more than cousins, they'd been good friends. I was afraid any relationship we might have would be stalled by our mutual love and admiration for Hannah. Perhaps I was wrong; however, I hadn't felt the spark of attraction that might have eventually flamed into romance, if I may be forgiven that cliché.

I took the plate of croissants into the small room reserved for staff breaks. Linda found me there.

"Don't you want one?" she asked.

"I do, but I'll have it later." I wasn't much of a

breakfast eater and had set a croissant aside in my office. "That was Hannah's cousin."

"So she said."

I set the plate down on the countertop next to the microwave. "It was very kind of her, don't you think?"

Linda avoided eye contact.

"What?"

When I caught her gaze, she smiled knowingly. "Winter was being more than kind, you realize. She's interested in you."

"In *me?*" I asked, playing dumb. I planted my hand on my chest as if I considered the idea preposterous.

Linda rolled her eyes. "She couldn't have been more blatant if she'd tried—and she's trying."

I grinned. "Yeah, I guess she is."

"Are you going to ask her out?"

I hadn't gotten that far. "I don't know. What do you think?" I wanted a woman's take on the situation, a woman's perspective. Linda had worked for me from the time I'd joined the practice and knew me well. She'd given me unstinting support during Hannah's illness; as Ritchie said, she'd been a rock. She was closer to my mother's age, and while I spoke to my parents in Arizona every other week, dating again wasn't a topic I'd discuss with either of them.

"What do I think?" Linda murmured. "I'm not sure. Are you attracted to Winter?"

"I suppose I could be," I said, although I really wasn't convinced of it.

Linda's brows gathered in a frown. "That isn't exactly a ringing endorsement."

"I don't really know her well enough to have formed much of an attraction," I hedged.

"Okay," Linda said, "how do you feel about *getting* to know her?"

That question was easier to answer. "I wouldn't mind." And it was true. At the very least, we could resume a friendship of sorts, this time without Hannah as our go-between.

"Then do it," my nurse said. "The ball is definitely in your court. The next move is up to you."

I had the distinct feeling that if I didn't follow through after Winter had taken the initiative, I probably wouldn't hear from her again, family connection or not.

I enjoyed Leanne Lancaster's company and had been giving serious thought to calling her. The reason for my hesitation was simple—I was afraid. I wasn't ready for this and neither was she. Leanne felt as emotionally raw from her divorce as I was a year after losing Hannah.

The strongest link between us was pain, and that wasn't the most solid basis for any sort of lasting bond. However, I sensed that we might be able to help each other heal. There's comfort in shared misery. Together we might even find a way to move beyond the pain to a new form of happiness—or contentment at any rate.

Hannah had chosen three women and now I'd met all of them. They were as different from one another as any three women could be. As far as I could tell, Hannah had included Macy Roth for comic relief. Hardly ever had anyone, male or female, irritated me more. Hannah had suggested that Macy would make me laugh; however, she'd been wrong. If anything, Macy left me with the urge to pull out my hair by the roots.

For all my musing I hadn't come to a firm decision about Winter or Leanne. I'd hire Macy to paint the mural, but not out of any genuine desire to know her. I'd spent maybe ten minutes in her company and had no doubt whatsoever about how I felt. She was off the list. The mural was a good idea, though, and if the photographs were any indication, her work was acceptable. I'd give her the job. I'd completed my duty as far as Hannah was concerned. I'd met Macy and made my decision.

That left Winter and Leanne. It was only fair I get to know them both, then make my choice. Or not.

I found a semblance of peace in that nondecision. A calmness of spirit. I wasn't sure I'd ever experience real peace again, but this felt close. I was satisfied with what I'd determined to do.

The rest of the day passed smoothly and I'd just

seen my last patient for the day, a six-year-old boy who'd managed to get a tiny toy car stuck up his nose. I showed him a couple of magic tricks I saved for occasions such as this, which helped him relax, and I was able to retrieve it from his sinus cavity.

Young Peter's awed reaction to my "magic" delighted me, and I was grinning as I walked out of the exam room.

Linda met me at the door. "This is your day for female visitors," she said, looking pleased with herself—as if she alone was responsible for bringing these women into my life.

I assumed it was Leanne Lancaster.

"She's brought a sketch for you."

Macy Roth.

I could've finished the week without another confrontation with that screwball and been happy.

"Is she waiting in my office?"

"She is."

I wanted to tell Linda to wipe that smirk off her face. Macy Roth was not a love interest, past, present or future.

When I entered my office I caught her leafing through a medical book. That annoyed me. It took a lot of nerve to remove a volume from my private library without asking permission first.

She glanced up and didn't reveal the slightest embarrassment.

I walked over, pulled the book out of her hands

and pointedly replaced it on the shelf. "You brought a sketch?" I asked.

"Yes, I put it on your desk."

I was curious about the type of scene she might have envisioned for my wall. If she was as imaginative as I supposed, the idea would be clever and amusing.

I had a small table in the room and rolled out the sketch, anchoring it with a paperweight and a book on opposite corners. One look at the ocean scene, and I frowned. She'd drawn a wave and in the crest of it were turtles and tropical fish of all sizes and colors. In the distance beyond the wave, a sailfish leaped into the air. There was a whale in the background.

"This isn't what I want," I said, trying to understand what I found so objectionable. I suspected it was more my attitude toward Macy than the sketch itself. Still, I felt the kids who came into my practice might think it wasn't interesting or whimsical or exotic enough. The mural was meant to entertain and distract them, not provide a zoology lesson.

"Why not?" she challenged.

"I just don't. It's not . . . kid-themed," I muttered.

"You told me to draw whatever I felt would work, and I did."

"True, and I apologize, but the ocean scene doesn't suit me," I said flatly. "I'd like another alternative." She was right; I'd basically given her free rein, but at the same time I retained approval. "Come up with a different approach."

"Fine," she said shortly. She reached for the sketch and rolled it up. "I don't have a problem with developing something else. However, before I spend several hours putting together a new scene, it would help if I had some idea of what you're looking for."

"I don't know. Zoo animals, I suppose."

"Zoo animals," she repeated, obviously disappointed in my answer. "I can do that . . . I guess."

"In a jungle scene," I added. "Gorillas, giraffes and lions should do nicely."

"You got it."

"When can I expect to see a new sketch?"

Macy paused, eyes on the ceiling as though mentally reviewing her commitments. "Does Monday afternoon work for you?"

I walked behind my desk to my appointment calendar and nodded, then wrote it in. "That should be fine. Make it 5:00 p.m."

Nodding, Macy stopped on her way to the door. "Are you *positive* you don't like the ocean scene?"

"Unfortunately, yes." My reaction had been immediate.

"I could throw in a ship. I'd thought of doing that and I didn't, and now I'm sorry."

"I wouldn't have liked it with the ship, either," I told her.

"Harvey liked it . . . well, as much as Harvey likes anything."

"Is Harvey one of your cats?" I remembered that Macy had several cats. Why that detail stuck in my mind I could only speculate. She talked about them as if they were human, which was odd enough, but soliciting a cat's views on a piece of art . . .

"Harvey is my neighbor, and he has exquisite taste."

This was apparently a dig at me for disliking the ocean scene. I recalled that she'd mentioned this Harvey in our first phone conversation. "No doubt he does, but it isn't his office where you'll be painting the mural."

"That's too bad," she muttered.

"One day another client might ask you for an ocean scene and you'll have it in your inventory."

She shrugged, but didn't respond.

I steered her toward the door, unwilling to continue the conversation. I wasn't interested in her next-door neighbor's opinion. The only opinion that mattered here was mine, and I didn't want the children who came into my office staring at fish.

"I'll have the jungle scene for your review on Monday," Macy said as she swept out of my office. "At five."

Feeling a twinge of guilt I realized my attitude wasn't entirely fair or open-minded. Macy was simply too . . . unconventional for me. Too erratic and unpredictable. In any case, I felt I'd done my duty by Hannah. From this point forward I'd concentrate my efforts on Winter and Leanne.

Thinking about Winter, I decided now was a good time to give her a call and thank her for the croissants. I waited until everyone had left the clinic, then closed my office door.

Surprisingly, I felt a sense of anticipation. I tried to think of something Winter and I might do together. I'd taken Leanne to dinner and, while that had been pleasant, I was looking for a different activity with Winter, since she owned a restaurant and eating out might be too much like work for her—too much like checking out the competition.

I called Winter's cell number; she answered on the second ring.

"It's Michael. I wanted to thank you again for the croissants," I began.

"You're very welcome."

She seemed pleased to hear from me, and that was encouraging. "The croissants disappeared so fast I was fortunate to get one." I'd eaten it with my lunch and savored every bite.

"There's always more where those came from," she teased.

I felt utterly inept at flirting, but stumbled ahead. "I was hoping, you know, that the two of us might get together soon."

"Ah, sure. When?"

"How about Sunday afternoon?" I tossed that

out, although I didn't have a single idea of what we might do.

"What do you suggest?"

"Well . . ." I thought for a moment. "If the weather's nice we could ride bikes." This was something Hannah and I used to enjoy. A surge of pain tightened my chest. I was surprised when the memory didn't hurt as much or last as long as I'd come to expect.

"I . . . don't have a bike," Winter said with what sounded like regret.

"Not to worry, I have an extra one in the garage. Actually, it belonged to Hannah." I figured Winter wouldn't mind borrowing Hannah's old bicycle.

"Okay, why not? But I have to warn you it's been years since I got on a bike."

"You'll pick it up right away," I assured her. "It really is true that once you've learned you never forget."

"That's good to know."

Already I was looking forward to the weekend.

We chatted for a few more minutes and then just before I was ready to hang up Winter said, "I'm glad you called."

"I am, too," I said and I meant it. Wherever our relationship went—whether we became close friends or casual ones, whether we experimented with romance or eventually fell in love—I was prepared to accept.

What would be would be.

Chapter Seventeen

I have to wear a helmet?" Winter asked.

"It's the law in King County," I explained. She seemed uncertain about every aspect of this venture. I was beginning to think taking out the bikes hadn't been such a great idea, after all. Winter had dressed in a matching pants outfit, and I worried that her cuff would get caught in the chain. By the time I noticed, it was too late to suggest she change clothes. I found a couple of metal pant clips and used them to secure the loose material, a concession to safety if not fashion. Her rhinestone-studded flip-flops weren't ideal for bike riding, either. I still had a pair of Hannah's biking shoes and recommended she wear those. Their feet seemed to be about the same size.

Since Winter hadn't cycled in years, I worked with her for several minutes until I was confident she wouldn't have a problem. Then we both climbed on our bikes and rode up and down the block before we set out beyond the neighborhood.

"How are you doing?" I called back to her.

"Great."

Her reply sounded tentative, so I made another circuit of the block, riding slowly. Hannah had been a competent cyclist, but it was unfair to compare Winter to her. I'd need to remind myself of that. I appreciated Winter's willingness to at least try. My hope was that in time she'd come to enjoy biking, which I loved.

I was surprised to realize how long it'd been since I'd last taken out my bike. Hannah and I had often talked about riding in the STP, the Seattle to Portland Bicycle Race held every July. It's a two-day event and we'd been gearing up for the ride when Hannah was diagnosed. She'd wanted me to participate, but I'd refused. It wouldn't have been any fun without her.

Ritchie rode a stationary bike at the gym, but I couldn't imagine him out on the streets in a serious ride. Not because he lacked athletic ability, but because he couldn't care less about cycling. Baseball was his sport and he was a rabid Seattle Mariners fan. He watched or attended every game the team played, memorized the stats and was a font of useless information. Useless, that was, in my opinion, although I'd never say that to Ritchie's face.

Absorbed in my own thoughts, I hadn't noticed that I'd gotten quite far ahead of Winter. I glanced over my shoulder and saw her wobbling danger-ously. I turned my bicycle, intent on rejoining her. Winter saw me turn and for whatever reason decided to stop.

I could see her start to fall, but I was unable to help. She couldn't get her foot released fast enough and as a result she crashed onto her side, the bicycle on top of her. It seemed to happen in slow motion, but I'm sure it didn't feel that way to Winter.

She cried out as she landed with a thud.

"Winter!" I pedaled to her side and was off my bike in a matter of seconds. Just as I'd feared, despite the clip, her pant cuff had gotten caught in the chain and had torn. I pulled away the bicycle and rested it against a tree, then did a quick visual exam. The skin on her elbow had been scraped and was bleeding, as was her knee, which appeared to be the worst of her injuries.

"Don't touch me!" She tensed as I bent down to examine her more thoroughly.

"I won't," I promised, looking in both directions to make sure no cars were coming.

Winter closed her eyes and released a shaky breath.

"Does anything feel broken?" I asked, quickly transitioning into doctor mode.

"No . . . nothing."

"Keep still for a moment. Concentrate. Where's the pain?"

"My elbow and knee—nothing's broken. I'm sure of it."

She struggled into a sitting position. When I tried to help, she shook her head, telling me she wanted to do this on her own.

She sat up slowly and, bending her arm, studied her elbow first. Then she stared down at her knee. I knew it must hurt. It wasn't as if we were kids and could easily recover from a fall. As adults we land a lot harder.

"Do you feel dizzy?" I asked, afraid she might have bumped her head. She was wearing Hannah's old helmet, but I had to ask.

"No."

"Light-headed?"

"No. The helmet saved me, I think."

"That's why we're supposed to use them." I've dealt with too many preventable head injuries in children who hadn't been wearing helmets.

Winter grinned. "You're not one of those men who take delight in saying *I told you so,* are you?"

I grinned back. "Every man lives for the opportunity."

"That's what I thought," she said, coming awkwardly to a stand.

"I'll take you to the house and patch up your wounds," I said.

Winter hobbled toward the house while I pushed both bikes. So much for that plan. Bike riding had been a disaster.

"I'm sorry, Winter."

"Why should you apologize? I'm the inept one."

"I should've suggested we do something else." I put the bikes in the garage, then joined her. With my arm around her waist, I led her into the kitchen and sat her down on a kitchen chair while I went in search of Band-Aids and antibiotic cream.

When I returned I had a fresh washcloth, too.

Next I ran cool water into a bowl and brought it over to the table where I'd set my supplies. I dabbed at her scraped elbow and knee, applied ointment and carefully bandaged them.

"I'm not a good patient," Winter said from between clenched teeth.

"On the contrary, you're an excellent patient."

She smiled and our eyes met.

Once I'd finished, I took away the water and the cloth and put everything back where it belonged. I hate to admit it, but I'm a neat freak, as Hannah rather unflatteringly described me. It's a habit I developed as a child, perhaps because my brother, with whom I shared a bedroom, was such a slob. Ever since then, I'd felt a need to have order around me.

"My mother always gave me a treat when I was hurt as a kid," Winter told me when I came back.

"What kind of treat?"

"Sometimes it was hot cocoa, other times a cookie. When I broke my arm she let me sleep in her bed and watch movies all day." Her face reddened and she immediately broke eye contact. "I wasn't asking to sleep in your bed, Michael."

I hadn't taken it that way and merely laughed. "Don't worry about it."

She thanked me with a lopsided smile.

"Would you like to watch a movie?" I offered. That was the only thing I could think of, probably because she'd just mentioned it.

"Do you have popcorn?"

"Let me check." Groceries were a hit-and-miss chore with me. I was thankful to discover an unopened box of microwave popcorn in the cupboard above the refrigerator. I didn't know how long it'd been there, but it served the purpose.

While I stood guard over it, Winter went through the stack of DVDs. I couldn't remember when I'd actually sat down and watched one, although we owned quite a few. Hannah was the movie lover, everything from black-and-white classics to foreign films to Hollywood blockbusters. I watched them with her—mainly to *be* with her—but movies seemed a waste of time to me.

Winter came into the kitchen, a DVD in her hand. "*The African Queen* is one of my favorites."

"Hannah's, too."

"I know. I'm guessing she bought it."

She had.

The popping slowed and then stopped, and the timer buzzed. I was grateful for the distraction. I didn't want to get caught up in memories of Hannah. I didn't think it was wise to drag her name into every conversation. Winter must have felt the same way because she didn't mention Hannah again.

The TV was in the family room and I inserted the movie, then sat down on the sofa next to Winter. I left several inches between us. She had her bowl of popcorn and I had mine.

It'd been probably four years since I'd seen the Humphrey Bogart and Katharine Hepburn movie. I'd forgotten what a moving love story it is. I did recall that Hannah invariably cried at the end.

As the credits rolled, Winter glanced in my direction. Neither of us had moved during the film. The same few inches still separated us.

"How are you feeling?" I asked.

"I'll survive."

"I've got some aspirin." I should've thought of it earlier. If she wasn't stiff and sore now, she would be soon.

She shook her head. "It hardly hurts at all."

"Well, tomorrow might be another story," I said, blaming myself regardless of her protests.

"As you might've guessed, I'm more of an inside woman," Winter announced. "I've always loved working in the kitchen and experimenting with recipes. I'm not really into sports."

Hannah had enjoyed cooking, too, but as far as sports went, she was game for anything. She had the spirit of an adventurer. Never once could I remember her holding back when I suggested we try something new, whether it was biking a hundred and fifty miles on a two-day trek to Oregon or signing us up for a river rafting trip.

"I might not be any good at sports, but I could whip up a dinner you'd rave about for weeks," Winter said.

"I'll bet you could." I hoped she didn't hear the

lack of enthusiasm in my voice. Since Hannah's charming dinner parties, I'd lost any interest in elaborate meals. Eating was just a means of fueling the body for me, not the soul.

"What would you like to do?" I asked.

"Do you play cards?"

"Not anymore." I used to play poker, of course, but not since Hannah got ill. "Sorry."

"Oh." Her disappointment was obvious.

"What do you do on your days off?" I asked.

"I putter around in my kitchen. I know!" Her eyes brightened. "How about if I make you dinner?"

"Don't you cook all week? You shouldn't have to do it on your day off."

"But it's what I love," she said. "When I'm at the café I'm stuck doing the paperwork, ordering, things like that. So I seldom get a chance to experiment in the kitchen anymore. There are a few dishes I've been eager to try, but it doesn't make sense to cook for one."

"I haven't been to the store in a while." I gestured for her to search through the fridge and cupboards if she wished, knowing she'd find mostly canned soup and a few frozen meals.

"Oh, that's part of the fun," she said. "I like grocery shopping."

"Okay, then. Let's go."

She grinned widely as I reached for my car keys. This wasn't how I'd envisioned spending our

Sunday afternoon, but if it was what she wanted I wasn't about to complain.

From the moment we stepped inside the store, it was clear that Winter was in her element. She maneuvered the aisles like a pro, pausing now and then to throw an item into the cart. She read labels, talked to the butcher requesting a special cut, and smelled and squeezed the fruit and vegetables. It was an experience just being with her.

Tagging along, I caught a bit of her enthusiasm. Passion is contagious.

"You've memorized the recipe?" I asked.

She stared at me as if I'd spoken a foreign language.

"You know," I said. "The recipe for this fabulous dinner you're cooking me."

"Ha!" she said with a laugh. "I don't have any recipe!"

"You said there was one you wanted to try."

"Well, yes. It's something I had not long ago while I was out with friends. I've been dying to reproduce it myself."

"Oh."

"Never mind—I promise it'll taste like a feast Henry VIII would've been proud to eat."

"Otherwise off with your head?" I joked, and she seemed to find that funny.

Back at the house, I unloaded the car while Winter set to work in the kitchen. She soon had the vegetables in the sink and started organizing ingredients on the counter. I saw the thick slices of fresh tuna and boneless chicken breasts and couldn't imagine what she might be planning with that combination.

"What can I do?" I asked, my hands in my back pockets. I'd never been much use in the kitchen.

She looked at me and for an instant I saw a flicker of sadness in her eyes.

"Were you thinking of Hannah just now?" I asked.

It did seem odd to see another woman in Hannah's kitchen, even if that woman was there by invitation. Almost immediately I realized I'd broken one of my own rules. I'd brought Hannah into our conversation, and I'd been determined not to do that.

"Not Hannah," Winter answered after a brief pause.

"Then who?"

"Pierre. He's the chef I mentioned. We used to love cooking together."

I nodded.

Winter turned abruptly away from me. "I think I told you Pierre and I . . . are taking a break from each other," she said. "Unfortunately it looks like it'll be a permanent one."

Winter was preparing a meal, indulging in her favorite pastime—which she used to share with the man she loved. I'd done the same thing when I suggested we take out the bikes. Hannah and I had often gone cycling on a Sunday afternoon, and it appeared that Winter and Pierre had spent their time together in the kitchen, doing something they were equally passionate about.

I could picture them working side by side, offering each other small tastes of their creations, arguing, laughing, kissing.

"What exactly happened with you and Pierre?" I asked.

She shrugged. "I don't know," she whispered.

Her voice registered such pain that I automatically took a step closer, and stopped myself just in time from wrapping my arms around her.

"I don't know," she said again. "I can't even begin to explain it."

Like me, like Leanne . . . Winter, too, was dealing with loss.

Chapter Eighteen

Grumbling the entire time, Macy did as Dr. Everett had requested and drew a jungle scene. The problem was that the man had no imagination. She'd met men like him before and found them uniformly boring. He obviously didn't have a sense of humor, either. In her humble opinion, the children's doctor could use a good laugh. He took everything far too seriously.

Monday afternoon, as promised, she showed up at his office—on time. He didn't seem impressed.

This ill-mannered physician hardly even noticed the effort she'd put into making sure she wasn't late.

In fact, Macy was kept waiting for five whole minutes. She could've used those extra minutes. Snowball hadn't eaten that morning, and Macy was concerned. He could be ill. Or mad. He seemed to think he was punishing Macy by not eating. How like a male to punish *himself* to spite her.

"Dr. Everett will see you now," his nurse told her, holding open the door to the inner sanctum.

Macy hadn't formed an opinion about this nurse. Her name tag identified her as Linda Barclay. The woman was certainly friendlier than the physician who employed her, but that wasn't saying much. However, based on a few comments she'd made, Macy suspected the nurse had a better sense of humor than the doctor.

"He's in his office," Linda said, pointing the way.

The last time she'd stopped by, Linda had escorted Macy directly into Dr. Everett's office; on this visit, she'd been left twiddling her thumbs in the waiting room. That was probably because Macy had taken it upon herself to read one of his precious medical books. He'd practically snatched the book out of her hands, not giving her the opportunity to explain why she'd taken it in the first place. She'd been studying the index because she wanted to look up certain symptoms. Harvey just didn't seem to be himself lately, and she was worried. He blamed his fainting spells on the fact that he hadn't eaten, but Macy thought it was more than low blood sugar. Besides, it'd happened again recently. On that occasion, she knew Harvey had eaten less than an hour earlier. Something else was responsible for all this, and her friend was too stubborn to make a doctor's appointment. Well, there were other ways to deal with this situation.

Between her cat and her neighbor, Macy was in need of medical advice, although she'd have to be crafty if she was going to get any valuable information from Dr. Everett. Granted, she'd already suggested an exchange of favors during their previous meeting, but he hadn't seemed enthusiastic. She'd have to handle him with finesse.

When Macy walked into his office, Michael was sitting behind his desk. He glanced up when she entered.

"I was on time," she told him pointedly.

He stared back at her, apparently unaware of the significance of this feat.

"I was late the first day we met, remember?"

"Oh, yes. By quite a bit, as I recall."

"But—" she raised her index finger "—I had a good excuse."

"Well, congratulations for being on time this afternoon." A hint of a smile touched his eyes.

Oh, what Macy would give to see him *really* smile. The urge to walk over and turn up the edges of his mouth with her fingertips was almost overwhelming. She cocked her head to one side as she tried to imagine what he'd look like amused.

"Macy?" he said, frowning. "You have the drawings?"

"Oh, yes. Sorry. I was trying to get a picture of you in my mind."

"I'm standing right here. Why would you want to do that?"

"I was trying to picture you happy. You know—smiling, maybe even laughing. You don't do that very often, do you?"

He turned away from her as though he found her exasperating.

"It's a shame," Macy felt obliged to tell him.

"That I don't smile?"

"Well, yes. It must be hard to frown all the time. I once read that it takes twice as many muscles to frown as it does to smile."

"Perhaps my lack of amusement has something to do with my limited patience."

That was a clear-cut reminder that she was there for a specific purpose.

"You were going to show me the new sketch for the mural. That *is* the reason you're here, correct?"

"I have the new sketch with me." The man was all business, which didn't bode well because she needed his help and wanted to propose an exchange, the "favor" she'd mentioned last week. While considering how best to broach the subject, she carefully removed the sketch, which she'd rolled into a tight scroll, from her backpack.

Dr. Everett took off the rubber band and unrolled the new sketch across the table. He secured it, then stepped back to examine her proposal.

"These animals are behind bars," he said with a grimace. He looked up at her, his frown deepening.

"You said you wanted zoo animals. I did what you asked," she said, trying not to sound defensive. "See the gorilla?"

"Why is he caged?"

"Have you visited a zoo lately?" She wasn't in favor of imprisoning wild animals, and this whole zoo concept had bothered her.

"I said I wanted zoo *animals*," he said, speaking slowly as if she was hard of hearing. "I didn't ask you to draw a zoo scene. You took me far too literally."

"I can paint it without the bars." She'd be happy to do that, in fact, but she'd wanted to give him precisely what he'd asked for. Apparently, he'd taken offense; maybe he didn't approve of zoos, either.

"I asked for a jungle scene."

"In a zoo," she added. "But like I said, I'll take

away the bars. Other than that, does this sketch *suit* you?" She wondered if he'd remember he'd used that very word in their previous meeting.

He went over each detail. "It does," he said slowly. "You're actually quite talented," he told her, and she wasn't sure whether to be pleased or insulted by the surprise in his voice.

"Thank you." A compliment—well, she'd settle for that.

"When would you like me to start?" she asked, eager now to get down to the negotiations. They'd already agreed on a price, although, as she'd told him, it was half of what she normally charged.

"You can begin this week if you like."

"Great. However . . ."

"How long do you think it'll take you to complete the project?" he asked.

Macy wasn't fooled. He wanted her in and out of his office as quickly as possible. Well, she wasn't keen on spending any more time than necessary with him, either.

"A couple of weeks, tops." She paused. "Um, if you'll recall, the figure I quoted you is half my usual fee." She gestured with one hand, but when she noticed how he glared at it, she immediately lowered it. "As you might also remember, that price is contingent on you doing me a favor."

Predictably, he frowned.

"I might be able to finish in ten days," she said, changing tactics.

"What's this *favor?*" he asked with unmistakable sarcasm.

"Just to see a patient."

"That's it?"

"That's it."

"Fine." He pulled open a desk drawer and took out his checkbook. "I'll give you fifty percent up front."

"Thanks." She'd hoped he'd pay her an advance.

He sat down at his desk and started to write the check. She watched for a moment before blurting out her question. "Do you make house calls?"

"House calls?"

"Yes. That's when a doctor visits a patient's home and diagnoses that patient in the comfort of his or her own environment."

He sighed. "I know what a house call is."

"I figured you would." She sent him a bright smile. "So, do you make them?"

"No, I don't," he said.

"But would you?" she asked hopefully.

"No."

"Don't you think it would be better to see patients when they're relaxed and comfortable?"

"Depends."

"Wouldn't you be able to make a more accurate assessment?"

"Not always. There are tests I couldn't run at a patient's house."

"But you could order those, right?" she persisted.

"Is there a reason you're asking me all these questions? Does it have to do with the patient you want me to see?"

"Y-e-s." She drawled the word, but didn't elaborate. She needed to line up her arguments first.

"I don't make house calls so it's a moot point," he said with finality.

"But you could."

"No," he said. "For malpractice insurance reasons it's out of the question."

"Oh."

He closed his checkbook and returned it to the top drawer.

"But what if we bartered for it?" Macy asked.

"That's irrelevant. As I explained, because of my insurance restrictions, it's impossible, no matter how you paid for it."

She bit her lip and tried a different approach. "I have a friend I want you to meet."

"Why?"

"Because he's sick and refuses to see a doctor."

"How old is your friend?"

"Eighty-six."

Dr. Everett's eyebrows rose. "In case you haven't noticed, I'm a pediatrician. I treat children. I have no expertise in geriatrics."

"That's all right," Macy said half-humorously. "Harvey sometimes says he's going through his second childhood."

The physician didn't even crack a smile. "I apologize, but I can't see your friend on a professional basis."

"Could you just meet him?"

"Socially I can meet anyone."

Macy clapped her hands. "That's perfect. Then I'll stick to my original agreement. I'll paint the mural at the price I quoted the other day. Otherwise . . . it would have to be more."

Dr. Everett closed his eyes, then opened them again. "Ms. Roth, first, your business practices are questionable, to say the least. Second, I have no intention of meeting your friend."

"Okay, if you insist I'll pay you, but the mural will be fourteen hundred dollars instead. I was giving you a fifty percent discount for meeting Harvey."

He exhaled in what seemed to be complete confusion. "You have no idea what you're asking me to do."

He was probably right, but Macy was desperate. "Harvey is a wonderful old man and I don't think he realizes how sick he is. He doesn't have anyone in the world. Except me—and Sammy."

"Sammy's his son? But you said—"

"No, he's a stray dog I rescued. I found him in the street. He would've been killed if I hadn't gone after him. I share him with Harvey." She didn't understand why it was so important that he hear every detail, but she couldn't make herself stop talking. Macy was sure that once Michael got to know Harvey, he wouldn't be able to refuse.

"At first Harvey didn't want anything to do with Sammy, but he needs someone with him and I can't be there as much I'd like. Sammy's great and I can tell he belonged to someone, so I put up notices hoping to find his rightful owner, but the truth is, I was just as glad no one claimed him because Sammy's such a good companion for Harvey." This last part was said in one gigantic breath.

"Ms. Roth—"

"Please," she said, willing to beg if necessary. "Harvey's like a grandfather to me. I love that old man and want him to live for many years to come. He's a war hero, you know."

"Ah . . ."

"Please. I'll paint the mural for free if you'll come and meet Harvey. That's all I want—for you to meet him. You don't have to listen to his heart or take his blood pressure or anything else that would put you at risk with the big powerful insurance company."

He hesitated and Macy could see he was thinking about it.

"Harvey never married," she said, rushing ahead with more reasons for him to meet her neighbor. "He was in World War II and fought in the South Pacific. He once told me he got malaria and was sick for months and then he was captured by the

Japanese and we both know those prison camps weren't like Camp Winnemucca where I went each summer as a kid."

"My grandfather was in the war, too," the doctor said quietly.

Again Macy could see that he was giving the matter serious consideration. Perhaps she'd misjudged him. She felt she was generally a good judge of character and wondered if she'd been too quick to find fault with Dr. Everett. "If this was your grandfather, wouldn't you want someone who cared about him to get a doctor to visit? Wouldn't you?"

Dr. Everett exhaled slowly. "Tell me what's going on with Harvey."

"That's just it," she cried. "I don't know! I think it must be his heart or it could be a recurrence of malaria. He has weak spells and sometimes faints, but he brushes off my concern."

"Describe one of these spells."

"Okay," she murmured. "The other day I found him slouched in his chair without his hat. He always wears his hat because he doesn't tolerate the sun very well. Sammy knew something was wrong, too, because he came to get me."

"The dog?"

"Yes. Harvey was too weak to stand up. He hadn't eaten in a while so I heated up soup and brought that to him, but his weakness was due to more than an empty stomach. There was another time he blamed the fact that he hadn't eaten, but I knew he had. These spells seem to be happening more and more. It's scaring me. Something's wrong, I can feel it."

The doctor didn't say anything for a long moment. "You're probably right that it's his heart."

"Will you please come?"

He met her eyes.

"You don't have to pay me any more for the mural than this—the three-fifty—if you'll agree to come and meet Harvey." She'd offered to do the whole mural for free, and she would if he insisted, but she really could use the money. "All you have to do is meet him. I'd like you to talk to him a bit, though. Maybe you can figure out what's wrong."

"I doubt meeting your friend will do much good, Macy."

"He might listen to you."

"About what?"

"Seeing a doctor. I mean, for a real appointment. A checkup."

"When's the last time he was in to see a doctor?"

Macy smiled. "I asked him that, too, and he said it was when he enlisted in the marines."

He smiled. Dr. Everett actually smiled.

"Wow," she said aloud.

"Wow, what?"

"You're quite good-looking when you smile."

He immediately frowned. "About your friend . . ."

"You'd be willing to meet Harvey?" she asked, interrupting him for fear he'd be motivated by the insurance company and their small print instead of his own compassion and better judgment.

"Fine. And I'll pay you for the mural at the price we discussed."

"Okay. Thank you," she remembered to add.

His eyes narrowed. "You being agreeable is a new experience."

"It's important to me that you meet Harvey."

"You really do love this old man."

"Yes," she said, nodding vigorously. "He means the world to me. You'll like him, too, only don't be offended if he's a bit brusque or short-tempered. That's just his way. He doesn't mean anything by it." Macy hoped Harvey wouldn't be in one of his moods. He could get downright cantankerous.

"All right, Macy," Dr. Everett said in a resigned voice. "As I told you, I'll meet your friend."

She folded her hands as though in prayer. "Thank you, oh, thank you so much."

"I can't promise I'll be able to diagnose what's wrong with him."

"I know, and I'm not asking you to do anything more than meet him because it could get you into trouble." She rushed around his desk and threw both arms around his neck. She could tell he didn't care for her show of gratitude, but she couldn't resist.

"Macy! Stop it!"

"Sorry, it's just that this means so much to me. Can you come next week? Monday?"

"I'm not sure yet. In any event, all I can do is convince, uh, Harvey to see a physician. I have a friend I'll recommend."

"That would be *perfect.*" She had a fleeting thought that maybe he could take a look at Snowball, too, but didn't mention that.

"Are we finished?" he asked.

"For now," she said. Macy felt wonderful. Everything had fallen into place exactly as it should.

Chapter Nineteen

Leanne Lancaster collected her mail on the way into her apartment. It was all she could afford. Due to the stalled economy, they'd lost money when they sold the house and, because of the renovation loan, hadn't had much equity, anyway. She'd signed a six-month lease on the apartment and eighteen months later she was still there. Her whole life seemed to be on hold.

She wished now that she hadn't made the effort to see Mark. The trip had only depressed her.

Even his physical appearance had been disheartening. The memory of Mark before prison—neat, well-dressed, confident—was a stark contrast to the man he was now. The shock of it continued to reverberate and left her sick at heart.

More for the pretense of companionship than any interest in current affairs, Leanne turned on the nightly news. She watched for five minutes and switched channels. If she was looking for something to raise her spirits, this clearly wasn't it. Instead, she tuned in to a game show and matched her trivia skills against the three contestants.

She lost. No surprise there.

She hadn't always been like this. Despite the fact that she worked with cancer patients, or possibly because of it, she used to be positive and optimistic, someone with an irrepressible sense of fun. Her personality had made her ideal for the job; she'd had the ability to help patients endure difficult treatments and, if terminal, to value the last months or weeks of their lives. People who walked through the oncology center's doors needed the medical staff to greet them with a positive outlook. These days with Leanne, they had to settle for compassion and gentleness. She smiled and said the right things, but her own life was a shambles.

The evening with Michael Everett had been a beacon in a dark, sad month. Her world had spiraled downward after seeing Mark. His rejection hadn't seemed real until he'd said it to her face. It was as if the last vestige of hope had been stolen from her. After that, any remnant of optimism had vanished. What she didn't understand was why she continued to care. She needed to wipe the slate clean and start again instead of allowing regret to define her mood.

The phone rang; Leanne glanced at the readout and saw that it was Muriel Lancaster, her former mother-in-law. "Hello?" Leanne answered as if she didn't know who was on the other line. She tried to sound cheerful. Undefeated.

"Oh, Leanne. I wasn't sure if you'd be home from work yet."

"I just walked in the door." That was a slight exaggeration. She'd been home long enough to know she couldn't match wits with the *Jeopardy!* contestants.

"We heard from Mark this week," Muriel said. "I . . . understand you went to see him."

Leanne swallowed hard. "That was a big mistake. I should've called first. . . . That would've been better than showing up unannounced."

Then she would've had some warning and could have made the much more sensible decision not to go.

"It went badly, then?" Muriel asked, but didn't wait for a response. "I was afraid of that."

"It was my fault." Which was true enough, since she shouldn't have gone in the first place.

"How are you holding up?"

"I'm fine," Leanne assured her. Smarter and wiser, anyway.

"Brian and I are planning to drive over to Seattle to visit Mark next weekend."

"But Mark's in Yakima."

"No—not anymore. He's finished his community service there, and he's back in the Seattle area."

"Well . . . it'll be a lovely drive," she said, wanting to change the subject. His parents lived east of the mountains in Spokane.

"We hoped . . . Do you think you'll be available, too? I can't recall the last time the two of us had a chance to really talk."

"Ah . . ." Leanne wasn't sure how to respond. She loved Muriel and Brian, Mark's father, but seeing them would serve no useful purpose.

"I understand if you have other plans. It is rather short notice," his mother said with some reluctance.

"Yes, sorry. Perhaps another time would be best." Leanne felt mildly guilty for putting her off, but also relieved.

The line went silent for a few seconds. "Brian and I decided we should come and see Mark. He seemed so depressed."

He wasn't the only one.

"This is very hard on Brian," Muriel said, lowering her voice. "He has trouble believing this could've happened to our family."

"I have trouble believing it, too," Leanne murmured.

"I know. I probably shouldn't have called. . . . It's just that I always feel better after we talk. I don't dare mention to Mark that the two of us still communicate. That would upset him." She paused. "I can't stand the fact that our children are having such a hard time. It doesn't seem fair, but then life isn't fair, is it?" Her voice cracked and she took in a deep, audible breath.

"I know Mark appreciates your love and support," Leanne said.

"Like I said, I always feel better after I talk to you," Muriel said.

"I do, too." Not only did she miss her mother-in-law, but Muriel was the one reliable source of information she had regarding her ex-husband.

"I'll phone again when we're back from seeing him, shall I?"

"Yes, please do." Mark wouldn't need to know, and Leanne wasn't foolish enough to pretend that she didn't want information.

She kept telling herself she should be over this. Her last visit—that was how she'd think of that confrontation from now on. Her *last* visit. Her last attempt at any kind of contact. Their relationship, or what little had remained of it, was done.

"Goodbye, Leanne, and thank you."

"You're welcome," she said, although she didn't know what Muriel had to thank her for.

An hour later, her stomach growled and she decided to make something for dinner. She cooked the same quantities as when she was married and froze the second portion. Cooking for one was ridiculous, hardly worth the bother. Unlike a lot of newly single women—or so she'd heard—she hadn't stopped with meal preparation. Funny how a little thing like that could help her emotionally, but it had. The routine itself—the shopping and planning, as well as the cooking—gave her home life a sense of order she'd been in danger of losing.

She sat down to a plate of clam spaghetti, which had been one of Mark's favorites. It was her own recipe, made with olive oil, clam juice, red pepper flakes and plenty of chopped garlic and onion. Spreading out a linen napkin on her lap, she sighed and tried to think of something pleasant.

Her evening with Michael Everett had actually turned out to be much more enjoyable than she'd expected. She'd felt a bond with him; perhaps surprisingly, they had a lot in common. He was a decent man who had yet to chart his way through the land of loss and grief. He'd already traveled some distance, as their evening together attested, but still had miles to go.

She hadn't heard from him since, and Leanne hadn't decided how she felt about that. For the first day or two after their date, she'd thought he might call her. He hadn't.

Sprinkling grated Parmesan on her spaghetti, Leanne reached for the stack of mail she'd brought in. The top envelope held a notice informing her that her car insurance premium was due. The next piece of mail was another bill, this time for her VISA card, and the last was a business-size envelope with a script that was achingly familiar.

Leanne's fork fell from her hand and tumbled onto the table.

For the first time since their divorce had been finalized, Mark had contacted her.

She tore open the envelope.

June 7
Leanne,

He didn't say *Dear* Leanne. Just her name, plain and simple. Drawing in her breath, she continued reading.

I've done a lot of thinking since your visit. I want to apologize for the way I behaved. It was a shock to see you. I wasn't prepared, emotionally or mentally.

She hadn't been prepared, either.

I believe I've figured out why you came here. You were looking to me for reassurance about this new relationship of yours. Leanne, it's what I've wanted for you all along. You deserve happiness, and I hope that's what he brings you. I'm the one responsible for the mess I'm in, not you. I'm deeply in debt and will pay for this error in judgment for the rest of my life. I'm the one who broke the law and was sentenced for my crimes. You did nothing wrong, so you shouldn't have to suffer.

It didn't matter that she was innocent. She was involved whether she wanted to be or not. She *was* suffering. Yes, Mark had stolen the funds, but she'd been affected by his actions. She wasn't behind bars and yet she felt like a prisoner all the same.

Get on with your life. What we once had was special, but it's over and there's no going back for either of us. Find a man, maybe this doctor, who'll love you and marry you and give you a family.

Leanne swallowed her tears. She wanted children. The oncology center was beside the fertility clinic and every day Leanne saw couples desperate for a child, willing to do anything in order to conceive. If that meant drugs, shots, tests, embarrassment, they'd submit themselves to it. Here she was, craving a child, and her husband— the man she'd always hoped would be the father of her children—was out of her life.

Before I close, I need to clear up one thing. I need to apologize. I led you to believe there'd been other women during our mar-riage. That was a lie. I was trying to convince you to hate me. Instead, all I did was cause you more pain. While I might have failed in many respects and sunk to levels I never knew I was capable of reaching, not once did I look at another woman. I wasn't even tempted. You were always my one and only, my wife.

Leanne smiled. She knew it; deep down she'd known he was lying. Even more than that, Mark hadn't been able to live with himself for having misled her. A great weight lifted from her heart.

That said, I hope and trust you'll be able to get past our divorce and begin a new life.

Leanne closed her eyes. She didn't know if she *could* do that, loving Mark the way she did.

This will be the last letter you receive from me. The last communication I will ever send you.
Mark

He hadn't ended with an endearment, either. Still, every word of his letter throbbed with love. He hadn't said he loved her, but he'd shown her.

This was all the proof she needed. Mark hadn't signed those divorce papers because he no longer loved her. He'd done it to protect her. He'd sacrificed his future for *her.*

He'd guessed correctly. She'd come to him looking for approval, for some indication from him that she was doing the right thing in accepting a date with Michael Everett. She'd gotten that approval now, in the form of a letter.

While she still had the courage, Leanne picked up the phone. She had Michael's cell phone number and she punched it out, held the receiver to her ear and waited.

"Hello." He sounded tentative.

"It's Leanne Lancaster," she said brightly. "I wanted to thank you for dinner the other night."

"I had a good time," he said.

"I did, too. Do you like crispy baked pork chops?" she asked. "Or we can have Italian food if you prefer."

"Ah . . . I don't know if I've ever tasted pork chops served that way," he said and seemed to find the question amusing. "I love Italian food, so either is fine by me."

"We'll probably have Italian then."

"Are you cooking?"

"I am. How about Sunday night, the twelfth, around six?"

"Works for me."

"Wonderful," she said. "I'll see you then."

"Sunday," he repeated.

"Oh," Leanne said suddenly. If Muriel

phoned—or impulsively dropped in, which she'd done once or twice—while Michael was visiting, it could be awkward. "Perhaps Monday would be better. Do you mind?"

"Not at all. Monday it is."

Leanne appreciated how accommodating he was. She hung up and resisted the urge to write Mark and let him know she'd followed his advice.

Chapter Twenty

I might bring someone home with me tonight," Macy told Harvey Monday morning. She stood on the other side of the white picket fence that separated their yards. Typical of her neighbor, he ignored her and continued watering the vegetable seedlings coming up in neat rows.

Macy was determined not to move until he responded. Two or three minutes later she was rewarded for her patience when he deigned to acknowledge her comment.

"Male or female?" Harvey asked without looking in her direction. He kept his back to her.

"Male."

That got Harvey's attention. He turned to face her, the hose, still spurting water, in his hand. "When did you meet him?"

"A while back," she said, not elaborating. "I want you to meet him, too."

"Why? Is he your boyfriend?"

"No."

"Then why are you bringing him to meet me?"

"He's a . . . sort of friend, nothing more. The thing is, I'm not even sure I like him."

Harvey made a scoffing sound and returned to his watering.

"I'm painting a mural in his office."

"Is he that persnickety doctor you talked about?"

"Yup." She grinned. "Persnickety. I love it. Not a word I've actually heard anyone say before."

"Then perhaps you should expand your vocabulary."

"Okay. Yes, he's that *punctilious* doctor I mentioned."

"The one who annoyed you."

That was putting it mildly. "He's the one."

Harvey snorted, but it could have been a laugh. Sometimes it was difficult to tell. "I'd be interested in meeting that young man."

Macy didn't question his sudden sociability. "You will tonight." This was working out beautifully. Macy would bring Michael by and introduce him to Harvey, and the two men would chat. Michael would ask a few subtle questions and learn what he needed to know so he could order the proper tests. Her next challenge would be to get Harvey to *take* those tests, but she'd deal with that when she got to it. "See you later," she said, waving goodbye.

Harvey grumbled something unintelligible.

Macy made sure Sammy and her three cats were fed, then took the bus to Michael's office, her supplies in a large canvas pouch.

When she arrived, Linda Barclay, Dr. Everett's nurse, let her in and accompanied her to the hallway. Macy removed the amended drawing from her bag, followed by paints, brushes, her purse, her lunch.

She was eager to begin the mural. She'd worked on the sketch over the weekend, adding several flourishes she thought Michael would like. Well, she hoped he would. Since their conversation on Thursday, she'd begun to think of him by his first name. And since she was passing him off as her "sort of friend" to Harvey, calling him Dr. Everett would be much too formal.

"The doctor isn't in yet," Linda told her as Macy unrolled the drawing.

"I can get started, though, can't I?"

The older woman shrugged. "I suppose that would be all right."

Macy still hadn't made up her mind about Michael's nurse. The woman stood guard over him as if he were royalty in need of protection. And yet, at times, Macy had the distinct impression that Linda, obviously no fool, might have taken a liking to her.

"I'm sure it will be, too," Macy said decisively. She'd struck her agreement with Michael and he'd approved her idea, minus the zoo bars.

The first order of business was to sketch in the background and the various animals. Since the wall had been freshly painted, or so she'd learned from Linda, Macy didn't have to prepare it and set about drawing with a thick lead pencil. She did everything freehand.

She'd just started when Michael showed up. He paused when he saw her.

"Good morning," she said cheerfully without interrupting her work.

"Morning."

He watched for a few minutes, although Macy didn't know what was so fascinating about a few lines. She was still sketching in the trees.

"Do you always hum while you draw?"

"Oh, do I?" Macy frowned. "No one's ever mentioned that before."

"You hum."

She turned and smiled warmly. "You'll notice I got here before you did this morning."

One side of his mouth lifted in a half smile, and Macy could see that getting him to relax would be a real test of her ability. She wasn't sure why she found it so important. She guessed it had to do with Hannah. If she'd loved Michael, and clearly she had, there must be more to him than he'd revealed so far.

"I'd like to get this done as quickly as possible," she told him. Of course, being paid when she was finished was a great incentive.

"Good idea."

"I added a few things to the scene if you want to check it out," she said and pointed to the sketch, which she'd rolled out on the floor. "See the baby giraffe? And the parrots?"

He stared down at it, then nodded. "I like it."

"I was hoping you would." She wiped her forearm across her brow. Her hair was tied back with a red Western-style bandanna. An apron covered her denim skirt and Mariners T-shirt, both faded from multiple washings. She didn't care if she got paint on them, but she liked the way the skirt allowed her freedom of movement.

He walked away and returned a couple of minutes later, entering the examination room at the opposite end of the hallway. Macy heard a little boy let out a wail and wondered what had caused him pain. Soon afterward, however, he was giggling. Macy smiled just listening to him. She wouldn't have guessed it, but Michael seemed to have a way with children.

Macy had hated visiting the doctor as a child and suspected other children felt the same terror she had. As the little boy left, he smiled shyly at Macy. Trailing behind his mother, he paused and studied the partial scene Macy had outlined.

"Do you see the zebra?" she asked, squatting down so they were at eye level.

He nodded excitedly. "The giraffe, too!"

"Cameron," his mother called, and he hurried

after her. When he reached the door, he turned and waved. Macy waved back.

She worked all morning without a break and was about to stop for lunch when Michael appeared. "I'm really going to have to ask you not to hum," he said.

"Oh, sorry."

"It's distracting to me and the staff. I don't mean to be difficult, but—"

"Don't worry about it. I didn't realize it was a problem. All you need to do is ask." She pinched her lips shut, then realized she could still hum.

"I'd appreciate it," he said pointedly. He went into his office and closed the door.

Macy stared at his door for a long time. She felt like sticking out her tongue, but didn't want to be a bad example to some suggestible young patient.

She ate a yogurt and fresh strawberries for lunch at a nearby park. When she came back, she saw that Michael's office door remained closed. She knocked lightly.

"Come in," he called.

Macy stepped inside and pulled the door behind her. Michael apparently ate lunch at his desk because there was an open container with a plastic fork poking out.

"I wanted to talk to you about this evening," she said.

"This evening?"

"Yes, you agreed to stop by my house and meet Harvey, my neighbor. He's the one—"

"I remember who Harvey is and Sammy and Puffball and—"

"Snowball."

"Whatever," he said with some impatience. "Now, what were you saying?"

"You were going to come by. We had a lengthy conversation about it. You haven't forgotten, have you?"

"I remember every word of our conversation. As I recall, we left it open-ended."

"But I said Monday," she insisted, mentally reviewing their exchange. "I know I did."

"Perhaps. However, I made no specific commitment."

That problem was easily solved. "Then how about tonight?"

"I have plans this evening."

"Oh." Well, so much for that. Still, Harvey was expecting to meet Michael and it would be a shame to disappoint him. "I don't suppose you could alter your plans slightly and stop by the house for a few minutes?" she asked hopefully. "I'm sure it wouldn't take long."

"Sorry, I can't."

"Drat." She sighed loudly. "But you *did* agree. I mean, this isn't a delaying tactic, is it? Because I'm really concerned about Harvey."

"Has there been another incident like the one you mentioned earlier?" Michael asked.

"Not that I know of, but then Harvey wouldn't tell me if there was." Her neighbor was stubborn in the extreme; he was also a cantankerous old fool. Hmm, Michael and Harvey should get along fine, seeing how similar they were.

"Does Wednesday fit with your schedule?" he asked, pulling out his cell phone and scrolling down.

"Anytime." She'd change whatever needed changing because this was too important to miss.

After they'd arranged a meeting on Wednesday, Macy returned to work, drawing into the late afternoon. Michael went into his office while she was putting the finishing touches on an elephant. He left his door open. She didn't intend to eavesdrop, but she couldn't help overhearing what he had to say. His "plans" appeared to be with someone named Leanne. No wonder meeting Harvey took second place—he was having dinner with this other woman.

Annoyed, yet aware that she was being unreasonable, Macy packed up when clinic hours were over and followed Linda Barclay out the door.

"The sketch is coming along nicely," Linda commented.

"Thanks." Macy was afraid she'd need to redo the entire afternoon's work. She felt it hadn't translated from her preliminary drawing to the wall as well as she'd hoped. It didn't help that she'd spent most of the afternoon brooding about Michael. She decided to blame her less-than-ideal work on the fact that she wasn't allowed to hum.

"Dr. Everett recently lost his wife," Linda said as they entered the elevator together.

"Yes," Macy told her. "I knew Hannah."

"You did?"

"I'd never met Michael. I saw him at the funeral. Wasn't it sad?"

"Oh, it was," Linda agreed. The elevator reached the bottom floor and they stepped out. "See you in the morning," she said as she headed toward the parking garage.

Macy walked to the bus stop, which was right outside the building. Using public transportation was so much easier than bringing her car and paying for parking. When she got home, she fed her cats and gave them some attention, then went out back. Harvey sat in his Adirondack chair, wearing his hat, a book propped open on his lap. She scrambled over the fence and joined him.

"Where's your friend?" he asked.

"He couldn't make it. He's coming on Wednesday instead."

"You don't sound happy about it," he said. "I'm used to turning down my hearing aid when you're around. What's wrong?"

"You know what's wrong—I don't like Michael."

"Really? Then he isn't much of a friend, is he?"

Sighing, Macy plopped down on the lawn next to Harvey and fanned out her skirt. The grass felt damp and cool against her skin. Sammy ambled over to lie beside her, resting his chin on her thigh.

"So, what's the problem with your boyfriend?" Harvey persisted.

"He most definitely is not my boyfriend," Macy said, frowning. "You know what he did?"

"I'm sure you'll tell me."

Harvey rarely showed even this much interest in any topic. She paused and regarded him suspiciously. Maybe he was feeling sick again, trying to distract her.

"What's the problem now?" he challenged.

"You. You're acting too friendly."

"Count your blessings."

Macy couldn't figure out what to make of this change in attitude. "You're not feeling well, are you?"

"I'm perfectly fine."

"No, you aren't." She wondered how long he'd been sitting in his chair.

"Don't tell me how I feel," he snapped.

Macy's fears lifted. "That's more like it," she said cheerfully.

"Leave an old man alone and take that mongrel with you."

"Sammy's yours now." She considered herself his coowner, or more accurately, one of his guardians. But Sammy's principal role was to be Harvey's companion.

"I don't want him."

"Too bad, he's part of the family."

"I thought you were looking for his owners. Seems to me you should've found 'em by now."

"No one claimed him."

"If he was mine, I wouldn't have claimed him, either," Harvey remarked.

"Harvey!" she cried, covering Sammy's ears. "You'll hurt his feelings. Everyone needs to be loved."

"Including you." He gave her a sly look. "I got a feeling about you and this doctor fellow."

"Me? Oh, please! We were talking about *Sammy*." And Harvey, too, but she dared not say that aloud.

"Yes, you," he said. "Here you are, complaining about the only man you've mentioned in months."

"He doesn't like me."

"I don't like you, either," Harvey muttered, "but that doesn't stop you from making a pest of your-self."

"With you I'm doing it for show."

"Are not," he insisted. "Now, tell me why you think this doctor isn't completely smitten with you."

"Smitten," she repeated and smiled just saying

241

the word. "Well, for one thing, he asked me not to hum. I like show tunes, so I hum when I paint, but he says it gets on his nerves."

"Seems to me you stirred him up."

She rolled her eyes. "We were supposed to get together tonight," she elaborated, wanting Harvey to understand how far off base he was. "Just as friends, you know. But now Michael has another . . . appointment."

"Didn't you say he was coming over on Wednesday?"

"Well, yes, but . . ."

"He probably has something important this evening. Doctors are busy people."

"He's got a date," Macy informed him primly. "I heard him talking to her. He asked if dinner was still on for tonight."

Harvey was undaunted. "Who said the dinner was with a woman?"

"I don't know many men named Leanne."

"Don't take it personally. He's seeing *you* on Wednesday."

"I still don't like him." She grinned. "Guess you'll have to marry me instead."

"Don't want to. Give him another chance."

"Don't want to," she echoed.

"So this doctor's playing the field. Good for him. If I was sixty years younger I would, too."

"Oh, Harvey. I told you—we're just friends." Even that was a stretch, but she didn't want

Harvey questioning why she'd invite a man she didn't like.

"Nope, I know the signs. You think I lived this long without kicking up my heels once in a while? I was quite the ladies' man in my younger days."

Smiling, Macy plucked a blade of grass. "I bet you were."

"Don't you get discouraged now, you hear me?"

"I'm not discouraged."

"Good. This doctor has the hots for you."

"The *hots?*" Macy laughed out loud. "Wait till you meet him. Then you'll see for yourself how wrong you are."

"Wanna bet? He sounds like exactly the right kind of man for you."

"We'd make a terrible couple. He's so . . . stuffy."

"Then he needs you." He turned and glared at her. "And you need him."

Macy shook her head. Even if she was attracted to Michael—and she wasn't admitting that at all—they were completely unsuited. Total opposites.

Just to take one example, she liked to hum and he liked to frown.

Chapter Twenty-One

I stopped at a wine "boutique" and picked up a bottle of champagne for dinner with Leanne. She'd be making either crispy pork chops or, more likely, something Italian. I was wandering around the store, trying to decide if I should bring red or white wine. The clerk, who came around the counter to offer assistance, suggested champagne.

"It isn't just for weddings, you know," he told me. "Champagne goes with everything." He recommended Drappier. I'd never heard of the brand, but I took him at his word and purchased the bottle.

When I arrived at Leanne's I was glad I'd gone to the trouble of buying something out of the ordinary. The aroma coming from her kitchen was delectable, and I sniffed appreciatively.

"I'm making an Italian dish," Leanne said as she led me into her apartment, "but my family background is German. My great-grandmother came through Ellis Island in the late 1890s. Apparently, she was a wonderful cook."

I was grateful for a homemade meal, especially after my excellent dinner with Winter. I'd forgotten how good it was to eat something that didn't come from the freezer or out of a can. And any meal I didn't have to fuss with was a major improvement over my own haphazard dinners.

"My grandmother used to make a pot roast

every Saturday," Leanne said. "She baked it in the oven with different vegetables and then parceled out the leftovers to whoever came for the meal. That sometimes meant a dozen people."

"That many?"

She smiled. "Always. Grandma never learned to cook for two. She made enough to feed a family of ten her whole life. No one complained—except Grandpa, who peeled the potatoes."

"Well, I may not be doing anything as useful as peeling potatoes, but I did bring this." I set the cold bottle of champagne on the kitchen counter.

"Thank you," Leanne said with another smile. She motioned toward the stove. "I hope you like lasagna."

"Sure do."

"I prepared it yesterday afternoon, so all I had to do was put it in the oven once I got home from work."

She moved to the cupboard and took down two wineglasses. "I apologize, but I don't have champagne flutes."

"These will do just as well." I tried to sound knowledgeable, as if I often served high-quality champagne and other wines. Actually, I'd gotten quite an education that afternoon and was intrigued by the number of wines available from every corner of the world. I'd return to that store, I decided. It was time I took an interest in something other than medicine.

While Leanne washed and dried the glasses, I removed the foil and the wire casing. I turned my back, thankful for the clerk's advice on how to remove the cork, which came out with a festive *pop*. I figured that made me look like an expert. If I'd been with Ritchie, I would've lifted the bottle high and demanded extravagant praise. But because I was playing the role of sophisticate, I acted as though this accomplishment was par for the course.

Speaking of Ritchie . . . I'd made the mistake of mentioning dinner with Leanne at the gym that morning. Naturally, my brother-in-law felt obliged to give me a list of *dos* and *don'ts*. This dinner was a much bigger deal than our first date. Tonight I'd been invited to Leanne's home and she was cooking for me.

According to Ritchie—when did *he* become so knowledgeable about dating etiquette?—this was a significant gesture on Leanne's part. In his view, making me dinner was a clear sign that she was willing to move forward with the relationship. I wasn't sure, despite Ritchie's insistence that I take her invitation seriously.

I poured us each a glass of Drappier and we sat down in her small living room. She had appetizer plates out with olives and roasted red peppers and two kinds of cheese. I leaned forward and speared an olive.

"I suppose you're wondering why I didn't

arrange this dinner for the weekend," she said, "since that's when I originally invited you."

I hadn't given it much thought; I'd surmised that she had other plans. Monday worked fine for me—regardless of Macy's assumptions. Like I said earlier, I didn't have what you'd call a busy social calendar.

"My mother-in-law phoned to tell me they were planning to visit Mark this weekend and that she'd get in touch with me while she was in town."

I didn't know if that required a response or not.

Leanne stared down at her champagne. "I . . . I didn't want her to call—or worse, drop by—in the middle of our dinner."

"I understand." It would've been awkward for us both. "Did she contact you?"

Leanne nodded. "She phoned me early Sunday evening."

Just about the time we would've been sitting down to eat.

"Muriel was terribly upset. Apparently, Mark's accepted a job that'll take him to Afghanistan."

"He joined the military?"

"No, this is a company the army's contracted with. Mark was rather vague on the details. All he'd tell his family is that the money will enable him to pay back what he . . . took and help with the fines. His sister tries to contribute, but she's having financial troubles of her own."

I could see the worry etched on her face. It was

more than obvious that she still had feelings for her ex-husband.

"He didn't want his mother to tell anyone, especially his sister and me, but she refused to make that promise."

"You're very concerned, aren't you?"

She lowered her head, and I noticed the way her hand tightened around the stem of her glass. "Yes. Muriel doesn't really know what Mark will be doing there, but we both suspect it doesn't have anything to do with accounting."

"I'm sorry to hear that," I said, hoping I sounded sympathetic. Discussing her ex-husband was uncomfortable, but I wasn't opposed to it. If she brought up the subject of Mark, then I could introduce Hannah into the conversation, too. That degree of honesty would probably be good for both of us.

The oven timer went off and Leanne leaped to her feet as if she welcomed the intrusion.

I stood, too. "Do you need any help?"

"No, but thanks." She was away for a short while. When she returned, she reached for her glass and sat back down. "The lasagna will have to wait for a few minutes. We're also having a salad."

I nodded. "Hannah used to love cooking, too," I said, and remembered the wonderful meals my wife had put together. She always felt it was important for me to follow a regular eating schedule, even during my residency, when the hours were crazy and days melded into one another until time lost all meaning. Often I had no idea what day of the week it was. Hannah brought meals to me at the hospital and cooked for the other residents, too. Everyone loved her. How could they not?

"This recipe is one I got from her."

"From Hannah," I breathed, abruptly drawn away from my musings.

"We were talking about our favorite dishes and she told me about this one. The next day, she handed me the recipe."

I was touched that Leanne had made it for me. At an earlier stage of my grief I might have found that presumptuous—or distressing. Now it warmed me with memories of Hannah and with gratitude toward Leanne.

While I ate another olive, Leanne set the salad bowl on the table. I rejoined her in the kitchen and we sat down at the small dinette table together.

She'd gone to considerable effort to make this meal as pleasant as possible. The salad, which included several leafy greens, was full of green peppers, red onions and radishes, plus pine nuts and goat cheese. The poppy-seed dressing tasted homemade.

"Another of Hannah's recipes?" I asked as I poured a small amount over the salad.

Leanne shook her head. "This one comes from my mother."

I licked some dressing off the end of my finger. "It's delicious."

"Thanks."

All at once we seemed to run out of things to say. Potential topics raced through my mind. If I was more interested in baseball, I could've discussed the Mariners, who'd played on both Saturday and Sunday. I couldn't recall who'd won either game, although Ritchie had gone on about it for several minutes that morning.

"Do you like baseball?" I asked, a bit desperately.

She looked up as if the question had startled her. "No, sorry. Do you?"

"Not really." We both fell silent.

"Most women seem to enjoy cooking," I said, trying again. "Hannah's cousin—" I stopped abruptly, realizing I'd sounded like an idiot. It wasn't a good idea to mention that Winter had made me dinner the week before.

Stupid, stupid, stupid.

One of Ritchie's cardinal rules of dating was not to talk about other women. It wasn't as though I considered Winter a real *date,* though. I was glad I hadn't said anything about her cooking for me to my brother-in-law. The less he knew the better.

Leanne seemed to be all out of conversation, too.

"Would you like more champagne?" I asked, eager for something to do.

"Yes, please."

We both stood at the same time. She opened the refrigerator and retrieved the champagne bottle and I refilled our glasses. While she was up, Leanne brought the casserole dish to the table, along with a loaf of warm, crisp bread.

We sat down again, and the silence seemed to yawn between us.

"How are things at the clinic?" she finally asked.

"I'm having a mural painted," I said. It was the first thought that came to mind.

I almost blurted out that the woman doing it was someone on Hannah's list. But that would've been even stupider than talking about Winter.

"Who's painting it?" Leanne asked. She seemed genuinely interested.

"Her name's Macy Roth. She's done several murals for businesses in the area." I described the jungle scene, with its baby animals and multicolored parrots. "Macy's quite a character. She doesn't have a normal nine-to-five job, which is no doubt for the best because she'd drive any employer insane."

"Why's that?"

"Where do you want me to start?" I leaned back in my chair and realized I was smiling. "To begin with, she's constantly late." Now, that was a bit unfair. Macy had been late for our first meeting, but she'd made a point of letting me know she'd been on time ever since, as if this was some impressive achievement.

251

"She seems to have a houseful of cats and dogs," I elaborated, "and she gives them ridiculous names."

"Such as?"

"Puffball—I think. And Sammy."

"That's not outlandish at all."

"Maybe not, but she refers to them as though they're human. I thought Sammy was her neighbor, only her neighbor is Harvey, who's in his eighties and going through his second childhood. That's in his own words, apparently." In my opinion, the two of them, Macy and Harvey, would be perfect together because Macy acted like a kid, too.

"I guess she's an eccentric artist type."

"*Eccentric* fits her to a tee." Or, as my father would say, her elevator doesn't go all the way to the top. He has dozens of expressions like that, and I smiled, remembering his sense of humor.

"She sounds like a lot of fun."

That was why Hannah had put Macy on her list. My loving, patient wife had viewed Macy as fun. I, on the other hand, saw her as a screwball. A flake. I didn't typically know people like that.

"How long is it going to take her to finish the mural?"

I shrugged. "A couple of weeks, or so she claims." I paused. "Did I mention that she hums while she works?" In all honesty, her humming wasn't nearly as irritating as I'd implied. Besides,

Les Misérables is one of my favorite musicals. I'd recognized "Master of the House" immediately.

Leanne seemed to find that amusing.

"Show tunes," I went on. "She says she's not aware of doing it, which is laughable. Then, before I can stop myself, I'm humming, too, and I have no musical ability whatsoever. Plus I have to listen to my staff joining in."

"I knew someone like Macy once. A nurse. Her name was Gayle and she was always singing. She'd also jump from one subject to the next without even the hint of a transition."

"That goes for Macy, too." The woman lived in her own world and anyone from planet Earth had to wonder what she was talking about.

I leaned closer to the table and offered Leanne my plate as she sliced the lasagna into squares. I waited until she'd served herself before I dug in. To say it was good would be an understatement of criminal proportions. I remembered eating this same meal with Hannah, and deeply appreciated Leanne's thoughtfulness in preparing it for me. I savored the second bite and the third. I devoured the lasagna and accepted another helping, which is something I rarely do.

Leanne talked about her friend Gayle, and I matched her stories, but mine were about my trials with Macy. Soon we were both relaxed and smiling at each other across the table.

"Would you like to go to a movie this

weekend?" I found myself asking as we lingered over coffee.

"Sure. Anything in particular you'd like to see?"

I didn't even know what was playing. "You decide."

"Action, comedy, drama? Do you have a preference?"

"What do you like?"

"Buttered popcorn."

I smiled. "Action, then. Something along the lines of *The Bourne Identity*." That was the last movie I'd seen, other than *The African Queen* with Winter the week before.

Ritchie's Rule #17: *Don't mention seeing a movie with Winter Adams while you're with Leanne.*

She suggested we have our coffee in the living room and because our conversation about quirky individuals seemed to have run its course, she turned on the television. We watched a news show and when it was over, I carried my empty mug into the kitchen.

"Thank you for dinner," I said and I hoped the simple words conveyed my very real gratitude.

"You aren't disappointed that I didn't bake crispy pork chops?" she teased.

"Not in the least."

"Maybe next time," she said.

"I'd love that," I told her.

"Sure."

Winter had promised to make me a pork roast soon; I just hoped I didn't get confused about who'd made what. Between the two, Winter and Leanne, I could find myself in trouble. Ritchie's Rule #23: *Keep track of meals and movies.*

"Do you want to give me a call before Saturday?" she asked as she held open the apartment door.

Suddenly, I couldn't remember why I'd need to call her.

She obviously noticed my blank look. "For the movie."

"Oh, right." I felt foolish, but Leanne put me at ease with her smile.

Once I was home and sitting in front of the TV with my feet up, I reconsidered that invitation to the movies. Quite frankly I don't know what had prompted me to suggest it. My plan had been to give myself a day or two to analyze the evening before I pursued the relationship any further.

Instead, I'd arranged another date. Perhaps I felt obligated to repay her for the meal. I didn't know.

Not until I turned in for the night did it occur to me that I'd spent most of the evening talking about Macy.

Chapter Twenty-Two

Alix Turner stuck her head inside Winter's tiny office at the French Café. "You have a visitor," she said. Judging by her smile, Alix seemed pleased about something. She was noticeably pregnant now, and the whole staff was thrilled. Everyone had adopted Alix and, while Winter had never given birth herself, she couldn't help offering dietary advice and concocting nutritious smoothies.

Jordan, who was the most attentive husband she'd ever seen, wanted Alix to stop working, but Alix had convinced him she could continue until she felt too uncomfortable to bake. She also served at the counter when Winter needed a substitute. There were only a few weeks left before her due date, and Winter suspected Alix would work right up until she went into labor. One thing was certain; this baby would have a number of doting godmothers, and she intended to be one of them. Alix's previous pregnancy had ended in an early miscarriage last summer. That accounted for the extra care Jordan and all her friends lavished on her now.

"A visitor?" Winter looked up from the food order she was about to complete. "Who is it?" she asked automatically. Even as she spoke, she wondered who'd feel a need to be announced. Michael or possibly—

"It's Pierre."

The pen Winter had been holding slipped from her fingers. "Pierre is *here?*"

"Should I send him in?" Alix asked, her smile widening. She'd always been a champion of his. At times Winter had actually been a little jealous of how well Pierre and Alix got along, of the easy camaraderie between them.

Now Pierre was here, when she least expected him. *Where* she least expected him. She remembered his anger when she'd dropped in to see him, the distant way he'd treated her. In Winter's opinion, he deserved the same treatment. She dared not let him see how glad she was, how happy his visit made her, how much she craved the sight of him. Contemplating her response, she leaned back in her chair. A moment later she decided he could wait.

"Tell him I'm busy with an order. I'll be out as soon as I'm done."

Alix frowned, her hands resting on her protruding stomach. "Are you sure?"

"I'm positive."

Alix left and, smiling to herself, Winter chewed on the end of the pen. So Pierre had actually made the effort to seek her out. This was an interesting development. But seeing how rude and unwelcoming he'd been, a lukewarm reception on her part seemed fitting. Although she suffered a twinge of doubt, she held firm.

She tried to concentrate on the order, but her mind kept drifting to Pierre. He'd never been a patient man and she guessed that after ten minutes he'd be furious. Good. Served him right.

When she felt he'd probably reached the end of his patience, Winter sauntered out of her office. She paused in the kitchen long enough to pour herself a cup of coffee and then casually walked around the counter to the front of the café. Pierre sat at a table next to the window, gazing out at Blossom Street. No one else was seated nearby, although there was a short line at the counter.

By ten-thirty, the morning crowd had dwindled to a handful who'd stopped in during their coffee breaks. In another hour, they'd get a rush of lunch orders. The soup du jour, baked potato sprinkled with grated cheddar cheese and fresh chives, was popular with her customers, so the café was bound to do brisk business.

Pierre looked up as she approached, and it gave her a degree of satisfaction to see his eyes narrow. His coffee cup was empty and the croissant only half-eaten.

"I hope you didn't find anything wrong with my croissant," she said as she slipped into the chair across from him.

"Quite the opposite. It was excellent as always." Pierre's spine was as stiff as his compliment.

Winter shrugged lightly. "I apologize for keeping you waiting."

His mouth tensed, and he shook his head as if he'd grown tired of the old games, the playacting they both indulged in. "Don't say things you don't mean."

"Like what?" She opened her eyes wide in exaggerated innocence.

"That you regret keeping me waiting. You did that intentionally and we both know it. You wanted me to be aware that you had more important tasks requiring your attention."

Winter didn't bother to deny it. She hadn't fooled him in the slightest. She'd meant to punish him. But the pleasure of vengeance had already begun to recede.

"What can I do for you?" Winter asked smoothly.

He didn't answer for a long time. "*Rien du tout. Nothing at all.*"

He started to rise, and Winter stretched out her arm, placing her hand over his. "Surely you had a reason for coming here."

Pierre had half risen from the chair. He sat back down, his dark eyes holding hers. "I thought we should talk."

She smiled and nodded, wanting to encourage him, wanting him to acknowledge that he missed her as much as she missed him. Nothing seemed truly right without Pierre and yet she wasn't sure how to make their relationship work.

Spending time with Michael Everett had been pleasant, but while she enjoyed his company, it was Pierre she loved, Pierre who was her soul mate, Pierre who was always on her mind.

After a lengthy hesitation, he said, "I came because I felt bad about the last time we spoke."

She frowned at the memory. "You were rude."

"I was busy," he snapped. "I had three banquets that evening, and two of the kitchen staff phoned in sick. What would you have me do? You could have checked with me first, could have given me some warning. You know what it's like in the kitchen."

"Why didn't you tell me this at the time?" If he could snap at her, she could snap back. Then, because she did know how crazy life could get in a large hotel kitchen, she added, "Okay, I should've phoned first. But I didn't deserve to have my head bitten off. Besides, if I *had* called, you wouldn't have answered and then I would've come anyway, so it's irrelevant."

"How do you know whether I would have answered or not?" he demanded. "To say I would ignore a call from you is an insult."

"Then consider yourself insulted." Winter drew in a deep breath and closed her eyes. It always ended like this. She'd be so happy to see Pierre, and then they'd start sniping at each other, and before she could figure out why, they'd be in the middle of an argument.

One look at Pierre told her he was as frustrated as she was.

"Why do we always fight?" she asked, sick at heart. No one else affected her this way. Only Pierre was capable of twisting her emotions into such an impossible knot.

Pierre was silent for a few seconds. "Why do we fight?" he repeated, as if he, too, had lost any hope of finding a solution. "If I had the answer to that, you and I would be married by now and starting our own family." His eyes went to the counter, where Alix was serving coffee and croissants.

They'd talked of marriage and children. That, at least, was a subject on which they could easily agree. It was everything else that ended in argument. Neither of them wanted this constant bickering and yet they seemed unable to avoid it.

"I suppose you expect an apology for what I said that afternoon," he muttered, returning to their earlier conversation. "Getting me to admit I was wrong seems inordinately important to you."

"You should apologize."

"What about *you?*" he blazed.

"What did I do that was so wrong?"

"Do you actually need me to tell you?"

"Yes, I do," Winter said.

"First of all, we both agreed upon no contact for three months. *N'est-ce pas?*"

Okay, she'd broken their agreement. So what? She'd had something to tell him and it seemed best to do it in person. "I had a reason."

"Sure you did. You wanted to shove the fact that you were dating some other man in my face."

"That is not true." She clenched her hands involuntarily. Pierre turned everything back on her, made everything her fault. He had no idea how unfair he was being, how unreasonable.

"Don't deceive yourself, Winter." He wagged his index finger as if he'd caught her in a lie. "That is *exactly* why you showed up on the most hectic day I've had all year."

"We'd never discussed it, and I felt you should know."

"Why? So I would miss you more? So I would beg you not to go out with this doctor? To remain faithful to me? If you're waiting for me to plead with you, you'll have a long wait."

"Fine, whatever."

"Fine with me, too." Pierre crossed his arms and scowled at her.

This was getting them nowhere. It felt as though they performed the same roles, recited the same lines, every time they were together. She'd grown so weary of it; Pierre had, too.

"If it makes you feel any better," she said, "you should know I've always been faithful to you."

He arched a brow, implying that was no concern of his.

His nonchalant attitude irritated her even more. "Don't you care if I date another man?" she asked.

He shrugged. "Why should I?"

"At one time we seriously considered getting married!"

"Thank God we didn't make that mistake."

His words were like a knife he'd sunk into her heart. Pierre knew how badly she'd wanted to marry him. Swallowing painfully, she asked, "Why do you have to say such ugly things to me?" She hated the small quaver in her voice.

"*Ma chérie,* be reasonable. If we'd married we'd have killed each other by now."

"That's not true!"

"Look at us," he said, gesturing toward her with one hand, then bringing it back to his chest. "We can't even have a conversation without aiming for each other's throat. Something is very wrong with us. I don't know what it is . . . I wish I did. I thought . . . I hoped that when we got back together the last time our problems had been resolved, but nothing's changed."

The sadness in his voice echoed her own feelings, although pride wouldn't allow her to show it.

"This three-month separation idea of yours is for the best."

Winter disagreed, but it was hard to admit that; as he'd pointed out, it *had* been her suggestion. She'd regretted it almost every day since. At the time she'd been so sure Pierre would fight to keep their relationship intact. Three months apart had felt like an eternity then. It still felt like one now. She'd been the first to break their agreement. That should've told him something about her feelings. She didn't know why it was like this with them. How she longed for the early days of their relationship, before they'd fallen into this pattern of destructive behavior, of belittling each other in this crazy reflexive way.

"So you want to continue with our separation?" she said.

Pierre flicked her an incredulous glance. "Of course, don't you?"

"Yes," she said, using the same tone. "But since you're here, when we agreed to have no contact—well, naturally I assumed you might've changed your mind."

"I didn't."

Winter managed to hide her disappointment. "S-o-o," she said, "you stopped by despite our decision not to see each other . . . to tell me we shouldn't see each other? Or was it because you were in the neighborhood and had a hankering for coffee and a croissant?"

"I already told you why," he said sharply. "To clear up any misconceptions from the day you came to see me."

"Misconceptions?" she repeated. "You couldn't have made your feelings any more obvious if I'd asked."

Pierre waited a heartbeat before responding. "Then we understand each other?"

"Well, actually, I don't."

"Do you need me to explain it to you again?"

"Maybe you should," she answered. Impatience seemed to radiate from him, making any kind of rational discussion impossible.

"I felt bad about that day and wanted to apologize," Pierre said.

"You *should* have felt bad." Winter regretted her words immediately.

Pierre's jaw hardened. "I can see it was a mistake to come here. It was an even bigger mistake to think the two of us could communicate. Our relationship didn't work before and it isn't working now. I'm afraid we were both fooling ourselves into believing we ever had a chance." He stood so abruptly that the chair wobbled before righting itself. "I won't say it was good to see you, because it wasn't. Frankly, this visit told me everything I needed to know," he said. "Everything I needed to remember." He started for the door.

At first, Winter was angry enough to let him go. But almost instantly she realized that if she allowed their conversation to end like this, the memory of it would always stand between them. She had to make at least an effort to reconcile.

She got up and hurried out the door. "Pierre!" she called, surprised to see that he was already halfway down the block.

He ignored her.

"Pierre," she called again, louder this time.

He paused, but didn't turn around.

Winter quickened her pace until she caught up with him. But then she didn't know what to say.

"I hate it when we fight," she blurted out, close to tears.

"Moi aussi," Pierre admitted, his shoulders slumping. "Me, too. Nothing ever changes with us. I love you and am crazy without you and then we're together for five minutes and I am crazy *with* you."

"I love you, too," she said in a low voice, "and yet sometimes I think I could hate you."

"We are not good together," he said, looking away from her, every syllable weighted with sadness.

She opened her mouth to disagree and found she couldn't.

Chapter Twenty-Three

When I got to the office Wednesday morning, I discovered Macy hard at work on the mural. She had her iPod plugged into her ears and seemed intent on her job. The sketch wasn't finished, but she'd made significant progress, which told me she'd been at work for several hours. And yet the office had opened just thirty minutes ago. I didn't understand how she could've accomplished so much in such a short time.

"She talked one of the security guards into letting her in early," Linda explained, reading my mind. She followed my gaze as Macy, oblivious to our scrutiny, continued drawing on the wall. "I don't know what she said to Larry."

"*Larry* let Macy into the office?" That particular guard was a stickler for rules. The fact that Macy had somehow persuaded him to allow her into the locked office was almost impossible to believe. I couldn't imagine what she'd said to him. For that matter, I'd rather *not* know.

Apparently, I made some movement that alerted Macy to my presence. The instant she saw me, she pulled out her earphones and gave me a dazzling smile.

"Good morning, Michael."

I nodded, a bit embarrassed to be referred to by my first name in front of Linda. "I understand you got here even before the staff," I said, striving to sound businesslike. I didn't want Linda or the others on staff to get any ideas.

"I had to because I wanted to make sure I'd be ready to leave when you were. I plan to finish the sketches today."

"It looks like you'll be able to start painting soon," I said.

She cocked her head to one side. "The more I thought about how I'd arranged the giraffes and the lion, the less happy I was with the sketch. I've already made changes, see?" She gestured toward the wall.

I didn't really notice that much of a difference, but then I hadn't paid close attention. Macy had shown me the drawing and I'd approved it. I wasn't going to stand over her and examine every line she drew.

"You'll be able to come home with me tonight, won't you?" she asked, her eyes imploring. "To meet Harvey."

I felt Linda's interest and tried to ignore my nurse. The truth was, I'd do just about anything to get out of this. "You need to make an appointment with a physician who specializes in geriatrics," I said.

Macy's eyes grew round. "Harvey will never keep the appointment. This is the only way. You said you would. You can't go back on your word now." Seeking reinforcements, Macy turned to Linda. "He promised."

"You promised," Linda repeated in a tone that told me she was enjoying this far more than she should.

"Traitor," I whispered. Her support of Macy's schemes surprised me. It wasn't like Linda to side with someone else against me. I wasn't sure I liked this change in my nurse, who seemed to be falling under Macy's spell. I couldn't figure out why everyone, including Hannah, thought so highly of her. Macy seemed like a generous young woman and she had a certain quirky charm, but after ten minutes I found her irritating in the extreme.

"You'll come, won't you?" she pleaded.

I opened my mouth, but before I could utter a word, Linda answered for me. "He'll be there." She shoved a file into my hands and steered me toward the first examination room.

Sure enough, by four-thirty I'd finished my scheduled appointments in record time. Linda had somehow managed to free up the late afternoon so all I had left to do was some minor paperwork.

When I walked out of my office, Macy was waiting for me in the reception area, her purse draped over her shoulder. She wore army-green pants and a yellow T-shirt with a butterfly print on it and a brown vest made of some shiny fabric I couldn't readily identify. As was often the case, her red hair was a tangle of unruly curls. She lit up like a neon sign the moment she saw me.

"Are you ready?" she asked.

I sighed. I wasn't keen to meet this neighbor of hers, and my guess was that Harvey felt the same way about me.

"Sure," I said. "Let's go."

"Is it okay if I ride with you? I took the bus this morning."

"No problem."

I led her across the street to the parking garage, which was a few blocks down from the gym where Ritchie and I worked out. Paul, the parking attendant, saw me with Macy and winked in my direction. It was all I could do not to stop and explain that in spite of what he thought, I wasn't romantically involved with Macy. But if I made an issue of it I'd only look foolish, so I resisted.

When I pushed the remote button to unlock the doors to my BMW, the lights blinked and Macy laughed softly.

"What's so funny?" I asked.

"You. You're so predictable."

"In what way?"

"The car. It's such a doctor car. And I bet it's spotless inside."

"Well, yes, but what's that got to do with anything?"

"Oh, nothing," she said. "It's just so . . . you."

I bit my tongue to keep from making some remark about how she dressed.

As I'd expected, Macy chatted nonstop from the moment she slid into the passenger seat. I heard about her cats and about Harvey and a number of other people, places and things. She bounced from one topic to the next, like Leanne's friend Gayle, without any detectable rhyme or reason. If I hadn't known better I would've said she was nervous, but that didn't make sense.

She directed me to her address and when we pulled up I was the one who laughed. The house resembled something out of a fairy tale. It was painted yellow and red. The yard was surrounded by a white picket fence with a gate, and flowers seemed to be blooming everywhere. She had huge pots on the front steps and the flower beds were ablaze with bright purple azaleas. I half expected Cinderella or Snow White to come waltzing out the door, greeting us with some chirpy song.

"What?" she asked, obviously unsure why I was so amused.

"The house."

"Oh, yes, isn't it divine? I inherited it from my grandmother."

"So you got your, uh, style from her?"

"Some," she agreed. "I repainted it last summer. A few of the neighbors made a bit of a fuss, but they got used to it after a while. Personally, I think it's inviting, don't you?"

"If I was eight, I would."

"Oh, stop," she said and laughed.

Apparently, she had no idea that I was serious. With a sense of resignation I climbed out of the car and shoved my hands in my pockets. Macy was already on the sidewalk, about to open the front gate, when she turned to look at me. "Don't worry about Sammy. His bark is worse than his bite."

No sooner had I stepped onto her property than a huge brown dog of indiscriminate pedigree came rushing toward me at full speed, barking loudly enough to hurt my ears. I braced myself, certain I was about to be tackled.

"Sammy," Macy said calmly. "This is a friend."

Sammy stopped in his tracks and stared up at me, his eyes filled with suspicion.

"Go ahead and pet him," Macy advised. "He's really gentle, but he's gotten rather protective lately." She opened the front door and the second she did three cats raced outside.

Macy bent down and petted each one, murmuring words of affection. "Meet Snowball, Lovie and Peace."

I felt a bit silly and, not knowing how else to respond, I waved.

"They've been cooped up inside all day," she explained as the cats twined themselves around her legs.

She led me into the house and, not surprisingly, it looked like a disaster site. She had a number of half-finished paintings propped up against the fireplace—or what I assumed was a fireplace. I didn't take time to study them, but each seemed different from the others. There was a landscape, a seascape and a still life—a fruit bowl with what appeared to be one huge pomegranate. There was also a portrait of a sleeping cat, the white fluffy one. None of these paintings was completed. This worried me. I hoped she understood that I wasn't paying her until the mural was done. Apparently, she saw where I was looking.

"I have a problem finishing . . . stuff."

"So I see."

"Don't worry about the mural, though," she told

me cheerfully. "My car insurance premium is due and I can't be late," she said, then added in a whisper she probably didn't think I'd hear, "Again."

I managed to hide a smile as I continued to survey the room. A laundry basket sat on her sofa, piled with either clean or dirty clothes, I couldn't tell which. The dining-room table was covered with books, newspapers, magazines and unopened mail. She'd tried to create orderly stacks, but either the cats had interfered with her efforts or the piles had gotten jumbled on their own.

We passed through the kitchen. The dishes had been washed and were set on a wire rack next to the sink. On a table in the small dining nook lay a hardcover book, opened and turned over to mark her place. I cringe whenever I see a book bent in such a fashion. I was sorely tempted to reach down and close it. This was a personal peeve of mine. I could see no reason to break a book's spine when a bookmark would serve just as well.

Looking out the window, Macy announced, "Harvey's out back, sitting in his chair. He spends far too much time doing that. He never used to." Worry tinged her voice. "I have a feeling he's had another bad day."

Even now I wasn't sure what she expected me to do. I'd talk to Harvey and determine what I could, but I had no promises to give her.

She grabbed my hand and pulled me toward the back door. "Let me introduce you."

"Okay, only—"

I wasn't allowed to finish before she half dragged me outside. "Harvey," she called. "I'd like you to meet Michael, the man I was telling you about." Then she turned to me and whispered, "This is just for show." With that, she looped her arms around my neck and kissed my cheek. Turning back to Harvey, she said, "You were right all along. I was besotted from the moment we met."

Besotted? Who used a word like *besotted?*

Harvey regarded me for a minute or so before he revealed any expression. It could have been a smile or a scowl, but frankly it was hard to distinguish which. "I can only imagine what she did to con you into coming by," he muttered.

"You're better off not knowing," I said.

He gave a snort of laughter, then gestured toward the house. "There's another chair over there. Help yourself." He looked at Macy next. "I've got a couple of beers in the fridge. Why don't you get them for us?"

She seemed more than eager to comply, even though he hadn't offered her one. "Coming right up."

We both climbed over the low fence, and Sammy jumped after us. She bounced into the house with the mutt close on her heels. The three cats had decided to stay at her place.

I carried the folding lawn chair next to Harvey

and sat down. Macy was back with the two beers, which she handed us. Then she disappeared again, leaping over the fence as if she'd done it a thousand times, which undoubtedly she had.

"So you're that doctor fellow she's been talking about," Harvey said. He took a swallow of beer and closed his eyes, either to savor the taste or allow a moment of pain to pass.

I took a sip of my own beer and had to admit it hit the spot.

"Before you start asking a lot of *discreet* questions, I should tell you I'm not going to make an appointment with any friends of yours. Nor am I willing to undergo any medical tests. I know what's wrong with me."

This was a relief. "So tell me and save me the bother of answering Macy's questions later."

"I'm dying," the old man said matter-of-factly. "It doesn't get much simpler than that."

"Of what?" I asked. Given his age, that seemed possible, and if he wasn't willing to have any tests or submit to a physical, I had no choice but to accept his self-diagnosis—at least until I saw firm evidence to the contrary.

"Can't say for sure. Cancer maybe, but it could be my heart."

"What are your symptoms?"

"Different ones. I get weak when I didn't used to. At first I thought it was my age, but now I know it's more than that. Used to be I could work in my yard all day and not get tired. Lately it's all I can do to water the garden. I have pains in my chest. No fever, though, which means it's not malaria."

"I suggest—"

"In case you didn't understand me before, I'll repeat myself. I'm not interested in anything you have to suggest that will lengthen my life. I've lived a lot of years. Like everyone else, I have a few regrets, but I'm ready to die."

"Macy—"

"It's time Macy learned she needs to let go of me."

"She loves you," I told him.

Harvey exhaled loudly as though burdened by her love. "She loves those cats of hers, too. Never met anyone quite like her. She collects animals and people the way someone else might collect baseball cards or ceramic frogs. I tried to discourage her when she moved in after her grandmother died. I think Lotty must've asked her to keep an eye on me. That would be just like the old bat. The last thing I need is Macy constantly fussing over me."

"I hear you."

The old man eyed me closely.

"My wife—"

"You're married?" Harvey interrupted. His gaze narrowed menacingly.

"Was. I'm a widower," I corrected. "Hannah, in

the end, didn't want any more medical intervention. No heroic measures."

"I remember—" he nodded in the direction of Macy's house "—she told me about your wife. I'm sorry for your loss."

"Thank you," I murmured. "I just wanted to let you know I understand how you feel."

"It's a matter of dignity. I prefer to face death on my own terms."

I remembered those had been Hannah's words, too. "Is there anything I can do to help with the pain?" I asked. The current drugs would ease his final months.

Harvey shook his head. "No, thanks."

Macy reappeared, carrying a platter with cheese and crackers. I watched as she popped a cracker in her mouth.

"I brought you a few munchies," she said.

"What for?" Harvey demanded.

"I thought you might be hungry," she said, smiling down at him, obviously accustomed to his gruff manner. She sat on the grass beside me.

"I'm not interested."

Harvey might not be, but I was. I reached for a slice of cheese.

"I wouldn't eat that one if I were you," Macy said in a muted voice.

"Why not?"

"I think Snowball licked it before I had a chance to shoo him away."

"Snowball is a he?" I probably should've asked why she hadn't just removed that piece of cheese from the plate. Instead, I was struck by the fact that the white puffball was male.

Macy stretched out her legs and leaned back on her hands. "He's never forgiven me for naming him that, either."

"Then change his name." The solution seemed simple.

"Can't. I tried, but I see him as Snowball, and nothing else seems to suit him now. Besides, all his medical records are in that name. It's too confusing to make the switch."

Harvey sighed. "Just accept what she says without asking a lot of questions. It's easier that way."

I could see his point.

Macy joined the conversation, telling us about the mural and the patients she'd seen coming in and out during the day. Sammy lay next to her, as close as he could get without sitting right on her.

It soon became apparent that Harvey had tired himself out and needed to go inside. I started to help him up, which he didn't appreciate, slapping my hand away. "Leave me alone," he snapped, "and allow an old man his pride."

Macy stood beside me and watched as her friend and neighbor walked slowly toward his house. The instant he was out of earshot, she bombarded me with questions.

"Well?" she asked, sounding nearly breathless.

"Can you tell what's making him so weak? He's sick, isn't he? I mean, really sick? Were you able to convince him to make a doctor's appointment? You led into that subtly, I hope."

"Let's go inside and talk," I said, dreading this conversation. I hadn't been eager to meet Harvey, but to my surprise I liked the old man.

I followed her lead, climbing over the low fence, Sammy by our side, accompanying us every step of the way.

"It's bad, isn't it? You don't need to mince words with me. I just want the truth. Don't be afraid to tell me." She was walking backward as we crossed her yard. We entered her small house through the back porch.

I gestured to a chair in the breakfast nook and, once she'd sat down, I pulled out the adjacent chair, turning so that I faced her directly.

She blinked at me. "He's dying, isn't he?"

I nodded rather than speak the words aloud.

"We've got to do something," she insisted, half rising out of her chair.

I gently placed my hands on her shoulders and pushed her down. "Macy, he knows he's dying and it's all right with him."

"It isn't with me!"

"Harvey's ready to die."

"He might be, but I'm not ready to lose him." Big tears welled up in her eyes, threatening to spill over.

"It's not really up to you."

"What do you mean?"

"At the end of her life, Hannah refused further chemotherapy," I told her, my voice low and to my embarrassment riddled with remembered pain. "She knew it was useless and asked me to let her die. I wanted to keep her with me as long as I could, but that would've been selfish. I had to accede to her wishes. Harvey is asking the same of you."

Macy sniffled and the cats gathered around her feet as if to offer comfort. Sammy stood guard and eyed me, his message clear—if I made one wrong move I'd pay.

"I'm sorry," I said and instinctively put my arms around her. Then for reasons I may never understand, I bent down, moving my head toward hers, and sought out her lips. We kissed. This wasn't a peck on the cheek or the friendly kiss I'd exchanged with Winter and Leanne. This was a Kiss with a capital *K*, a real kiss that shocked me to the very marrow of my bones.

We broke apart as if we'd suddenly realized what we were doing. Macy looked, if anything, even more unsettled than I felt.

"Thank you," she whispered.

"For what?" She couldn't possibly be thanking me for the kiss.

"For spending time with Harvey and for telling me about Hannah's request."

"Sure," I said, striving for levity. "Happy to help."

I left shortly afterward, confused about what had made me kiss Macy and, more importantly, why I'd enjoyed it so much.

Chapter Twenty-Four

I didn't sleep well that night. I wasn't surprised when Macy didn't show up on Thursday. By her own admission she wasn't good at completing projects. But this mysterious absence was due to more than that. I knew it in my gut, the same way I knew the kiss we shared was special.

"Have you heard from Macy today?" I asked Linda. I didn't want to say too much but I was curious. She might have called with a plausible excuse that Linda hadn't bothered to pass on.

"No. You mean you haven't, either?" Linda's eyes narrowed slightly. "You didn't say anything to upset her, did you?"

"Me?" I asked. I shot Linda a hard look, but not because I was angry. I might be her employer, but every so often she slipped into the role of substitute mother. I was astonished at how willing Linda was to come to Macy's defense.

I tried to minimize my interest by saying in a calmer voice, "I'm sure Macy will be in later this afternoon. If not, she'll be here tomorrow."

"I'm sure she will," Linda said, then added, "We just love her."

I looked to my trusted nurse for an explanation. I didn't quite understand how this had happened. Had they *all* fallen for Macy? In less than two weeks?

Linda's mouth quirked with the beginnings of a smile. "Well, first, I don't suppose you've noticed, but she chats with all the children before and after their visits."

Linda was right; I hadn't noticed.

"It's like watching you with the kids. They take to Macy immediately."

That made sense now that she'd mentioned it. As I'd observed before, Macy was like a child in her whimsies and enthusiasms. "What does she talk to them about?"

"All sorts of things. With the Branson boy, she showed him the lion hiding in the grass, and with the Farinelli girl she chatted about hair clips. She and Ellen Roche discussed dogs at great length. The children relax and laugh, and it makes their visits here less stressful. I haven't figured Macy out, but I like her."

I liked her, too, and it was starting to concern me.

"She's funny. And generous." Apparently, Linda wasn't finished singing Macy's praises. "The other morning she brought in homemade granola bars for everyone. Did you try one?" When I shook my head, she went on. "Too bad. Anyway, Macy said the recipe began as a treat for her bird feeder and she just kept throwing stuff in. It tasted so good, she turned it into granola bars and bought birdseed for the feeder."

I grinned, although I was determined not to let Linda—or anyone else—know what was happening between Macy and me. Not that anything *was* happening. But I'd actually kissed a woman I professed to dislike. To complicate the situation, I hadn't stopped thinking about that kiss. Correction, I *couldn't* stop thinking about it. An even bigger mystery was the fact that it had felt so . . . I'll admit it—kissing Macy felt *right*. Everything about the two of us together was so wrong, it simply hadn't occurred to me that I'd enjoy holding her in my arms. Kissing her . . .

The rest of the day I felt a sense of expectation. No one needed to spell out what caused this feeling. I was waiting for Macy, and that just plain annoyed me.

She never did show up.

Friday morning I arrived at the gym in a bad mood. It didn't take Ritchie long to comment.

"What's with you, man?"

I mumbled something noncommittal about lack of sleep, which was true enough. I did my regular three-mile jog on the treadmill, speeding up the pace so I finished a minute earlier than usual.

I was in the shower by the time Ritchie appeared in the change room. He made some remark I didn't catch and I ignored him. To my surprise he was smiling when we met at the lockers. I'd assumed he'd give me a wide berth, which was what I wanted. Instead, he was chortling away, acting as if he knew something I didn't.

"I've seen that look before," Ritchie said.

"What look?" I asked, letting my impatience show.

"The one you're wearing. You've got a woman on your mind, and I'll bet I know who it is."

I could see there was no use trying to keep this to myself, so I blurted it out. "I kissed Macy."

My brother-in-law hooted. "I *knew* it." He aimed his index finger at me. "Didn't I say so? Didn't I tell you that you've got a thing for her? Would you admit it? Oh, no, not you. Not the great Dr. E."

"You haven't even met her," I reminded him.

"True."

"Then how can you claim you've known all along that I have this so-called thing for her?"

"Easy," Ritchie said, opening his locker door and turning his back to me. "You talk about her constantly."

"Because she irritates me."

Ritchie threw me a knowing look over his shoulder. "Irritates you enough to kiss her."

True. But I'd rather not discuss it anymore.

"So, you kissed her," Ritchie went on. "Why is that such a big deal?"

"This was a real kiss," I muttered. "Not a friendly little peck on the cheek."

"In other words, you sucked face."

I cast him a pained look. "How old are you? Fourteen?"

Ritchie shrugged off my censure. "Why are you so shaken up? You kissed her. You've kissed other women since Hannah died. Right?"

I sat down on the bench and leaned forward, resting my elbows on my knees. "Those weren't real kisses. That kiss with Macy was hot." I paused for a moment, trying to explain. "I always thought I'd feel guilty if I ever kissed another woman. *Really* kissed her, I mean."

"And you didn't?"

"No, and that bothers me." There was a whole lot that bothered me about that kiss. The fact that I wasn't consumed by guilt was merely the first of a long list.

"You *want* to feel guilty?" Ritchie demanded. "Do you think Hannah's looking down on you in disapproval? Is that it?"

"No." I shook my head for emphasis. "I don't know what I feel." That was a big part of the problem. What I'd expected to feel was regret and it hadn't happened.

"I guessed all along that Macy was the one," he crowed again.

"She isn't." I stood and reached for my jacket. I was sorry I'd said anything because Ritchie just wouldn't drop it.

"You enjoyed kissing her, didn't you?"

I could feel it coming. I decided then and there not to answer.

"Kissing her has you all twisted up inside and now you're confused."

He got that right. I was more than confused, I was completely bewildered by what had taken place between Macy and me. "I'm not even sure I like her," I said.

"Oh, you like her," Ritchie insisted in that annoying way of his.

I refuse to believe I'm that easily read. Ritchie's my closest friend, but there are times he can be a real pain in the butt.

"Do you have plans for tonight?" Ritchie asked as we left the gym.

Today was Friday, when I used to volunteer at the free medical clinic until the incident with Shamika and her abuser. A replacement had been found and in some ways that was probably best.

"I'm going to call Leanne," I said, and instantly felt relieved at having made a decision. No, at having made *that* decision. We were supposed to talk about seeing a movie this weekend, anyway.

Ritchie scratched his chin. "Leanne?" he repeated. "Not Macy."

"Definitely not Macy." I needed time to clear my head and half hoped she wouldn't be at the office today, either.

Uncharacteristically, Ritchie refrained from

launching into another series of questions and comments.

"See you Monday," he said once we were outside. He began walking toward his office.

"Catch up with you then." I took off in the opposite direction.

I hoofed it the few blocks to my office building and glared at Larry the security guard as I went in. I wanted him to know I didn't appreciate the fact that he'd let Macy into the clinic before office hours. With everyone else Larry was inflexible; with Macy he'd been prepared to bend the rules. As far as I was concerned, Macy got her own way far too often. She wouldn't with me again.

Just as I'd feared, she was at the clinic when I got there. She had her earphones plugged in and if she noticed my arrival she gave no indication. That suited me; the less contact I had with her the better.

"What time did Macy deign to show up?" I asked Linda.

"About ten minutes ago. What makes you ask?"

I wasn't accustomed to having Linda question my questions. "Nothing," I murmured and hurried toward my office where I put on my white jacket and slipped the stethoscope around my neck before going to the first exam room.

By noon it was apparent that Macy had made substantial progress on the mural. The sketch was completely finished now and she'd started painting. The colors she'd chosen were bright and bold, acrylics rather than oils. The entire office seemed enthralled with her work, judging by all the chatter about what a wonderful job she was doing.

I should've been pleased but in my present frame of mind, I was only interested in finding fault with her. She was impeding me, not physically, but emotionally. Having her so close made me uncomfortable.

I wanted her out of my proximity and, even more, out of my head. What troubled me most was how much I thought about that kiss and the way it'd made me feel alive again. I couldn't get past the idea that, regardless of what Hannah had said in her letter, I didn't have any right to feel like that. Alive, when Hannah wasn't.

Every time I fantasized about kissing Macy again, I felt as if I was losing control of who I was. I hated that sensation and I wanted to shake it off.

At lunchtime, I left my office door open and reached for the phone. I knew Macy was within earshot because she was sitting with Linda. The other staff members had gathered around her like those jungle creatures she'd painted converging at a water hole. I could hear their banter and high spirits.

I usually close my office door during our lunch break. I value the peace and use that hour to make phone calls, many of which have to be done in private. However, I wanted, *needed,* Macy to hear me talking to Leanne.

I got hold of Leanne on her cell phone.

"Hello, Michael," she said, and the welcome in her voice felt like a soothing balm.

"How have you been?"

"I'm doing well, and you?"

"I'm fine," I said, wondering how long we'd carry on this mundane conversation.

"I was going to call you," she said. "About the movie. Sorry I haven't gotten around to it. But I do want to go. Would you rather we went on Saturday or Sunday?"

"What about this evening? Are you free?"

"Sure," Leanne said. "Do you still want to see an action film? There's that new Tarantino. I'll cover my eyes during the violent parts."

"Sounds like it's not the kind of movie you're fond of."

She hesitated. "The truth is, I don't think I'd be good company at any movie. I've been depressed for the past couple of days. I told you Mark's in Afghanistan? He just got there. His mother gave me his e-mail address and I wrote to him. He . . . blocked my name so anything I send him will be automatically returned."

"Ouch."

"Yeah, that's exactly the way I felt."

"Did you find out what he's doing there?"

"He . . . he's working as a helicopter mechanic

for one of the big contractors there. A friend of his got him on."

"A helicopter mechanic?" That seemed odd, since Mark was an accountant.

"He worked on helicopters when he was in the army. Then, later, after he finished his tour of duty, he went into accounting and became a CPA. We met while he was taking classes and got married a year later."

Of course, it made sense that he couldn't continue as a CPA with embezzling charges against him.

"Muriel—that's his mother—said he took the job because it's so lucrative and he'll be able to pay off the hospital and the fine—but this is a war zone. I'm worried about him. Maybe I shouldn't be . . . but I can't help it."

In similar circumstances, I'd be worried, too. "I'm sorry, Leanne."

"I probably shouldn't have said anything."

"Let me take your mind off Mark," I said. "Let's go out for dinner," I suggested. "I owe you a meal."

"Oh, Michael, you don't owe me anything."

"I'd *like* to take you to dinner," I said. "How about if we meet after work, have dinner and look over the movies? We'll make a decision together."

"Okay. Thank you."

I appreciated her willingness. Partly because I figured Macy, not to mention Linda, was listening,

I went on to talk about the meal she'd prepared for me. "I really enjoyed having an honest-to-good-ness home-cooked dinner," I said.

I must have overdone it; the next thing I knew, Linda was standing outside my office, closing the door.

"Having you over gave me a good excuse to turn on the oven," Leanne said, and I could hear the smile in her voice. "I'm still dining on the left-overs. This recipe freezes well. I should've sent some home with you."

"That wasn't necessary." I could feel how red my face was. In my awkward attempt to send a message to Macy, I'd embarrassed myself in front of my entire staff. I'd also taken advantage of Leanne's friendship. I was ashamed of myself and wanted to blame Macy; however, I was the one at fault and I knew it.

Fifteen minutes later I stepped out of the office ready to meet my first patient of the afternoon. Linda handed over the file and stared at me accus-ingly.

I met her look straight on. "You have something you want to say?" I asked.

"Macy left."

I glanced behind her and noticed that the wall was only about a quarter finished. "And your point is?"

"My point is," she said stiffly, "she got your message."

"I don't know what you're talking about." Pride wouldn't let me own up to my poorly disguised scheme.

Linda didn't answer. She scowled at me and shook her head. I wasn't having a good day and being rebuked by someone I respected made me feel worse than ever.

I was still astonished by how completely Macy had won over Linda—and not just Linda, either. There was everyone on my staff and the security guard, and Ritchie championed her, too. The woman appeared to have magical powers. Which was fitting, I thought wryly, considering her fairy-tale house.

Okay, fine, Macy was a good person. I'd agree with that. Hannah might've believed Macy would make me laugh, but my dear wife hadn't realized how utterly mismatched Macy and I were.

The kiss was a fluke and wouldn't be repeated. That was the end of that. Leanne and I would go to dinner and I'd make an effort to get to know her. Based on how this evening went, I might even ask her to attend the awards banquet with me two weeks from now.

Chapter Twenty-Five

M acy would've left Michael's office early that afternoon, anyway. She'd been contracted to record another radio ad at two o'clock. This one was for a big charity event to be held in July. The producer said her voice was pleasant and engaging, and the more commercials she read, the more familiar she'd become to the listening audience. According to him, a recognizable voice evoked a sense of trust.

The money wouldn't buy her a vacation home in the San Juan Islands, but it was decent. The only reason Macy had stayed at Michael's office for lunch was that she enjoyed his staff.

She left the office at precisely 12:55 p.m. and went to retrieve her bike. Larry, the guy in security, had promised to keep an eye on it for her. The middle-aged retired military man was a sweetheart. She didn't understand why almost everyone seemed so wary of him. The guy had a big heart and he loved cats.

"You ready for your bike, Macy?" Larry asked as she approached his desk.

"Please, and again, thanks so much."

"No problem. Anytime you need me to look after something, you let me know. I'll lock it up, and it'll be safer than inside Fort Knox."

Despite feeling so dispirited, she managed a

smile. She followed Larry into the basement. He'd confided in her that after retiring from the air force, he'd taken the security job to help his youngest daughter with college expenses.

"He doesn't like me."

"Who, Macy?"

"Oh, sorry, I didn't realize I'd spoken out loud. I do that sometimes." Living with cats, Macy habitually verbalized her thoughts and often without being aware of it. "I guess I'm not his type. After Hannah and all."

"Did you say something?"

"No, no, sorry, it's nothing." Except that it bothered her, especially after the way Michael had kissed her. She just wasn't good with romantic relationships. They hadn't worked out before, so her expectations weren't high when it came to Michael, either. That kiss, though . . . A single kiss and it'd been so exciting. So exquisite.

For hours afterward she'd walked around in a daze. It was as though she was fourteen all over again, when Tommy Whittier had kissed her for the first time. The only time, actually. She'd loved Tommy with all the passion in her teenage heart. His kiss had stayed with her all these years and now . . . now Michael's kiss was the first to match that incredible sensation. Why, oh, why did it have to be him?

Larry got her bicycle and, after securing her helmet, she was off to the recording studio. As she hit the Seattle streets, her mind spun as fast as the wheels of her bike.

Michael couldn't have been any more obvious about his feelings if he'd rented a billboard. He wasn't interested. She'd heard his phone conversation loud and clear, just like he'd intended. He wanted her to know he had another date with the woman called Leanne. Even the sound of her name was elegant and refined. Macy had gotten her own name when her mother went into labor while shopping. She supposed she should be grateful it hadn't happened at Neiman Marcus. Macy would admit she was neither sophisticated nor stylish. She'd never fit in with his friends.

That kiss, though, had surprised her. Michael's reaction told her he'd been equally taken aback. He wanted her to know it had been an accident, and that he regretted it.

She didn't.

Macy didn't realize how upset she was until she arrived at the recording studio and had no recollection of getting there. She'd pedaled through maybe a dozen streets, and the entire time she'd thought of Michael.

Fine, she decided. He didn't have to tell her twice. She'd do everything within her power to stay out of his way. He wouldn't even know she was there. As quickly as possible she'd finish— yes, finish—that darn mural and that would be it. They need never see each other again.

The recording session didn't go as well as the previous one and Macy had to read the commercial twice as often as any of her other bookings.

The producer wasn't pleased. On her way out the door, he patted her shoulder and reassured her that everyone had an off day now and then. He followed that by letting her know he wouldn't be as forgiving the next time.

Wonderful.

She might lose the best-paying job she'd found to date and all because of Dr. Michael Everett.

Macy climbed on her bike, grateful she could just go home. She hadn't talked to Harvey since Wednesday. He'd been avoiding her and she was going to put an end to that. Now more than ever, Macy was determined to persuade him not to give up on life. He was the only family she had in the area, since her parents had retired to New Mexico and her brother lived in Hawaii. Okay, so Harvey wasn't actual family; it just felt as though he was. He'd squirm and fuss if she ever told him, but he was grandfather and friend in one, and she loved him.

Macy was less than a mile from the house when it happened, although she wasn't quite sure how. What she remembered later was that one moment she was on her bicycle, and the next she was jolted from behind. Before she had time to react or even brace herself, she went flying over the handlebars.

She landed hard on the asphalt and must have

blacked out for a second. When she came to, she heard the sound of screeching brakes and loud voices. A man was bending over her and yelling for someone to call 9-1-1.

From then on, all she felt was pain. White-hot pain in her head, her arms, her legs. A group of people gathered around her and everyone seemed to be giving her advice.

"Don't move until the aid car gets here."

"Take deep breaths."

"Don't close your eyes."

Macy tried to do what everyone asked, but it was impossible.

A siren wailed in the distance. Then two men arrived and a blood-pressure cuff was slapped on her upper arm. Her neck was secured in a brace and she was being lifted. When she glanced down, she saw her bicycle helmet lying on the ground. It looked as if someone had taken a sledgehammer to it.

The paramedic seemed busy, but she had an important question and grabbed his sleeve, holding on until he turned to her.

"Yes?" he said. He seemed annoyed that she'd interrupted his work.

"Is that *my* blood on the pavement?" She'd always been a little squeamish about the sight of blood.

He nodded.

"Is my bike in any better shape than the

helmet?" That bike had cost more than she could really afford and she'd hate to lose it.

"Afraid not. Listen, I'd rather you didn't talk."

"Okay." She closed her eyes. The pain was bad. She wasn't kidding herself about that. She could deal with it more easily when she didn't have to look at anything or anyone. Instead, she concentrated on taking one breath at a time.

The paramedic asked questions, which she did her best to answer. The aid-car siren screamed as it wove in and out of traffic. The next thing Macy knew, they were at the hospital and everything started again.

She was examined by a doctor, who ordered a battery of tests. Macy was wheeled into X-ray, then taken for an MRI. They stitched her up and she had bandages on her head, her knees and her arms. There wasn't a single spot on her entire body that didn't throb with pain, despite the medication.

Everything hurt, up to and including her eyelids. People stood around her and spoke, acting like she wasn't even in the room. They were all saying how fortunate she was. From where she was lying, with her head pounding as though someone had put it in a vise, she didn't feel too fortunate.

A familiar voice joined the others. Certain she must be hearing wrong, Macy forced her eyes open and looked up.

"Michael?" she whispered, shocked to see him.

Without answering, he took her hand and wrapped his fingers around hers. His hold was tight and yet his touch was the most comforting one she'd received.

"What are you doing here?" she asked. How could he have known she'd been in an accident?

"You gave them my name," he told her.

"I . . . couldn't have. I did?"

"It's all right. I came as soon as the hospital phoned." He stroked her head. "I'll be back after I speak with the attending physician. Will you be okay?"

She nodded, stunned that she didn't remember mentioning Michael's name. The paramedics had asked so many questions; she seemed to recall that, among other things, they'd asked who they should contact on her behalf. Had she really said Michael?

She was mortified to realize that of all the people in the world she'd given them Michael's name. Perhaps she'd said he was her physician. That was it.

Maybe.

The reality of time escaped her; he could have been away two hours or fifteen minutes. When he returned, she stared up at him, hardly knowing what to say. She felt dreadful that she'd taken him from the office.

"Were you just here or was that a long time ago?" she asked him.

"About five minutes."

"Oh. It must be the pain."

"Probably. But the Tylenol should kick in soon."

"Can I get out of here? Someone needs to feed the cats, and then there's Sammy. Harvey depends on me to feed him. Sammy's fifty percent Harvey's dog but he—I mean Harvey—refuses to admit it. So Sammy comes to visit and stays for dinner every night." She paused. "He usually eats on the porch. Because of the cats."

"I'm taking you home."

Macy felt tears in her eyes, so grateful that she was close to dissolving with emotion. "I'm s-sorry to trouble you."

"It's no trouble."

"Wh-what about your date?"

"I phoned Leanne. We put it off until tomorrow."

"Oh . . . sorry."

"Stop apologizing."

"Okay. Except that I feel responsible and you made such a point of arranging this date with her . . . I know it's important to you."

Michael pressed his finger to her lips. "Stop."

"I didn't mean to give them your name," she mumbled against his finger. "I must've been talking to myself again."

He sent her an odd look. "Don't explain that."

The ride to her house was miserable and seemed to take forever. While he drove, Michael gave her a detailed medical report. Most of what he said went over her head. Basically, nothing was broken. She had several deep cuts. That much Macy knew, although she barely remembered being stitched up. The primary concern was the possibility of concussion, he explained. She needed someone to stay the night with her.

"I'll call a friend," she told Michael. Joy Williamson could probably come over. Or maybe Sherry Franklin . . .

"No, I can do it," he said.

"You?"

"I know what to look for. I'll be waking you every few hours and checking your eyes. To see if your pupils are dilated."

Once they got to the house, Michael helped her out of the car. Wearing an unusually worried expression, Harvey stood on her porch and held open the front door. Sammy immediately started to whine. Her cats didn't seem to care what the problem was; they didn't take kindly to having their dinner delayed. But that was cats for you.

"I'll get you into bed and then feed them," Michael promised.

Macy tried to assure the cats that food was forthcoming, but Snowball, Lovie and Peace weren't interested in excuses. When her cats were cranky, they let everyone in the vicinity know.

Michael discreetly helped her change into a nightgown—really an oversize T-shirt with pictures of kittens all over it. Once she was settled in bed, her head nestled in the pillows, Macy was almost comfortable. She could hear Michael and Harvey talking in the living room, but their voices were too low to distinguish the words.

"Talk louder," she called out and winced at the sound of her own voice. If she was the main topic of conversation, she figured she had a right to hear what was being said.

The two men were silent then or they'd moved out of earshot—it was difficult to tell from her bedroom. The oddest things were going through her mind and she must have fallen asleep because when she opened her eyes Michael was standing over her. The curtains had been drawn, and he'd turned on the bedside lamp.

She blinked, blinded by the light, and blurted out, "Mom was right. I should've worn new underwear."

"Why?"

"Because I was in an accident. My mother told me that putting on nice underwear's important in case I'm in an accident."

Michael seemed to find that amusing, although she didn't understand why.

Another time he helped her up and into the bathroom, then stood outside the door, giving her privacy. He was so gentle with her.

"Where are you sleeping?" she asked as he supported her with an arm about her waist. They slowly made their way back into the bedroom.

"On the sofa."

"Oh, dear. That's Lovie's bed."

"So I discovered."

Macy felt the need to explain.

"I tried to convince her to sleep elsewhere when I got the new sofa," Macy said. "But she made it clear that she'd slept on the old one and she was sleeping on this one, too, and she didn't care how much I paid for it."

Another smile.

Macy tilted her head to the side. "You're quite handsome when you smile. Did I tell you that before?" Reaching out she touched his cheek with the tips of her fingers. His face was bristly because he needed a shave. "You should smile more often."

"I'll take it under advisement."

The final time he woke her it was around four in the morning. His clothes were badly wrinkled and he looked as if he hadn't slept all night.

When Macy woke on her own, it was six. She sat up carefully and waited for the pain to assault her. The throbbing in her head was nearly gone. Although every muscle in her body cried out in protest, she moved her legs, first one and then the other, over the side of the bed. She sat there for several minutes until she'd regained her bearings.

When she felt brave enough, she stood, holding on to her nightstand with both hands. Once she was upright, she felt more confident. Taking baby steps she walked out of her bedroom and into the living room and saw Michael sprawled on her sofa. One arm was flung above his head and one leg draped over the edge, with his foot resting on the braided rug. Lovie and Peace were sleeping on his chest. Snowball lay on the back of the sofa, curled up in a fluffy white ball. Sammy was asleep, too, snoring softly next to the coffee table. The cats had apparently called a truce and permitted him to spend the night.

Lovie woke up first. On seeing Macy, she stood and stretched, arching her back and digging her nails into Michael's shirt. His eyes flew open and, when he saw Macy in her kitten shirt, he smiled.

"You shouldn't be up," he said.

"But I am."

He sat up awkwardly, displacing the two cats. "How do you feel?"

"Like I took a flying leap off my bicycle. How do I look?"

He grinned almost boyishly. "Like you took a flying leap off your bicycle."

Standing now, he ran his fingers through his already disheveled hair. "I could use some coffee."

"Me, too." It suddenly occurred to her that Michael had probably missed dinner on account of her. "When's the last time you ate?"

"I found something in your refrigerator."

Macy went still. "What did it taste like?"

"I don't know. I think it was leftover salmon casserole."

"It wasn't. That was cat food."

His expression was priceless. His eyes widened and he made jerky movements with his tongue against his lips, as though attempting to banish the taste from his mouth.

If it hadn't hurt so much to move, Macy would've laughed. Instead, she held up her hand. "I often make my own, so don't worry. You weren't eating processed cat food. Didn't you find it a bit blah?"

"Not really. It was good, but no wonder the cats were all over me."

When she moved toward the coffeemaker, Michael stopped her. "I'll make it."

"Thank you."

"Once it's finished brewing, I need to get home. After I have a cup, of course."

Macy nodded. "I don't know how to thank you."

He seemed eager to be on his way. The coffeepot was only half full when he grabbed mugs for each of them. He gulped his down, then started for the door.

He hesitated. "Promise you'll call me if you need anything," he said.

"Sure." She didn't want him to leave and yet she could hardly believe he'd been here at all.

"Harvey said he'd check on you later this morning."

Macy sat in a kitchen chair, cradling the mug between her hands. The cats were at her feet. Sammy, too. "Thank you," she whispered. "I'm so . . . sorry to have been such a bother."

Michael cupped one side of her face. He looked down at her and for the briefest moment she thought he might kiss her again. That was what she wanted him to do. He didn't. "You were no bother, Macy. None whatsoever. I'm just grateful you weren't badly injured."

Then he walked through the living room to the front door, skirting paintings and piles of books and the laundry basket that now sat on the floor.

Fastidious Dr. Everett maneuvering through the chaos of her home. That one image epitomized the differences between them.

Macy's heart sank.

Chapter Twenty-Six

When I left Macy, I was convinced she'd be perfectly fine without me. She revealed no signs of having suffered a concussion, and she should recover fully in the next week, with a few scars to show for the experience. I insisted she take a couple of days off and not worry about completing the mural until she felt up to it.

I needed to get away—because I'd been tempted to kiss her . . . again. I couldn't understand it, and yet I was drawn to her. Several times during the night I'd stood and watched her sleep. Once I pressed my lips to her forehead in a chaste good-night kiss, then quickly, guiltily, hurried away from her room.

From Macy's I went to a drive-through latte stand and ordered a double espresso. I sat in the car in a nearby parking lot, sipping my coffee. I needed the additional caffeine to kick me into gear. Sleeping on a sofa with two cats on my chest and one just above my head, not to mention a dog on the carpet beside me, wasn't the ideal condition for peaceful slumber. Besides, the dog snored.

A second sip of the espresso started to revive me. I closed my eyes and remembered how I'd reacted when I got the call that Macy had been injured. The hospital hadn't given me any details. I was well aware that the administration's policy was not to relay a patient's medical condition over the phone, yet I'd demanded to know the extent of her injuries. It didn't matter; they wouldn't tell me.

Except for a few occasions in Hannah's last months, I can't remember getting to the hospital faster in my ten years as a physician. My heart felt like it might explode by the time I made it to the E.R. In the beginning I was afraid Macy had been seriously hurt and then, when I learned the true extent of her injuries, I was so angry with her I could barely speak. Thankfully she'd been unable to ascertain my mood. I wanted to grab her by the shoulders and shake her for riding her bike in the crazy Seattle traffic, especially during rush hour. She should know better!

Shock, fear, anger, relief and finally acceptance. I felt each one of those emotions more powerfully than I'd felt anything since Hannah's death. These stages were classic reactions to the news of trauma, whether accident or illness. I'd often seen families shift from one stage to the next while dealing with some health crisis. I'd gone through it myself when Hannah was first diagnosed. I was unprepared and frankly unwilling to feel these same gut-wrenching emotions for Macy . . . and yet I had.

I'd set my cell phone to wake me every two hours so I could check her for signs of concussion. Thank God there hadn't been any. Thank God her injuries weren't worse.

Interesting that I'd turned to God in gratitude on this particular night.

I don't have a good relationship with Him. Hannah was big on faith. Not religion, but faith. She believed, and while I'd been raised by religious parents who dragged me to church, I'd abandoned even the vestiges of belief when Hannah got sick.

I was still angry with God. Angry with the world. Just plain angry at Hannah's death. She was the most decent human being I'd ever known. Surely there was someone else, some low-life He could easily have substituted. Oh, no, He had to take Hannah. Forgiveness for this plan of His wasn't coming anytime soon. Now here I was, thanking Him for sparing Macy.

What upset me was that I didn't actually know what I felt for Macy. For reasons I had yet to understand, I did feel some sort of . . . attachment to her. I wasn't happy about it. But the feelings were there and they were gaining intensity.

I sipped the coffee, which had cooled considerably, making me wonder how long I'd been sitting in the parking lot analyzing what had taken place during the night. Trying to figure out how my emotions had undergone such a transformation. How I'd moved from resistance to . . . acceptance of this woman in my life. From annoyance to— what? Fascination.

Once I got home I read the paper, then put on my shorts and running shoes and hit the pavement. Physical exertion always helps me sort out my problems.

This time, however, it didn't work. All I could think about was Macy. How was she doing on her own with those cats of hers and Sammy? What about the old man? I shouldn't have left her. I should phone and make sure she was all right.

Macy. Macy. Macy.

Her name reverberated in my head with every step I took.

And no matter how fast I ran, I couldn't get her out of my mind.

The first thing I did when I returned home, sweating and panting, was stumble toward the phone. I had her number written on a pad next to it and dialed, still gasping for breath.

Harvey answered.

"How's Macy?" I asked, instantly alarmed that her neighbor was at the house this early. It was barely nine.

"You took off like a bat out of hell," Harvey said. "What got into you?"

"I had an appointment," I lied. The truth was, I ran every Saturday and did consider it a standing appointment—with myself. Okay, I ran *almost* every Saturday. "Let me talk to Macy."

"I can't."

"Why not?"

"She's taking a shower."

"Is the door open?" Harvey's hearing wasn't that great and, if Macy passed out, it could be some time before he noticed and called for help.

I immediately asked another question. "Did she remember to cover her stitches so they wouldn't get wet?" I'd gone over the instructions with her last night, but she'd been pretty much out of it and might have forgotten. I berated myself for not reviewing them this morning; I'd been in too much of a hurry.

"Don't shout at me," Harvey barked.

"I'm not shouting," I said, and I wasn't.

"Yes, you are, and furthermore I can only answer one question at a time. No, the bathroom door isn't open. I'm not a voyeur!"

"She could pass out!"

"Macy? She's not the type."

"It isn't a *type*," I said, doing my best to remain calm. "Macy got a hard knock to the head."

"If you're so worried about her, why did you leave?"

"I probably shouldn't have," I admitted.

To my surprise Harvey laughed. "She'll do that to you," he said.

"Say that again," I said, uncertain what he meant.

"Macy," he told me. "She wears you down. When she first moved here, I did everything I could to discourage her. I didn't need her to be my friend. I didn't want anything to do with her, wacky dame that she is. I built that fence for a reason.

"She overlooked every rebuff. I ignored her when she stopped by to visit. I didn't say a word, and you know what? I doubt she even noticed. She chattered away, talked about everything under the sun. If I told her to scat, she'd disappear for a few minutes and then come back with something for me to eat. She'd always say she got cranky when she was hungry, too. I doubt that girl's been cranky a day in her life."

I could hear the affection in his voice. This was an unusually long speech for Harvey.

"How are you feeling?" I asked him.

Harvey snorted. "Don't change the subject."

I was beginning to grow concerned about the old coot. He wanted to deal with death on his own terms, but that didn't mean it had to be painful—or happen any sooner than necessary. If I could steer him toward a physician, I would.

"Macy's wearing you down, same as me," Harvey insisted. "I can see it in your eyes. You're falling for her, and all I can say is God help you."

"Don't be ridiculous," I scoffed.

"Don't worry. I won't say anything to her about it."

"How's she doing?" I asked again.

"It's hard to keep her still."

"Do your best," I told him and didn't envy him the task.

"You coming back or not?" Harvey demanded.

I briefly toyed with the idea and quickly decided against it. "Not."

Harvey chuckled. "Thought as much. Yup, I was right. She's got you wrapped around her little finger, just like she does me. Fight it all you want, but it's not going to do you a bit of good."

Before I could tell him how wrong he was, Harvey disconnected the line.

For half a second I was tempted to call back and argue with him. Fortunately, common sense took over and I walked away from the phone.

When I stepped out of the shower, I felt refreshed. From this point forward, I was determined to avoid Macy and Harvey, too. She could finish the mural, I'd pay her what I owed and I wouldn't see her again. That decision brought me a measure of relief. No woman who wasn't Hannah was going to dominate my thoughts. Especially one as reckless and unpredictable as Macy. I meant it, too.

I'd agreed to pick up Leanne at six. Truthfully, I was grateful to have a reason to get out of the house. Two or three times during the day, despite keeping busy, I'd felt the urge to check on Macy again. The woman was becoming a habit, an addiction I had to break.

Leanne was ready when I got to her apartment. She opened the door and smiled at me. "How's your injured friend?" she asked.

"Better, thanks." I didn't want to go into details.

She smiled, and I was reminded that she was an exceptionally lovely woman. I once again considered asking her to attend that awards dinner with me, but once again held off. It wasn't for a couple of weeks. There was no rush.

"Have you picked out a movie?" I asked. I was fine with whatever she chose. When Hannah was alive, we used to take turns choosing. I actually enjoyed a few "chick flicks" and she'd sat through more than one techno-thriller.

"I thought we should do that together," Leanne

said. She had the paper spread out across the kitchen counter and we stood there and reviewed the listings.

In the end we decided to watch a new movie that was being compared to last year's Academy Award winner. Neither of us had seen it and, frankly, I wasn't sure I'd like it. Still, it was getting great reviews, so others must have found it entertaining and meaningful.

She suggested we attend the movie, then figure out what we wanted to do about dinner. At the theater, I purchased our tickets, after which I stood in a long line to get us a large buttered popcorn. As we sat through the movie, which took place in India, my mind drifted frequently as I contemplated giving up my medical practice and volunteering to serve in a third world country. The need was huge, I'd tell myself, and then . . . then I'd be pulled right back into the plot.

I mentioned dinner as we strolled out of the multiplex.

"After all that popcorn I couldn't eat a thing."

I'd certainly gobbled my share and I wasn't hungry, either, but I didn't want the evening to end. However, spending time with Leanne wasn't the only reason. My fear was that once I got home, I wouldn't be able to resist calling Macy.

"How about if we have a cup of coffee," Leanne said. "I'd like to hear what you think."

"Think? About what?"

"The movie."

"Oh . . . of course." I hadn't really formed an opinion. I hadn't watched it consistently or paid very careful attention.

We found a café that had outdoor seating and ordered cappuccinos, then made small talk until our coffees arrived.

"I really enjoyed the film," Leanne said. "I liked how they set everything up from the very first scene. You could feel the lead character's isolation and it foreshadowed where the story was going."

I nodded, although I hadn't really been aware of that.

Leanne was quite knowledgeable about story structure and plot. She spoke for several minutes, then stopped, looking embarrassed. "Oh, Michael, I'm so sorry," she murmured, staring down into her half-filled mug.

"Sorry?" I repeated. "For what?"

"For talking on and on like that and not giving you a chance to say anything."

I smiled and squeezed her hand. "I appreciated hearing your insights. If you hadn't mentioned it, I would never have noticed how well the various plotlines were connected. And I thoroughly enjoyed seeing you this animated." Unlike me, she was a pretty sophisticated filmgoer. Come to think of it, Hannah used to have insights like that, too. She'd joked more than once that I only appreciated the gasoline explosions. Not true!

Leanne exhaled and seemed relieved that I hadn't been offended. "Mark and I used to watch a lot of movies together," she told me. "He has an incredible memory for facts about actors, directors and producers. I used to try and stump him, but he always outdid me." She grew sad and lowered her eyes. "I wonder if the army shows movies over in Afghanistan. Even if they do, I don't know if Mark would have access to them. Not that I'd find out from him."

I wasn't sure what to tell her, so I changed the subject and probably not with a lot of finesse. "Hannah loved to cry at the movies." I never understood it. If the movie had a happy-ever-after ending, she'd weep because she was happy. If some tragedy befell the protagonist, she could go through an entire wad of tissues.

Leanne smiled. "That sounds like Hannah."

"What about you?" I asked.

"No," she admitted. "I'm not much of a crier."

We talked for a while longer; after an hour or so, we decided to leave.

Because our order was small, I left a generous tip for the waiter. I was about to suggest we take a stroll along the waterfront or ride the monorail to the Seattle Center, site of the 1962 World's Fair. That event had put Seattle on the map, my father had told me. Then Leanne yawned, a clear signal that she was ready to go home. I might not be able to decipher the finer points of a movie plot, but I could tell when a woman was eager for my company and when she wasn't.

We walked back to where I'd parked the car and I opened her door. It was still light out, but at this time of year, the sun didn't set until almost nine-thirty.

When we were close to her complex, Leanne glanced at me and said, "You don't need to walk me to my apartment."

"You want me just to drop you off?"

"Sure. Don't go to any trouble."

In other words, she wanted to make a quick escape. I'd be lying if I said my ego hadn't taken a hit. It wasn't that I intended to invite myself in to spend the night, but it would've been nice if she'd shown *some* sign of having enjoyed our time together.

"The curb will be fine," she said next.

"Okay."

Leanne must have detected my disappointment because she turned to look at me. "Michael, oh, my goodness, I'm being rude! Forgive me, please. Would you like to come up?"

"No, that's okay. I have things to do." Another lie.

"I can't believe I was so thoughtless."

"Leanne," I said, "it's okay. Really." I was sincere about that. If I'd accepted her invitation it would've been for the wrong reasons. I'd hoped to distract myself to avoid thinking about Macy. My motives weren't exactly pristine.

I pulled up to the curb.

"I had a wonderful time," Leanne said with a little too much enthusiasm.

"Me, too."

I started to get out of the car to open her door, but Leanne placed her hand on my arm and stopped me.

When I turned back she offered me a soft smile, slipped her arms around my neck and kissed me. The kiss was lengthy and passionate, as if she was trying to prove how much she'd enjoyed my company. When she finished I realized we'd both been trying too hard to find something that just wasn't there.

She knew it.

So did I.

Chapter Twenty-Seven

Have I ever asked anything of you before?" Ritchie asked, his breath coming in gasps as he kept pace with the treadmill. Usually he had his ears plugged with his iPod, but this morning he'd decided to hound me into rejoining the weekly poker match.

I pretended not to hear him.

"Michael." He tried again.

I glanced in his direction. "To answer your question, yes, you have. In fact, you seem to constantly be asking me to do one thing or another."

"It's a poker game. You used to love poker."

"I was young and foolish."

"So, what changed?" Ritchie asked, cocking one thick eyebrow.

I sighed. Okay, so Ritchie wanted me to sit in for Bill, whose wife had recently given birth to twins. Bill had taken my spot in the weekly game two years earlier, and now, with the demands of a young family, he felt he needed to bow out.

Ritchie was right; I really had liked my time with the guys. One night a week we set aside the concerns of our offices, our patients, taxes, malpractice insurance and everything else. One night a week we simply had fun, enjoying one another and our game of Texas Hold'em.

I don't mean to brag, but I'm fairly good at cards. However, I cared far more about the camaraderie I had with the guys than taking their quarters.

I might not be a tournament-quality player, but I could generally count on beating my friends and feeling superior for a couple of minutes. Patrick, Steve and Ritchie used to say I was lucky.

I didn't feel so lucky when Hannah learned she had cancer.

I quit playing after she was diagnosed. I didn't feel I could leave her for even one night. Because the cancer hadn't been detected until she was at stage four, I knew we had a struggle ahead of us. Hannah knew it, too; otherwise, she would've protested me giving up my poker night.

I'm not going to say it wasn't hard to abandon the game and my time with these friends. They were my buddies, who knew me better than anyone, other than Hannah. Other than family. I wasn't sure why I hadn't gone back. Well, for one thing, Ritchie had found a replacement and it didn't seem fair to show up a year later and announce that I'd returned and Bill would have to leave. On the other hand, we could've played with five, and Ritchie had invited me more than once. I'd always declined; I had no real desire to play. After a few times, Ritchie had stopped asking. Until this morning.

"Will you come?" Ritchie pressed. "We need you, man."

"I don't know." The same reluctance filled me, even if I couldn't explain why I was avoiding something I'd once enjoyed so much.

"When *will* you know?" Ritchie demanded.

This sounded like a schoolyard conversation. "Soon," I said.

"Call me before two—otherwise, I'll get someone else."

Ritchie was upset, and that was rare for him. Hannah and her brother had the same easygoing disposition. My indecision irritated him and he had no qualms about letting me know that. If I could've told him why I felt so reluctant, I would have.

When I got to the office, the first thing I did was

look at the mural. Macy hadn't been back since the accident, which meant she was still laid up. I'd checked in with Harvey a couple of times to see how she was doing. According to her neighbor, Macy was up and about, but still sore and miserable.

"When's Macy coming in?" Linda asked.

"I don't know," I snapped.

Linda's eyes widened and she glared at me. "There's no need to be rude," she snapped back.

"I'm sorry." I apologized rather than allow any dissension between us. "I haven't been in touch with Macy. When we spoke, I told her she could finish the mural as soon as she's up to it."

"You mean you haven't talked to her since the accident?"

"No. Not since Saturday, anyhow." My source had been her cantankerous neighbor, who seemed to take great delight in my interest.

"It's already Wednesday—I expected her back by now," Linda murmured. She shook her head and cast me a look similar to one my mother had used when I was a kid—the one that said she was disappointed in me.

I'd assumed Macy would want to finish the mural right away. I missed seeing her at the office, although I was only now admitting it. "She'll return as soon as she's ready," I told Linda.

"By the way, Dr. O'Malley phoned," Linda said. "I left the message on your desk."

"Thanks."

I entered my office, then sat down and reached for the pink slip. But it wasn't Patrick I was thinking about. Macy was front and center in my thoughts. I didn't like it, but I couldn't ignore this curiosity.

Before I had time to reconsider, I grabbed the phone and called Harvey. I'd already talked to him twice in the past four days, and both conversations had annoyed me. Still, that wasn't enough to dissuade me from phoning a third time. I needed to know that Macy was getting better, but I was determined not to call her.

"Yes?" Harvey barked into the receiver.

"This is Dr. Everett."

"I know who it is," he returned in the same bad mood he usually displayed.

"I'm calling to see how Macy is."

"Why don't you bother her instead of me? I'm not her nurse."

"I realize that," I said, clenching my teeth, "but you're her neighbor and her friend."

"I wouldn't be if I had a choice."

"How's she healing?"

He hesitated. "Not sure."

"Why not?" It sounded as if Harvey was in pain again. I wished he'd let me help him, the stubborn old fool.

"It isn't like I'm keeping tabs on her."

I was beginning to feel concerned. "You've seen her in the past twenty-four hours, haven't you?"

"Yeah," he muttered.

"How does she look?"

"All right, I guess. Black-and-blue. She's limping a bit, but that seems to be improving. I don't understand why you keep bugging me when she's got her own phone."

"I figured you'd be honest with me," I said, and while there was some truth to that, it wasn't the real reason I'd called him. I knew if I spoke to Macy directly, I'd find an excuse to visit—and if I went to see her, I'd end up kissing her again. That was not going to happen.

"You don't want to talk to Macy because you're falling for her."

Rather than address that comment, I chose to overlook it entirely. I wasn't arguing with Harvey. "If Macy needs anything, let me know."

"She won't, and even if she did I wouldn't call you."

The line was abruptly disconnected and I sat back in my leather chair, mulling over the conversation. I agreed with Harvey; I needed to call Macy myself, although I was reluctant to do so. My reasons were too complicated to explain to anyone else, especially a cranky old man who seemed increasingly scornful of me.

My next call was to Patrick who, besides being my friend and partner, was one of the poker group. I had a patient waiting, but with Patrick I knew I'd be on and off the phone in under a minute.

"I got your message," I said.

"You going to the game tonight?"

"I haven't decided."

"What's wrong with you, Michael? Are you afraid Hannah wouldn't want you to have fun?"

"Ah . . ." The comment felt like a slug in the gut.

"I've got to go. Listen," Patrick continued, "you have to be there tonight. No excuses, understand?"

"Okay, okay."

The line went dead. A tingling feeling raced down my spine. Had Patrick hit on something I hadn't considered? Ritchie and Patrick were telling me essentially the same thing. It went without saying that if Hannah were alive, she'd be the first one to encourage me to rejoin my friends.

At noon, I told Ritchie I'd be at his house by six-thirty. I could tell he was pleased. The more I thought about it, the more I looked forward to being with the guys again. It would be like old times—we'd laugh, exchange stories, eat pizza and drink beer. Then we'd play cards until we ran out of quarters—or I walked away, my pockets jingling with change.

I showed up fifteen minutes early.

"Glad you're here," Ritchie said. Max came downstairs and gave me a high five before racing back up. Without asking, Ritchie handed me a beer. "Pizza's on the way."

"With anchovies?"

"Would I order one without?"

"That's what I was hoping you'd say."

Hannah and Steph detested anchovies, and whenever the four of us ordered pizza, Ritchie and I made sure we shared one with double anchovies, just to prove that we were real men. We told little Max that the fish put hair on our chests, which was why the women refused to eat them. The joke was inane, but it always made us laugh.

Patrick got there next, and when he saw me he grinned. "About time," he said.

Steve was the last to arrive. He pulled into the driveway and the pizza delivery kid pulled in right behind him. Five minutes later, we each had a cold beer and a slice of pizza. The stories started and before long I was laughing so hard my sides hurt.

I felt almost as if I'd never been away. It'd been nearly two years since I'd played poker. Two years. That seemed impossible now that I realized how much I'd missed it.

We played until eleven. Steve won, and all I could say was that I'd gotten rusty and I'd get my money back the following week.

Just before we were ready to call it quits, Steve said, "I brought a welcome-back gift for Michael." He spoke in formal tones, and everyone looked in his direction.

My friend, an internal medicine specialist, was smiling from ear to ear.

"For me?" I asked in a falsetto voice, hoping it wasn't a practical joke.

"I was at a medical conference in Miami last weekend," Steve said, "and I picked these up while I was there." He opened a plain brown paper bag and with considerable ceremony laid out four fat cigars. "They're Cuban," he said proudly.

"You sure about that?" Patrick had always been the skeptic of the group.

"Smoke one and then you tell me," was Steve's comeback.

"Cuban?" I repeated. "Aren't they illegal?"

"Don't ask, brother, just enjoy."

"Yeah, Everett, don't look a gift horse in the mouth." This came from Ritchie, who already had the cigar clamped between his teeth.

I agreed. Who was I to question when and how Steve had procured these cigars? I bit off the end and lit up, too. The aroma from Ritchie's cigar wafted toward me. I closed my eyes as the sheer pleasure of it overtook me.

"Even if this isn't Cuban, it's still the best cigar I've ever had," Ritchie said appreciatively.

The four of us sat back, and although none of us smoked, once or twice a year we indulged in a cigar. Apparently, the tradition had continued without me.

"It's good to have you back," Steve said. He held out the cigar as if toasting me with the finest whiskey.

"Hear, hear," Patrick said.

"I'll second that," Ritchie added.

I looked around the room at my friends and felt their welcome. "It's good to be back," I told them and I meant it.

We sat there talking for another thirty minutes and then, because we all had to be at the office or hospital early the next morning, we called it a night.

On the drive home, I turned up the radio and sang golden oldies at the top of my voice. Once I got to the house, I was too keyed up and happy to sleep.

Happy.

I hadn't been truly happy since before Hannah died. The feeling now left me light-headed. I wandered from room to room and put in a CD—Neil Young's *Harvest Moon*, which Hannah had loved. If there'd been a woman nearby I would've asked her to dance.

As she did far too often, Macy drifted into my mind. I had the strongest urge to phone her. High on everything that had happened this evening, I wasn't thinking clearly. I was . . . happy, and I experienced a compelling need to tell someone how I felt.

Macy was the only person I could think of. I knew I'd regret this come morning. However, that wasn't enough to dissuade me.

I reached for the phone, then sank down onto the

sofa and dialed. The phone rang four times before she answered.

"Hello."

She sounded groggy. I'd obviously awakened her.

Now that she was on the line, I couldn't seem to speak. My first instinct was to hang up. But that would've been childish and I couldn't make myself do it.

"Macy," I croaked.

"Michael, is that you?"

"I'm afraid so," I admitted.

"Is anything wrong?" she asked. "It's the middle of the night."

"I know."

"Is it Harvey?"

I snickered and said, "That old man's too mean to die."

"Michael, that isn't true! Not once you get to know him."

I didn't want to argue.

"Why are you calling me so late?"

"I'm happy." That was probably the most irrational reply I could've given her and yet it was the truth.

"Happy?"

"I played poker with my friends."

"I assume there's some significance to this."

"It's the first time I've been with the guys since . . . since Hannah was diagnosed with cancer."

"Ah," she said, as if she automatically understood what this meant. "You had a good time, didn't you?"

"Steve brought us Cuban cigars." I closed my eyes and was forced to confront a truth that shook me to the very core of my being. If Macy had been in the same room with me I would've made love to her. To Macy. Not Hannah. Macy.

My eyes flew open. "I didn't mean that," I said, fearing I'd spoken out loud.

"Mean what? That you smoked the cigar?"

"Not that . . . something else."

She giggled as though she found my chatter amusing. "How much have you had to drink?"

"Not enough," I said. "Go back to bed, Macy, and forget I called."

"Are you sure that's what you want me to do?"

"Very sure."

"In a minute," she insisted. "In the morning, I want you to remember that you called me tonight."

"Why is that?"

"Because I'm happy, too."

My smile disappeared. I was in trouble here and sinking fast.

"I'll be in tomorrow to work on the mural."

"There's no need to rush—especially if you're still feeling sore."

"I was feeling terrible earlier this evening," Macy said, "but I'm not anymore. I'm so glad you phoned, Michael. I'll see you first thing in the morning."

Chapter Twenty-Eight

Although I had difficulty admitting it, I was looking forward to seeing Macy in the morning. Still high from the poker game with my friends, I walked into the office with a bounce to my step. Linda immediately noticed my good mood. She raised her head and stared at me.

"Is Macy here yet?" I asked.

"She's coming in today?"

"That's what she said," I told her.

"Well, she hasn't shown up yet."

I nodded and continued down the hallway, pausing long enough to take a fresh look at the half-finished mural. I appreciated Macy's talent anew, and wondered why I'd ever thought she was merely an adequate artist. As my staff kept marveling, she'd done a splendid job. I'd seen how well children and adults alike responded to the painting. I'd watched the kids glow with delight and point to various animals among the vibrant jungle foliage.

The painting had a curious effect on everyone, from my staff whose mood had brightened perceptibly to my patients who seemed livelier, less apprehensive. Or maybe the change had been in me.

I *was* different, I realized. And it was because of Macy. That made me question whether I was falling in love with her, as her neighbor claimed. A protest reverberated instantly in my head.

A relationship with Macy would never work. By her own admission, she wasn't good at relationships. Besides, Macy and I were worlds apart in every possible way. I liked things orderly while she seemed to thrive on chaos. I was probably ten years older than she was. I tended to be self-contained and she . . . well, Macy shared everything. No, I couldn't ever see this working, regardless of Hannah's opinion.

Okay, okay, I was willing to admit the attraction was there; neither of us could deny it. We'd kissed once and I'd felt that kiss in every cell of my being.

I moved on to my office; Linda came over to hand me Cody Goetz's file. The boy needed a health form filled in for an overnight summer camp he'd be attending. Linda didn't say anything but scrutinized me so intently, I grew uncomfortable.

I reached briskly for my stethoscope and jacket and headed toward the exam room where Cody, my first patient of the day, was waiting.

By ten o'clock, when Macy still hadn't appeared, I was beginning to feel concerned.

Despite knowing how unsuited we were, I wanted to see her. I even wanted to hear her infernal humming. I just wanted her with me, close to me. Because she made me feel *alive.* It wasn't simply about attraction in a sexual sense; it was bigger than that—the attraction of one life to another.

Hannah had been so right. In her letter she'd said that her life had ended, but that mine would go on. In the fourteen months since I'd laid her to rest, I'd lived in a state of limbo, shuffling from one day to the next, doing my utmost to hang on to the past, clinging to memories, to Hannah.

How well she knew me, how well she'd known how I'd react once she left this world. But for the first time since I'd lost her, I felt not only alive, but—to my complete surprise—happy. I saw now that her letter had freed me; it'd given me permission to live. The letter, with her list, was a testament of her love. I would always cherish the years I had with Hannah. But now I could find love again, find happiness, experience everything life had to offer. Without guilt and without regrets.

At eleven I took a short break between patients and phoned Macy's house. No one answered, which most likely meant she was on her way. Joyful expectation spread through me. I knew my staff would welcome her back with enthusiasm— and chocolate. I'd seen her name on a box of Mount Rainier mint truffles.

By lunchtime my patience had worn thin. Where *was* Macy? I'd assumed she'd meant to start work in the morning. Had I misunderstood her? No, I clearly recalled her telling me she'd show up first thing. I also remembered my excitement at the prospect of seeing her so soon.

As it turned out Macy didn't arrive until almost two. She burst into the office, wearing a rainbow of colors. Linda and the others gathered around her, acting as if she'd been away for months instead of days, bombarding her with questions. She was like sunshine exploding across a dark horizon, flooding the earth with light and life and laughter.

While she answered their questions and hugged each person, I noticed that her gaze sought me out. Her eyes were warm and full of unspoken affection.

The best I could offer her was a faint grin. After a respectable length of time, the staff drifted back to their jobs, and I finally approached her. "I thought you said you'd be here this morning," I said. I immediately felt that remark had been too miserly, but she didn't react.

"Oh, Michael," she said, still smiling. "I had the most fabulous morning. I can't wait to tell you about it."

"You'll have to tell him later," Linda said, placing her hands on my shoulders and steering me away. "Right now, Dr. Everett has to get back to his patients."

"Okay, okay." I glanced over my shoulder and nearly drowned in Macy's smile. It was all I could do to focus on my work.

Our eyes stayed connected for a moment and then she picked up her paintbrush and I went into the exam room to check on Ted Malcom, a five-year-old who'd broken his right leg falling off a swing set. He'd destroyed three casts in less than a month, which was something of a feat. The poor kid wanted to play with his friends, run and swim in the summer sunshine. He tried to do all those things despite the cast, which was repeatedly ruined by water and rough treatment.

His mother was frustrated with her son and worried about his recovery.

"Hi, Lucy," I said as I knelt down in front of the boy. His mom smiled tightly.

"Ted," I began.

"Yes, Doctor."

"I think I see the problem here."

Ted looked at the floor. "I don't want to wear a cast."

"I wouldn't, either. You can have a lot more fun without a cast weighing down your leg, can't you?"

With his head so low his chin was practically on his chest, Ted asked, "Are you mad at me? My mom is." He squinted up at her through his lashes.

"I'm not mad," I told him, "because as I said, I think I understand the problem. This cast is boring. You need it decorated."

"Decorated?"

I got up and opened the door. "Macy, could you step in here for a moment?"

She looked confused, but did as I asked. I explained the situation to her and, as I spoke, I saw her eyes light up. "I have just the solution," she declared.

"You do?" Ted asked.

"Let me get my supplies."

I left the three of them and went into the adjoining exam room. I saw three patients, one after another, and when I returned to the first room, Macy was nearly finished. She'd painted dinosaurs of different kinds all around the cast, cleverly positioning them.

"Do you like it?" I asked Ted.

He grinned from ear to ear. "It's way cool."

"Cool enough for your friends to admire?"

He nodded eagerly.

"That's what I thought, too. Do you want to keep this one?"

Again he nodded.

"Perfect. I'll see you back here when it's ready to come off."

He grinned again and we bumped fists and added a high five.

Ted's mother grasped my arm. "Thank you for coming up with this. And, Macy, thank *you*. It's a work of art. Would you sign it, please?"

Macy shrugged off the praise, but used my pen to write her signature on the cast. She collected her paints and returned to the hallway. I was feeling good about my solution for Ted and wanted to thank Macy myself. But when I went in search of her, I discovered she'd gone for the day.

"What do you mean she's gone?" I asked Linda in bewilderment. "Did she have another appointment?"

"Not that she said." Linda appeared as baffled as I was. "I have a feeling Macy does that fairly often."

"Leaves for no reason? Why?" I didn't understand it, but I shouldn't have been surprised. Macy had warned me, after all, that she frequently lost interest in projects halfway through.

"I don't think she knows. But then again . . . maybe she does."

Linda liked to speak in cryptic sentences. "What does that mean?" I asked bluntly.

"She likes you."

"So she avoids me?" Which, of course, was the same thing I'd done after her accident.

"Maybe you should just ask Macy," Linda advised.

"Ask her what?" I said. "Ask her about being here one minute and gone the next?" I despaired of ever understanding Macy. Give me a cranky four-year-old any day.

Linda patted my arm sympathetically, then clapped a file in my outstretched hands. "Talk to her and you'll both feel better."

An hour later, I tried Macy's home phone. She didn't answer. Nor did she pick up thirty minutes after that. When I was done for the day, I decided to stop by her house and find out what was going on. I hoped Linda's advice worked. Maybe I'd invite Macy to dinner. . . .

By the time I parked in front of her house, I was happily anticipating an evening in her company. As Hannah had promised, when Macy wasn't frustrating me, she did make me smile.

I let myself through her gate and walked up the sidewalk to her front door. I rang the bell and waited. A cat, Peace, I believe, leaped onto the living room windowsill. Peering into the house, I saw the other two cats asleep on the sofa. Macy was nowhere in sight.

"You looking for Macy?" Harvey called from his porch. Sammy stood at his side, tail wagging furiously. "In case you're too dumb to figure it out, she isn't home."

"Where is she?" I asked, choosing to overlook the insult.

He didn't answer. "I wondered if you'd come by," he said in the gruff tone I'd come to expect from him. "If I was twenty years younger I'd punch your lights out."

I bounded down Macy's steps and hurried around to his porch.

"Okay, forty years younger," he amended. "What did you say to Macy, anyway? I've never seen her this upset, outside of losing her grandmother, that is."

I wasn't spilling my guts to this old coot. "I didn't say anything."

"In case you don't know it, young man, Macy is mighty special. I can't understand why she cares about you, but then I don't know why she pesters me with all this attention, either."

"Did she say when she'd be back?" I asked, more eager to learn what she was upset about than to discuss his theories about her emotional attachments.

He shook his head. "You want to come inside for a beer?" he asked abruptly.

"Okay. As a matter of fact, I'd love one." I had nothing more pressing to do and Macy would return eventually; I might as well stay here.

"Good." When he held open the screen door, Sammy and I trotted into the house. Lowering himself onto his recliner, Harvey told me to retrieve the beers. When I joined him, he turned off the evening news. I sat down across from him on the couch, while Sammy lay on the rug, next to Harvey's chair.

"You had dinner?" I asked.

"Don't have much of an appetite these days."

"How about a pizza?"

He considered the suggestion, then shrugged. "Sounds as good as anything else."

I took out my cell. After more than a year of fending for myself, I had my favorite pizza delivery service on speed dial. I ordered the usual, then sat back and relaxed, gulping down a refreshing mouthful of beer.

"She has a private place she'll go for a few hours when she's upset," Harvey said. "Don't know where it is. She's never told me, but my guess is she likes to walk along the Hood Canal. I'm sure she'll be back soon—those cats want feeding."

I put down my beer. "You love her, don't you?" Most of the time, the old man pretended otherwise.

He snorted and looked me in the eye. "So do you."

I began to argue and realized I was no different than Harvey. I hid my feelings, too, dodged emotions and their uncertainty, their messiness. Hannah had been the keeper of our emotional life. Now I was finding my way through this strange new existence.

Harvey's eyes pierced straight through me. "Admit it. You love her."

"Yeah, I guess I do," I said reluctantly.

The old man shook his head. "Damn shame," he muttered.

"What is?"

"She loves you, too. I'd always sort of hoped she'd marry me," he said. His serious expression shocked me until I realized he was joking. Harvey joking? That was a switch.

He grinned and it seemed as though his facial

muscles were stiff, unaccustomed to smiling. What I'd done to deserve his smile I couldn't begin to guess.

I sat on the couch with my beer as we waited for our promised thirty-minutes-or-it's-free pizza delivery. "Before she died, my wife wrote me a letter," I said, unsure what had prompted this sudden confidence.

Then, before I could decide whether I should, I told Harvey everything. After having read Hannah's letter countless times, I repeated it to him almost verbatim.

Harvey listened, not interrupting even once to ask questions.

"It took me a long time to understand why Hannah included Macy," I finished.

He arched his brows as if to say that was the stupidest remark he'd ever heard. "You'll figure it out soon enough. You're still young. In another thirty years, you might wise up."

I laughed. He meant it as an insult, but I didn't take offense.

"You married a wise woman," he said next.

"I did." When people mentioned Hannah, I used to feel overwhelmed by grief and sadness. All I could think about was what I'd lost. Now I was starting to understand what I'd been given in the years we'd had. That time together had been a priceless gift.

Another thought struck me and it was like being

prodded out of sleep into wakefulness. A moment later I was on my feet.

"You going somewhere?" Harvey asked.

"No . . . I was thinking." My mind was still spinning. *I'd been given another chance.* Macy was that chance. Through Hannah's wisdom and the grace of God, I'd found Macy.

A car door closing caught my attention and I reached for my wallet to pay for the pizza.

"It's Macy," Harvey announced, looking out the window.

I didn't need him to say another word. Opening the door, I ran down the steps.

Macy stopped when she saw me. She seemed to brace herself, as if she felt apprehensive about what I'd say.

I didn't hesitate. I ran down the walk and straight toward her. Not giving her a second to protest, I slid my arms around her waist and lifted her from the sidewalk. Then I buried my face in her shoulder and breathed in the scent of lavender and paint and Macy. . . .

"I'm sorry I left," she whispered. "I had to get away."

"Why?"

"I was . . . afraid."

"Of me?" I asked.

"Yes. No. I'm afraid of falling in love with you."

I set her on the ground and held her face in my hands. "Am I so terrible?"

"Oh, no! You're wonderful. Too wonderful."

"Oh, Macy . . ."

"You'll get tired of me and angry because . . . I'm different."

"You're beautiful."

"But—"

"Would you please stop talking so I can kiss you?"

She smiled, and before she could say anything else, I lowered my mouth to hers.

Chapter Twenty-Nine

Monday afternoon Leanne's cell phone rang while she was on her lunch break. After a bowl of chicken soup in the hospital cafeteria, she'd gone for a walk. The last week of June was cool and a little blustery; according to the calendar summer had begun the previous week, but it didn't really arrive in the Pacific Northwest until the latter part of July. Still, she needed the exercise, so she'd brought a heavy sweater to wear outside.

She'd made her way from the hospital and strolled through the shopping complex at Pacific Place. She didn't need anything, nor could she afford much, but browsing through the stores gave her a chance to think.

She hadn't heard from Michael Everett in a couple of weeks and realized the attraction just wasn't there. Thankfully, they both recognized it.

When her phone rang, Leanne fumbled in her purse to retrieve it. She didn't take the time to check her small display screen, afraid the caller might hang up.

"Hello," she said breathlessly.

"Leanne, this is Muriel. I apologize for disturbing you."

Her mother-in-law didn't sound like herself. Her voice quavered as if she'd been crying.

"I'm glad you phoned," Leanne assured her as she continued walking.

"How are you?"

Leanne left the shopping complex and stood on the street, where telephone reception was better. "Okay, and you?"

Muriel didn't respond.

"Is everything all right?" Leanne asked during the awkward pause that followed.

Muriel still didn't answer and Leanne wondered if the call had been disconnected. "Muriel? Are you there?"

"Yes, I'm here."

"Is it Brian?" Her father-in-law was in good health as far as Leanne knew, but she hadn't seen him in nearly two years.

"No," Muriel said in the same odd tone she'd used earlier.

"Is . . . is it . . ."

It suddenly came to her that Muriel would phone

in the middle of a workday only if something had happened to Mark. She clenched her cell phone more tightly. The street noise made it almost impossible to hear.

"We . . . got some news this afternoon—about Mark—and I thought you'd want to know," she said in a leaden voice.

Leanne's legs felt weak. Fortunately, there was a bus stop nearby; she staggered toward the bench and slumped onto it.

"Tell me," Leanne pleaded.

"McPherson, the company that employs Mark, contacted us an hour ago. Mark did warn us before he left that there'd be risks, but . . . but we assumed, the way everyone does, I suppose, that he'd be safe inside the army compound. It *should* be safe there, don't you think?"

"Yes, of course." Why in heaven's name was Muriel dragging this out? *Tell me!* It was all Leanne could do not to scream at her.

Some of the expression had returned to Muriel's voice. "Mark knew several of the military men in Afghanistan from when he was in the service. One of them is a helicopter pilot. About the same age as Mark, married and a father. I believe Mark told us he has two little girls. I don't recall how old they are. Then again, Mark might not have said. I don't remember now."

Leanne's hand flew to her mouth and she closed her eyes.

"His name was Alan," Muriel said. Her voice shook.

"*Was?* Alan's dead?"

"Yes."

Leanne swallowed painfully. "Alan . . . wasn't alone, was he?"

"No . . ."

The grip she had on her cell phone threatened to crush it. "Was . . . Mark with him?"

Muriel's answer came in the form of a sob. "Yes!"

Leanne could hardly breathe. Her mother-in-law was crying. Finally, when she couldn't bear it any longer, Leanne blurted out the question. "Is he dead? Just tell me if Mark's dead."

"We don't know. . . . Apparently, Mark went out with Alan and another mechanic because Alan was having engine problems and Mark couldn't figure out what was wrong. He thought if he heard the engine in flight, he'd know where to look— only, when they left the compound, they came under immediate fire and went down. Then . . . when the second chopper got to the one Mark and Alan were in, they found Alan had died in the crash."

"And Mark?" she asked. "What about Mark?"

"He wasn't there. Neither was the other man."

"Mark was *captured?*" That scenario was truly terrifying. Leanne was well aware of what might happen once the enemy got hold of him. The evening news had been filled with nightmarish accounts of beheadings and brutal beatings. The fact that these men and women weren't military, were just contract workers, didn't seem to matter.

"We don't know what's going on," Muriel told her again. "The company's promised us they're doing everything in their power to rescue Mark."

"He should never have been in that helicopter in the first place," Leanne cried, lashing out in her pain.

Muriel sobbed. "I . . . I agree."

The silence stretched between them. Leanne was afraid to close her eyes for fear of the appalling images that would come to life.

"I felt you'd want to know," Muriel said again.

"Thank you."

They disconnected, but for a long time Leanne held on to her cell. She struggled to assimilate this terrible news. Ever since her divorce, her family and friends had insisted she should get on with her life. Her counselor, too, had advised her to focus on the future.

Leanne had done that, or tried to. She'd gotten involved in the Kids with Cancer program and had organized the volunteers for the picnic. She'd gone out with friends, joined a reading group, taken a class on new cancer therapies. She'd dated Michael Everett. Nothing had worked. Nothing had eased the ache in her heart. She loved Mark. She'd never stopped loving him. She realized it the Sunday she'd driven to Yakima; she knew it when she heard he'd taken a job in Afghanistan.

Now it might be too late to tell him she still cared, still needed him. She'd followed everyone's advice, did her best to move on, and to a certain extent she had.

As soon as she returned to the hospital, she went to see her supervisor.

Janet glanced up from her desk and frowned. "Leanne, what's wrong?"

"I need a leave of absence as soon as possible," Leanne said, unable to keep the tremor out of her voice.

"What's wrong?" Janet asked again, sounding alarmed.

Leanne told her about Muriel's call.

"What will you do? Where will you go?"

Leanne didn't have an answer. "I don't know yet . . . but I'm too upset to be any good to anyone here. I need to be where I can get information about Mark, no matter what it is."

"Where would that be?"

Janet forced her to think logically. "With his parents in Spokane." She took a deep breath. "They shouldn't be alone."

"Then that's where you need to go."

Leanne nodded, grateful that her friend understood.

"Go home," Janet said. "Now."

"But my patients—"

Janet removed her glasses and set them aside. "I'll take over for the rest of the day and I'll arrange your leave. Like you said, you're too emotional to work right now. I'll call you once I've talked to HR."

"Thank you," Leanne whispered. Janet had helped her figure out what to do. Sometime in the next few days, she'd leave to be with Mark's family. They'd support one another through this.

Janet stood and hugged her. "Do you have any idea how long you'll be away?"

"No . . ."

"I'll be praying for you and Mark and your family."

"Thank you."

Leanne didn't remember the drive home or dragging her suitcase out of the spare-room closet. She'd just finished packing when she got a call from Janet telling her that the leave of absence had been arranged.

"Keep us updated," Janet said.

"I will and thank you so much."

Ten minutes later, she let the building super know she'd be away. Then she carried her suitcase outside and thrust it in the trunk of her car.

Not until she was in the driver's seat did she think to call her former in-laws to explain her intentions.

Shuffling through her purse, she searched for her cell phone. It wasn't in the side pocket where she normally kept it. When she finally located it in the bottom of her purse, she heaved a sigh of relief. Her fear was that, traumatized as she was, she'd left it at the bus stop.

Holding it gratefully with both hands, she pressed the button that would redial the number of the last call received. Brian Lancaster answered on the first ring.

"Hello?" He sounded anxious, no doubt worried that this was the call he'd been dreading.

"It's Leanne."

Brian took an audible breath. "Muriel phoned you?"

"Yes." She didn't elaborate. "I'm driving to Spokane. Can I stay with you and Muriel until . . . until . . ." She left the rest unsaid and held her own breath; she felt as if her lungs might explode.

"Should you be driving?" he asked. Brian was the practical one in the family. Levelheaded, competent, rational, and Leanne admired him. Mark was a lot like his father.

She released her breath. "Probably not, but I'm coming, anyway."

"Will anything I say stop you?"

"No."

Brian's voice cracked. "I think we all need to be prepared for the worst. Come. Stay as long as you like. Muriel needs you and, frankly, I don't think I can help her get over the death of our son. . . ."

Brian had always been strong, the dock

everyone had tied their boats to in the crazy storm that had struck their family. He'd stood by Mark, hired a good attorney for his son, helped his daughter settle into a new life and remained the bulwark of strength they all relied on. But this— the thought of losing Mark, his only son—was more than even he could bear.

"I'm on my way," Leanne whispered.

After a long pause, he whispered back. "Thank you."

Chapter Thirty

Macy and I never really got a chance to talk in any detail about why she'd suddenly disappeared from my office or where she'd gone the previous Friday. I thought it had something to do with one of her many auditions. But then the pizza arrived and the two of us joined Harvey and chatted happily over dinner and beer.

When we'd finished, I helped clean up and then we went to Macy's to feed the animals. I'd never considered myself a cat person, but I realized it was because I hadn't been around them very often. I was becoming fond of Macy's three, and they seemed to reciprocate the sentiment. Sammy had accepted me, too, so I was friends with all the furry denizens of 255 Jackson Avenue, all the creatures who seemed to understand that I loved Macy as much as they did.

Once they were fed, Macy and I cuddled on her sofa and watched television. Instead of talking about her insecurities, trying to deal with the differences between us, we kissed. Soon coherent thought vanished. Soon all I could think about was how good it felt to have this woman in my arms. This warm, whimsical, vibrant woman.

My feelings for Macy had intensified since her accident. In the past few days, I'd found that my thoughts constantly turned toward her: what she was doing, who she was rescuing—even what she was humming. She's such a natural with people; kids and animals love her. Macy's impulsive and nonconformist, yet that's all part of her appeal.

Unlike Macy, I rarely act on impulse, but I did the next Tuesday morning. Macy had a radio spot she was recording today; yesterday she'd had another audition—a callback, she'd told me proudly. I wanted to give her a gift; I wanted her to know how glad I was that she'd come into my life. The idea of replacing her bicycle occurred to me, and I remembered the small shop where I'd purchased the bikes for Hannah and me.

As I'd hoped, they were still in business. I called the store and described Macy's unique personality; Mel Wellborn, the owner, laughed and said he had just the bike for her. I looked at the picture on his Web site and had to agree. It was pink with orange tassels on the handlebars and lime-green pedals. Apparently, a clown had special-ordered it and then changed his mind. Mel quoted a price that made my head spin, but I couldn't refuse. The picture on the Internet proclaimed that this was the perfect bike for Macy, so I bought it and was told I could pick it up that evening.

I called her during my lunch break. Fortunately—since, predictably, she didn't have a cell phone—she hadn't left for the studio yet. "Are you going to be home tonight?" I asked.

"Yes . . ."

The hesitation in her voice gave me pause. "I'd like to stop by."

"Okay."

"Are you sure you aren't too busy?" I asked.

"Michael, I want to see you."

"I can come another night if you prefer."

"No . . . no. I have something I'm dying to tell you." Her voice bubbled with excitement.

"Tell me now," I urged.

"I want to wait until I see you. This is just the most wonderful thing that's happened to me since . . . since I met you."

Her words brought me a sense of contentment. "Meeting you has been wonderful for me, too, Macy."

Macy went from effusive to silent. "Do you mean that, Michael?" she asked after a moment.

"With all my heart."

She was quiet again.

"What time will you be home?" I asked.

"The earliest I can make it is six—make that six-thirty in case I'm late leaving the studio. I really am trying to be on time, you know."

"I do know," I assured her.

After a few words of farewell, I hung up the phone, but my hand stayed on the receiver, as though I could hold on to that connection with Macy.

After more than a year of lonely grief, of self-imposed isolation, I found that I craved the company of others. Craved evenings with Macy and her menagerie of people and pets, playing poker with my friends, laughing again. Because of Macy I'd stepped out of the shadows.

At the end of the day I left the office as early as possible, then drove straight to the bicycle shop to get Macy's gift. Mel was an older guy who, like many small-business owners, offered great personal service. I hadn't considered how I'd transport the bike, so I had to purchase a bike carrier for the car, which I hoped Macy and I would put to good use.

Mel installed the carrier, and I loaded up the bike, driving first to the wine boutique, then to Macy's house. I could hardly wait to see her face suffused with delight when she saw this crazy bike.

Her car was parked outside, so I knew she was home. I pulled in behind her. These days I smiled when I saw her house with the bright red shutters and the white picket fence. Even now, it looked like something out of a fairy tale to me. I could believe that one day I'd find Sleeping Beauty inside having tea with Cinderella—and Macy.

Before I'd climbed out of the car, Macy opened her front door and dashed down the steps. By the time I made it through the gate, she'd launched herself into my embrace, twining her arms around my neck. I grabbed her by the waist and swung her around.

"I'm so *glad* you're here," she said fervently.

I kissed her because it was impossible not to. I couldn't be this close to her and resist. But she was so lovely I had trouble taking my eyes off her, even to kiss her.

"I want to tell you my news," she said, breaking off the kiss.

I set her back down on the sidewalk and waited for her to speak. But before she did, she placed her hands on either side of my face and kissed me again.

"So tell me," I urged, loving her enthusiasm for life, loving everything about her.

"I got a part in a local TV commercial!" she said. "I get to be a shopper at the Safeway store."

"A shopper?"

"I push a cart down the aisle and take a box of breakfast cereal from a display at the end of the aisle and put it in my cart. I'm supposed to look pleasantly surprised at the discounted price and from there, I move the cart off screen."

I did my best to look impressed. "Congratulations!"

"The production company is taping it a week from Friday."

"Fabulous."

"If I do well, I might get a speaking role next. No guarantees, of course. The man who produces the radio ads I do recommended me for this. Is that fantastic or what?"

"It is," I told her. She'd explained to me that working in television was high on her list of career goals. And, of course, she had more of those than most people.

"I heard from the TV people this morning that I got the job. Then I did a radio spot for a landscaping service. Oh, and I should be completely finished the mural by the end of the week."

She bounced from one subject to the next with hardly a breath in between.

We'd been standing on the walkway leading to her porch, so she hadn't noticed the pink bicycle attached to my car.

"I brought you something," I said.

"What?" Her eyes grew huge with curiosity.

I ran my hands down the length of her arms, my gaze never leaving her face. I wanted to see her reaction when she first caught sight of the bicycle. "Look behind me. At the car."

She frowned. "You brought me a car?"

"No." I laughed. "The bicycle at the back of my car."

Her face exploded with reaction. She covered her mouth with her fingers, then raced to my car. "Oh, Michael, pink! I love pink."

I helped her remove it from the carrier and let her examine all the features. She laughed at the tassels and the white basket I'd had attached to the front. White with pink flowers!

"I've always wanted a pink bicycle," she told me breathlessly.

"You like it?"

"Are you kidding? I love it! I absolutely love it. Thank you, oh, thank you so much." Once again her arms were around me—not that I was complaining. Her spontaneous joy filled me with joy, too. I was still unaccustomed to emotion like this. It burned in my chest the same way as tears did, and now I understood why people sometimes cry out of happiness.

After Macy had studied every inch of the bicycle, I handed it to her. She immediately hopped on and started pedaling down the empty sidewalk. She wore a skirt and her slim legs pumped the lime-green pedals as her laughter echoed along the street.

The moment he saw her, Sammy jumped down from Harvey's porch to chase after her, barking wildly. She braked and got off, pausing to crouch and rub Sammy's ears. Then she walked the bicycle back to me. She kept her gaze on the ground and I felt a stab of fear.

"What's wrong?"

"Michael," she whispered, close to tears. "Thank you so much."

"Don't cry, please." I shook my head. "I just wanted to give you something special, and your bicycle was ruined."

Tears spilled from her eyes. I'd never seen Macy cry before, and I wasn't sure what to say. Or do. I felt completely helpless. "Macy . . ."

"I'm so afraid of what'll happen if I fall in love with you. But I . . . think it's too late."

"Is loving me so bad?" I asked gently.

"Oh, no! It's just that you're an important doctor and, well, look at me," she said, gesturing at her white-and-purple saddle shoes with their pom-pom laces. "You're dignified and I'm . . . me."

"I'm falling in love with funny, undignified you and that's a good thing."

She brought one hand to her mouth and hid a sob. "That'll change, though. Men think I'm fun and different, and then they get to know me and after a while they decide I'm . . . annoying. Or silly. And I couldn't stand it if that happened with you."

I clasped her shoulders. "Nothing's going to change my mind about you, Macy. Understand?"

She nodded.

"Come on," I said and took the bike from her. I leaned it against the fence and we sat together on the top step of her porch. Sammy lay at my feet with his chin on my shoe. I stroked his thick fur and he groaned softly, a sound that expressed content-ment. A dog or cat asked for so little, I thought—food, shelter, affection—and gave so much.

Meanwhile Macy continued to sniffle.

"I want to tell you something," I finally said. I'd decided it was time Macy knew about Hannah's list, so I told her how I'd come to make that phone call all those weeks ago.

She listened intently as I described what Hannah had written. Her eyes revealed astonishment when I explained that Hannah had given me her name.

"Me?" she said, her hand pressed to her heart. "She gave you *my* name?"

"Yes, you. In the beginning I was sure she'd made a mistake—or was playing a trick on me."

Macy laughed. "Either one might be true."

"But there's no mistake, no trick. Hannah was right about everything. You *have* taught me to laugh again, to enjoy life. When I'm with you I feel happy I'm alive. You are so generous and kind. You make me want to be a better person."

"Oh, Michael . . . I don't think anyone's ever said anything lovelier to me in my whole life."

I had to make an effort to keep from hugging her and kissing her again. I was afraid that once we started we wouldn't be able to stop.

Macy rested her forehead against my shoulder. "Hannah was one of the wisest, most generous women I've ever known."

I nodded. Hannah had understood that I'd need encouragement to move into the next stage of my life. She'd released me to love again, but she'd gone a step further. I felt a fresh sense of appreciation that Hannah had steered me toward Macy.

"There's an awards banquet a week from Friday," I told her. "I'm nominated for Pediatrician of the Year, and I'd like it very much if you'd come with me." I'd dreaded this evening until I'd asked Macy to join me. It would mean everything to share this night with her, to have her at my side, win or lose.

"This is a formal dinner?" she asked. She seemed more than a little nervous.

"Unfortunately, yes."

"I won't embarrass you?"

"No," I said, laughing at the thought. Macy was Macy. If she chose to show up in a pink taffeta gown and ballet slippers, that would be fine with me. If she wore a clown suit that wouldn't bother me, either, as long as she was by my side.

"Oh, Michael, I can't believe this is happening. You're truly falling in love with me?"

"Yes, Macy."

Her look was serious now, if a bit fearful. "I fell in love with you the night you stayed here after the accident. Any man who'd put up with me, the cats and Harvey is a prince in my book. *My* prince."

I grinned. "This is the perfect house for a prince

to find his princess," I said. A princess in disguise. The accident had been a turning point for me, as well. I remembered the fear I'd experienced when I received the call that Macy had been hurt. The thought of losing her had clarified everything. That accident had shown me what my heart had been trying to tell me from the day I met her.

Because I'm a stubborn, willful man, I hadn't been ready to accept that I'd fallen for Macy. I tried to get her out of my head, out of my life, but nothing had worked. Now I was grateful my puny efforts hadn't succeeded.

The problem was that I'd grown comfortable wallowing in pain, comfortable with the anger I felt at losing Hannah. I was at ease with my grief. But Macy had changed that. Falling in love with her meant I had to let go of my grief and, shockingly, that was hard. I had to reach out toward life and, frankly, I found *that* frightening.

We had dinner together. Macy insisted on cooking, with my assistance. We worked side by side in her kitchen, laughing and teasing each other, interspersing our tasks with lengthy kisses. The radio played rock favorites from the seventies and eighties, and we managed to dance and sing while we assembled the ingredients for the salmon casserole. Apparently, this recipe wasn't all that different from the one she sometimes made for her cats, because Lovie, Peace and Snowball meowed at us in three-part harmony. Macy put me in charge of the salad. The lettuce was from Harvey's garden.

"Should I set the table?" I asked when I'd finished tossing everything in the large ceramic bowl. Not that I could see the table. Macy had stacked newspapers and books and accumulated *stuff* on top of it. I started shifting things into new piles on the floor. I made a heroic attempt not to wince as I did so and consoled myself that the floor was scrupulously clean.

The oven timer went off, and Macy removed the casserole, then took over rearranging the books and papers.

After that, she tried the salmon dish and blinked. "Oh, dear, I think I might've mixed up the recipes."

That wouldn't surprise me, seeing how often we'd stopped to kiss during our preparations.

"I'm afraid this might be the one I use for making cat food. Oh, well. It wouldn't be the first time." She laughed. "Just kidding."

"It wouldn't be the first time for me, either," I said wryly. "At least we have a fine Merlot to wash it down."

If someone had asked me what dinner tasted like, I couldn't really have said—except that the casserole was better than cat food. What I remember most was how much I enjoyed being with Macy. I helped wash the dishes after the meal and afterward we watched TV, sitting on the sofa with the three cats piled on our laps. Sammy was keeping Harvey company tonight. Needless to say, we paid far more attention to each other than the medical drama on the screen.

Much later, as I drove home, I realized I wanted every night to be like this. No one could be more shocked than I was at the speed with which things had changed. But despite our differences, despite *everything,* I was certain of my feelings.

The following afternoon, before I joined Patrick, Ritchie and Steve for our poker night, I stopped at the jeweler's and picked out an engagement ring. I planned to ask Macy to marry me the night of the awards dinner.

Because I spent so long at the jeweler's, I was late for poker.

"Where've you been?" Ritchie asked when I got to his house. The others were already there.

"It's not like you to be late," Patrick said.

"I had something to do."

"What?"

I might as well own up. "I've decided to ask Macy to marry me."

Ritchie's eyes widened and he immediately glanced at my left hand. Earlier that day I'd taken off my wedding ring—the one Hannah had placed on my finger. For me removing the ring was a momentous act, not something I'd done lightly. Still, I expected Ritchie to tell me it was too soon and that I needed to think this over.

But he didn't. "You sure?" was all he said.

"As sure as the day I asked Hannah."

"Didn't I tell you?" Ritchie grinned. "I knew all along it would be her."

I think Hannah did, too.

Chapter Thirty-One

Winter stared at the computer screen, rereading Pierre's e-mail. He'd written to remind her that their three-month separation was about to end and asked if she still wanted to meet on July 1 to discuss their options. Unless, of course, she had a new relationship with that doctor she'd mentioned.

Winter had only talked to Michael Everett briefly in the past few weeks. They'd both made an effort, but it was clear right from the start that they'd never be a couple. Winter blamed herself. She loved Pierre, and because of that, she hadn't been truly open, truly receptive, to a new relationship. She couldn't be. Despite their differences, despite their constant bickering and their breakups, she was still in love with Pierre. The Sunday afternoon she'd spent with Michael, cooking him dinner, she hadn't been able to think about anything except the hours she and Pierre had spent in her kitchen. In retrospect she knew she'd been trying to replicate those times, but it hadn't worked. Michael wasn't Pierre. And she . . . well, she wasn't Hannah.

Nothing had changed between her and Pierre. She hadn't been in touch with him since their last confrontation, but he was never far from her thoughts. How was it that two people who loved each other so much could be so miserable together—and just as unhappy apart?

Neither of them had been able to accept defeat, and yet, sadly, there didn't seem to be a solution for them. People who were in love should bring out the best in each other, but it was the opposite with them. She detested the woman she became when she was with him.

Sitting in her small office at the French Café, she told herself it was time to make a decision. They couldn't go on like this. Either they ended it for good or they figured out how to make it work. Winter was willing to do whatever it took—if only she knew what. And how. The problem was that they both kept doing the same things, fighting over the same issues. She'd read somewhere that the definition of insanity was doing the same thing over and over, but expecting a different result. That must mean they were both crazy.

Yes, it was time to decide. "Make it or break it" time.

Pierre's e-mail message was simple and succinct, with no indication of his feelings.

Winter wasn't sure how to answer. They *should* meet. They should talk. They had to decide whether to try yet again or end it entirely.

Deep in thought, she didn't immediately hear Alix knock at the half-open office door. Alix knocked again, and Winter turned to see her standing there, holding a mug. She gestured her in. Alix's movements were cumbersome, reminding Winter that there were only a few weeks left before her due date. Winter was proud of Alix and Jordan, and she envied them, too. They'd survived the miscarriage last year without losing hope or faith. Now their first baby was about to be born.

Jordan had refinished a used crib and set it up in the nursery this past weekend. Alix had been knitting for weeks, as had everyone at A Good Yarn.

"Winter?" Alix said hesitantly. "I thought you could use this," she said, offering her the mug of coffee.

"How nice. Thanks." She reached out a hand for the mug and managed a half smile.

Alix lingered in the doorway. "Is everything all right?"

"Sure. What makes you think it isn't?" she asked with forced brightness.

"Well, for one thing, you've been sitting in here for the past thirty minutes, doing nothing but staring at that computer screen."

"Oh."

"Is the café not doing well?"

"Actually, revenue is up fifteen percent compared to last year at this time." The croissants had always been popular. And starting in May the café had added a ten-minute carryout lunch, which consisted of homemade soup and a freshly baked herb scone. That had proved to be highly successful; many office and retail employees ordered lunch and were then able to walk to the nearby park and eat there or meet friends. Winter planned to continue the quick lunch throughout the year.

"Is it Pierre?" Alix asked softly.

Reluctantly, Winter nodded. She swallowed the lump in her throat. "I love him, but . . . but we can't seem to make our relationship work, no matter how hard we try."

Alix stepped into the office. "I don't know if you're aware that Jordan and I went through a rough patch when we were first married."

Winter didn't, but pretended she did.

"My own parents never provided a very positive example of how married people should communicate, and I'm afraid I wasn't always as good a wife as I wanted to be," Alix admitted sheepishly.

Winter remembered that Alix had made several costly mistakes at work before she'd become pregnant—mistakes like leaving out a key ingredient. Winter had talked with her, and Alix had taken their talk to heart and made an effort to improve. Winter had never once regretted keeping her on staff.

Alix gazed down at the floor. "I hate to tell you this, but I was the biggest shrew ever. I had a habit of not telling Jordan what I wanted, because I believed he should already know. He was my husband and, if he loved me, he should automatically be aware of my needs. Well, not surprisingly, that wasn't too effective."

Winter looked at her thoughtfully. Her own problems with Pierre came down to communication, too. Jordan was a minister, and she wondered if that accounted for his greater willingness—or perhaps ability—to work out the difficulties in his marriage.

"This pregnancy hasn't been easy, either, especially after we lost the first one. I'm still not confident about the kind of mother I'll be. All my fears seemed to coalesce into this continuous bad attitude toward Jordan. I can't believe he put up with me."

She smiled and glanced up. "Don't get me wrong. Jordan's no saint and he contributed to his share of arguments, but he never let things get out of hand. No matter how unreasonable I became."

"So what changed?" Most of this was news to Winter. Alix was a private person and if something bothered her she kept it to herself. Winter recognized that there was a reason Alix had chosen to bring up such a personal subject now.

"I realize I might not be a perfect mother, but I'm determined to be a good one. I love my baby. It's amazing to me that I can love him this much and he has yet to be born. Jordan feels the same.

He's so excited. I wish you could see him. Every night he puts his hand on my belly and prays for the baby and then kisses him good-night."

"That's sweet." Winter knew Alix was confiding a part of herself she never had before. "You're telling me this because you think your experience can help Pierre and me?"

Alix pulled out a chair and sat down. "After the morning sickness passed, I felt dreadful about the way I'd treated Jordan. He put up with my moods and was gentle and caring through the worst of it." She grimaced in obvious embarrassment. "One morning after I threw up I blamed him for everything. I even called him a bunch of names and told him our love life was over. I didn't mean it and felt horrible about it after I got to work."

Winter stifled a laugh and leaned back in her chair.

"I called Jordan, but he was out with his father. After I finished here, I went over to my in-laws' house and Susan—my mother-in-law—and I had a long talk. Susan's become like a mother to me. She listened to everything. The advice she gave me might help you and Pierre, too."

At this point, Winter was willing to listen to just about anything. She straightened again, her interest piqued. "Okay, let's hear it."

"I know you and Pierre are meeting next week."

She frowned. "Who told you that?"

Alix pointed to the office door. "It's on your calendar, along with the work schedule for July."

"Oh." Winter must have posted it there three months ago.

"Have you thought about what you're going to say?" Alix asked.

Winter shook her head. "It seems like mission impossible. I love him and at the same time I don't think anyone can upset me faster than Pierre. He's wonderful one minute and completely irrational the next."

"Aren't we all?" Alix asked and laughed.

Winter agreed, but true as that was, it did nothing to improve the situation.

"When I spoke to Susan about my bad moods and the way Jordan so often seemed to disappoint me," Alix continued, "she told me what she did as a young married woman. It really helped us."

"Then tell me," Winter urged. "Please. I'm desperate."

Alix nodded. "Okay. She got a notebook and made a list of all the things her husband did that irritated her on one half of a page. She left the other half blank. I'll get to that in a minute."

"A list." Winter could see where this was going and wasn't sure it would make any difference. She knew Pierre's good traits and his bad ones, too. They seemed about equal.

"What does Pierre do that bothers you the most?"

His bad habits were in the forefront of her mind. She'd dwelled on them far too often to have forgotten. "Well, for one thing, he can be moody after work. If he has a bad day, he takes it out on me. He gets upset at the most innocent comment and becomes completely unreasonable. He's like a little kid who doesn't get his own way." Just thinking about it upset her all over again. "Then ten minutes later, it's as if nothing happened and I'm supposed to forget everything he said and did."

"I've been there with the irrational moods," Alix said. "Write that down," she instructed, pointing to the pad in front of Winter. "But first draw a line down the middle of the sheet."

She turned to a blank page and divided it, then dutifully wrote out her complaint. "I know it's petty, but it really upsets me that he eats standing up. After I've cooked him a fantastic meal, the least he can do is sit down at the table with me and savor every bite. Really, is that too much to ask?"

"Put that down, too. Anything else?"

This was only the beginning. "As a matter of fact, yes. He's the most untidy person I've ever met. He leaves stuff wherever it falls and then accuses me of hiding it from him."

"That's a good one. Put it on the list."

Winter was really getting involved in this now. "He thinks he's a better chef than me."

"No way!" Alix was appropriately horrified.

"Okay, so he attended a fancy culinary institute, but my training was excellent, too, even if it was from a local school."

Alix pointed to the pad and Winter wrote it down in bold capital letters.

"Anything else?"

"Oh, yes." She went on for three or four minutes, adding items to her growing list.

"That's it?" Alix asked.

"Isn't it enough?"

"I want to make sure you think of everything."

Chewing on the end of her pen, Winter shook her head. "No, that's it."

She looked at her list. Articulating Pierre's faults, seeing them all in one place, made her recognize anew how unsuited they were. The situation seemed hopeless, which disheartened her even more.

"I suppose you want me to list his good qualities now." At the moment, Winter couldn't think of a single one. Not after making this lengthy list of his flaws, which seemed to outweigh everything else. How could she love a man who was completely unreasonable, short-tempered, inconsiderate and a slob?

"I don't want you to list his good points, because I think you'll have a difficult time finding any," Alix said. "I know that's how I felt when I was talking to Jordan's mother."

Winter nearly laughed out loud. "You're so right."

"Instead, do what Susan did and write down how *you* react when Pierre behaves the way he does. Start with the first one. What happens when he's moody and unreasonable at the end of the day?"

Winter stared at her friend. "What happens?" she echoed. "I'm not sure what you mean."

"Do you get moody and unreasonable back?"

"I guess so. If he snaps at me, I snap at him. I don't deserve to take the brunt of his bad moods. No one does."

"Write that across from your point about his mood swings."

Winter did, and remembered the argument they'd had in late March, which had led to the current separation. Pierre had been upset about some incident at the restaurant where he'd been working. Winter couldn't even recall what it was. He'd come over to her place that evening and growled at her and she'd growled right back. Their disagreements usually began that way. She'd look forward to seeing him all day and, five minutes after he arrived, they'd be yelling at each other.

"What do you do when he stands while he's eating the meal you've prepared?"

"I . . ." Winter slowly wrote it on the pad. "I insist that he sit down."

"What about the messes he makes?"

"I've bribed and pleaded and begged him to pick

up his own stuff. I am not his maid and I am not his mother."

"Exactly."

Winter made another notation on the second side of the pad.

"Okay, read me what you've put as your reactions to the first few things that bother you about Pierre."

"Okay." Winter read them aloud. "I get angry back at him. I demand that he sit down, and I bribe and plead with him."

Alix crossed her arms and nodded. "Okay, Pierre upsets you, and you become angry, demanding and manipulative. Do I have that right?"

Hearing it put that way was like seeing something from a completely different vantage point and Winter suddenly realized the role *she'd* played in their difficulties. "Yes, you're right." Hard as it was to admit, she had to agree. "The problem is, I don't know what to do about it." She sighed. "He just makes me so mad. Maybe I'm not helping the situation but . . ."

"If Pierre's cranky and upset," Alix said, "you should let him rant and get it out of his system. That's what Jordan did with me. He listened sympathetically and, when I was finished, he gave me a hug." She grinned. "Well, it wasn't always like that. We both had to work at it. After speaking to Jordan's mother, I saw that my reactions contributed to our troubles. Our conversation that day changed our marriage. I'll always be grateful to Susan."

"Your mother-in-law is a smart woman," Winter said. No wonder Pierre couldn't get away from her fast enough. She harped, pouted, retaliated. It wasn't a pretty picture.

As for his own outbursts, Pierre was seldom angry for long. Once he'd vented, it was over for him—but not for her. Perhaps things could change if her reactions to him did.

"He eats standing up out of habit," Winter murmured. "He tastes food in the kitchen at work and he's on his feet, so it's natural for him to do it at home, too."

"What can you do to get him to sit down?"

"Well, I know that getting angry doesn't work. Perhaps if I tell him the meal's ready and politely ask him to sit with me."

"You could try that. Or you could stand and join him," Alix suggested.

Winter laughed, and for the first time since their separation, she felt real hope.

"How'd your mother-in-law figure all this out?" Winter asked.

Alix shrugged. "Her own experience. That, and because she's talked to so many young wives with similar problems."

"Sounds like you married into a great family."

Alix nodded in agreement. "Jordan's a good

husband and he'll be a wonderful father." Alix relaxed in her chair and folded her hands over her stomach. "Talking with Susan helped me confront my fears about motherhood, too. Like I said earlier, I might not be a perfect mother, but I intend to be the best one possible."

"I think your baby's fortunate to have two loving parents."

Winter's compliment produced a huge smile from Alix. "Thank you, Winter."

"And thank *you* for these ideas. Hey, if you ever decide to change careers—not that I want you to—you could be a counselor."

Still smiling, Alix left the office, and Winter got up to close the door. She returned to her computer and sent Pierre a message saying simply that she looked forward to their meeting next week.

Then she began to plan her first stand-up dinner with Pierre.

Chapter Thirty-Two

The week passed quickly. I was busy and so was Macy. She had a couple of radio spots that paid the bills for all her animals' vaccinations. She was also helping her friend Sherry Franklin at a local craft show. Sher was a potter who relied on Macy at these events; one day soon, I hoped to see her in action, charming hordes of people into buying Sher's cat-shaped mugs and bowls. Macy had done some work on the mural, but I didn't mind that its completion was delayed by these other commitments. It just meant I'd have her at the clinic longer. In any case, we'd managed to talk every day and see each other three separate evenings. Thursday, the night before the awards dinner, Macy showed me the dress she planned to wear.

She sat me down on her sofa, and with all three cats around me, one on each side and Snowball on the back of the sofa, I waited patiently for the grand unveiling. Sammy rested at my feet, his chin on my shoes. It was a characteristic posture of his and one that, according to Macy, signified his approval of me.

When Macy appeared I nearly slid off the sofa. In a word, Macy's dress was stunning. I'm not much for fashion and I couldn't name a designer if my life depended on it, but I knew this dress was out of the ordinary. She'd purchased it at a tremendous discount while modeling for a catalog shoot.

Seeing Macy in that dress took my breath away. "I'll be the envy of every man there," I told her. "You could walk on the red carpet at the Oscars and not be out of place."

Macy blushed with pleasure.

At one time I'd dreaded this whole outing, but now I regarded it with a pleasurable sense of anticipation. I'd be proud to have Macy with me tomorrow evening. Ritchie had purchased tickets for himself and Steph, and Patrick would be at my table, as well as his wife, Melanie. So would our third partner, Yvette Schauer, and her husband. This would be the ideal opportunity to introduce Macy. And of course, I had the ring for later. I pictured Macy and me toasting each other with champagne, imagined slipping the diamond on her finger . . .

Macy stroked the dress. "It hardly cost anything and I bought it on faith that one day I'd have somewhere special to wear it."

Apparently, buying things on faith was a habit of hers. "Faith, not trust?" I asked.

"No, faith," she insisted. "The way I figured it, if this dress came to my attention, then there'd be an occasion when I'd need it." She fanned out the skirt at her sides. "Now I *do* have an occasion to wear it. Same with the dog food."

"Dog food? What's the connection between this dress and dog food?"

"There isn't one. But you see, about a month before I found Sammy, I happened upon a closeout sale on dog food and bought a twenty-five-pound bag. Naturally I didn't know at the time that Sammy would turn up in my life, so when he did, I was prepared. Well, sort of."

"Sort of?" I wondered where this answer would lead our conversation. Macy was unlike anyone I'd ever known and she saw the world in what I could only describe as a very individual way. The more I was around her the more I was enthralled. I'd grieved for Hannah so long and so intensely that I'd forgotten how addictive joy could be.

"Well," she went on to explain, "the night I found Sammy I'd forgotten about the dog food and fed him the same thing I do the cats. He was too hungry to be choosy, but all along I had that twenty-five-pound bag of kibble on the back porch and I'd completely forgotten about it. I remembered it the next afternoon. He was a happy camper after that."

I had to laugh. "That explains it, then."

"Will the dress do?" she asked, whirling around one last time to offer me a full view.

"It's perfect." And it was.

She made an elegant little curtsy in response.

"Shall I pick you up at five-thirty?" I asked, reaching down to pet Sammy. "The dinner starts at seven, but there's a social hour first."

"Could you come at five forty-five?" she asked.

I frowned, suddenly suspicious. "Is there something you're not telling me?"

She avoided eye contact. "The shoot for the TV commercial is tomorrow."

I exhaled slowly as understanding dawned. I remembered now. Of course this new job was important to Macy, but tomorrow's dinner was important to me. Important to both of us, although she didn't know that yet. "You're afraid the taping might run late?"

She nodded. "We're supposed to be done by five, but there are no guarantees."

I mulled it over, then gave her a reassuring smile. "We'll make it work."

"How?"

"I'll go on to the dinner ahead of you, and you can join me once you're done, no matter how late it is." This was a sensible compromise. I'd rather have Macy with me when I arrived, but that couldn't be helped. And afterward, I'd bring her back to my house—Hannah's house—for the first time. Because soon, I hoped, it would be Macy's, too.

"You don't mind?" she breathed.

"It'll be fine." Seeing the relief on her face was all the reward I needed. Although I wouldn't object if she wanted to express her gratitude in other ways . . .

As if reading my thoughts, Macy threw her arms around me and brought her mouth to mine. I pulled her into my lap and kissed her repeatedly, unzipping the back of her dress. While my hands explored her slim body, she smiled and spread happy kisses over my face. I could see that my life with Macy was going to be a wild ride—one I was eager to experience.

Friday night, I arrived at the hotel as scheduled and made excuses for Macy. All during the cocktail hour, I watched and waited expectantly. Obviously, the TV shoot had gone on much longer than planned. I could only imagine how nerve-racking this must be for her.

She still hadn't appeared when the ballroom doors were opened, but I wasn't too concerned, even though the crowd had begun to file in.

"You sure she's coming?" Ritchie muttered, following me into the ballroom. This was a question he'd asked more than once.

"She'll be here," I said confidently as we wove between tables looking for our assigned seating. The room was filling up quickly.

Because I'd been nominated for this award, my table was close to the front of the massive ballroom. I'd told Macy that the table number was listed on the dinner ticket and hoped she'd notice it.

"Is she perpetually late?" Ritchie asked as we found our place.

"She has a part in a commercial," I said. I'd explained as much several times.

We sat down with one empty space next to me. The salads were already on the table and the noise of clanking silverware and conversation rose to the vaulted ceiling. I'd selected my seat so I had a view of the door. I wanted to see Macy as soon as she came in.

The poached salmon with wild rice and asparagus was brought out by an army of servers in white jackets. As they moved smoothly about the ballroom, I became aware of a commotion in the back. The noise level instantly fell as half the room turned to find out what had caused the ruckus.

I swallowed tightly, instinctively knowing this involved Macy.

"If you'll excuse me a moment?" I said to my friends. I set my linen napkin beside my plate and stood.

Sure enough, it was Macy. She stood at the entrance to the ballroom, arguing with one of the security guards. I blinked when I saw her. The dress she'd previewed for me the night before was nowhere in sight. Instead, she had on a housedress that resembled something my grandmother might have worn. She clutched a large purse to her chest as though it held every valuable she possessed.

"Macy," I said. "Is there a problem?" I directed the question to the guard.

"Michael! Oh, thank goodness you're here. Would you kindly inform this . . . this man," she said in righteous tones, "that I am *not* a street person trying to crash this dinner and that I'm your invited guest?"

The man employed by the hotel regarded me skeptically. "Is she with you?"

"She is." I placed my arm protectively around Macy's shoulders. "Do you have your dinner ticket?"

"I . . . I couldn't find it." She draped the oversize purse over her arm and let it dangle.

"Not to worry," I said, frowning at the security guard. "If need be, I'll purchase another."

"That won't be necessary," he said and walked off.

Seeing how upset Macy was and because the two of us had become the focus of attention—I gently eased her into the lobby and away from the ballroom.

"Oh, Michael, I'm so sorry."

"What happened?" I asked as I hugged her close.

She trembled in my arms. "The taping went much later than I expected," she whispered.

That much I'd figured out.

"I guess you didn't have time to change clothes." She must've been wearing what she'd had on for the commercial shoot.

Macy nodded, her face against my shoulder. "I didn't know I was doing *two* scenes. The first was the modern-day grocery store and the second was from the 1960s. If I'd gone home and changed, I would've missed the dinner entirely."

"It's all right."

"No, it isn't," she said, sounding close to tears. "All I've done is embarrass you. I can't stay."

"Of course you can. I want you to meet my friends. I'm not embarrassed—I'm proud of you."

She shook her head. "I can't . . . I'm sorry. I've ruined everything."

Clasping her shoulders, I held her back from me and looked down into her face. "Don't be silly," I said, reaching for her hands. "Come inside with me and have some dinner. You'll feel better once you do."

"I can't. . . . I shouldn't have come, but I couldn't let you down . . . I just couldn't." She buried her face in her hands, and, seeing how distraught she was, I realized it would be even more upsetting for her to walk through the ballroom in full view of everyone.

"Do you want to go home?" I asked.

"Yes," she said in a high-pitched squeak.

Reluctantly, I nodded. I put my arms around her again, hoping to comfort and reassure her.

We stood entwined that way for perhaps a minute—until we were interrupted by Ritchie, rushing out of the ballroom. "Michael! They're getting ready to announce the awards."

"Okay. I'll be there."

Macy broke the embrace and smiled up at me. "I'm fine. Go back inside."

Ritchie looked at Macy and then at me, then back at Macy. He pulled me aside. "*This* is Macy?" he asked as though he couldn't believe his eyes.

"She came directly from the commercial shoot," I told him.

"Oh." He regarded me thoughtfully. Then in a lower voice, he asked, "Hannah's Macy?"

"No," I said, "my Macy."

"Oh."

I'd rarely seen my brother-in-law at a loss for words, but Ritchie clearly wasn't sure what to say. He opened his mouth, closed it again, then turned away, disappearing inside the ballroom.

"That was my brother-in-law," I said. "I didn't think you wanted me to introduce you just yet."

She nodded mutely.

"I'll stop by the house when I'm finished here," I promised her. My proposal could wait for another time.

Macy stared up at me, her eyes bright with unshed tears, then flung her arms around my neck and kissed me hard. The tears were flowing in earnest when she released me. Before I could say anything she fled down the hallway.

Her tears, and the desperate way she'd kissed me, alerted me to the fact that something was wrong. I would have followed her if I hadn't heard my name over the speakers. When I stepped back into the ballroom, I saw people glancing in my direction and discovered I'd won the award.

The rest of the evening was like a bad dream. I kept looking for an excuse to leave, but I was thwarted at every turn. Because I was the winner, I had to remain after the banquet for a short interview with the *Seattle Times*. Then the photographer showed up. When I left the hotel, it was almost eleven.

But I didn't care how late it was. I was going to Macy's house.

Despite the positive events of the evening, I had an anxious feeling about Macy. As soon as I pulled up in front of her fairy-tale house, I noticed that all the lights were off. Only the porch was illuminated.

Undaunted, I climbed out of the car and hurried up the sidewalk. As I neared the front door, I saw an envelope taped to the screen door, addressed to me.

I couldn't forget that my relationship with Macy had begun with another letter. The one from Hannah. Standing directly under the porch light, I ripped open the envelope and withdrew the single sheet of paper.

July 2
Michael,
  I can't do it. I'm so sorry.

Can't do what? I wondered.

Hannah made a mistake. I'm not the right kind of woman for you. I'll embarrass and humiliate you the way I did tonight.

She hadn't embarrassed me. When I discovered I'd fallen in love with Macy, I'd accepted that she was herself, her quirky, madcap, independent self. Those were the very qualities I now found so attractive, so appealing. So different from me.

I don't want to see you again. I know you probably think I'm being emotional and that this is an impulsive decision on my part. It isn't. I'm taking the cats and leaving for a while. This is for the best.

Best for whom? Not me. My initial reaction was to argue, except that I didn't have anyone to argue with.

I don't know when I'll be back but I can assure you it won't be soon. Put me out of your mind and look for a woman more suited to your world. And thank you, oh, thank you for loving me. I just wish I could be different.
Macy
P.S. Sammy's with Harvey. I hope you'll keep an eye on them both.

I read the letter a second time, crumpled it and dropped it on the porch before I turned and walked away.

Macy wanted to get out of my life. It was what I suspected she'd do after disappearing from my office that day—was it only two weeks ago? This was a pattern of hers. Uncompleted paintings and unfinished relationships.

Hannah had gotten it all wrong.

Chapter Thirty-Three

Mark's sister sat across from Leanne in the Lancasters' kitchen. It was after midnight and, while his parents had gone to their bedroom, Leanne doubted that either of them slept.

Mark had been missing in Afghanistan for a week—the longest week of Leanne's life. A day earlier, the country had celebrated the Fourth of July and the fireworks display had lit up the evening sky. The Lancaster family felt they had little to celebrate, and yet they'd stood with Denise's daughters and made a small display of patriotism for the sake of the children, who didn't fully understand what had taken place.

So far, the disappearance of two Americans in Afghanistan had been kept out of the news. For that Leanne was grateful, although she wasn't sure whether McPherson would be able to keep the incident under wraps much longer. She feared that in short order the information would be uncovered by the press. Then any privacy would be destroyed and the men's safety might well be compromised.

In contrast to last evening's loud fireworks, now there was only silence in the darkness of the summer night. The kitchen seemed to vibrate with stress as the two women sat there.

Denise had come to Spokane the Friday before

the holiday. She and her daughters slept in the spare bedroom. Until they'd arrived, Leanne had slept there, but she'd given it up for her sister-in-law and nieces. For the past three nights she'd bunked down on the living room sofa.

She needed to go back to Seattle. She couldn't continue putting her life on hold. Although the company had been good about updating the family, there was no real news. Her sense of hope escalated with each phone call and then plummeted just as quickly. No one slept for more than a few hours at a time. The only positive note was that while they were together, they could buoy one another's spirits.

"I suppose we should talk about . . . you know," Denise said reluctantly, cradling her coffee mug with both hands.

"I suppose," Leanne said, although she'd rather not. Still, everything that had happened was directly connected to Denise. The two women had never discussed it, and Leanne didn't see how talking about it now would serve any useful purpose, but she couldn't refuse.

Denise squirmed in her chair, not meeting Leanne's eyes. After several uncomfortable seconds, she blurted out, "I didn't know what Mark had done!"

"I realize that," Leanne assured her calmly.

"I knew if I didn't get away, Darrin would do something terrible, that he'd hurt us. He . . . he had before. No one knew besides Mark. I couldn't tell Mom and Dad, couldn't ask them for help. I had nowhere else to turn. My parents had pleaded with me not to marry Darrin and they were right."

Leanne saw that Denise's hands were clenched and her knuckles had gone white. "I've wanted to kick myself a thousand times for my rebellious attitude. I thought they were just being overprotective. Daddy disliked Darrin the moment they met."

So had Leanne. The man was manipulative, self-absorbed, domineering and irrational. She'd only met Denise's husband once, and she'd immediately assessed his personality. Mark's sister had been blinded by infatuation—or, as she'd hinted, by immaturity. Mark hadn't liked Darrin any more than Leanne had, but in his unswerving loyalty to Denise he'd defended her choice.

"At the time," Denise was saying, "I figured no man would ever be good enough for daddy's little girl, so I ignored his advice." She hung her head, and her long, straight, brown hair fell forward. "I've paid dearly for that."

Mark had, too, but Leanne prevented herself from saying so. The one concrete thing Denise had done to help her brother had been to plead for a lesser sentence. Because of that, Mark had gotten a year in prison instead of five. Still, the price had been far too high and, even now, Mark continued to pay.

"You have every right to be angry with me," Denise said.

"I am," Leanne told her frankly, "but I'm trying to forgive you." It wasn't easy, though, and Denise obviously understood that.

"I haven't forgiven myself. Trust me, if there was a way to relive the past I'd do it." She shook her head. "If Mark's—"

"Don't say it," Leanne insisted.

"Okay," Denise said. "But I believe he's alive. I can feel it—can't you?"

Unfortunately, Leanne couldn't. All she felt was terror and fear, pressing on her chest like bricks.

Denise darted her a look. "I'm not sure if anyone told you, but Darrin's in prison now for assaulting a woman he dated after our divorce."

Leanne glanced up. "I didn't know." That didn't change the past, but it did reveal the desperate situation Denise had faced when she left her husband.

"I couldn't have escaped him without Mark." She sobbed and Leanne realized how much Denise, too, was suffering. It wasn't fair that she and Mark had paid for his sister's bad decisions, but there was no going back.

Denise reached across the table as if to take Leanne's hand, but then drew back. "I'll pay back every penny, I swear I will. I'll do anything I can to make this right."

Money alone wasn't going to repay this debt.

Denise knew that. But there was no point in mentioning it.

"I will," Denise repeated.

"I know," Leanne whispered, because that seemed important to Denise.

"I'm so sorry, so sorry," Denise said, sobbing freely now, her thin shoulders heaving. "Please, please, say you can forgive me."

Leanne stretched one hand across the table and grabbed Denise's arm. "I forgive you. . . ."

Denise looked up then, her face streaked with tears. "It just never seems to end. Mark took that assignment in Afghanistan because of me . . . and now . . . now—" She couldn't finish.

Getting up from her chair, Leanne walked around the table and slid her arm around Denise's shoulders. She made comforting sounds, gently rocking the young woman as Denise wept bitter tears.

It took a long time for Denise to stop crying. Leanne's heart went out to everyone in Mark's family for the pain Denise's marriage had brought upon them all. The one piece of good news was the fact that Darrin was in prison.

"If we lost Mark . . ."

"Stop it!" Leanne cried. She couldn't lose Mark. He had to be alive. She had to believe that somehow he'd make it through this ordeal. The company and the military were doing everything possible to rescue him.

"We *have* to believe Mark will survive this," she said. Trusting, hoping, praying—for now, that was all they could do.

"I know . . . I know." Denise seemed to find a tiny bit of courage deep inside herself. She wiped the tears from her face and straightened. "You're right. If for no other reason than to keep up Mom and Dad's spirits, we have to believe. But I do think he's alive, I really do."

They hugged each other and, soon after that, Leanne retired to her sofa bed, sleeping fitfully. The next morning, she made the decision to return to Seattle and her job. The farewells were hard, and they clung to one another for long minutes.

"I'll always consider you the sister I never had," Denise whispered as they hugged. After loading her vehicle, Leanne headed back to Seattle with tears clouding her eyes.

News of Mark's rescue reached her two days later. Muriel Lancaster phoned, sobbing with joy and relief. Mark had been rescued by Special Forces, who said it was a miracle that both men were alive. Because she was so overcome with emotion, Muriel couldn't answer Leanne's questions.

That night Leanne slept a solid eleven hours, not waking even once. She didn't expect to hear from Mark personally. She had every reason to assume his attitude toward her hadn't changed. None of that mattered, however, because Mark was *alive*.

Nearly two weeks passed. Muriel gave Leanne

regular updates on Mark's condition. He'd been severely beaten and was in bad shape when rescued. After being stabilized by the medics, Mark was flown back to the States. McPherson flew his parents to the Washington, D.C., hospital where Mark was receiving treatment. A short while later, he was released. Muriel kept her informed, but Leanne recognized that her mother-in-law did so without Mark's knowledge or consent.

Tuesday afternoon, nearly three weeks after Mark's rescue, Leanne stopped in the cafeteria to grab soup and a sandwich for lunch. She often ate on the hospital patio. It was early August now, a beautiful day with cloudless blue skies and a gentle breeze wafting in off Puget Sound.

She found her favorite spot on a concrete ledge under a dogwood tree. Sometimes friends joined her and, while she never rejected their company, she was just as happy to eat alone.

No sooner had she settled down and opened her soup container than she noticed a man in a wheelchair with his back toward her. She lowered her spoon as a tingling sensation went through her.

The man reminded her of Mark.

The width of his shoulders, his hair with the small cowlick she'd loved to run her fingers through . . . But the last thing Leanne had heard, only two days ago, was that Mark was at a rehab facility on the east coast, recovering from his injuries.

Was it possible? *Could* this be Mark? If her ex-husband was at the hospital, presumably it was because he planned to approach her. Perhaps he hadn't seen her enter the patio area. Perhaps he was waiting for her.

Leanne was afraid her mind was playing tricks on her. Mark was always in her thoughts, so it stood to reason that she'd look for hints of him in every man she saw.

Still . . .

When she couldn't stand it any longer, she got up, discarded the remains of her lunch, then walked over to the table with the big sun-bleached umbrella.

It was Mark.

His face revealed evidence of his capture. His jaw had been broken—his mouth was wired partially shut—and one side of his face was swollen and bruised. His left arm was in a cast. Just seeing him with these injuries unloosed all the grief in her heart. She couldn't bear the thought of the man she loved in such pain.

He glanced up and smiled crookedly. "Would you care to join me?" he asked, gesturing to the opposite side of the table. His voice was slightly muffled, and he seemed to have some difficulty speaking.

Leanne tried to respond, but couldn't. After two or three futile attempts, she finally managed to ask, "What are you doing here?"

She hadn't meant to sound unwelcoming, but thankfully he didn't take offence.

"I came to see you."

That was the only logical explanation and yet she couldn't understand it. A hundred questions circled her mind and she could hardly sort out which one to ask first.

All of a sudden, it became more important to tell him one simple truth than to ask any of her questions. "I love you," she whispered brokenly. "I never stopped loving you. We both made mistakes—"

"We did," he said and, reaching across the table with his free hand, he took hers. Like teenagers they held hands, fingers gripping tightly.

For a long moment neither spoke.

"You went to stay with my parents," he eventually said.

A huge lump had formed in her throat and all she could do was nod.

"Dad said you kept their spirits up until Denise got there."

"I tried," she said hoarsely.

"While I was held captive, all I could think about was you," Mark told her. His thumb grazed the top of her hand. "It didn't matter how often they beat me, I kept telling myself I had to stay alive because I needed to get home to you."

"You're home now." She placed her other hand over their clasped ones.

"There's never been anyone but you, Leanne. There never will be anyone but you."

"Why did you ever say otherwise?" He'd withdrawn those words, but the lie still upset her.

"I was afraid you might come back, and I wouldn't have the strength to send you away a second time."

"Oh, Mark."

"I knew it was wrong. The hurt in your eyes tormented me for days. That's why I sent you that letter. I was always faithful to you, Leanne. Then and now."

She leaned forward and touched her forehead to his.

"The doctors said I shouldn't come, but I couldn't stay away any longer."

She laid her hand lightly on his swollen jaw. "Oh, Mark." Chills shot through her at the thought of his suffering.

His hand covered hers, and he brushed the tears from her cheeks. "You are so beautiful."

Somehow she managed to laugh. "Sure I am. My eyes are red and watering and my nose is probably running."

"Beautiful," he insisted.

All of a sudden Leanne sensed someone behind her. She twisted around and saw Denise.

"Do you two lovebirds want me to disappear for a while or is it safe to join you?"

Leanne stood and hugged her sister-in-law.

"She drove me over from Spokane," Mark explained. "I flew in yesterday," he added.

"He would've found a way to get to you, with or without me. I figured it was the least I could do." She looked from one to the other. "I owe you both so much. I wanted to help fix things for you." A slow smile came into play. "Although I have to say you don't seem to need much help."

"Where are the girls?" Leanne asked.

"With Mom and Dad in Spokane."

Leanne sat down, her hand once again holding Mark's. She needed to be close to him, needed to touch him, in order to believe he was really here. With her.

"Did you ask her?" Denise directed the question to Mark. Then, not waiting for a response, she said, "As you might've noticed, it's a bit difficult for him to speak."

"Denise," Mark warned in a low growl.

His sister ignored him. "He wants to ask you to marry him, but first he wants to know if you're interested in that doctor you mentioned. I told him you weren't, but he wants to hear it from you."

"Denise!" This time his growl was louder.

"Oh, hush. If I left this to you, you'd mess it up for sure." Denise winked at Leanne. "You love my brother, don't you?"

"Yes," Leanne said, laughing softly.

"Told you so," Mark's sister said to him in a

know-it-all tone. She turned to Leanne. "And you'd remarry him in a heartbeat."

"I would."

"That's what I thought." She exhaled loudly. "Well, then, my work here is done. Oh, just one more thing."

"What?" Mark said impatiently.

"My girls could do with a cousin. Don't keep them waiting too long."

Mark gave a strangled laugh. "We'll get on that."

"Yes, we will," Leanne promised.

Her soon-to-be husband raised her palm to his lips and dropped a kiss there.

Leanne had her husband back, and her world had been set right. This time she wasn't taking anything for granted. This time, when they spoke their vows, it would be forever.

Chapter Thirty-Four

The first week after Macy left town, I went to her house every day. On the weekend, I was there two or three times. When it became apparent that she truly meant what she'd said and would be gone for an extended period, I cut back on my visits.

The second week I came by twice. A man on the neighborhood watch committee questioned me one evening. After that, I figured I'd better make myself scarce.

The third week, I was over only once and then, after a month, I didn't go back. Yes, Macy had meant what she'd said. I tucked the ring in the back of a drawer and tried to forget about it. I should have returned it; sooner or later I would.

My only consolation came from Harvey. I spoke to him every day that first week, although it did little good. The two of us were like wolves howling at the moon, miserable and lost without Macy. I have to admit that by the end of July I was pretty pathetic.

"Has she ever done anything like this before?" I asked her cantankerous next-door neighbor that first week. I recalled that day in mid-June, when she'd taken off and not come home until evening.

"Oh, she'd leave for a few hours when she got upset. She has that place she goes when she needs to think, but she's never been gone this long. My guess is she went somewhere else," Harvey said.

"Where would she go?"

"If I knew that," he yelled, "I'd go after her myself!"

"What about her family?"

Harvey shrugged. "Doubtful. If she did go to her parents' in New Mexico, her mother would likely send her right back."

Harvey's suspicions proved correct. When I called her parents, I learned that Macy hadn't been in touch in several weeks. I explained who I was and said I loved Macy. Her mother had never heard of me. That was another big dent to my pride. By then, it had received so many dents I was beginning to feel like a car abandoned at the junkyard. I asked Mrs. Roth to contact me if she talked to her daughter. She didn't call and I could only assume Macy hadn't gone running to her family for solace.

"How's Sammy doing without Macy?" I asked Harvey the second week. She'd taken the three cats with her, wherever she might be.

"He misses her as much as you and I do," the old man said starkly.

The third week, Harvey called me after ten one evening, so excited I had difficulty understanding him. "Turn on channel thirteen," he finally said, enunciating slowly and clearly as if I were some backward pupil.

As it happened, I had my TV on and flipped to the proper channel just in time to catch the end of the grocery-store commercial that had caused Macy such trouble. Seeing her in that 1960s costume again set my heart racing.

"You see her?" Harvey demanded.

"Yes."

"Looks good, doesn't she?"

I nodded, knowing Harvey couldn't see my response. But that was okay because he knew how I felt. I was so hungry for the sight of Macy, I would've crawled inside the TV set if I could have.

"Miss her, don't you?" he said with surprising gentleness.

"More than I could ever have guessed. You?"

"She's a pest." He sighed. "Never thought I'd say this, but it's downright lonely around this place without her."

"At least you've got Sammy."

"If you want him, come and get him," Harvey retorted. "He's all yours."

That was an empty promise if I'd ever heard one. "No, you keep him," I said.

"Sammy's company, all right," Harvey said next. "But half the time he's over at Macy's door, whining because he misses her and those darn cats. I swear I've never seen anything like it."

I was whining myself.

"You coming by tomorrow?" Harvey asked.

I squared my shoulders and my resolve. "No."

"Why not?"

"She isn't there, is she?"

"Not yet."

"Then I can't see any point in coming by." My friendship with Harvey was a good reason, but I preferred to keep in touch with him by phone. It was just too painful to visit her house, her neighborhood.

"You want me to call when she comes back?"

I had to give that some consideration. "No, I don't think so." I didn't mean to have a defeatist attitude, but I'd done all I could. As far as I was concerned, it was Macy's turn.

"No?" Harvey echoed in disbelief. "What's the matter with you, boy?"

First, I don't like being referred to as a *boy,* and secondly, Macy had been clear about what she wanted. And what she didn't want. The way I saw it, if she couldn't love me enough to see past our differences, a relationship between us had no potential.

"I gave it my best shot, Harvey," I said. "Macy doesn't want to be part of my life, so I'd better live with her decision."

"She loves you," he argued. "But she's afraid. She's never been in love like this before."

"I have," I reminded him. I knew what it meant to love someone else, the way Hannah had loved me, and this wasn't it. Macy might *think* she was in love with me, but her actions certainly contradicted that.

"Let the girl have a second chance," Harvey said.

I smiled at his feeble attempt to patch things up. He could argue all he wanted, but his arguments were irrelevant, since Macy was nowhere to be found.

I insisted I was done with Macy; nevertheless, I sat up for several hours, staring at the TV, flipping channels, looking for a repeat of the Safeway commercial just to see her again.

That said, I do have my pride. To prove I was getting over her, I accepted a blind date and actually had a semi-enjoyable evening. The woman, Carrie, was a friend of Melanie's, Patrick's wife. Carrie was a perfectly nice person, but she wasn't Macy. She had an easy laugh but she didn't make *me* laugh, didn't make me think or challenge me. Nor did she try to feed me cat food or drag in a stray dog to love and protect.

One date was all it took. I realized I wasn't nearly as over Macy as I'd hoped.

What particularly disturbed me was the fact that Macy had never finished the mural. It remained three-quarters completed. Every time I walked past it, I looked at that jungle scene, those parrots and that baby giraffe, and thought of Macy.

Nearly everything in her life seemed to be like this unfinished painting. She had good intentions, but one thing or another kept her from following through with what she started. Apparently, this translated into relationships, as well. I was just another unfinished project discarded along with the mural on my wall.

My guess was that this inability to complete anything went back to her childhood. In one of those lengthy phone conversations, during which we chatted for three or four hours, I'd learned that Macy had always been considered a bit odd by her family. They had little patience with her often-roundabout approach to things and her idiosyncratic views. And they rarely showed much interest in any project she undertook. The only person who understood and appreciated her had been her grandmother. I'd come to love her quirky nature, but I couldn't get past her ability to walk away from people and projects.

Linda caught me staring at the mural the first week of August. "Do you want me to find someone to finish it?" she asked.

"No, thanks."

"It's funny, isn't it, how she simply vanished like that?"

Funny isn't the word I would've used. "Yeah," I said and headed for my next appointment.

"Before you go in there, I need to tell you this is a new patient. He's, well, a bit of an unusual case."

I nodded. "Thanks for the warning." She wore a strange expression and I couldn't help wondering what was so different about this new patient. I soon found out.

When I walked into the room, I found Harvey sitting on the exam table, his legs dangling down so far they touched the floor. "Harvey," I said, unable to disguise my shock.

"I made my appointment like everyone else," he grumbled, crossing his arms over his chest in a defensive gesture.

"I'd like to remind you that I'm a pediatrician."

"And I'd like to remind *you* that I came at my appointment time. Don't tell me you're going to refuse me treatment."

"No." If Harvey was seeking medical help, I'd do everything I could, and that included referring him to a specialist. If necessary, I'd personally escort him to every appointment. I'd come to love this old man as much as Macy did, probably more. I wouldn't turn my back on him the way she had.

"You'd better sit down," he said.

"That bad, huh?" I teased. Because of the chest pains he'd occasionally mentioned, I suspected the problem was with Harvey's heart, although he didn't seem any worse than the day we'd met.

I plugged my stethoscope into my ears. "Let's start by listening to your heart."

"I'm not here about my heart."

"All right," I said, removing the stethoscope. "Why *are* you here?"

Harvey took a moment to answer. He nailed me to the stool with his piercing gaze, then said, "Macy's back."

I was glad I was sitting down. Still, I couldn't immediately form the words to question him. "When did that happen?" I finally asked.

"Couple of days ago. She doesn't look good, either."

"Oh." I was reluctant to show interest, but at the same time I was curious. I just didn't want Harvey to know it.

The old guy frowned at me, but I wasn't intimidated. I'd learned months ago that he was all growl and no bite.

"She's lost weight and she didn't have any to lose." Lips pinched, he shook his head. "She's nothing but skin and bones."

"I'm sorry to hear that." And I was. "Where did she go?"

"To a friend's place on the other side of the mountains, near Wenatchee."

She'd never mentioned a friend near Wenatchee. I wondered if this person was male or female.

"I told her about you hanging around the place for a month or so."

I'd rather he hadn't; nevertheless, I was curious to know her reaction.

"And?" I asked in a bored voice. I doubt I'd fooled him but my pride demanded the pretense.

"She didn't say anything."

That figured. "I'll bet Sammy was pleased to see her."

"And her him. Those two were glued to each other for a whole day. I don't understand it."

"She rescued him. Sammy owes her. What's there to understand?"

"I wasn't talking about Sammy and Macy," he snapped. "I mean Sammy and those cats of hers. You'd have thought they were best friends. They were all over him and Sammy just stood there, happy as a clam at high tide, letting those blasted cats weave in and around his legs. I wouldn't have believed it if I hadn't seen it with my own eyes."

Despite my determination not to, I smiled.

Everything had felt out of kilter while Macy was away. And now she was back—but it didn't matter. It couldn't matter.

"So?" Harvey said none too gently.

"So, *what?*"

"Are you going to see her?"

"Nope."

"Why not?"

"I wasn't the one who ran away."

"That didn't stop you the first week. You practically lived at my house. I can remember a couple of times I had to escort you to the door because it was past my bedtime."

"That was before," I said.

He narrowed his eyes. "Before what?"

"Before—" I looked at him pointedly "—I came to my senses."

Harvey shook his head slowly from side to side. "It seems to me you've *lost* your senses."

"Macy has a habit of running away whenever she's confronted with anything difficult or boring or unpleasant. I'm not chasing after her, Harvey. If she loves me, she'll come to me."

His frown darkened. "Cut her some slack."

"I did. I gave her a month. Now it's up to her."

He didn't like it, but I could see he wasn't going to argue. I guessed he'd talked to Macy and learned what I already knew. Macy might be full of energy, crackling with life and unexpected ideas, but she was afraid of commitment, afraid of love. If my feelings for her weren't enough to give her the courage to face me, then nothing I said or did would make any difference.

"The two of you are more trouble than you're worth," he said with a disgruntled snort.

"No doubt." I could appreciate that it had taken a great deal for Harvey to make an appointment to see me. He knew that if he'd phoned, it would've been a short conversation. This way, he could see my reaction for himself and gauge how likely it was that his efforts would bring Macy and me back together.

"You want me to examine you?" I didn't wait for an answer. I inserted my stethoscope's earpieces again. "Since you're paying for this appointment, you should make it worth your while."

"You're charging me?" he asked in an outraged voice.

Apparently, he hadn't considered this until now. "It's our policy to charge for office visits, so in a word, yes. I'm charging you. Or Medicare, as the case may be."

"You got to be kidding! No wonder people say no good deed goes unpunished."

I listened to his heart. "Not bad," I told him. There was a strong, steady beat. I listened again, then moved the stethoscope around to his back. "Take a deep breath," I instructed. His lungs, too, sounded fine.

"I'm doing all right," he muttered when I checked his reflexes. "I've decided I'm not dying."

"Glad to hear it."

"Well, not yet, anyway. Those chest pains? They went away. Must've been indigestion from eating cat food."

I couldn't suppress a grin.

"I'd like to run a couple of blood tests," I said. "Just to make sure your latest self-diagnosis is correct." I now suspected his fainting spells had been caused by hypoglycemia and I wanted to confirm that.

"No way."

"You afraid of giving me a little blood, Harvey? If you do it, you'll get a sticker for your forehead and a lollipop."

He didn't respond for a moment, then sighed in resignation. "Why didn't you say so earlier?"

"Good boy." As I said it, I had a clear memory of the time he'd called me "boy" and how I'd felt about it.

"I'm a long way from being a boy," he grumbled.

"Uh-huh." I patted him on the back and helped him off the examination table, aiding him with his balance. "Didn't you tell Macy you're in your second childhood? Just think of this as your annual checkup before you hit puberty."

He grumbled again, but I could tell he was amused. And he did let Linda take his blood.

The next morning when I met Ritchie at the gym, I knew it was a mistake to say anything about Macy. But I hadn't slept well, and when he prodded me about that, I blurted it out.

"She's back?" my brother-in-law said, half jogging, half running on the treadmill.

I pretended I hadn't heard him, running at my own pace. We were on machines that stood side by side.

"You talked to her?"

"No. I don't plan to, either."

Ritchie slowed his speed. "You honestly intend to stay away?"

"Yup."

To my surprise, he didn't have an automatic comeback. I glanced over at him and saw that he was studying me.

"I don't get it, man."

"What don't you get?" I was foolish enough to ask.

"You. Macy disappears and you moon after her for weeks. In case you aren't aware of it, you were miserable and you made everyone else miserable, too."

"I apologized for that." Unfortunately, Ritchie had been on the receiving end of my bad mood for much of that time. Fortunately, however, he's a good friend and he put up with me.

"Yeah, you apologized, but it wasn't enough."

"What more do you want?" I asked. This was probably going to cost me.

"One thing."

"Okay, name it."

"Ask yourself what Hannah would want you to do."

I stopped running and nearly lost my balance as the treadmill shot me backward. At least I had the presence of mind to grab the handlebars.

"That was below the belt," I muttered.

"Think about it," Ritchie said.

What *would* Hannah want me to do? Good question.

Well, she'd just have to tell me.

Chapter Thirty-Five

Winter and Pierre were sprawled at opposite ends of the leather sofa in her condo. Their feet met in the middle and they both had cookbooks propped on their laps.

Winter dropped her book on the floor with a thud. "What about a cold avocado soup for lunch?" It was early Sunday afternoon, a lazy summer Sunday with flawless August weather.

"Blended with buttermilk?"

"And fresh lime juice," Winter suggested. "Add a little salt, and ooh-la-la!"

"Sounds *délicieux*. But—" he raised his eyebrows "—the soup might be too thick, depending on how much avocado you use."

"Ah." Winter nodded. "I have a secret ingredient."

Pierre's cell phone rang and he reached inside his pocket.

Winter could tell from the way he stiffened that it was bad news. He listened for a few minutes, then stood and walked over to the window. He started pacing, back and forth, back and forth.

She sat up and watched him.

Frowning, Pierre swore and snapped his cell phone shut before shoving it in his pocket.

"What's the matter?" she asked.

"I work with a group of *imbéciles,*" he shouted. "Where do they find these people? I would assume I could have one day off, but, oh, no." He stormed into the kitchen. "Where is my book?" he demanded. *"Mon cahier?"*

"What book?"

"The one I had with me earlier, of course. My *book.*"

Winter didn't think it was her responsibility to keep track of his book. Besides, it wasn't really a book, but a notebook, one he always carried with him.

"Pierre."

"Can't you see I'm in a rush?"

She inhaled and closed her eyes. This was a telling moment. She could respond with anger or she could remain calm. Her instinct was to return tit for tat, but experience told her that would only exacerbate the problem.

She walked into the kitchen, where he was tossing papers to and fro, searching for his "book."

"Let me help," she offered.

"Did you hide it from me?"

Normally she'd be infuriated by his ridiculous accusation. Instead, she laughed.

He turned and regarded her suspiciously.

"Is this what you're looking for?" she asked, holding up his notebook. He'd left it on the table in plain sight.

He grinned and put out his hand. She held the notebook out of reach. "It's going to cost you."

A smile crinkled the corners of his eyes and then faded. "Our Sunday afternoon is ruined."

"There'll be other afternoons."

Pierre threw his arms around her. "Thank you."

"No, thank Alix's mother-in-law."

"Her mother-in-law?"

"Never mind," she said, touching her lips to his.

He left shortly afterward, and Winter settled back on the sofa. For the past six weeks, she and Pierre had been dating. This time, they hadn't made the mistake of moving ahead too quickly.

During the initial meeting after their three-month break, Pierre had been guarded and brusque. He seemed determined to end their relationship until Winter had coerced him into trying the exercise Alix had taught her. When Pierre saw how he reacted to things that bothered him about Winter, his eyes, too, had been opened. Now, a month later, their relationship wasn't without problems, and breaking old habits required constant effort, but it was working. Winter was happier than she'd been all year.

She fell asleep on the sofa and was awakened by Pierre's kiss an hour later. She wrapped her arms around his neck and savored everything about him—his strong, solid body, his warm clean scent, the steady beating of his heart.

"Mmm. This is a lovely way to wake up."

Pierre chuckled.

Winter's phone pealed in the background.

"Not again," Pierre moaned. "Don't answer it."

"Pierre, I have to. It could be important." She didn't remind him that she hadn't asked him not to answer *his* phone earlier.

He released her with obvious reluctance, and she grabbed the phone just before it went to voice mail.

"Alix is having her baby!" Lydia from A Good Yarn said excitedly. "She called a few minutes ago and she's in labor."

"I thought Jordan was supposed to call."

"He didn't, but you know Jordan when it comes to this baby—he can't think straight. Alix sounded a lot calmer than he did." Lydia laughed. "I could hear him in the background insisting she get off the phone, that they had to get to the hospital."

"Their baby's going to be one spoiled infant."

Winter intended to do a fair amount of that spoiling herself.

"Right now Jordan's a nervous wreck," Lydia said.

"Of course he is. He's a first-time father and with what happened before—well, it's understandable." They talked a while longer and then Winter ended the conversation. "Thanks for letting me know. Call me if you hear anything and I'll do the same."

Pierre and Winter made the avocado soup, and it was as delicious as Winter had known it would be. Pierre laughed at her "secret ingredient," which was ice cubes. She added ten to the recipe, using the ice to both cool and thin out the avocado and buttermilk blend. She also added an extra cup of milk and served the soup with crumbled blue cheese.

Pierre made chicken curry sandwiches to complement it. Halfway through lunch, Winter set down her spoon and lowered her half-eaten sandwich to her plate.

"What's wrong?" Pierre asked. "Too much curry in the chicken?"

"No, it's perfect." Pierre was a master at gauging spices.

"Then what is it?"

"I'm worried about Alix," Winter murmured.

"Women have babies every day. There's nothing to worry about."

Winter hoped that was true. "It's just . . . a feeling I have." She stood and walked aimlessly around the kitchen. A moment later, she'd made a decision. "I want to go to the hospital."

"*Mais, ce temps—c'est pour la famille*. A time like this is for family," he translated.

"I *am* Alix's family. She doesn't have anyone except us—the people of Blossom Street who love her."

Pierre considered her words, then slowly nodded. "Would you like me to accompany you?"

She nodded with relief. "I was hoping you'd offer."

"For you, my love, anything."

Winter put their dirty dishes in the sink while Pierre dealt with the leftovers. She collected her purse and they headed out together.

For some reason she felt less worried when they arrived at the hospital. Perhaps that was simply because she was *doing* something now, even if that something was just waiting in a different place. To her surprise she discovered the waiting room was full. She recognized Larry and Susan Turner, who were sitting across from Lydia Goetz and Casey, her thirteen-year-old daughter.

"Hi, Winter." Lydia smiled when she saw her. She was a lovely woman, a two-time cancer survivor whose petite, delicate beauty belied her emotional strength. "I told Casey you wouldn't be able to stay away, either, and I was right."

"Mom's always right," Casey said teasingly.

"And don't you forget it."

Winter knew that Lydia and her husband, Brad, had adopted the girl the year before. She'd started off as a foster child and, over the summer, the family had grown to love her. The girl had become close to Alix and often stopped at the café to chat with her. Casey must be anxious for news of the baby's birth.

"You all know Pierre, don't you?" Winter asked, stepping over to where the Turners had gathered.

Larry stood, and Pierre shook hands with Jordan's father. "We met at the wedding," Larry said. "This is our first grandchild," he added nervously.

"Bonne chance," Pierre said. "I'm wishing you the best."

"Would you two stop?" Susan said with a laugh. "Everything's going to be fine." She had a crochet project on her lap, and Winter could see that Casey had brought her knitting.

Following Winter's gaze, Casey said, "I'm making the baby a blanket. Mom's helping me." Then under her breath, she muttered, "I'm better at crochet than knitting. Aunt Margaret even said so."

"How's it going with Alix?" Winter asked, directing the question to Susan.

"Jordan was back to give us a report about half an hour ago. Alix is well—and the baby should be born soon."

Just then, as if he'd been summoned, Jordan burst through the swinging doors and threw his arms in the air. "We have a son!"

"A son," Susan echoed. She pressed both hands to her mouth and her eyes instantly filled with tears.

"A grandson," Larry said as though in shock.

"Healthy as a horse, too, if his bellow is anything to go by," Jordan said, his voice elated. "He weighed in at seven pounds, nine ounces."

"August eighth is a great day to be born," Casey said.

"You know anyone born on that day?" Winter asked.

"Alix's baby."

Winter grinned. "Right."

"Do you have a name picked out yet?" Susan asked.

Winter remembered that Alix and Jordan had kept their choices a secret, not wanting any pressure from even the people they loved.

Jordan smiled. "Thomas Lawrence."

"Thomas Lawrence," Winter repeated.

"After her brother," Lydia said quietly.

Winter looked at her for an explanation.

"Alix had an older brother who died," Lydia told her. "She named her son after her brother."

Jordan nodded. "And after my father."

"I'm deeply honored," Larry whispered. He seemed very emotional and close to tears.

"When can we see Alix and the baby?" Casey asked, sitting on the edge of her seat. "I want to show her the blanket."

"It'll probably be a while yet," Lydia said. "They need to wash the baby and do some tests."

"Oh."

"You'll have plenty of time to visit Alix later," Lydia promised.

The two of them stood, and Winter did, as well. Susan and Larry hugged Jordan, and Casey and Lydia did, too.

Jordan turned toward Winter, his arms out-stretched. "Thank you so much for coming."

"I love Alix," Winter said.

"I know, and you've been wonderful to her. She loves you right back," Jordan said, pulling her toward him. "Thank you all for being here. I'll be sure to tell Alix."

"Please do, and give her my love." She kissed his cheek, then turned and joined Pierre.

Pierre reached for her hand and they walked to the elevator.

It was difficult to leave. Winter glanced over her shoulder and saw Larry and Susan still congratu-lating their son.

On the way out of the hospital Winter felt euphoric. Pierre slipped his arm around her waist as they strolled toward the parking complex.

"I'm so happy for Alix and Jordan," she said. "Just so happy."

"I am, too." Pierre stopped suddenly and drew her to a halt. "We should have a baby," he said.

"What?" Winter chuckled. "Pierre, we'd want to be married first, wouldn't we?"

"But of course."

"And we'd want to be absolutely certain we were bringing a child into a healthy relationship. A loving one."

"Naturally," he agreed.

Winter looked up at this man she so desperately loved. "Just a minute . . . Pierre, are you asking me to marry you?"

"*Oui.* Which means yes, *mon amour améri-caine.*"

She nudged him. "That much French I know. But Pierre, is this what you want?"

"More than I realized. I want to have children with you, Winter, and to love you with the same love I saw in that young father's eyes. We have some distance to go, but you and me—well, I believe we can do this. Six months ago, six weeks, I could not have said that, but I can now."

Winter flung her arms around his neck. "Yes, *mon amour français,* I believe we can."

Chapter Thirty-Six

S he's here!" Linda Barclay said, stepping into my office a week after Harvey had told me about Macy's return. Seven long days. My nurse shut the door behind her, and as if I needed to be informed who *she* was, added, "Macy's here."

"Oh?" I looked up from my half-eaten lunch. I pretended not to be interested. "What does she want?"

The question appeared to confuse Linda. "I don't think she *wants* anything."

"Then what's she doing here?"

Linda motioned helplessly. "She's here to finish the mural. She's got her paints. Right now she's saying hello to everyone. I . . . I thought you'd want to know."

"It doesn't matter to me," I said coldly. As for the mural, I'd grown accustomed to seeing it unfinished. It even had a certain appeal that way. I'd come to accept that it would probably stay exactly as it was, and that was fine by me. I no longer expected Macy to finish anything she started. That included the mural *and* me. This was a pattern; when situations grew too intense or uncomfortable, she simply walked away.

That left a question as to why she'd returned and then the answer came to me. Instinctively, I realized she wasn't back out of any desire to see me. After all these weeks she probably needed the money to catch up on her bills. Accepting that as the most likely explanation, I opened my top desk drawer and pulled out my checkbook.

"What are you doing?" Linda asked suspiciously.

"What does it look like? I'm writing a check for the remainder of what I owe her." I signed my name with a great deal of flair, ripped off the check and set it on the desk. "I'd appreciate it if you'd see that she gets paid when she's finished the mural."

"Michael!" Linda cried, hands on her hips.

She hardly ever addressed me in that tone, and I automatically glanced up. "What?" I asked. Paying a supplier for services rendered wasn't an unusual request.

"You need to give it to her yourself."

"No can do. I have a busy afternoon."

"No busier than usual."

"Fine, have it your way," I said, unwilling to fight about this. "If you won't give her the check, I'll ask one of the others to do it." I refused to be thwarted. I refused to see Macy. I didn't want to speak to her, either.

"She isn't here because of the mural," Linda told me.

I knew otherwise. Remembering how close Macy lived to the edge financially, I was well aware that six weeks without income must have played havoc with her bank account. That check was the sole reason she'd swallowed her pride and walked in here today. If she expected me to make a scene, then she'd be disappointed. Or relieved. I didn't care which. As far as I was concerned, she was invisible.

Rather than continue the argument, I walked out from behind my desk and found the receptionist. "Would you kindly see that Ms. Roth receives this check before she leaves?"

"Ah . . . sure." Her eyes connected with someone behind me. Linda, no doubt.

I chose to ignore them both. Without another word, I went back to my office, walking directly past Macy. From her position on the floor, paintbrush in hand, she looked up at me. I felt her gaze as powerfully as a caress. It took a great deal of strength to pretend she meant nothing. Once back in my office I closed the door.

My first appointment of the afternoon was with Ryan Clawson, who had an infected big toe. I cleaned it and wrote out a prescription for antibiotics, then wrapped his foot. Taking my pen I drew smiley faces on his other four toes and made up a story about the "Toed" family to keep the boy entertained. Ryan at six had been frightened and nervous, but he'd held up bravely, even giggling at my nonsense. After giving his mother instructions on how to care for his foot, I helped Ryan down from the exam table.

"Who's the lady outside?" he asked, looking up at me.

"Nurse Linda?"

"No, the lady painting the wall."

"That's Macy," I said, trying not to grit my teeth. Was there no escaping her?

"She's nice."

Rather than respond verbally, I managed a smile.

"She said you'd help my foot feel better. She said I should be brave and I was, wasn't I?"

"Yes, you were." I was sure this was Macy's way of sending me a message. Well, she could send all the cryptic messages she wanted, but I wasn't responding. I had nothing to say.

"Can I tell her how brave I was?"

"By all means." I held open the door for Ryan and his mother. Without glancing in Macy's direction, I went to the next room, where I was to examine a suspected case of poison ivy.

By the time I'd finished my afternoon appointments, Macy had completed the painting and disappeared, which was exactly what I'd expected. I'd certainly called that one. She'd taken the money and run. No surprise there.

Rather than risk an unintentional meeting, I returned to my office and shut the door once again. It was after five and I was looking over lab results when I heard someone knocking. Assuming it was Linda, I called out, "Come in."

The door opened and Macy stepped inside.

So she hadn't hightailed it out of the office, after all. Leaning back in my chair I feigned irritation. "Yes?" I said shortly. I wanted it known that I wasn't pleased to see her.

She stepped forward and set the check on my desk. "You don't owe me anything."

I wasn't going to be drawn into an argument, and yet I felt obliged to pay her. Picking up the check, I handed it back. "Did I not agree to pay you seven hundred dollars for the mural?"

"You did."

"Then what's the problem?" I wanted her out of my office as quickly as possible. I continued to hold out the check, which she ignored.

"I didn't finish the mural in a timely manner."

"But you did finish it."

"Besides, you made a house call to see Harvey, remember?"

"It wasn't a house call," I insisted. The last thing I needed was my insurance company getting wind of the fact that I'd broken a cardinal rule. My malpractice premiums were already more than my college loan payments had been. I didn't need a rate hike because Macy couldn't keep her mouth shut.

"You held up your end of the bargain. I'm doing the same."

I gestured toward her dismissively, the check still in my hand. "It was nothing. Take this and cash it in good conscience."

"I can't do that."

"Fine, then," I said as though bored. I tore it up and let the pieces flutter into the wastebasket.

Still, Macy didn't leave. She stood awkwardly on the other side of my desk, shuffling her feet nervously while I acted as if she wasn't there. Finally I couldn't stand it anymore.

"Was there something else?" I asked, making my voice as flat as I could.

"Ah . . . Harvey said you stopped by every day for the first week."

I didn't bother denying it. "More fool me."

"Would it help if I told you I was sorry?" She bit her lower lip, something I'd seen her do any number of times. It always made me want to kiss her, to ease away her anxiety. Instead, I looked down at the lab reports on my desk.

"Michael, I really am sorry."

I glanced up then and saw her big eyes staring back at me, silently pleading. I exhaled slowly. "I'm sure you are," I said.

"Does an apology help?" she asked.

"No."

"Oh."

This had gone on long enough. I walked over to the door and opened it. To my shock Linda, the receptionist and two other staff members stood on the other side, listening in on our conversation. They each wore a stunned look and instantly scattered. If I hadn't been so unprepared, I would have laughed. Well, maybe not.

"I remember Hannah," Macy said.

My hand remained on the knob, my back to Macy. I felt a surge of anger. It wasn't fair to bring up Hannah's name! "I think it would be best if you left now."

But Macy didn't leave. "I don't have a lot of friends." She hesitated, then amended the statement. "That isn't what I meant—I have lots of friends, but most of them are more . . . acquaintances. I considered Hannah a friend, a true friend. I loved everything about her. The way she laughed wasn't like anyone else I ever knew. I enjoyed the sound of it so much I'd do just about anything to hear it."

"It really is time for you to go," I said again, my voice gaining conviction.

"I know. I probably should, but I can't make myself do it."

"Do you want me to call security?"

"You could, but I should remind you that Larry likes me."

She was quickly gaining the upper hand and I resented it. I opened my mouth to tell her I'd request someone else, when she interrupted me.

"No one's ever loved me the way you do . . . did."

That was her reason for abandoning me? It didn't make sense. Not for a moment.

"Oh, my grandmother. And maybe Harvey, although he'd never admit it."

"You're telling me this . . . why?"

"Because your love frightened me. I didn't know what to do or how to act. It overwhelmed me, just like Hannah's friendship did."

"You ran away from her, too?"

"No."

Liar. Other than at Hannah's funeral, I'd never seen Macy, never even met her. "I don't remember you coming to visit her."

"I didn't," she confessed.

That said it all.

"I couldn't bear to see her so gravely ill, not Hannah. So I sent her things."

"Things?"

"I wrote her poems and mailed her letters and pictures of Snowball and Lovie. And I knit her socks. And a shawl."

I frowned. I suddenly remembered those multi-colored socks and the letters; they'd made Hannah smile, when it didn't seem possible I'd ever see her smile again. Without my knowing it, Macy had given me a gift I'd never expected.

I swallowed hard and turned to face her. "Thank you."

She shrugged off my appreciation. "If you don't want to see me anymore, I'll accept that, I really will, but I'm hoping you'll give me another chance."

"So you can walk out on me again? So you can disappear at the first sign of trouble? So you can leave one more issue in your life unresolved? No thanks, Macy. I've learned my lesson."

She nodded sadly. "Thank you for loving me for that little while, Michael," she said. "It means more than you'll ever realize."

She walked past me, over to the door.

Without even knowing that I intended to do it, I reached out and touched her hand. I had the sinking sensation that if I let Macy walk away from me again, I'd always regret it, always wonder what we might've had together.

After a moment, she turned back to face me, her eyes alight with hope. She must have read the love in my eyes because she sobbed and then walked into my arms as if that was where she belonged, where she was meant to be.

I grabbed her blouse and bunched it up in the back as I held her against me and breathed in the scent and feel of her. I closed my eyes and savored just having her in my arms.

"I need you, Macy." *What would Hannah want?* Ritchie had asked me that. Now I had an answer. Hannah had known I'd fall in love with Macy. Knew she'd be the perfect balance for me. Knew that Macy would teach me to laugh again.

"I need you, too," she whispered.

We kissed then, with a hunger that threatened to consume us both. Her hands were in my hair, roving over my neck and down my back, restless in their movements. It would've been so easy to lead her to the sofa and make love to her right there in my office. Thankfully common sense prevailed.

Once I'd regained control, I felt it was important to clear up a few things. "When we're married, I'm not living in that fairy-tale house. I've got a very nice place and—"

"Uh-uh. We can't leave Harvey," she said firmly. She broke away and leaned back just far enough to study me. "I'll paint the house any color you want except white."

"I like white," I protested. "But you're right about Harvey."

"Green, then."

"I am not living in a green house."

"You really should give red and yellow a chance. You'd get used to it."

"No, I won't." I wanted her to understand that I had my limits.

"Okay, I'll paint it white, but I won't like it and neither will my cats. They missed you, by the way."

"Sure they did." If they missed anything it was sleeping on my chest and digging their claws into me in the middle of the night just to see how loud I'd yelp.

"I want babies," Macy said. "Lots of babies."

"We'll negotiate that."

"Girls first. Two, I think, and then boys."

"We generally don't have a say in which comes first—boys or girls."